Assuming the game was finished, Kate pushed a path through the mud towards the steps to her right. But the men quickly followed and pinned her against the side of the pool.

'What do you want now?' she asked, a high note of alarm in her voice.

That earlier mood of hostility which had frightened her so much was now back, bringing a madness to their eyes and harsh, sadistic grins to their lips. They spun her round until her back was towards them, and then brutal fingers were probing her forbidden zone, rubbing and poking until she yelped with discomfort.

'Oh, no,' Kate protested. 'I draw the line at *that*.'

Her firm tone could have left them in little doubt that what they wanted was not an option in this game of erotica, but they chose to ignore her.

'Oh, God, no . . . I said "No",' she shrieked . . .

Also by Scott Owen
in New English Library paperback

Blue Squad

The 69 Club

Scott Owen

NEW ENGLISH LIBRARY
Hodder and Stoughton

First published in 1998
by Hodder and Stoughton
A division of Hodder Headline PLC

A New English Library paperback

10 9 8 7 6 5 4 3 2 1

British Library Cataloguing in Publication Data

A CIP catalogue record for this title is available
from the British Library.

ISBN 0 340 68573 5

Typeset by Avon Dataset Ltd, Bidford-on-Avon, Warks

Printed and bound in Great Britain by
Clays Ltd, St Ives plc

Hodder and Stoughton
A division of Hodder Headline PLC
338 Euston Road
London NW1 3BH

CHAPTER 1

When the rasping zip of a fly rang out loudly to her left, Kate Highlands's groin gave a delicious flutter; and although her eyes had not yet adjusted to the sensuous half-light in the private bar, she swivelled around in her seat and searched for the source of that provocative sound.

A young couple were perched on bar stools a few yards away: the man, darkly handsome; the girl, a gorgeous blonde. Kate sipped her drink and kept a surreptitious eye on the girl's scarlet-tipped fingers snaking their way into the man's open flies, causing him to squirm and sigh as they gripped their excited quarry.

Unable to look away, Kate openly studied the girl; she was in her twenties with a pretty face and large breasts which all the time threatened to escape from the low bodice of her tiny dress. Her long shapely legs were open and just a hint of black briefs could be seen at her crotch.

Kate tried to concentrate on her vodka and tonic but soon her gaze was wandering back to the lovers, dragged there by the man's muted cries of pleasure. The girl was tenderly pulling free his throbbing cock and a frantic edge crept into his groans when her long fingers took to toying with it and the palm of her free hand teased its quivering tip with slow, circular movements.

His dark lustful eyes, his hugely kissable mouth pulled

back over perfect white teeth, and the massive dimensions of his magnificent cock all conspired to bring a fierce trembling to Kate's vagina. Giving up all pretence now of simply enjoying her drink, she pushed the glass aside and turned fully to watch the sexy show.

The man's eager hand was travelling along the soft, tanned skin of the girl's thigh, and once at her crotch he delved enthusiastically inside her knickers. Kate's breath caught in her throat when thick blonde pubic hair came into view, only to disappear again beneath the man's groping hand.

The girl threw back her head and incoherent murmurs escaped on a sigh as she gave herself up to the sweet sensations between her legs, her hands all the while working industriously on the man's shaft. Kate strained forward to catch the garbled words now tumbling from her full lips.

'You've got a beautiful cock,' she was moaning. 'I'd love it inside me.'

Rising passion brought a growl to her throat, cutting off the words in an instant, and the girl leapt to her feet and pushed down her briefs. The man's desire was fuelled still further when she pulled up her diminutive dress and exposed the blood-red vaginal lips peeking coyly through their blonde nest.

It was then that a hush crept over the crowded bar, broken only by the soft clink of glasses being hurriedly returned to the counter, and Kate realised that she was not the only voyeur in the room. Indeed, all eyes were on the girl who was hastily removing the man's trousers. Almost as one the crowd pushed forward and formed a tight circle around them.

Kate jumped down from her stool and wormed her way

to the front, peering first at the man's aroused member which was so swollen that its taut skin seemed in danger of tearing, and then at the inviting cleft nestling between the girl's legs.

'Screw her,' a man shouted from the back.

The girl somehow regained her senses and started playing to her audience. With a cheeky wink she sashayed towards the pool table and, selecting one of the coloured balls, she pursed her scarlet lips and kissed it, her willing tongue flicking out and sliding over its smooth surface. The ball was then tossed across the green baize and it clattered noisily into one of the pockets.

Catcalls and whistles reverberated around the room when the girl climbed onto the edge of the table, pulled up her dress, and spread her long legs wide. The man made for the table, his massive shaft rippling with excitement, and positioned himself between her thighs. She slowly inched forward until her wanton crack was rubbing against his huge cockhead; and she let out an ecstatic 'yes' when, with a loud grunt, he pushed himself home. Straight away he fell into a steady, determined rhythm and brought loud gasps from the girl as her pleasure zone was stretched to its limit.

Kate swallowed loudly and ran her tongue around her lips. She could feel her vagina jumping, twitching, the wet crack rubbing against the silky material of her panties and spreading her love juice.

At the pool table the man was pounding away inside the girl; and she was pushing back, moving her body in time with his until their strangled screams met in a crescendo of joy.

'Mr Dixon will see you now.'

The whispered voice made Kate jump. Tearing her eyes

away from the copulating couple, she found herself staring into the face of a dark-skinned woman of around thirty-five whose huge, sultry eyes flashed with excitement. 'Or would you rather watch the end of the show first?'

In the background the lovers were groaning and thrashing about, flesh slapping on flesh, and Kate sensed that they were both close to orgasm.

'Yes,' she said in a hoarse whisper, 'I think I would.'

Several girls had moved forward and were caressing the man, exploring his testicles, flirting with his anus, their feathery fingertips teasing his thighs while he continued to thrust into the tight cavern.

Kate could almost feel the exquisite sensations rising from the friction as his hard shaft travelled in and out of the girl's vaginal embrace. She found her hand wandering toward the itch at her own crotch and massaged the coarse nest between her legs as best she could through the thin material of her skirt and panties.

'Pull it out,' someone shouted to the man. 'Let's see you come.'

Although mesmerized he nevertheless withdrew and, turning slightly so that all could see, began pulling roughly at his cock until an ocean of sperm gushed all over the girl.

'We'd better leave now,' the woman whispered. 'This is a brothel, and it looks like there's about to be an orgy.'

Kate's eyes grew large with incredulity. 'The 69 Club's a brothel?'

'That's right – at least, the upper floor is. Our members usually enjoy a drink in here and then meander upstairs to sample our other delights.' She grinned. 'Obviously those two couldn't wait.'

Even as Kate followed her to the door, couples were

pairing off and intimately fondling each other. A fierce blush was burning her cheeks as they pushed their way through the crowd, and she was glad when they reached a cool corridor at the rear of the building. The woman turned to face her.

'I'm Maria,' she announced with a warm smile. 'I suppose you could say I'm the Madam.'

Kate inclined her head. 'It's nice to meet you,' she said, striving to appear nonchalant. 'Can you tell me what Mr Dixon wants to see me about?'

'Since you joined the 69 Club – three months ago, I believe – it's come to Mr Dixon's attention that you're a private investigator, and he wants to hire your services.'

'I see.'

Kate was intrigued, and she followed Maria along a seemingly endless winding corridor which led to the bowels of the building.

The orgy was in full swing, and above the clamour of impassioned cries, Maria went on, 'Mr Dixon, like myself, is Spanish by origin which means that he has a passionate nature and is totally without inhibitions. At the moment he's enjoying a massage, so I do hope that what you're about to witness won't embarrass you.'

Kate laughed. 'After what I've just seen in the bar? I hardly think so.'

Maria stopped by a door and ushered Kate into a large, impressive room. Dixon was lying on a long table, stomach down and completely naked. His tall, muscular body was being kneaded and rubbed by two nude girls. Both were long-legged, possibly mid-twenties, with large, firm breasts which rose and fell while they worked. The thick nests of hair between those shapely legs confirmed that both were natural blondes.

No one seemed to notice Kate's entrance into the room, and as she watched one of the girls climbed on to the table and straddled Dixon's legs so that she could rub her vagina against the hairy skin of his thigh.

Maria motioned for Kate to stay at the door and then approached the table with a bold step.

'Kate Highlands is here to see you,' she whispered in his ear.

Dixon turned his head and fixed Kate with an amused gaze. Once again a blush threatened to spoil the look of her carefully applied make-up; the man was so very handsome with skin tanned to a rich mahogany. His bone structure was perfect and made more interesting by a slightly hooked nose. Kate shifted uncomfortably from one foot to the other as his heavy-lidded eyes, dark brown and unfathomable, appraised her. Very slowly those eyes feasted on her legs and devoured her torso before finally coming to rest on her face. White, even teeth flashed as he smiled.

'Miss Highlands, how nice to meet you. I have a rather unusual assignment to offer—' He stopped abruptly and turned to glare at the girl still masturbating against his leg. 'Stop that, Nicky. Now.'

But the girl merely whimpered and murmured, 'Make my pussy happy,' as she fucked his thigh with added urgency.

'Wait.'

His barked command had the desired effect and the girl climbed from the table, pouting and petulant, as Dixon returned his attention to Kate.

'I want you to locate a business associate of mine, Miss Highlands. A man by the name of Laurence Wilson. He has taken something belonging to me—' That spark of

amusement was back in his eyes. 'He may be hard to trace, and you may have to use your body in the quest.'

Kate's jaw dropped. 'And why should I have to do that?'

Suddenly Dixon turned on to his back and Kate got her first look at his large, fully erect penis. While she stared fixedly at the bulging purple tip that so regally crowned his hard shaft, Dixon signalled to Maria who immediately stepped forward and took a slip of paper from his hand.

'On that is the fee I am prepared to pay. Give it to her, Maria.'

Kate took the proffered note as the blonde Nicky bent forward and expertly sucked Dixon's trembling penis between her moist lips. Kate unfolded the slip of paper and gave it a perfunctory glance before returning her attention to the table.

Without once slackening her oral grip on his cock, the girl clambered on to the table and manoeuvred herself around until her vagina was rubbing against his waiting mouth. Once in position she tantalised and teased, refusing to stay still long enough for his darting tongue to penetrate that heavenly slit between her legs.

It was then that something clicked in Kate's consciousness and quickly brought her mind back to the slip of paper. Peering at it eagerly she counted the number of noughts again and again until her eyes bulged with disbelief. Mr Dixon was prepared to pay one million pounds for her services. One million pounds. Kate swallowed loudly.

'God, that's so good,' Nicky called out as Dixon's rough tongue finally made contact with her fiery clitoris. She threw back her head, savouring the pleasure for a few seconds, and then attended once more to his swollen member.

While his lips laboured diligently between her legs, so Nicky returned the compliment with a frenzied mouth fuck. Her saliva ran in torrents down his enlivened shaft and settled around his jumping testicles where the other girl was lapping avidly and all the while fingering her own neglected crack.

Nicky was now gyrating her body against his face, no longer denying him access to her secret spot, but increasing the pressure of his tongue and lips on the inflamed button that protruded from the glistening folds of her sex. The sensations were exquisite and her mouth abandoned his cockhead as she gave loud voice to her delight.

But the magnificent penis was not neglected for long, for she continued to tug it with her right hand, the strokes long and fast, while her left was gently squeezing his balls and preparing to milk him dry when the moment came.

The second girl, with access to those heavy bags now gone, was feverishly working on his anus. Kate could see her deft tongue flicking out with relentless vigour while Dixon writhed and squirmed and murmured in the sea of sweet sensations that threatened to engulf him. And above it all the sound of slurping fingers increased when the girl forced a fourth inside herself and resumed her solitary pleasuring.

Maria gave a discreet cough. 'Now you know why it's called the 69 Club. I think it's time we left. Please follow me.'

'Wait a minute,' Kate whispered, indicating the piece of paper.

But she was shushed into silence and ushered towards the door. Still viewing the spectacle taking place on the table, Kate allowed herself to be propelled into the corridor. Three people were about to be made joyously happy,

but the sight was blocked from her view when Maria closed the door behind them. Kate spun round to face the woman in the dimly-lit corridor.

'Is this some sort of joke?' she demanded, holding up the slip of paper.

Maria shook her head. 'James Dixon never jokes about money. If you agree to take the assignment then half a million pounds will be paid into your bank account immediately. You will get the balance on completion.'

Kate bit her lower lip and tried to take in the enormity of Dixon's proposition. It disturbed her; so too did the close presence of the dark and sexy Maria.

'I'll let Mr Dixon know,' she managed to say.

'No, from now on you'll be dealing with me.'

'Fine.'

Kate made to walk away but the woman blocked her path, causing their breasts to touch for a fleeting second. Highly embarrassed, she turned away. Her discomfort only increased when sounds accompanying Dixon's climax drifted from the room.

'If you wish to accept the job you must come back in two days' time so that I can give you lessons—' She paused, and a knowing smile touched her lips. '—lessons in the art of lust.'

'For God's sake,' Kate retorted. 'I know how to screw, if that's what you're talking about.'

Maria laughed softly. 'Poor Kate, there's really no need to be so uptight. My guess is you'd love to screw, but you don't know how.'

Kate turned away sharply so that Maria would not see the confusion in her eyes.

'I would say that you've never reached orgasm during sex, and there are many things you would love to try but

you think they are taboo. How am I doing?'

Kate exhaled loudly and refused to answer.

'I was watching you while we were in the room,' Maria went on. 'I could see that James Dixon's beautiful cock excited you. And so did the girls' bodies – isn't that right, Kate? You liked their large breasts and their juicy pussies, didn't you?'

Laughing softly, Maria moved away and leant against the wall, her deep brown eyes openly mocking when Kate made no attempt to leave.

'This is getting silly,' she protested, fidgeting on the spot.

'Why don't you admit it, Kate? You want to try sex with another woman, but you have a mental block about it which probably goes back to when you were a young girl. Perhaps you tried it then, but it failed to live up to expectations.'

Suddenly she reached forward and rested a hand on Kate's breast, her index finger lazily circling the nipple.

'Don't,' Kate moaned. But even so she made no attempt to push the hand away.

'Do you really want me to stop? Do you?'

Maria was now standing so close that Kate could feel her hot breath on her cheek. And still the fingers continued their relentless exploration of her breasts, bringing tremors of pleasure to her spine and an unfamiliar hardness to her nipples.

'Do you want me to go further, Kate?'

The words were murmured on a low sensuous breath which tickled her ear, bringing a delicious rush of adrenalin to her groin and an excruciating ache to her vagina.

Kate's intended rebuff caught in her throat and her large breasts heaved as she fought for air. She felt wholly

at the mercy of this exotic and intriguing woman and could feel an uncanny mix of fear and excitement building in the pit of her stomach as Maria's hand wandered down and travelled still further, caressing the taut young flesh beneath her dress.

'I can smell the heady scent of your cunt,' she said, her hand straying between Kate's legs, feeling, probing, gauging the steamy place which lay hidden away beneath her formal outfit.

Kate opened her mouth to make a feeble protest, but her words were stifled by Maria's warm, moist lips touching her own. The move was made too quickly for her to pull away and in that cool, gloomy corridor Kate found herself responding, pushing back hard against the force of the kiss and opening her mouth to welcome the touch and taste of Maria's demanding tongue.

A shiver of anticipation brought goose bumps to her skin when Maria's hand stole to her thigh and moved up, until it touched the silk of her panties, causing the lips of her sex to open and emit a flood of torrid love juices.

Kate gasped for air when their lips parted. She felt she was drowning, becoming swamped by wave upon wave of erotic expectation as they built with each touch of Maria's confident fingers. They were feeling her crack through the thin silk, stroking the coarse hair, and with each thrilling brush the doors to her velvet cavern opened ever wider.

The gusset was pushed aside and Kate held her breath, knowing that this madness should be brought to a stop, but longing for Maria's intimate caress. After what seemed like an eternity, cool fingers picked a way through the hairy bush and found the hot crack concealed in its midst. Immediately, its gorged lips pulled back to reveal Kate's

crimson clitoris which seemed to lunge forward as if to greet these most welcome of visitors.

A finger circled the tiny bud, hardly touching but teasing mercilessly, until it itched and grew bigger in an attempt to reach its tormentor. The flirting finger stayed outside its reach but eventually slid along Kate's wet trench in search of the opening to her magical place.

Kate gave in fully to her carnal desires and leant back against the wall, her legs spread wide. She was panting, silently praying that the finger exploring the entrance to her burning slit might be pushed inside and worked to and fro.

'You've got a beautiful little cunt,' Maria whispered. 'If you let me, I can teach you how to use it.'

Kate responded with a breathless moan.

'I'll show you how to use your hands, and your mouth, too – men love to have their cocks sucked.'

The wet fingers edged between Kate's buttocks and teased the puckered opening of her anus.

'And I'll teach you how to use this really secret place. If you let me, Kate, I'll show you how to use the whole of your gorgeous body to make a man happy.'

The hand strayed back to Kate's vagina.

'And lastly I'll teach you how to enjoy sex with another woman. Would you like that?'

Kate knew she was fast losing control but was powerless to stop the heavenly responses which burned feverishly at the nub of her sex. All rational thought dictated that she should call a halt, but she was in the grip of something far more powerful than logic.

Reaching down, she grasped Maria's wrist and tried to manoeuvre the woman's finger into her vagina. Maria gave a loud, triumphant laugh and pushed into Kate's tight hole,

feeling around its soft, cushiony walls as she entered.

'Make me happy,' was Kate's plaintive cry. 'Please, Maria, make me happy.'

'What do you want?'

'I . . . I want you to finger me.'

Maria set to work, fucking with slow, even strokes. Kate whimpered and her pretty face broke into a grateful grin, for the terrible ache in her crack was gone, chased away by a burgeoning heat which grew with each thrust and which promised an almighty eruption of pleasure.

'That's more like it,' Maria purred. 'I just knew that behind your prim facade you were a really sexy girl. Just remember, the dirtier you're willing to be, the more enjoyable sex becomes.'

As the finger-fuck gathered momentum, Kate's senses began to spiral. An acute burning sensation began in her middle and grew hotter and hotter still until it threatened to explode. Kate relaxed and waited; she was about to experience her first orgasm and she was determined to enjoy it to the full. But then the warmth subsided, began to slip away, and a curse left her lips on a panicked breath.

Without breaking her rhythm, Maria set a second finger to work on Kate's clitoris, which was scorching and so ready to be molested. Straight away that luscious heat was back, only stronger this time, and even as Kate wished fervently for it to increase, a gigantic wave of pleasure surged through her groin. The feeling was divine and Kate was about to cry out with pure joy when Maria's finger stilled and immediately thwarted the impending climax.

'Why have you stopped?' Kate screamed. 'Make me come, Maria. You must—'

But the hand was withdrawn from Kate's briefs. Maria stepped back, and her voice held a hard edge as she said,

'Oh, no, Kate. You must realise that when you're dealing with us you must first supply us with what we want. Then, and only then, will you get what you want.'

Kate was close to tears as she straightened up and adjusted her clothing.

'I refuse to let you use me in this way,' she spat. 'I'll think over Mr Dixon's offer and let you know what I decide.'

Maria laughed. 'Smell yourself,' she said, thrusting a finger to Kate's nose. 'Believe me, it's a scent and taste you'll come to love.'

Although unwilling, Kate was forced to breathe in the intoxicating perfume of her own love juices but, determined this time to hold on to her self-control, she slapped the hand away.

'I'll let you know,' she repeated, with as much dignity as she could muster.

As she strode off along the corridor – the clatter of her high heels echoing from all corners – the uncomfortable feel of her wet knickers served as a taunting reminder of how easily she had fallen under the woman's spell, of how desperately she had wanted to come.

'I look forward to seeing you in two days' time,' Maria called after her.

CHAPTER 2

The woman's confident tone and the lilting laughter behind the words annoyed Kate immensely; and that annoyance was plain to see in her body language as she hurried up the wooden stairs. She was still furious when she collected her battered Mini from the car park and sat looking at the elegant building.

She had joined The 69 Club because it was trendy, and because she thought it would be a good place to go for a drink after work. Everyone who was anyone went there – now she knew why. How could she have been so naive? Why hadn't she ever wondered why all those people continually trooped up the back stairs, only to return a while later, exhausted and dishevelled? And how dare that woman take advantage of her in the way that she did?

Pushing the car into gear, Kate moved off with her hand lingering longer than was necessary on the knob of the gear lever. Suddenly hot, she snatched the hand away and silently cursed as she quickly unfastened the top buttons of her blouse.

Her mind should have been on the one million pounds that to all intents and purposes had just been flung into her lap, but it remained firmly fixed on the crack between her legs which had refused to stop twitching ever since its awakening at the gifted hands of Maria.

The fact that the woman had been so accurate in her assessment of Kate's sex life – or lack of it – only served to fuel her boiling anger. Yet as she manoeuvred the car along the quiet city streets, Kate found herself admitting for the very first time that the total lack of orgasms within her relationships troubled her greatly.

She did get pleasure from sex; quite a lot, in fact. She loved to watch a sleepy, shrivelled cock grow into a big, hard, throbbing rod within the seconds it took for her to drop her knickers. And she loved to see the uninhibited pleasure on a man's face at the moment he spurted inside her. Those small delights were exciting, and Kate had always thought they were enough to satisfy – until now.

She parked the car and ran up the back stairs to the flat, her mind still filled with Maria, her anger still seething. The tiresome woman had even been right about Kate's hunger for lesbian sex. She *had* tried it years ago and, yes, it *had* promised so much. But it had ended in nothing more than acute embarrassment and a deep feeling of shame on both sides.

Kate slammed her way into the flat and promptly pulled off her clammy briefs. Then, muttering hotly, she flung the contemptible garment into the washing basket. The air was heavy with her own musky odour. Just a few hours before she would have found that scent repulsive, but now it was somehow titillating, and caused a strange excitement to grow in her middle.

In the living room she smoked two cigarettes and knocked back a large vodka and tonic as she tried to collect her thoughts. Something from the past kept creeping back into her mind. It was her mother's chiding voice reciting the monologue that, way back, had been forced repeatedly into her psyche: *sex is disgusting, Kate. A woman must agree*

*to sex only when she is married, and for no other reason than
to give pleasure to her husband – never forget that.*

She supposed she had always known – subconsciously,
at least – that those words were responsible for her constant inability to climax. Thanks a lot, mother.

In a fit of frustration, Kate hurled her empty glass onto
the settee and strutted into the bedroom to prepare for a
shower. She undressed slowly and studied her naked
reflection in the dressing table mirror.

She was a pretty girl who looked younger than her
twenty-five years. Her short, blonde hair framed a small
oval face which was dominated by impossibly large blue
eyes. Her sweet, freckled nose turned up slightly and
seemed at odds with her full sensuous lips. She somehow
managed to look both vulnerable and provocative at the
same time.

Never one to pay much attention to her body, she nevertheless knew that hers was a figure which men craved
after. Her large breasts were firm with rosy nipples that
stood proud and her flat, hard stomach gave way to wide
hips which swept down towards long, shapely legs topped
by a thick triangle of blonde hair which fully hid the very
best of her assets.

She had denied herself so many things. *And why*? she
thought angrily. Partly because deep down she had felt
those pleasures to be wrong, but mostly because she
couldn't cope with the prospect of gratification eluding her
yet again.

Try as she might, Kate couldn't help dwelling on the
sensations so easily evoked by Maria's sliding fingers and
as she remembered, her hands crept stealthily up to her
breasts to caress the nipples. Their movements were soft
at first, tentative, but then the crimson gems were pinched

lightly between fingers and thumbs until they grew larger than they had ever been before and tingled deliciously beneath her touch.

With a deep sigh she slid a hand down over her stomach and, fighting off a twinge of guilt, recalled the pleasure she had felt when Maria's hand had come to rest between her buttocks. Her fingers were now pushing their way through the blonde bush at her groin which was still wet from that unspeakable incident in the dark corridor.

The trench of her vagina was hot and still oozing the cream of her desires as a finger stole across the blossoming love bud. Her legs went weak as it expanded in response to her touch, and Kate thrilled at the lewd expression on the face of the woman reflected in the mirror.

'Oh, God,' she whimpered, her voice hoarse.

Her fingers kept up their persistent attack on the wet pussy and it fought back, twitching and trembling, as if begging for something to fill it. Her legs were now shaking so much that she was forced to lie on the bed. Positioning herself so that she could watch her reflection, she spread her legs apart and stroked her grateful slit until the lips widened to reveal the glistening entrance to her tunnel of love.

Desperate for satisfaction but still fearing disappointment, Kate allowed the middle finger of her right hand to slide inside. Straight away the silky walls tightened in a warm embrace, and a thousand nerve endings stirred into a frenzy of tingling as the finger moved steadily in and out.

Kate closed her eyes and as her other hand crept towards her anus she thought about Maria. The furrow between her buttocks was slippery with her juices and the steamy stickiness seemed to enhance her pleasure. The anal opening itself felt like a mouth pursed in righteous

indignation and Kate giggled at the crazy metaphor as she fondled herself there, while a second finger delved into her velvet crack.

Very soon that longed-for heat returned to the centre of her body as erotic fantasies ran through her mind, each one tumbling over the last as her brain raced. She fucked faster, using a third finger now, stretching her pleasure pit to its limit.

All of a sudden, thoughts of the dusky Maria were pushed aside by a clear picture of her closest friends, Pearl and Nigel. They had been light-heartedly pestering her for months now to join in a threesome. She always refused, of course, never causing offence but always firm nevertheless. But now her flight of fancy was taking her into their bedroom, with the three of them naked on the bed.

The burning in her crack was becoming too much to bear and Kate increased the speed of the sweet finger-fuck. She tossed about on the bed, her head jerking from side to side. The hand between her legs was a blur as the heat became red hot. Then, without warning, it exploded like a huge firework in her groin, sending mild shooting stars of ecstasy far and wide.

'Oh, yes, yes,' she cried, rolling about on the bed, her fingers still moving until the last dying ember had expired.

For the very first time Kate had managed to bring herself to climax. The feelings had been weak – the earth certainly hadn't moved – but the pleasure was enough to melt the tensions that had built up since her meeting with the illustrious Mr Dixon.

Almost in a daze, Kate wandered through to the living room for a drink and a cigarette. Then, still breathing heavily, she returned to the bedroom and sprawled out on the bed. Every time she raised her hand to drag on the

cigarette, the heady aroma of her love juice floated into her nostrils. Stubbing it out quickly, she brought the finger to her lips and sucked on it, enjoying the taste, until it was clean.

While she was finishing her drink an impulsive thought pushed to the forefront of Kate's mind and refused to budge. And before she had time to think better of it she was off the bed, a huge smile on her face, and was reaching for the telephone receiver on the bedside table.

The number was quickly punched out and the ringing tone was in her ear. She glanced at the clock. It was eleven-thirty p.m. and she worried briefly about the lateness of the hour. But then the connection was made and a breezy voice answered.

'Hello?'

'Hi, Pearl, it's Kate. I'm not disturbing you, am I?'

The loud dirty laugh which was so typical of the woman thundered into Kate's ear, as she answered, 'Of course not, we're just having a threesome, that's all.'

'I might have guessed. Is she pretty?'

'It's not a she,' Pearl giggled. 'My turn this week, sweetie, so I've got two big pricks to play with.'

Just then Kate heard a male voice in the background, and once again Pearl dissolved into a fit of giggling.

'Who was that?' she asked, already sure of the answer.

'It was Nigel, sweetie, asking as usual if you'd like to come and join in.'

'Not tonight, I'm bushed,' Kate murmured, stretching out on the bed. 'But I wouldn't mind meeting up with the two of you in the morning. We might even arrange a little sex romp – who knows?'

There followed a stunned silence from Pearl's end, and then she said, 'Are you kidding, Kate? Nigel's been trying

to get inside your knickers for months.'

Now it was Kate's turn to giggle. 'You don't have to remind me. I just feel randy all of a sudden – God knows why.' She paused. 'And it's not just Nigel I want to have fun with.'

A sceptical gasp travelled down the line. 'I don't believe this. Am I hearing you right? None of the girls we've been with have ever agreed to that.'

'You heard right, Pearl. So I'll meet you at the park tomorrow morning and we can discuss it. Say about ten o'clock – okay?'

'God, I'm so turned on. I can't wait to tell Nigel.'

'Good, see you in the morning.'

Kate replaced the receiver and stifled a yawn. She was suddenly sleepy; contented and sleepy. And with thoughts of one million pounds going around inside her pretty head, she lay back and closed her eyes.

CHAPTER 3

Kate awoke next morning to find the weather warm, but dull and overcast – a perfect day for a frolic in the park. After a leisurely shower she chose her clothes with care, finally settling on a loose-fitting white dress which buttoned down the front. Her briefs were also white and small enough to hug the slight bulge of her pubis and allow her blonde pussy hair to spill from their sides.

Her bra, stockings and suspender belt were all returned to the drawer – she wouldn't be needing them – and the top three buttons of the dress were opened to allow a generous view of her soft creamy cleavage.

During the short drive to the park Kate reflected on the carefree marriage of Pearl and Nigel. The three had met a few months ago when Pearl answered Kate's advertisement for a freelance typist. She was a tall, slim woman in her thirties, with cropped black hair, a cheeky tomboy face, and a hugely desirable body.

It was not long before Kate was invited around to her house for dinner, and there she met Nigel. Also in his thirties, he had thick auburn hair and large brown eyes that seemed to undress every woman he met. His physique was well-proportioned, and he had a very impressive bulge in the front of his trousers which were always worn tight to accentuate that most precious of attributes.

That dinner was the first of many, and Kate soon realised that they were obsessed with sex. They would undress for the flimsiest of reasons: maybe the weather was too hot, or they needed to throw off the earthly restrictions of the spirit (both were deeply into transcendental meditation). Whatever the excuse, Kate would almost curl up with embarrassment as Pearl wandered around in tiny bra and pants, and Nigel stripped down to his ridiculously small tanga briefs.

He never missed an opportunity to put their conversations onto a sexual footing, and whenever they played cards, would always sternly warn that if she lost then Kate would have to play with his cock. It was a threat she always resisted, along with their light-hearted offers for a little fun in bed.

But that episode at the 69 Club had changed Kate forever. Her libido had undergone a complete metamorphosis and for the first time in her life she felt liberated and without guilt of any sort.

She parked the car in a side street and plotted her tactics. She wanted to thrill and flirt until they were on the edge of their seats, panting for it; then, and only then, would she deliver.

She had chosen the park for two reasons. Firstly, in such a public place Nigel would be unable to pull down her knickers and pounce; even he would have to show restraint in such circumstances. And secondly, there was a strong element of danger attached to the venue. They could be seen – watched surreptitiously. The thought excited Kate; made her tingle with anticipation, and there was a spring in her step as she hurried towards the large iron gates.

Pearl and Nigel were already waiting just inside the park

as Kate headed towards them, a warm smile playing on her lips.

'Hi,' she said, coming to a halt with legs apart and hands on hips.

Nigel looked at the darkening sky and pulled a face. 'Why don't we all go to our house, or maybe to your flat?'

'Oh, no, I want some sex fun in the open air,' Kate countered. 'Well, I must say you both look very nice.'

Nigel was today brandishing his bulge in small blue shorts which matched his light blue sports shirt. Pearl – looking nervous, Kate noticed – was a vision in a short pastel pink wrap-over dress which was held together by a tied belt at the waist. Kate leant forward and planted a casual kiss on her cheek.

'Come on then, you two, let's go and have a coffee.'

In total charge now, she led them to a small cafe by the bandstand. The limited space was crowded but they managed to find an empty table in the far corner. While Nigel ordered the coffee, all the time complaining to his wife that this was a wind-up, Kate excused herself and went into the nearby lavatory. Wasting no time she removed her knickers and stuffed them into her shoulder bag. Then, after checking her make-up in the badly scratched wall mirror, she returned to the table and found Nigel and Pearl already sipping their coffee.

Laughing inwardly at their forlorn expressions she took her seat between them, quick to note that whatever might take place beneath the table would be well hidden from prying eyes.

'Nigel reckons you're winding us up,' Pearl remarked, with a good-natured grin.

Kate made no reply but took a sip of her coffee and at the same time placed a hand on Pearl's knee. The woman

gave a derisory chortle and was about to make a wry comment to Nigel when the hand began its journey towards her luscious thigh.

The change in Pearl's expression alerted Nigel and his eyes grew bright with interest as he glanced down in time to see the tops of her stockings and their black suspenders come into view.

'Jesus,' he breathed, as Kate's hand touched the tanned skin beyond the stocking tops.

His wife, having recovered from the shock, eased forward and opened her legs wide. Now it was Kate's turn to be startled for her friend was naked beneath the dress, and for the first time she found herself face to face with Pearl's quivering nest.

Her inquisitive fingers reached out, of their own accord, and ruffled the thick, coarse hair which covered that most desirable prize. She could feel the well-hidden cleft, and her jaw dropped in surprise when Pearl used both hands to hold the lips of her vagina apart and brazenly display herself.

The invitation in the woman's eyes was plain and Kate watched Nigel's face closely while she fingered his wife's pussy. His gaze remained glued to the sliding finger that was causing Pearl to groan and whimper, the woman now totally oblivious to all others in the cafe.

'Shush,' Kate whispered. 'Someone might hear you.'

Immediately Pearl released herself and brought both hands to her face, hiding her expression and stifling the sounds of rising passion that threatened to escape from her lips.

Kate glanced around the cafe. At first she thought that no one had noticed the erotic goings-on taking place beneath the table and she was about to return her attention

fully to Pearl's enlivened crack when she noticed two young boys sitting directly opposite at the far end. They were both about eighteen and were staring across with curious expressions.

She was certain that they couldn't see anything; they must have guessed, from Pearl's kittenish purrs, that something sexy was happening. She shot them a cheeky smile and they swiftly turned away, their young faces flushed with embarrassment.

Turning her gaze back to Nigel she found he was lovingly stroking his bulge which was now enormous as his erect penis strained against the cotton shorts, his eyes still fixed on his wife's groin. All of a sudden a powerful feeling of authority swept over Kate. Here she was in a public place, skilfully bringing Pearl to a crashing climax while Nigel, his cock swollen with desperation, could only look on.

Pearl squirmed frantically against the exquisite feel of Kate's finger and her quiet mewings reached a crescendo. Sensing she was almost there, Kate whispered to Nigel, 'Show us your cock.'

Without a moment's hesitation he opened his flies and, turning his back on the crowd, released a quite magnificent shaft which must have been a good seven inches long. Kate's gaze took in every inch of the horny spectacle, and she urged Pearl to open her eyes and take a look. She did, and the sight was enough to take her over the brink of orgasm. Bucking wildly, with her hot cavern literally devouring the foraging finger, Pearl's hands once more leapt to her face as, in ranting whispers, she told that she was coming and begged Kate to go faster and make her happy.

Timing it to perfection, Kate pushed a second finger

into the burning slit and was met by a surge of love juice as Pearl's legs trembled and shook with the violent ferocity of the come.

Hiding a victorious grin Kate glanced across to the young boys and felt a surge of disappointment when they got to their feet as if to leave. But her spirits soon lifted for instead of heading for the door they pushed their way to the counter and ordered more coffee. And better still, when the coffee was poured, they made for a table just feet away from Kate's. Things could soon start to get interesting, she pondered happily.

Throughout all of this Kate had repeatedly transferred saliva to Nigel's trembling shaft and now it was liberally coated. Pearl had at last recovered and she pushed her chair back to watch the action.

Kate lit a cigarette and casually blew smoke towards the ceiling while her free hand acquainted itself with the excited cock. She stroked it lightly at first, gently rubbing her palm across the bulging tip until Nigel was wriggling about on the seat.

Using every ounce of restraint, he managed to keep his expression impassive and his hands resting lightly around the coffee cup while his rampant organ remained at the mercy of Kate's teasing movements. Very slowly she took him in her hand and her eyes grew large as the huge cock expanded still further with each forceful pull. But that fleeting look of surprise was all that betrayed her lusty actions at Nigel's groin for she continually smoked and chatted to him as if they were simply friends taking coffee together. Their hushed conversation was far from innocent, however.

'Pearl's always telling me about your gorgeous prick,' she said, her fingers tightening their grip as she rubbed

harder while still maintaining the same slow rhythm. 'And I must say, it is rather divine.'

Nigel tried to lift the coffee cup but his hand was trembling too much and he coughed to cover a groan. The two boys were openly staring, their eyes wide and incredulous. Kate flashed them a grin and intensified her efforts on Nigel's throbbing shaft.

'Do you know, Nigel, I've wanted to play with this for a long time – ever since Pearl told me you keep on and on about wanting to screw me.'

She was treating the cock to furious jerks now, and the strain of having to appear casual was showing clearly on poor Nigel's face. His legs began to shake uncontrollably as the increased friction turned his cockhead into an ecstatic mass of tingling nerve endings. Sinking his teeth hard into his bottom lip, Nigel stared straight ahead with unseeing eyes; and when a high colour crept into his face Kate knew he wouldn't hold out much longer. It was then that she decided to hurry things along.

'I was really flattered when Pearl told me how much you want my hot cunt,' she cooed. 'After all, I've only got what she's got.'

She stubbed out her cigarette and pulled up her skirt to expose the blonde bush in her lap.

'See, Nigel, that's all it is.'

The sight of her vagina proved too much. Nigel swallowed loudly and his body went rigid as a torrent of sperm gushed from his throbbing member. Kate heard the first jet hit the underside of the metal table and promptly wrapped a hand around the tip to catch the hot, sticky liquid in her palm.

Nigel sank back in the chair, his breath coming in short, shallow gasps. He watched, spell-bound, as Kate took a

tissue from her pocket and unhurriedly mopped herself clean. At the next table, the two boys stared in earnest disbelief, both unable to wrench their eyes away from the sperm-soaked tissue which was casually tossed into the ashtray.

'There,' she said, smiling. 'You two must realise I'm not winding you up now, so shall we go and find a quiet place and get on with some really horny fun?'

They opened their mouths to speak, but when no words came they simply nodded.

'Great,' Kate said, cheerfully. 'Pearl, come to the loo with me before we go.'

Straight away the woman got to her feet, and when Kate followed suit she held up her dress just long enough for the boys to get a fleeting glimpse of her silky pussy hair. Their young faces were flushed with excitement as she grabbed Pearl's arm and guided her towards the lavatory. The minute they were inside Pearl spun round to face her.

'I can't believe what we've just done out there,' she said, her voice alive with exhilaration.

Kate gave a throaty laugh and pulled her into the nearest cubicle. Pearl was still giggling when the bolt of the door was pushed home. They stood facing each other in the confined space, neither of them sure of the next step. It was Kate who broke the embarrassed silence.

'Did you notice those two young boys at the next table?'

'No, why?'

'They saw everything.' She laughed. 'They were straining their eyes so much I thought they were going to burst a blood vessel or something.'

Pearl's jaw sagged open. 'They saw everything? You mean, they saw me . . . they saw us?'

Kate's face broke into an impish grin as she nodded.

'Bloody hell,' Pearl said, shaking her head. But then she giggled. 'I must have been too busy to notice.'

'Anyway, it looks like we're going to have an audience for our little romp,' Kate observed. 'Maybe we could get them to join in the fun.'

The lewd expression which flitted across Pearl's face suggested that the idea was a a good one.

'I know that Nigel and I have done some really wild things but honestly, Kate, I never thought anything like this would happen to us.'

Before she could say more Kate surprised them both by taking a bold step forward and brushing the woman's lips with her own. This was unexplored territory for Kate, and it was only her highly charged libido which had allowed it to happen. The kiss was tentative, experimental, but Pearl's enthusiastic response incited Kate's passions and soon they were both lost in the torrid urgency of the embrace.

Pearl's heart skipped a beat at the feel of Kate's hand working stealthily up to her crotch, and she gasped for air when their lips finally parted. She was breathing heavily and offered no resistance when warm fingers touched her wet, aching sex before moving on towards her buttocks and the hidden channel between them.

'You've got a lovely arse. I really fancy it,' Kate whispered. 'Why don't you take off your dress?'

She continued to fondle the juicy crack as Pearl fumbled with her tied belt. She whimpered with frustration when the knot refused to come apart, but finally the dress gaped open. Kate helped her out of it and they watched with mounting anticipation as it fell to the floor. Then Pearl struggled out of her bra and stood before her in the

confined space, naked but for stockings and suspender belt.

Her small breasts jutted out, with nipples that were pert and provocative as they rose and fell in time with her heaving breath. Her enticing vagina was still wet from its orgasm in the cafe and its thick pubic hair lay plastered to her skin, highlighting the swollen, protruding lips and the inviting dip of her entrance.

Kate had never been so turned on. It felt as if the whole of her body's energies were concentrated on achieving sexual satisfaction; nothing else mattered, and all she could think of was the frisky cleft between her legs, which would no longer be ignored. She instinctively knew what must come next, but as she was new to lesbian affairs Kate had little idea of how to achieve it.

Willing herself to relax and allowing her desires to dictate events, Kate ordered Pearl to sit on the lavatory seat. Pearl needed little encouragement to spread her legs wide. Indeed, she brought her heels up onto the seat and looked at Kate with big, imploring eyes.

Kneeling down between those open legs, Kate planted gentle kisses on Pearl's tanned thighs. She took her time, advancing on the hungry slit with excruciating slowness. Getting closer, closer; drawn by its strong scent. And then she was upon it, running her tongue through the soaked hairs while Pearl babbled incomprehensible words and panted, moaned and whimpered. And then she let out a cry, unmindful of passers-by, when Kate kissed the glistening lips of her jumping, twitching sex. She kissed it as she would another mouth, long and lingering, relishing the salty taste which stung her lips.

'Lick me,' Pearl implored. 'Please, lick me.'

Kate's tongue probed the moist slit, thrilling at its

warmth, at the smooth feel of its silky walls, and she sank her fingers into Pearl's thighs, forcing them even further apart.

Leaving the depths of the yielding cavern, Kate set off along the wet trench in search of its hidden love bud, and soon her rough tongue was sliding across it.

'You're there,' Pearl murmured joyously. 'Oh God, that's wonderful.'

The crimson button grew larger with each careful lick, and while Kate concentrated her efforts on that sensitive spot she pushed a hand between Pearl's buttocks and started to explore. The channel was saturated with a sexy blend of saliva and love juice, which acted as a fine lubricant for her fingers as they travelled backwards and forwards over the forbidden entrance.

Pearl responded enthusiastically, bucking beneath her, rubbing her hot crack against Kate's lips and uttering tiny animal grunts of ecstasy. Urged on by that dramatic reaction, Kate furthered her exploration by delving into the tight hole. As the tip of her finger gently probed and her tongue kept up its relentless attack on the swollen clitoris, Pearl was transported to a higher level of bliss and a spectacular climax was hers for the taking. She bucked wildly for several moments, completely out of control. And then, suddenly breathless, she became still, her body limp.

Kate got to her feet and gazed down at the gratified look which she alone had placed on her friend's beautiful face. Pearl opened her eyes and grinned broadly.

'You're a dirty cow, Kate. I've never felt so excited.'

'You ain't seen nothing yet, kid.'

She held out a hand and Pearl was pulled to her feet where she tottered on unsteady legs.

'Would you like me to do the same for you?' she asked, shyly. 'Don't expect too much, though. I mean, I've never done it before, so I wouldn't be as good as you.'

A feeling of pride crept over Kate. Should she let on that it was her first time, too? No, let them think she was experienced. Let them lie in bed at night, wondering what she might be getting up to. It was nice to have the upper hand for once.

'I'd like you to do it, Pearl, but not here. Do it while Nigel's screwing you from behind. And after that, perhaps he could have me – what do you think?'

Pearl laughed while she pulled on her dress. 'To tell you the truth I'd forgotten all about Nigel having to dip his wick. Honestly, Kate, after what you've just done I don't know how much more I can take.'

'And, don't forget, we've got two young men to take care of as well,' Kate said, stepping out of the cubicle to wash her hands. 'Although how we're going to bring them into our little game is beyond me at the moment.'

'Well, if Nigel runs true to form he'll drop off to sleep immediately after he's had us,' Pearl said.

'Ah, now that might be useful.' Kate turned to Pearl, her eyes sparkling with excitement. 'I really fancy some young cock. Don't you?'

Pearl giggled. 'You're really awful. Let's go and get Nigel. I want to get on with this.'

'Don't forget to give the boys a flash every now and again,' Kate said, with a worldly wink. 'Just to keep them interested.'

CHAPTER 4

Back in the cafe Nigel was moodily nursing his coffee cup, and he shot them an impatient look as they picked a path back to their table.

'Where have you two been?'

'Girl talk,' was Pearl's cryptic reply. 'Move over, Nigel, I want to get my bag.'

She leant across his chair and took her time in retrieving the shoulder bag as her tiny dress rode up and granted the boys an uninterrupted view of her hairy patch. Their lusty gulps were plainly audible above the clinking crockery and the low rumble of conversation.

'I've got a big hard-on,' Nigel said, with hope ringing loud in his tone.

'You won't have for long,' Kate promised.

'That's what I like to hear,' he said, grinning broadly and attempting to hide his bulge.

At the door Kate glanced back and was pleased to see the two boys trailing behind at a discreet distance.

She led them to a lake which was heavily wooded on one side for she had already decided that this would be the perfect place for their erotic encounter. On the pretext of fiddling with her shoe, Kate waited for the boys to catch up. She needed to be sure they would see her going into the wood. Suddenly they wandered into view and immedi-

ately stopped, shuffling their feet and waiting for her to move on.

Nigel led the way through thick undergrowth, gallantly holding back tree branches for the girls to pass under. Deep inside the wood they came upon a small clearing, with a larger area just beyond. While the others passed through to the larger space, Kate waited until she could hear tell-tale sounds from the boys. Pretty soon snapping twigs could be heard and then the rustle of vegetation. Kate smiled.

'Right, shall we all strip off?' she said, brightly.

Nigel was already tearing at the zipper on his shorts and as they slid to the ground his massive cock reared up and pointed towards the heavens. Kate chuckled merrily as the last of her buttons was undone and the dress was idly discarded, while Pearl swore softly and repeatedly at the catch on her suspender belt until it too was thrown aside.

Kate made a beeline for Nigel who was gazing with pride at the cock he held so tenderly in his hand. Taking hold of the generous shaft, she slid her fingers over its surface and marvelled at its thick veins and huge throbbing tip which was purple with lust as he drank in the beauty of her naked body.

All three were breathing heavily as they stood in a small circle while their hands roamed over one another's bodies like snakes writhing in a pit. Kate was fascinated by Nigel's shaft. She rubbed it gently and tiny shivers of delight travelled down her spine every time the foreskin rolled back to reveal the jaunty, quivering head.

Both Pearl and Nigel were toying with her vagina and in no time at all it was throbbing with such intense heat that Kate imagined it might ignite. Pearl was slowly

fingering the lavish tunnel and was clearly enchanted by the tightness which grasped and hung on to her fingers each time they probed and withdrew.

Nigel was pampering her clitoris with fingertips that were thick with her love cream. Now and then he would teasingly slide them along her cunt lips and away from the fiery button. But they would always return, like moths around a flame, bringing earthy groans charging up from the depths of Kate's delicate throat.

The feelings brought on by those fervent fingers were so intensely erotic that she was tempted to let them go on forever, but the itch so deep inside her became a torment that demanded satisfaction.

'Your cock's so big, Nigel,' she heard herself saying. 'I want it inside me.'

Suddenly the hands were taken away and she was standing on tip-toe with her hairy patch just touching the bulging tip of his weapon, openly inviting Nigel to thrust himself inside. He willingly accepted, but he was taller than Kate and therefore was unable to manoeuvre his excited shaft through the doors to her velvet tunnel. After several abortive attempts they were both trembling with frustration.

Kate quickly took his hand and led him towards a fallen tree. There she lay back against one of the large branches, but even before she was settled Nigel was pushing forward.

'Hold on,' she giggled, breathlessly. 'Give me time to spread my legs for you.'

Before her smooth thighs were apart Nigel was kneeling between them, prodding his penis into the wetness of her vagina. She reached down and guided him to the opening, and then their rapturous cries mingled in that still, quiet place as he pushed into her tight sheath.

It was soon obvious that he was far too excited to worry about technique and he thrust viciously with little regard for the hard wood scraping the soft skin of her back. He was ecstatic, delirious with excitement, and murmured continually about the intense feelings in his cock.

Despite her considerable discomfort Kate found her feelings of arousal spiralling, spurred on by the fact that Pearl was positively drooling at the action. She began to push back, her bare bottom bouncing off the hard branch and sending slight tremors of pain through her middle. Sadly, it was a move she soon regretted for her frenzied fucking immediately pushed Nigel towards a staggering climax and she was left aching with frustration when his hot seed began to spurt.

'That was fantastic to watch,' Pearl enthused. 'I love it when another woman gets Nigel so hot.'

She rushed forward and, kneeling before him, set about sucking his sagging cock into full hardness again. Kate felt sperm running in rivulets down the insides of her thighs as she watched Pearl working on her husband with hands and mouth. She suddenly felt in the way and hurriedly pulled on her dress before wandering off into the woods.

Soon she had worked her way around to the small clearing and it was there, with sounds of their lovemaking ringing off the trees, that Kate remembered the boys. Moving cautiously, she picked a path through the bushes until she had them in her sights. They were intent on watching Pearl and Nigel as they rolled on the floor, a profusion of limbs.

Each boy was masturbating vigorously, with shorts and pants around his ankles. Luckily, Kate had a sideways view of them and she marvelled at the size of their eager young

tools. There was something quite filthy about spying on these strangers as they unashamedly pleasured themselves in such a public place.

Her own pleasure zone ached with unfulfilled desire, and the agony only worsened when Pearl screamed out that she was coming. Kate's sharp intake of breath must have alerted the young men because suddenly two frightened faces were turned in her direction and their jaws sagged in unison when they caught sight of her.

One of the boys was fair-haired, with eyes widened by panic, and he hurriedly pulled up his shorts and ran off through the undergrowth. But the other boy, who was dark and interesting, stood up, remaining rooted to the spot.

'I'm sorry,' Kate began, lamely. 'We only came into the wood to have some fun. I didn't mean to disturb yours.'

She found it impossible to wrench her eyes away from his penis. It must have been at least eight inches long, and it was still swollen despite the surprise of discovery. She wandered across and, standing behind him, allowed her warm breath to play on his neck while she watched Pearl and Nigel.

'It's so exciting to watch couples having sex, isn't it?' she said, her voice deep and throaty.

The boy could only nod his agreement, and Kate could feel goose bumps rising on his skin as she ran a hand along his thigh.

'I've already been screwed, but I still feel horny,' she breathed. 'So I can't imagine how you must feel.'

She very gently probed his ear with her tongue, and the boy let out a soft moan as she pushed her large breasts against his back and lifted her dress so that soft pubic hair could brush against his buttocks. Soon his breathing was

ragged and Kate took to stroking the tops of his thighs while she nibbled at his neck.

'Do you want me to play with you?' she whispered. 'Shall I make your lovely cock feel good?'

The boy gave a tentative nod and then began to moan as her long fingers curled around his eager shaft. Kate could feel it throbbing vigorously against her palm, and the sensation fuelled the fire between her legs.

Her first hefty pull galvanized the boy, and he kicked off his shorts and opened his legs in one smooth movement. Still standing behind him, Kate could see his large balls swinging as she rubbed his gorgeous cock. Her own plaything was streaming with love juice, and some of it spilled on to the boy's buttocks as she moved closer to watch her expert hand fuck.

Watching Pearl and Nigel no longer seemed of interest, and he stood with eyes tightly shut and his head swaying from side to side as she rubbed him towards bliss.

'I really want you,' she murmured. 'My tight little hole can't get enough cock.'

The boy groaned and she pulled harder, longing to see him ejaculate.

'Go on, shoot,' she encouraged. 'Then I'll get you hard again and you can screw me.'

Explicit curses left the boy's mouth on jagged breaths, and then hot seed was flying from his tip and splattering on to the leaves of nearby bushes. He was still gasping and shaking when Kate released him. With obvious difficulty he turned to face her. His eyes were glazed, but she noticed with some relief that his sexy equipment was still large and hungry.

'You are a dirty boy,' she said, smiling. 'I'll have to make sure that goes down before I let you go.'

'Did you mean it?' he asked, with a touching eagerness. 'Can I really have you?'

'Of course,' she giggled. 'Didn't I tell you I can't get enough of it?'

She so wanted to appear carefree, nonchalant, but the sheer want in the slit at her groin was overpowering. With great haste she bent over in front of him and pulled up her dress. She heard him whistle softly at the sight of her sticky nest and then he stepped forward to savour her delights.

Kate reached between her legs to guide him to the spot, all the time worrying that her cavern would be too small to accommodate such a massive shaft, but was surprised by the ease with which she opened up to accept him. The boy pushed himself in to the very root of his cock, then stood still for a second as he acquainted himself with the feel of her rich warmth. But then he was pumping away and gripping her thighs.

Kate winced as his fingers dug into her flesh; but every man she had ever fucked had thrust with the same enthusiasm, so she always assumed that this was the way it was meant to be. She would simply have to grin and bear it. Opening her legs wider, she wriggled her bottom to entice him on.

'That's great,' she purred. 'Really screw me.'

The boy could hardly believe his luck. Was he really fucking this beautiful woman in the open air? If it was all a dream then he would enjoy it to the full. Without breaking his rhythm he widened his stance to give himself a more even balance, and with the help of his powerful thigh muscles he rammed into Kate, totally unmindful of her discomfort. Indeed, with only a limited experience to draw upon, he presumed that the harder a

man thrust, the greater was the woman's satisfaction.

The boy's crude technique would win him few notches on his belt and yet Kate relished the sleazy encounter. She didn't even know his name, for Christ's sake. To be screwing with a total stranger in a public park was more than enough to get her juices flowing.

Deep within her middle something stirred and started to build, holding the promise of fulfilment for her poor frustrated vagina. Pleas to God jostled with harsh expletives to be first out of her mouth as Kate verbalized her joy when the orgasm gained strength. Her crack was getting hotter and hotter, the wondrous heat overflowing into her groin like hefty waves from a broiling sea.

But then the feelings subsided and Kate almost wept with disappointment. It was as if her sexual plateau had been reached and the only way left to her now was down. The boy was still fucking, still gripping her thighs, his highly fit young body covered in sweat, and defeat mingled with regret in Kate's heart as the walls of her tunnel became sticky with his milky seed.

When the very last drop had left his industrious balls he pulled out of her with a tiny plop and gathered up his shorts, all the while backing away.

'Thank you. Thank you,' he mumbled.

The boy made to turn away but stumbled over some bushes. Righting himself quickly, a bright flush colouring his cheeks, he hurried off.

Kate suddenly felt very weary as she straightened up. Taking a tissue from her pocket, she cleaned away the mess between her legs. The sight of his sperm only added to her sense of longing and yet the strong desire to plunge comforting fingers into her yearning crack was pushed aside.

Once again fulfilment had eluded her, and with a heavy heart she wandered back to the large clearing. Nigel had indeed stayed true to form – he was sprawled out on the soft grass, snoring contentedly. Pearl was sitting beside him, enjoying a cigarette, and her face broke into a warm smile as Kate squatted down at her side.

'I heard you enjoying yourself with one of the young lads,' she teased.

Kate fixed a knowing grin on her lips, and said, 'I heard you coming, as well.'

'I didn't come,' Pearl said in a conspiratorial whisper.

'But I heard you shouting that you were.'

She laughed. 'Oh, I always do that because I know it's what Nigel wants to hear. If you ask me, sweetie, the whole climax during intercourse thing is one big fallacy.'

Kate felt her spirits sinking. 'What about when we were together at the cafe? Were you pretending then?'

'When you were licking my pussy, you mean?' A wistful light entered her eyes. 'No, Kate, I didn't have to pretend then. It was so dirty, and I wanted it so much.'

'Don't you ever come during a screw?' Kate asked, trying to keep her tone conversational.

Pearl shrugged. 'Not very often, no. Look, the conclusion I've reached is that my body is just a tool that men use for their own gratification. What's the point in chasing something that doesn't exist?'

Without another word Kate stood up and pulled her briefs from her shoulder bag. She put them on and her vagina seemed about ready to burst as the soft material brushed lightly against her pubic bush.

'I'll make my way back,' she called over her shoulder as she flounced away.

Although her spirits were at an all time low, Kate drew

some comfort from the fact that Maria was in for a big surprise. She didn't need lessons in the art of lust. In a matter of hours she'd had sex with Pearl and Nigel, not to mention the young stranger who had taken her from behind. Yes, that bitch of a woman would be forced to admit that Kate knew exactly how to use her body to give pleasure to another – man or woman.

'Oh, Christ,' she exclaimed. 'I just wish I could bloody well come.'

That evening Kate got very drunk. The last thing she needed was a night of tossing and turning in a lonely bed, so at least the alcohol assured her of a few hours' sleep. Next morning, however, she was punished by a terrible hangover and was relieved when Maria telephoned to put her appointment back to four o'clock that afternoon.

'You wait, Maria,' she murmured, replacing the receiver. 'You just wait.'

CHAPTER 5

Maria led the way along the endless, winding corridors at the 69 Club, chatting continually in a most friendly manner. It would seem that she had forgotten Kate's rather brusque departure after their last meeting.

They stopped outside a plain teak door, and Kate could feel her anger rising as Maria scrutinized her appearance, as if she were no more than a useful commodity.

'Your first lesson will concentrate on the many and varied ways of giving oral sex to a man,' she said.

'I already know how,' Kate snapped back.

'You may think you do, but I'd be willing to bet you have very little idea.' She smiled and gave Kate's arm a comforting pat. 'You must regard me as a friend, Kate. There are so many techniques a woman can use to make a man's prick happy, and the more skills you learn, the more likely they are to divulge their secrets ... such as the exact location of Laurence Wilson.'

Kate lowered her eyes. 'All right, you win.'

'Good.'

Maria opened the door to reveal three naked men lying on single beds. All were young and well-built, and their sleeping weapons began to stir and harden when Kate walked in.

'Strip, Kate,' Maria ordered. 'Show the boys what you've got for them.'

Kate's nervous fingers fumbled with the buttons of her shirt, causing her to redden with embarrassment. Relief fought with mild humiliation when it finally floated to the floor. The men whistled their appreciation of her sumptuous breasts and shy nipples, which seemed to shrink away from the three admiring glances.

When she dropped her skirt and stepped out of it their loud cheers only served to strengthen her feelings of degradation. Still, one million pounds was a sum which didn't come along every day, so the quicker she learnt how to swallow her pride, the better.

Now only her tiny briefs remained, and Kate could feel all eyes upon her. She dearly wanted to give a good show, make the most of it as an experienced strip-tease artiste would, but instead she simply pushed the panties down her long legs and stood with her hands primly hiding the blonde nest at her crotch.

'That's better. Now we can begin,' Maria said as she strode to the nearest bed. 'Kate, this gorgeous young man is Sean.'

Feeling utterly self-conscious and more than a little ridiculous, Kate padded across to the bed. Sean grinned up at her. He was a good-looking blond with bulging muscles, and his throbbing penis betrayed the fact that he was feeling extremely randy. Kate was struggling to drag her gaze away from the delectable demon in his lap when Maria solved the problem by handing her a carton of double cream.

'Spread this over Sean's cock,' she said, 'and then I'll show you how to lick and suck it off.'

Kate's nervousness was still apparent and, when she

clumsily pulled off the lid, the whole tub almost landed on the floor at her feet. Taking a deep breath, she plunged her fingers into the chilled cream and gently spread it over Sean's twitching shaft.

'Cover his balls, as well,' Maria said.

Sighing inwardly, Kate scooped out the last of the cream and advanced on his full sac.

It was a good three hours before she was allowed to leave the room and in that time Kate had given ten blow jobs, and her fingers – not to mention her tongue – had probed some very intimate places. The experience had proved to be a real eye-opener and, although she would never have admitted such a thing to Maria, Kate now saw where she went wrong during all of her previous attempts at oral sex.

Her mouth and hands ached almost as much as her frustrated pussy. All that time spent with three hunky men and a sexy Latin lady, and not even a fingertip went anywhere near her hungry crack. Surely that was cruelty at its most harsh.

It was that thought which accounted for Maria's sympathetic glance as she led Kate to another room which was furnished quite simply, with a single bed and an armchair positioned in front of a large television set. Kate could see a small kitchen beyond an open door to her right

'Sit,' Maria said, pointing to the armchair.

Kate sat submissively, realising with a start that she was no longer conscious of her nakedness.

'Did you find that useful?' Maria asked.

'Very useful, I must admit.'

'Good,' she said, studying Kate closely. 'Tell me something – you've never come, have you?'

Kate opened her mouth, intent on uttering a firm denial,

so was as surprised as Maria when a huge sob emerged
instead and hot tears streamed down her face. Maria
crouched at her side and listened while she poured out
the events of the past few days.

'I see,' she said, at last. 'And all that has left you feeling
unfulfilled—'

Kate's tiny, 'Yes,' brought more tears flooding out.

'You have the potential to be a very dirty girl, but there
are so many inhibitions we need to break down first.'

'Was Pearl right, Maria? Is complete satisfaction for a
woman just a fallacy?'

'Of course not,' she said, kindly. 'I'd say you're not
frustrated enough and it's that fact which is stopping your
orgasms. Your hairy crack must be so excited that all
thoughts are driven from your mind. Then, and only then,
will instinct take over and you won't simply be lying there
thinking will I come or won't I.'

'I wish I could believe you,' Kate sniffed.

'But you can, my love, you can.'

She was finding Maria's almost motherly manner quite
soothing and therefore what came next took Kate completely off guard. The woman squatted before her, pulled
up her tight skirt and pushed down her frilly knickers to
display her secret love spot. The hair around the vagina
was cut short and did little to conceal the pouting lips of
her glistening entrance.

'There, Kate,' her hypnotic voice cooed, 'your first
reaction was to look away, but if you could just be honest
with yourself you'd find that you want to play with me,
finger me, lick me, taste my beautiful juices on your lips.'

'Can I?' There was a faint note of pleading in the request.

Maria shook her head and pulled up her knickers.

'I'm afraid not. The fact that you turned away proves

that you're not ready. Listen, will you put yourself in my hands for two days?'

'Yes, yes I will,' Kate answered, eagerly.

'Most of that time will be spent here, by yourself,' Maria warned. 'You'll be watching videos that we beam through to you. But by the end of your time here I promise that you'll be like a bitch on heat. You'll experience climax after delicious climax.'

Kate looked puzzled and opened her mouth to speak.

'Just trust me,' Maria persisted. 'There's alcohol and cigarettes, food in the fridge, and the bathroom is through there,' she said, pointing to a door on their left. 'You were selected very carefully for this job, Kate, and now you must be trained.'

She thought it over for a few moments and then nodded her agreement.

'Good, I'll leave you to it, then.' At the door, Maria turned to face her. 'Watch the screen, Kate. Watch the screen.'

The woman left and when Kate heard a key turn in the lock something close to panic touched her spine. Was she their prisoner? Were Maria's kind words merely lies, uttered to give her a false sense of security?

She was about to rise from the chair when her attention was caught by the flickering television screen. Naked bodies rushed towards her; groups of people kissing and fondling; couples locked in energetic intercourse. The images did not linger long enough for Kate to study them, but then the picture settled and became a Victorian lady of obvious breeding. She was standing behind a screen, and the sound of water slurping its way into a tin bath could be heard.

The woman looked to be in her late-thirties and was

dressed in a tight bodice trimmed with delicate lace work, and cotton drawers that reached her ankles. With a sensuous slowness she removed the bodice. Once free of their restraint, her full breasts bobbed enticingly as she slipped off the long drawers. Kate let out an unconscious gasp when she saw the thick nest of hair between her legs.

'Johnson,' the woman called. 'Is my bath ready?'

'Yes, Madam,' a young, husky voice called back.

'Then go and wait in the corridor while I see if there's enough water in it.'

A door could be heard to open and close, and then the woman appeared from behind the screen. She skipped delicately across the room and stepped into the bath. Once settled in the deep water she set about lathering herself until the water was cloudy with soap suds. Then she lay back, a smile resting on her lips.

A few seconds elapsed before she rang a hand bell. Johnson entered the room almost immediately. He was twenty years old and ruggedly handsome, dressed in thick flannel trousers and a collarless shirt.

'Yes, Madam?' he enquired, his deep blue eyes sweeping over the bath in an attempt to catch a glimpse of the woman's body beneath the soapy depths.

'More water,' she ordered, tersely.

He crossed straightaway to an open fire in a huge grate and took an urn of water from the hob. Careful not to spill a drop, he returned to the bath and gingerly poured it at her feet. As the clear water eddied around the woman it was easy to make out the hair between her legs and her pink nipples, which were already aroused and swollen.

'Is that all, Madam?' he asked, his voice quite hoarse.

'No, I would like you to wash my back.'

'But, Madam—' he said, glancing towards the door with a panicked expression.

'Do as I say,' she ordered, sitting up and fully displaying her breasts before leaning forward. 'Hurry, hurry, the soap is somewhere in the bath.'

Johnson rolled up his shirt sleeve and plunged an arm into the warm water, feeling around for the bar of soap.

'It's between my legs, Johnson,' she said, in a taunting tone. 'It's right at the top of my legs.'

The bulge in Johnson's trousers grew rapidly until his rod was sticking out like a huge flagpole, stretching the rough flannel of his trousers.

Madam eyed it hungrily as he splashed around in the water, still searching for the soap. Suddenly she gave a shriek of horror.

'Johnson, how dare you touch me in such an intimate place. Only my dear husband is allowed to fondle my quim.'

'I'm sorry, Madam, it . . . it was the soap,' he stammered.

'It was not the soap,' she scolded, lightly. 'It was your hand which touched my most private of parts. And look at your big rod sticking out. Goodness only knows what terrible thoughts you are harbouring.' The expectant grin that was kept from her mouth was shining brightly in her eyes as she murmured, 'I think you had better remove your trousers, in the hope that shame will force the enormous thing to go down.'

Johnson took two steps back and unfastened his leather belt. Although his movements were totally servile, desire loomed large on his face as, with eyes narrowed, he licked his tempting lips. Madam's gaze was steadily aimed at his groin, and her pretty bosom rose and fell with ardent anticipation.

Finally the trousers were lying in a heap around his

ankles and Madam's eyes widened with astonishment for Johnson was not wearing undergarments. His cock, now free of its shackles, was standing to attention. It jerked and swayed before her eyes, as if wanting to show all angles of itself for her consideration.

Pulling herself to a sitting position, she leant forward for a closer look at the solid shaft. It pleased her greatly as it pranced about like a strutting stallion. But her expression remained harsh and the corners of her mouth dipped with spurious distaste when Johnson stepped out of the trousers, the hurried motion prompting his heavy balls to swing freely like an erotic pendulum.

'It is such a distasteful thing,' she muttered, huskily. 'And the smell offends my nostrils. I think I had better wash it.'

Snatching the proffered soap from Johnson's trembling hand, she briskly worked up a good lather, her gaze never once straying from the magnificent object of her desires.

Kate was highly aroused as she allowed the video to claim the whole of her attention, and was quite oblivious to the fact that her fingers were constantly stroking her thighs and rubbing at the coarse hair around her crack.

'Come here,' Madam commanded, her aroused nipples fiery with want.

Johnson shuffled forward and let out a low moan when her tiny, delicate hands stroked his excited member, causing it to quiver and jump with renewed fervour.

'Wash my breasts for me,' she breathed, grasping him fully and rubbing with a slow, tormenting rhythm.

His soapy hands brought a joyous groan from her throat as they slid over the huge mounds and took to circling her hardened nipples.

'What began as an innocent bath,' she said in a breath-

less whisper, 'has released the demon in me, and I am overcome with shame. Letting you play with my tits while I rub your heavenly cock is not something I should allow to happen. But, try as I might to be a God-fearing woman, the wanton desires of my quim make me use the language of a kitchen maid.'

A long sigh left her lips as she closed her eyes and gave herself up to the teasing feel of his fingers which became more earnest with each divine pull on his cock.

'God forgive me, but I need a good rogering every night. I use all my strength to resist that urge but you, Johnson, you have released a devil and now you must quieten it.'

Water splashed over the sides of the bath as she spread her legs and urged him to wash her wicked place. Johnson leant towards her, and as he did so an unquenchable desire seized her hand and forced her to increase the speed of her hand fuck. The suddenness of the move brought a mighty gasp from the depths of his throat and an angry flush to his cockhead which grew larger as each stroke led him nearer to orgasm. With eyes tightly closed and lips pulled back in the throes of passion, he reached into the water and felt for her silky slit.

'Oh Johnson, I am lost now,' she panted, as a large, rough finger was pushed inside. 'I cannot wait for this to be over so that I can return to my normal self.'

With an eagerness which was at odds with her words, Madam plunged a hand into the water and grasped his wrist in an effort to work his finger faster...

Kate let out a groan of disappointment when the television screen went blank. But, within seconds, another video started. This one was to do with two women in their thirties who were setting out to seduce a young man who worked in their office. Although it held her interest, it

didn't have the same appeal as the Victorian saga.

She was all too aware of the scent rising from her smouldering crack but resisted the urge to dip her fingers into the hair-covered honey pot and then suck them clean. However, the desire to do so remained with her while she poured a large vodka and tonic and lit a cigarette.

CHAPTER 6

In a room two doors along the corridor Maria was sitting with James Dixon, watching Kate's progress on closed circuit television.

'She's not as interested in this one,' Dixon remarked.

'I don't think she is, no, but it's enough to keep her ticking over,' Maria replied, still studying the monitor. 'She really is a beautiful girl.'

'Yes, she is.'

Dixon's heavy-lidded eyes filled with lust as he stared at Kate reclining in the chair, her legs wide open and inviting.

'The Victorian video gets really horny,' he said. 'I suggest that we show Miss Highlands another extract in one hour's time, when she's had a few more drinks and is ready for bed.'

'Good idea,' Maria said, rising from the chair. 'Now, perhaps you'd like to sit back and let me relax you.'

'Maria, you have the best mouth in the business,' he sighed, as she unfastened his trousers.

By the time Kate had finished two more drinks her head was spinning pleasantly and her mind was drifting towards sleep. The television screen had been blank for the past ten minutes so she assumed that the show was over for the day.

Getting to her feet, yawning and stretching languidly, she wandered across to the bed and was just pulling back the duvet when sounds from the television filled the small room.

'Johnson,' a female voice called out, 'I feel the need to stand up so that you can wash my quim.'

Kate raced back to the chair and settled down just as Madam stood up in the bath tub. Water cascaded from her body and was still running down in rivulets when Johnson's hand went between her legs. Her thick pubic hair was bedraggled, so Kate had a good view of the vigorous fingering Johnson was administering to his horny mistress.

His big rod swayed back and forth as he manoeuvred the finger in and out of her tight little hole. Every so often she would grasp his wrist and show him the speed she needed. Soon she was gasping and groaning, splashing about in the water, seemingly incapable of remaining still.

'Oh, Johnson,' she panted, 'you have made my eager cunt go so hot and I cannot deny you any longer, although I know I should. But you must promise that if I let you roger me, you will remove your big weapon before you shoot your seed, for I do not want to be with child.'

'I will, Madam,' he promised. 'Oh, I will.'

She smiled her gratitude and lay back in the bath, her eyes inviting him to take her. Hurriedly he climbed in and positioned himself on top as she opened her legs.

'My,' she said, 'your cock is so huge. I don't know if I can spread my legs wide enough to grant it entry.'

In a frenzy of activity Johnson mounted and began to ride. Their violent movements, as he thrust forward and she pushed back, caused the bath water to well up in the tub and splash onto the tiled floor.

'Do it even faster,' she begged.

Mounting excitement gripped Kate as she watched the sizzling scene. Unable to deny herself any longer, she allowed a hand to creep between her legs, letting out a thankful groan when her fingers found her clitoris.

Johnson's body was a blur of movement as he fucked, while his mistress cried out in ecstasy as the power of her second orgasm swept away her senses. But the cry changed to one of disappointment when he pulled out and towered above her with sperm gushing from the rude tip of his elated cock. Four large blobs landed in the water and floated on the surface while he stood fighting for breath, his wet shirt clinging to his highly muscled torso.

'Oh, thank you,' she cooed. 'A most pleasant experience, but it did not last anywhere near long enough. Perhaps you could help me up and we could dry each other.'

By now Kate was unashamedly pandering to her clitoris, using her middle finger to give the crimson bud the attention it craved. And tiny shocks of pleasure were coursing through her middle as she watched the couple on the screen drying each other off.

Madam was kneeling in front of Johnson, and when she finally threw the towel to one side his rock-hard pole was just inches away from her full lips. It was so easy for Kate to sense the woman's warm breath surrounding it, playing on his testicles.

'I would be powerless to resist if you decided to push your huge weapon into my mouth,' she purred. 'I would be forced to suck it until it spat down my throat.'

Johnson gave a lustful growl as he pushed forward, thrusting his enlarged tip between her willing lips. Grasping his shaft to prevent it from entering her throat, Madam started to suck while her free hand slipped between his buttocks to probe and caress. She sucked expertly for

almost ten minutes, all the time teasing his balls and fondling his anus until his expression was one of demented bliss.

He repeatedly begged her to go faster, but she kept up the same determined rhythm, tormenting him with it as she became drunk with the power being exerted by her salacious mouth. He begged for her to make him come, but his pleas were met with the same slow, sensuous movements until, in desperation, he grabbed handfuls of her hair and rammed his prick in and out of her mouth.

Madam's muffled cries of joy urged him on and soon his moment of release was close. Johnson thrust faster and then he was groaning and crying out with triumph, while his mistress eagerly swallowed his hot seed.

Kate had four fingers inside herself, up to the knuckles, and was about to lose what little control she had left, but her eyes never left the screen for a second.

'I have caused you displeasure,' Madam said, rising to her feet. 'I have tormented your shaft for my own amusement, for it is nice to have a man begging me to make him come. But I took the game too far and now I must pay the awful price.' She promptly lay on the floor and allowed her legs to part. 'You have my permission to do whatever you will, no matter how vile it may be, until you are fully satisfied.'

Tears sprang to Kate's eyes when the screen went blank once more, and she sprang to her feet and hurled her empty glass across the room. It hit the wall and shattered, as she screamed,' I want it, you bastards, I want it.'

She paced around the flat for what seemed like an age and finally came to rest by the armchair, an idea springing to the surface of her mind. The chair had a hard wooden arm and she reached out to feel the intriguing coarseness

of the material with which it was covered. For many moments she gazed at it, her fingers toying with the rough knots that held the material in place.

Unmindful now of the camera which she had assumed was fixed on her every action, she straddled the arm and tentatively rubbed her vagina against it. Each push caused the roughness of the fabric to open up her pouting lips and brush against her clitoris.

'Oh, that's it,' she called out, frenzied. 'I want it. I bloody want it.'

'So do I, Miss Highlands,' Dixon said as he turned off the closed circuit television.

'Tomorrow she'll be ready,' Maria said. 'And then she can start the job.'

They were both naked now, and their expressions suggested that they were eager for fulfilment.

'We'll let her have breakfast and then show her the final instalment,' Dixon said, as he sprawled out on top of his bed.

Watching Kate had left him with a full, throbbing erection, and Maria knew only too well that her day would not end until it had subsided. She climbed on top and guided his quivering cock to the place he had christened, the tight pit of pleasure.

CHAPTER 7

Kate was awake early. She glanced at her watch, then stumbled from the bed and headed for the shower on shaky legs.

While the exhilarating coolness of the water brought her body quickly back to life and the previous evening's events clear in her mind, a faint flush of guilt made her face redden and burn, but the soapy water soon washed it away. If she had to resort to lewd antics, then all the blame must rest at Maria's door. For was it not she who had orchestrated the whole bizarre scenario – Maria and Mr Dixon? She was merely obeying orders, and therefore was totally beyond reproach.

As she dried her hair, Kate became aware for the first time that she was locked in the room without one single item of clothing. That fact, coupled with the hour upon hour of sexy videos she was forced to watch, would have anyone acting out of character.

Feeling better about herself she wandered into the compact kitchen in search of breakfast. While coffee bubbled in the percolator she rummaged in the cabinet and found a box of cornflakes. They would do. The tiny fridge was well stocked with milk, eggs, bacon, and cheese.

She took out a carton of milk and was about to close the door when something caught her eye. Lying in the salad

tray was a large cucumber. Her eyes dancing with devilment, Kate picked it up and started to rub it as she would a penis. Feeling rather foolish, she looked around the kitchen for any tell- tale camera eyes and then pushed the vegetable between her lips, surprised that this ridiculous act should bring a flutter to her vagina.

For a few moment she worked her mouth backwards and forwards along its green surface and then, feeling like a naughty girl, she positioned it near the entrance to her crack.

'Oh, no, Kate,' she murmured, giggling. 'That's going too far.'

She wolfed down the cornflakes, enjoyed the fine coffee and was smoking her first cigarette of the day when her hand kept straying to the cucumber which was lying at her side on the table. She seemed unable to resist, and as she fondled and played with it, a happy smile was on her lips.

But then she heard a click which meant that the television had come on. Kate almost stumbled and fell in her haste to get into the room, and she whooped with joy when a picture of Johnson and his lusty mistress filled the screen. As she settled into the armchair, so the action began.

Madam was still lying on the floor with her legs spread wide, her hairy nest on full display.

'But you must lick me first,' she implored, 'because that is something my husband refuses to do.'

With an eagerness which delighted her, Johnson crawled between her thighs and promptly buried his face into her bush, his tongue searching for her hot slit straight away. The expression on Madam's face betrayed the fact that he had found it and was in the process of administering a furious licking.

'Oh, my goodness,' she cried, as she writhed. 'I did not think it was possible for anything to be so pleasant, but it only makes my little crack crave for something far larger.'

As those words filled the room, Madam thrust her legs straight up in the air so that Johnson's probing tongue could delve deeper. She opened her legs wider and shrieked that she was coming, but he kept up his assault until she became still and languid beneath him. And even then he kept on, moving down to her buttocks and slipping his tongue towards the puckered hole.

'Oh, no, sir, I beg you not to take me there,' she murmured, the horror in her voice outweighed by the look of sheer enjoyment on her face. 'Please, such things defile a lady.'

Her feeble protests seemed to encourage him, and his kisses became more intense as she rubbed her arse against his face. Still complaining about his boldness, Madam turned over and thrust her buttocks into the air, brazenly holding the cheeks open with eager fingers. The camera was perfectly angled to pick up Johnson's tongue pushing into the tight orifice, and all the while his mistress begged for more.

But then the picture faded and Kate was yet again left watching a blank screen. This time, instead of venting her annoyance, she flounced into the kitchen and returned wielding the cucumber. Finding a comfortable position in the armchair, she brought her heels up on to the seat and thew her legs apart, then placed the tip of the vegetable inside her crack and worked it like a dildo.

Although no more than an inch was penetrating she found the sensation rather pleasant and so continued to slide it in and out. Her eyes had closed and her lips were

moving in silent mutterings as she imagined that the cucumber was Johnson's superb rod.

A sound from the television set made her jump and that tiny movement allowed another inch of green prick to slide inside her tunnel. Content to leave it in there, she settled back and concentrated on the screen.

Johnson was vigorously fingering his mistress's bottom while she protested in a joyous voice.

'I pray to God that you will not put your weapon in there after you have used my tight quim again, Johnson. I pray to the good Lord that it will sag and go down after you have come again.'

Johnson sat up. There was a depraved look on his face as he studied his mistress's ungainly position. Her buttocks were still in the air and her legs were open and waiting. He lunged forward and her hand promptly appeared between them to guide him to her pleasure point. After rubbing his tip against the wicked entrance of her arse, leaving him in little doubt as to what she wanted, she guided him towards the enticing lips of her quim and beseeched him to push it home.

He entered her with a loud grunt, ramming in all eight inches until her ecstatic screams reached a crescendo. Very slowly he withdrew and then pushed the hard tool home again, gradually increasing his speed until finally he was pumping into her like a crazed monster, thrusting with all his might as she beat a triumphant tattoo on the bare floor with her clenched fists.

'I must confess, Johnson, this is the best fuck I have ever experienced,' she gasped, wriggling her bottom to meet his thrusts. 'Oh, dear Lord, your cock is making me come again.'

Her cries were now of unconcealed joy as Johnson

stepped up the battle at her crotch, his breathing ragged, his face wet with sweat.

'Let me leave it in, Madam,' he implored. 'My shaft is about to burst.'

'Oh, yes, fill me with your gift, Johnson, fill me with your precious gift.'

He trembled as if with a fever, his whole body affected by the force of his imminent climax, and then his aching balls discharged their load deep within her valley.

Without even realizing, Kate had pushed another two inches of cucumber inside herself, and was working it furiously while she watched the video, totally entranced.

Johnson and his mistress were on their feet, facing each other.

'At this moment I do not care about anything,' she confessed, with a grateful smile. 'And for you, my dear Johnson, I will always drop my drawers, and I will always let you leave your cock in when it comes.' She glanced down and giggled. 'It does take a lot to make it go down, and yet I am sure I can conquer it.'

His penis was in fact sagging from the pounding it had taken, but it soon hardened again when Madam began to spread cool grease along its scorched surface. When it was thick with the oily substance and was once more pointing towards the heavens, she scooped more from the jar and, with a wicked smile touching her sensuous lips, reached behind and delved between her buttocks.

The smile was still there as she said, 'Now you can visit my most private of places.'

With that she bent over and grasped her shins. Johnson stood behind her, gazing avidly at her body: at the thick hair between her legs which was sticky with his residue; the doors to her obliging tunnel which had pleasured him

beyond belief; and finally, the cleft between her buttocks which she continually stroked as she squirmed with delight. That dark hole now drew him like a magnet.

Taking hold of his cock, Johnson placed the massive tip at its door. Would her tightness yield before his burgeoning rod? He stood motionless for a long moment, savouring the delight that was so close.

'Do not be gentle,' she told him. 'I want you to be rough and brutal with my comely arse.'

Inspired by her vulgar words and bawdy tone, Johnson pushed into the grasping passage and did not stop until his swinging balls were slapping against the creamy softness of her buttocks. She yelped with pain while he grunted with satisfaction.

Kate worked six inches of the cucumber into her yearning pussy, spurred on by the action on the screen. She wanted to close her eyes and enjoy the sensation of the substitute prick as it grew hot and wet and glided exquisitely over her pleasure zones again and again, but she also wanted to watch the movie. Gradually, though, her eyelids closed of their own accord, and the whole of her world became the disgusting sounds of the video and the intense pleasure building up in her vagina.

'Now that the pain has gone,' Madam was saying, 'the feeling is such a sweet one. Especially when you toy with my hot quim at the same time.'

Johnson was whimpering at the feel of her, at the tightness of her arse which was eroding his control. By the sounds, Kate guessed that he was really slamming into the woman, but their delirious jangle of cries soon faded into the distance, drowned out by Kate's own laboured breath.

Something wonderful was happening between her legs.

That delightful itch was intensifying, taking over her whole being. Kate was on a roller-coaster, heading for bliss, and in her eagerness to arrive there she pushed in the cucumber as far as it would go, massaging each and every one of her pleasure spots until the full length of her tunnel was a mass of rapturous nerve endings, all seemingly contracting as one to hug the cause of their pleasure.

The heat in her middle throbbed in time with her racing heartbeat. It felt like a tidal wave of warmth pounding against a dam, threatening to break it. Some spilled over the top and a mild electric shock travelled through her groin. But this time the pleasant feeling only served as a spur for Kate to intensify her efforts. She was fucking herself with total abandon, her free hand toying with her arse and wallowing in the sex juice which was flooding the pulsing channel of her buttocks.

Again the warmth edged nearer to climax, closer, closer, almost at the top. While the cucumber continued to rub her cunt into a frenzy, two fingers were let loose on Kate's pleading clitoris. They stroked, teased, pinched and rolled the neglected swelling, dragging from its impassioned centre sensations so intense that they were almost painful.

She was approaching the summit now and Kate dared not breathe, concentrating fully on the sexual energy unleashed at her crotch. But then the feelings weakened and began to slip away.

'Oh, God, no.'

Kate's call was frenzied and, pushing the cucumber faster, she pinched her clitoris between finger and thumb until it burned and throbbed. The climactic sensations had all but faded when they came rushing back, swamping everything in their path, gushing over and flooding her

groin with a sizzling orgasm which could no longer be denied.

'I'm coming,' she screamed.

Jumping to her feet and standing with legs apart, Kate thrust the cucumber into her burning slit, forcing every drop of hot come to pour out of her joyous tunnel. Then, totally breathless, she became still and opened her eyes. Maria was standing beside the closed door, utterly absorbed in the erotic spectacle.

'That was good to watch, Kate.'

'When did you . . . I mean, how long—?'

'Long enough,' she replied, walking to her side and taking the cucumber from her grasp. 'I'm beginning to feel quite randy.'

Kate laughed and felt between her legs. 'I'm beginning to feel bruised.'

'You were rougher than most men would have been. Sit down and I'll put some cream on for you.'

Maria disappeared into the bathroom, then came back seconds later with a bottle of baby lotion. Kate flopped into the chair and spread her legs for Maria to kneel between. She shuddered slightly when the cool oil was gently massaged into the aching lips of her sex.

'It's not too bad. You haven't harmed yourself,' Maria assured her. Then she giggled. 'I can't believe how wet you are.'

The cream was administered to all parts of Kate's vagina before the woman spoke again.

'By the way,' she said, 'I've paid half a million pounds into your bank account. In fact, I was so sure you'd come through, I did it yesterday.'

Kate laughed and shook her head. 'The money side hasn't sunk in yet. I mean, one million pounds! This whole

thing is just so surreal. Am I really a millionaire?'

'Not yet. There's the little job to do for Mr Dixon first, don't forget. Now, tomorrow you start work for Earl Barton. He's a writer of erotica and you will be his typist.'

Kate's eyebrows rose in surprise.

'Yes, it should be a fun job,' Maria said, grinning. 'Seriously though, you're to take the job because Laurence Wilson stayed with Barton for several weeks recently, but unfortunately he had moved on by the time Mr Dixon became aware of the fact. So, Barton is the only lead you have, and he may be reluctant to part with any information because he and Wilson are good friends. So, it's up to you to unearth what you can.'

By now Maria was crouching in front of Kate, whose eyes were fixed on the gusset of her white knickers, which was stained with her love juices. She was stroking Kate's vagina and thrilling inwardly at the look of lust in her lovely eyes.

'Now I must warn you that Barton thinks his typists should take their knickers off as part of the job. And he does write superb erotica, so you may well find yourself doing just that.' She smiled. 'He has a son of eighteen who is very shy and withdrawn, and a daughter of nineteen. The girl is important – she had sex with Wilson on a regular basis when he was staying at the house. She's a dirty little madam, but one who tends to use sex to exert power over men rather than for enjoyment. Anyway, we believe all three of them know where Wilson went after he left their house, and it's up to you to get them to part with that information.'

Kate nodded, her gaze still glued to Maria's crotch, and she said, 'One million pounds is a hell of a lot of money. This Wilson must have taken something very valuable to Mr Dixon.'

Maria simply shrugged. 'Mr Dixon is a rich and power-ful man. If someone stole a pound from him, he would spend a million to get it back, just to prove that no one could take anything away from him.' She followed the line of Kate's eyes and laughed. 'Do you like what you can see, Kate? Do my wet panties turn you on?'

She nodded.

'They're wet because I enjoyed watching you with the cucumber,' she whispered, reaching a hand up her skirt and pulling the gusset to one side. 'Do you like what I've got?'

Kate did indeed like the dark skin, and the black hair that surrounded her proud, glistening lips.

'Yes,' she said, her voice faltering.

'Good. You did not look away this time,' Maria mur-mured softly. 'Is that because you want it?'

'Could we? Could we have fun, I mean?'

Maria shook her head and rose slowly to her feet. 'No, but I do promise you that before too long we will enjoy each other's bodies.'

Kelt felt a surge of disappointment when the woman crossed to the door.

'I will arrange to have your clothes sent up, along with the address of your new employer.' Her smile was warm. 'Good luck, Kate.'

The door was closed quietly and Kate stared at it for many moments before gazing around the room with a heavy heart. It had been such a happy place for her and now that the time had come she didn't want to leave it. But she was a private investigator, here to do a job for which she would be amply rewarded. And as Maria had implied, there would be time for sex later. Kate could hardly wait.

CHAPTER 8

Early next morning Kate arrived at Earl Barton's plush mews house. She was met at the door by a young girl with flowing blonde hair and a shapely figure. She was dressed in a flimsy bra and panties and a toothbrush stuck out of her pretty mouth.

'Yes,' she asked sullenly, toothpaste around her mouth.

'I'm Kate Highlands,' she said, with a bright smile. 'I'm here to work for Mr Barton.'

'Oh yeh, come on in.'

Kate crossed the threshold as the girl called, 'Dad, the typist's here.' Then, without another word, she bounded off up the stairs.

A man wandered out of a room on Kate's left. He was tall and well built, with long auburn hair which covered his ears and spilled sexily over his collar. Kate felt that his face had a rugged appeal, and her vagina twitched when his deep brown eyes rested on her face.

'Hi, there, I'm Earl,' he said, extending a hand. 'Excuse Donna, won't you? Sometimes I think she's hardly civilized. But what can I do? – I'm only her father.'

He stood back and studied Kate while she laughed politely.

'My, you are formally dressed,' he said, taking in her long black skirt and prim white blouse.

'I like to look nice,' she countered.

'Good, that's good.' He clapped his hands briskly. 'Right, then, I've got to go out now, so I'll show you to the study and, well, let you get on with it.'

'Okay.'

Kate followed him across the hall and into a small room dominated by carved wooden panels which covered each wall. In one corner a battered desk was home to an elderly word processor.

'This is it,' he said, pulling out the chair for her. 'I don't know if you've ever typed erotica before?'

'No, I haven't, but I shall treat it just like any other job,' was her short reply as she sat down.

'Jolly well done.' He placed his hands on the desk and leant towards her. 'I do like my typists to tell me if my work causes them to, well, get aroused. It's the way I judge if it's any good or not.'

She could smell the strong masculine scent that permeated through his spicy aftershave, which was pleasant enough in itself. That, and the boyish glint in his gorgeous eyes, broke through her defences and brought a grin to her lips.

'I'll give you my assessment of it, then.'

'Good.' He scooped up his leather jacket from the desk and pointed to a pile of papers. 'That's the manuscript. Why don't you read through some of it first, get the feel of it?'

Kate waited until he had left the room and closed the door behind him, and then picked up the first handwritten page. The book was entitled *Susie's Amorous Encounters*, and was quite bulky. It was just as well she had kept her typing up to scratch. Kate settled back and read the brief extract on the fly leaf.

'He penetrated her with seven inches of throbbing flesh. She could feel it twitching with excitement as it pushed into her hairy nest. Her vaginal muscles contracted immediately, gripping it tightly in welcome as the man worked to and fro. She had no idea who he was, what he was, and that only added to the pleasure of the event.

It had all happened so suddenly. They had kissed just once, and during that kiss his hand stole up her skirt, expecting to be met with firm resistance. When none came, his free hand fumbled with the zip of his trousers until finally he managed to push it down and release his trembling penis.

The woman lifted her skirt and held it aloft in a token of surrender, standing passively while he wrenched her knickers from that most intimate of places. Freeing one leg, she stood on tip-toe, spreading her legs wide so he could manoeuvre himself into her warmth.

And that was how she found herself being screwed silly in the cramped toilet of a train which was travelling at ninety miles an hour.'

Intrigued, Kate picked up the next page, the start of the first chapter, and as she scanned the words she realized that this job would keep her sexual urge very much at the forefront of her mind. Grinning widely at the thought, she began to read.

'The girl was sitting with the boy in the middle of a huge field and, as the long grass swayed in a slight breeze, it was obvious that they had just finished a rather frenzied sex session. The girl's short skirt was pulled up, and she was enjoying the feel of the cool air caressing her young, ripe vagina. The boy was gazing at it avidly.

"Go on," she cajoled. "It should be a giggle, not to mention really horny fun."

She was eighteen years old, with long blonde hair and a well-developed body. Her eyes were blue and sparkling, her turned up nose small and cute, and she had the type of mouth that made men yearn for oral sex.

"I don't know, Susie," the boy replied, his attractive face marred by a frown. "Why do you want us to seduce our teachers, in any case?"

"Just to see if we can." She gave an infectious laugh. "It's to give us a feeling of power. They'd be taking a chance, wouldn't they? They'd risk losing their jobs, and all that. Oh, come on Greg, let's have some fun."

"But it wouldn't be fun if they turned us down," he said, still frowning. "We'd look silly, and then we'd be the ones in trouble."

"Miss Phipps is always hanging around the changing rooms and showers at the gym. You know she is. She's always watching you boys undressing. You only have to look in her eyes to see that she wants it. Oh, say yes, Greg. She's got a gorgeous pair of tits, and I bet her pussy's really hungry for it."

The boy still looked doubtful. "What about you with Mr Steel?"

"Just you leave him to me," she replied, confidently. "He won't stand a chance once he sees my hot little crack and knows it's willing. Think about it, Greg. If we can get those two going, who knows what we could do? We could even arrange an orgy with some of the other kids there."

Greg glanced around the field, deep in thought; he was a sensible boy who knew his limitations. Still, he could see the potential of what Susie was suggesting. But could they pull it off?

While he mulled over the problem, Susie impatiently crawled between his legs and opened his flies. With young

fingers that were already expert, she coaxed his cock through the opening and rolled it between her cool palms. Greg lay back and arched his body so that Susie could undo his trousers and pull them down.

Tenderly, she kissed his quivering tip and ran her tongue around it while Greg tried to push it into her mouth. She laughed, pulling her head back to thwart his efforts.

"Do it Susie, please."

"No," she teased, "not until you say 'yes'."

She was rubbing his eager shaft, a bewitching light in her eyes, and very soon he was panting and bucking up and down in an effort to fuck back.

"Say yes, Greg, and I'll let you come in my mouth."

"Yes," he wailed, bringing both hands to his face. "I'll do anything you say. But please, just suck me."

With a tiny smile of victory playing around her mouth, Susie leant forward and pressed her lips against his tip then deliberately pulled away, staying just beyond his reach.

"Go on, then," she murmured, playfully. "Push your prick in."

Greg lunged towards her and pushed until the lips grudgingly parted, and he thrilled at the feel of her teeth lightly chaffing the sensitive skin of his cock as it entered. The feeling was so entrancing that he began to whimper straight away, a sound which turned into a deep moan when she started to slide her lips along the whole of his length.

Susie had sucked cock many times before and knew just how to make her mouth resemble the tightest of vaginas, and knew too that the use of her teasing tongue on his tip could drive a man wild. Her technique was superb and it ensured that Greg would be forever at her

heel and desperate for the next journey to Heaven.

At precisely the right moment Susie allowed her free hand to meander towards his aching balls, and Greg stiffened with anticipation for the move could only heighten his already spiralling pleasure. Cupping them in her palm, Susie squeezed them with a tenderness that was almost sublime, helping his milky seed on its swift journey to the back of her throat.

Susie savoured the bitter taste of his essence before swallowing greedily, and an inward smile burst in her breast at the sight of Greg's rapturous expression. She knew only too well that as long as men needed to discharge their sperm into a tight orifice, they would do as she desired.'

Kate let out a long, low whistle and replaced the pages on the desk. Her vagina was pounding and her knickers were wet. It was an enjoyable feeling and she had a strong urge to touch herself there, but resisted. There was a time and a place for everything, and now was not it.

As she reached for the next few pages it struck her that the physical description of Susie fitted exactly that of Barton's daughter, Donna, and she momentarily wondered whether the character was in any way based on the girl. She also pondered on the fact that most women, after spending the day reading and typing this stuff, would be more than ready to drop their knickers; in fact she imagined that it would be near impossible to keep them on. Still that was one of the reasons why she was here. Settling back in the chair, she turned to the next page.

'Susie felt so good the next morning as she hurried along the corridor towards Mr Steel's study. She had spent the

previous evening with Greg, drinking lager and planning the seduction of their unsuspecting tutors. Greg had wanted sex again – he couldn't get enough – but Susie had remained firm, saying that they both needed to feel really randy in the morning.

She fleetingly wondered what Greg would now be doing to lure Miss Phipps into his amorous trap. One glance at his naked organ would be enough to ensure her total capitulation, but how would he bring that about? A devilish smile touched her lips as her mind dwelt once more on her own mission.

She had spent ages rummaging through her wardrobe that morning, for her outfit needed to be perfect for the job in hand – not too sexy, but at the same time revealing enough to have Mr Steel drooling at his desk.

Her panties were of red lace, delicate and completely see-through. There was a strip of silk at the gusset, but it stopped short of her pubic hair so the thick bush was in full view, adding a sordid touch to the tiny garment as it escaped through the open weave.

The matching bra was equally flimsy, and its half cups were an added bonus. Susie was proud of her breasts. The ripe mounds stood, haughty and flirtatious, defying gravity as teenagers' did. Their nipples were huge and permanently erect, as if continually begging to be sucked. Susie couldn't wait to see the lust in Mr Steel's eyes when those gems poked brazenly over the top of the sexy bra and drew *his* mouth towards them.

Her dress was also red, a plain shift of the thinnest Jersey wool, which clung to her curves like a second skin. Mr Steel would *have* to notice her in that outfit, and the rest could be left to her wily nature.

So obsessed with sex was Susie that she found it quite

normal to be constantly soaking between the legs. The lips of her vagina were all the while engorged and ready to open up, so they couldn't help but rub against her knickers as she walked, adding to her perpetual state of arousal.

Arriving at the study, she knocked lightly and waited for Mr Steel's call to enter. The moment she walked into the room his eyes travelled the whole length of her body, openly devouring the feast before them. Susie was thrilled; this was going to be easier than she'd thought.

Mr Steel swallowed loudly and averted his gaze. He found that being in charge of a class of eighteen year-olds was a difficult task, for he had a very active sex drive. There was an added complication in the fact that he was tall, well muscled, and darkly handsome. He was, in fact, the very type of man for whom young girls very quickly developed crushes. To be in such close proximity day after day was enough to test a saint but, so far, he had managed to keep all relationships on a firm student–teacher basis. Well, almost.

He liked the scent of a young girl – the fresh, raw aroma which caused the blood to flow hot in his veins. But best of all, he liked to smell them after a long, hectic session in the gym; then his eager nostrils feasted unashamedly on the odour of their young, sweaty vaginas.

Yes, his was a job which ensured that the rampant tiger between his legs was always half erect, always keen to pounce. And the girls were aware of it; aware too that they were the reason for his hardly contained excitement as their gazes rested unceasingly upon the intriguing bulge in his trousers. He had thought, more than once, that if he could only devise a way of making the words on the blackboard even half as interesting as his crotch then his yearly exam results would top all other subjects by a mile.

Now here was Susie, the raunchiest of the lot, mincing her way towards his desk. With a weary sigh Mr Steel tore his eyes away from her breasts and focused on her face.

"Sit down, Susie," he said, kindly.

"Thank you, sir."

She settled in the chair, lazily crossing one long leg over the other, the soft wool dress riding up to show an ample amount of luscious thigh. Mr Steel let out another long breath and loosened his tie a little.

"Now, what can I do for you?"

Susie looked him directly in the eye and cleared her throat. "I've just been elected to represent the students, sir, and Mandy Thompson has complained to me that you tried to have sex with her."

All colour drained from Mr Steel's face.

Meanwhile, Miss Phipps was strolling through the boys' changing rooms in the pavilion as she often did. She had no right to be there, of course, but the place seemed to draw her like a magnet.

Earlier on the boys were playing cricket, but they must have finished sooner than usual because, to her dismay, she found the block almost deserted. Her spirits soared, however, on hearing the hiss of water coming from the shower room. Greg was the only boy in there, and through the screen door she could see the opaque outline of his fine, young body.

A familiar fluttering and twitching began inside her knickers as she watched him lather his muscular torso, getting nearer and nearer to the dangling cock which reached halfway down his thighs. Then, as if catching her unspoken wish, he reached down and gripped the sleepy member with a soapy hand.

Miss Phipps shivered in delight as it grew larger with each caress, and she positively swooned when it reached its full proportions. The cock was enormous – the biggest she had ever seen – and so thick. Oh, if only she could touch the divine creation. If only . . .

She knew she should go now, just run out into the open air and leave the boy to his dastardly self-abuse, but she couldn't. She had taken root right there on the cold stone floor and was completely at the mercy of that vision of young manhood before her eyes.

Miss Phipps had to stifle a gasp when Greg put down the soap and concentrated wholly on pleasuring the wonderful plaything which was always ready to bring him joy. The feeling inside her knickers intensified as she watched him pulling ever harder at his huge tool, and the battle inside herself continued. But she had not had sex for three whole months and there was no way she could walk away from such a lewd show. She would watch, she promised herself, but that was as far as it would go – this time.

"Go on," she whispered. "Jerk it right off. Go on."

As if to oblige, Greg's hand started to move faster. Then suddenly he stopped. And before Miss Phipps could rally her senses, he had turned off the shower and opened the cubicle door. There he was, mere feet away, with nothing between her and his deep chest, his flat, hard stomach that bulged with rippling muscles, and his quivering shaft which almost took her breath away.

A smile came to his lips as she gazed at it, fighting the urge to rush forward and finish what he had started.

"I'm so sorry," she stammered, before turning and fleeing.

Outside, with the cool air easing the frantic burning of

her cheeks, she sat on the grass in front of the sports hall and smoked a cigarette, attempting to put her emotions into some sort of rational order.

This was like history repeating itself, she thought, glumly. Her panties were soaking wet, just like the first time. And that's why she'd been forced to remove them. If only she hadn't done that.'

CHAPTER 9

'Why?' Kate murmured. 'What could have happened that was so awful?'

The text left poor Miss Phipps agonizing outside the sports hall and Kate desperate to know about her previous transgression. Never mind, all would be revealed – she was confident of that.

In the meantime, she had Susie and Mr Steel to entertain her. Making herself comfortable again, she read on.

'Susie felt a feeling of total power sweep over her as she watched a ghostly pallor rise up on Mr Steel's face.

"Yes," she went on, "Mandy claims you took her out for a walk—"

"Only to celebrate her exam results," he interjected.

"That's as maybe." She took a bundle of papers from her briefcase and studied them. "Now, she claims that you bought her a meal and made her drink a lot of wine – which, I might add, she's not used to, as you knew – and by the time you left the restaurant she was no longer in full control of herself."

"Oh, come on, that's just not true," he scoffed. "She kept asking me to buy her drinks."

"Let me finish, please," Susie said, holding up a hand. "This part of it is in Mandy's own words. And I quote: 'he

started to drive me home, and I was worried about my parents seeing me drunk so Mr Steel suggested that we park in a quiet spot until I'd sobered up a bit. He pulled into a big lay-by and straightaway he started to kiss me and play with my tits through my dress. I didn't object to this, I even pulled my bra up so my tits were out of the cups, and I let him put his hand down the front of my dress.

" 'Because I was drunk I didn't realise he'd got his prick out until he made me put my hand on it. That's how he did it, he put my hand on it and made me wrap my fingers all the way around it. I wasn't myself so I started playing with it and telling Mr Steel it was a lot bigger than my boyfriend's. He seemed very interested to hear what I got up to with Paul, and I told him that I let him screw me whenever he wanted to. He then asked me if I ever gave him head, and I said I would never do that for a man because the thought of sucking a dick revolted me.

" 'My head was clearing a little by this time and it was then that I began to realize that Mr Steel had planned this whole thing. He got me drunk on purpose so that he could seduce me. He kept asking if I'd suck him off, and when I kept refusing he got really nasty.' "

Susie shot him a brief look of disdain, and Mr Steel could only shake his head in disagreement.

"I'll go on, shall I, sir? Mandy said: 'I was really frightened by this time, and I realised I'd have to offer him something or he might hurt me. So I asked if he'd like me to rub him right off. He thought about it for a few minutes and then agreed, but said I'd have to do it with my knickers.

" 'I was panicking a bit, by now, and when I took my panties off I tried to make sure he wouldn't see what I'd got. But he wasn't having any of that. He made me sit forward in the seat while he pulled my skirt up, and then

he kept rubbing my panties between my legs until they were really wet. I felt I just had to do what he said, because if I didn't then something terrible might happen to me.

" 'After that, I started to jerk him off with my wet panties. He kept moaning and groaning, and all the time he was playing with my hairy crack and telling me how he'd love to have me. I rubbed really hard and kept pushing my tongue in his ear because I wanted to get it over with. But it was ten minutes before he came in my knickers. There was so much of it; I thought he was never going to stop.

" 'I hoped it was all over then, but he tried to pull me on top of him so he could screw me. His dick was still massive, and I could feel it about to go up my pussy. I think that's when I told him I'd scream if he didn't stop. Anyway, he pushed me off and said if I ever told anybody about this he'd hurt me. I had to promise I wouldn't tell before he'd take me home.' "

Susie looked up from the papers, her eyebrows raised inquiringly.

"But, it's not true," he said, firmly.

"You're saying none of this happened?" Susie pressed. "You're saying Mandy made the whole thing up?"

"No, no. I'm saying Mandy made all the running. Look, I'll admit that when we first pulled into the lay-by I kissed her, and I played with her breasts, but only because she'd been coming on to me all night. She was feeling my legs and making suggestive remarks the whole time. That's the truth, Susie, you've got to believe me. It was Mandy who unfastened my trousers. For God's sake, I'm not made of iron – she was coming on to me and stupidly I responded."

"So, Mandy's description of what happened in the car is accurate, then?" Susie persisted.

"More or less," he agreed, with a dismal nod. "Except that *she* tried to climb on top of *me*, and that's when I finally saw sense and told her to stop."

Susie sneered. "That doesn't sound very likely . . . sir."

"Either way, I'm in trouble if you go to the Headmaster with this."

"Too true," she said brightly, "but there might just be a way for you to stop that happening."

Susie pretended to scrutinize the papers as she waited for the meaning of her words to become clear. When she glanced up there was a look of total relief on Mr Steel's handsome face.'

Kate fanned herself with the pages, realising full well that her high colour had nothing whatsoever to do with the temperature in the room.

'This stuff is really filthy,' she murmured aloud. 'I'd better remember to bring several changes of underwear tomorrow.'

She left the study and wandered through to the kitchen in search of coffee. Donna was pouring some from the pot, still dressed in bra and pants, while a good looking young man sat at the breakfast bar.

'Hi, I'm Kate,' she said, favouring him with a sunny grin.

Donna sneered, while the boy gave her a shy smile.

'Now, I know your sister's name is Donna, but I don't know yours, I'm afraid.'

'It's Matthew,' he replied, haltingly.

Donna looked on, her contempt for Kate deepening, and said, 'This is Dad's latest screw, Matthew. The latest in a long line of brainless, randy cows.'

In that second something snapped inside Kate's head. Without time for thought, she strode across the kitchen

and slapped Donna hard across the face. The girl's coffee cup crashed to the floor and she recoiled, surprise and pain jostling for a place on her pretty features.

'What do you think you're doing?' she screamed, as she side-stepped the pool of coffee at her feet.

'I think we'd better have some ground rules,' Kate spat from behind a pointed finger. 'When you're dealing with me, young lady, you keep a civil tongue in your head. Do you understand?'

The girl seemed about to deliver a cutting response, but she burst into tears instead and ran from the room, shouting, 'I'll have your job for this.'

Matthew sat there, applauding wildly. 'Well done, it's about time somebody put my dear sister in her place.'

Kate poured herself a coffee and sat facing him. 'Not a very good start to the job, though, is it?'

'Don't worry about it. Dad'll understand.'

They chatted about things in general while Kate drank her coffee, and after a few minutes she had dumped her initial impression of the boy. He may well be shy at first meeting, but he was also witty, intelligent, and very easy to talk to. As she replaced her mug on the breakfast bar, she glanced at him.

'Matthew,' she said, trying her best to sound casual, 'I think a friend of mine stayed here a little while back ... Laurence Wilson.'

'Yeh, he did. He's a nice guy. We used to go bowling together.'

'You don't know where he's gone, do you? Only he left something at my flat and I want to give it back.'

'No idea,' he said, with a shrug. 'He left in a real hurry, as I remember, right in the middle of dinner one night.'

'Oh, well, I'm sure he'll catch up with me, sooner or

later.' She stood up and viewed the mess on the floor. 'I suppose I'd better mop that coffee up.'

'Leave it, I'll do it.'

'Thanks. Anyway, nice meeting you.'

She hurried back across the hall, quite relieved that she hadn't found out the whereabouts of Wilson, for that would have meant missing the next instalment of the book. Once in the study, she grabbed the next few pages and settled into the chair.

'Miss Phipps smoked the cigarette right down to the tip and then lit another straight away. At least she hadn't gone as far as she did at the last school. She had always hung around the boys' changing rooms and had often been rewarded with a good view of a fine young dick, which had usually hardened once the boy saw that she was looking at it.

But the incident at her last school had been a terrible mistake. She had stood in the shower room on that occasion, and had surreptitiously watched a boy playing with himself, as Greg had done. She had been thrilled by the fervent way in which he pulled his splendid prick, and utterly mesmerised by the speed of his hand and the look of absolute joy on his face. The mere memory was enough to bring a tingling to her crack and a hot flush to her face.

Like Greg he had stopped suddenly and found her watching, but whereas Greg had proudly displayed himself to her, that boy had tried to hide his throbbing shaft behind trembling hands. She should have run away, but was so aroused, so hungry for sex that her desperate libido forced her feet forward and she approached the naked boy, with sweet anticipation rising in her middle, and knocked his hands away.

In a husky voice she reprimanded him and told him to report to her after school had finished. Her knickers were drenched so she took them off, and the thought of seeing the boy after school was enough to keep her excitement at fever pitch throughout the rest of the day.

At last the other students rushed off home and the boy was shuffling across the classroom with an expression of deep shame etched on to his face. Miss Phipps sat before him on a high stool, and kept him waiting for a long time while she pretended to mark some papers. Finally she put them on the desk and was twiddling the pen between her long fingers. She let it go, and it landed on the floor at his feet.

The boy was ordered to pick it up. As he bent down to retrieve it, Miss Phipps opened her legs and granted him a long and lingering look at her hairy crack. The events of the next thirty minutes were to stay with her and excite her for the rest of her life, for the romp ended with her bending over the desk, totally naked, while the boy took her from behind.

That experience had been beyond belief. She had never been fucked so well, had never had such a powerful climax. She had always yearned for it to happen again. And today it almost did.

But Miss Phipps knew that she must try and exert some control over her riotous sex urge because that time, although no one have ever been able to prove anything, the gossip had finally forced her to leave the school and move to another county. And she didn't want that to happen again.

She glanced up just as Greg was leaving the sports hall, and the breath caught in her throat when he strode purposefully in her direction.

"I'm sorry about what I was doing in there, Miss Phipps. I didn't know you were watching."

He was staring at the ground, and she thought how young and innocent he looked – just like the other boy.

"It's quite all right," she said, her breath quickening. "I expect boys of your age to do it. There's nothing unnatural about it, after all."

"I feel such a prat though."

She smiled. "Let's keep it our secret then, shall we?"

"You're really great, did you know that? I never expected a teacher to understand."

He started to walk away and, although her heart sank, a tiny voice in Miss Phipps' brain screamed for her to let him go. But the sight of his trim young buttocks filling out the tight trousers, the perfect shape of his torso, and the memory of his swollen shaft set her mind racing. Her own aching sex secreted more love cream into her knickers.

Let him go, the voice repeated, let him go. But it was too late.

"Oh, Greg—" she called.

He turned rather eagerly. Or did she imagine it?

"What are you doing this afternoon?"

He shrugged. "Nothing. I've got a free lesson."

"Me too," she said, strolling to his side. "Would you like to come for a walk with me?"

"Yes, all right."

"Just give me time to go to the loo," she said, hastily backing away. "I won't be a minute. There's something really urgent I want to discuss with you."

She hurried into the building and as soon as the cubicle door was safely locked Miss Phipps scrambled out of her knickers and held them to her face. The heady perfume sent her senses reeling . . .'

CHAPTER 10

Kate was debating whether she should read on or start the typing when she became aware that she was being watched. Turning quickly, she found Earl Barton standing in the doorway.

'What do you think of it?' he asked.

'It's horny stuff,' she admitted, with a laugh. 'Really horny.'

'Good.'

He studied her for a while, his divine eyes bringing a redness to her cheeks. Finally, he said, 'I hear you had a little run in with Donna.'

Feeling that her sitting position put her at a disadvantage, Kate rose from the chair and stood defiantly by the desk.

'Yes, I did, Mr Barton. I don't like people being rude to me. It's something I won't tolerate. I'll leave if you want me to.'

'That won't be necessary,' he said, waving a hand dismissively. 'I dare say Donna had it coming. But I'd like to make clear the things she said to you. It's true that I have sex with most of the women who type my work, but it doesn't come with the job. Now, I don't know how you feel about sex—'

'I like it,' she said. 'In fact, when I'm in the mood I can't

get enough of it. But I do like it to be my choice.'

'That's fine, then. That's exactly how it is here. Right, Miss Highlands, would you stay and have dinner with me tonight?'

'All right,' she said, smiling. 'Yes, I think I'd like that.'

'That's splendid.' He approached the desk. 'Now, let's see where you've got to. Ah, yes, Miss Phipps, do you want to start typing, or would you rather carry on reading?'

She lowered her eyes. 'I'd like to carry on reading, if that's all right. I'm quite eager to find out what happens to Susie and Greg.'

He grinned. 'Splendid. That's exactly the answer I wanted. I just hope I catch you when you can't get enough of it, because something tells me you're a very dirty girl, Kate Highlands.'

'I can be, Mr Barton,' she said, her eyes flirting, 'when the mood takes me.'

When the door closed behind him all thoughts of Laurence Wilson were driven from her mind. As she picked up the next section of the book Kate realized she was addicted to the characters in the story, all of whom were living out their fantasies in such a lascivious yet wholly believable manner.

It took her by surprise to find that she was still with the sex-starved Miss Phipps; she expected the next chapter to start with Susie and the redoubtable Mr Steel. Eagerly, she read on.

'Greg had already guessed that Miss Phipps would want him to play an innocent schoolboy and he decided to go along with it. After all, it wasn't every day an older woman set out to seduce him.

He could actually smell the want in her; it oozed from

that tight crack at her crotch and seemed to waft around him as no other woman's scent had ever done. Just to be with her was giving him a full, throbbing erection which was beginning to hurt as he walked along. He noticed that her eyes kept straying towards it, and those fevered glances fuelled his mounting excitement until his cock felt as if it were on fire.

They strolled across the fields in companionable silence while the school building was still in view. And all the time Greg watched the teacher from the corner of his eye. In the course of a few hundred yards her entire character had undergone a complete change. She was no longer the prim and proper Miss Phipps; now her bottom wriggled sexily as she walked, and she kept shooting teasing little glances which promised that this was something more than a chaste walk in the countryside.

When they came to a stile, Greg vaulted over and gallantly held out a hand to help her across. She took it with a smile and, pushing her dress up between her legs and affording him a good view of her most shapely thighs, she clambered over.

By now he was eager to get things moving and was racking his brains for something to say.

"I'm sorry about what you saw me doing," he began, lamely.

Miss Phipps slipped her hand in his as they walked, and for some reason Greg found it so exhilarating to have his fingers intertwined with hers.

"It's all right," she assured him. "By the way, how often do you do that to yourself?"

"What, wank, you mean? Oh, sorry, I shouldn't have said that."

She gave a lilting laugh. "Don't worry, I know what it's

called. Now, come on, how often do you do it?"

"Two or three times a day. Whenever I think about sex, I suppose. I really did think you'd tell me off, you know."

"What? In this day and age?" she said, surprise widening her eyes. "Mind you, it was different years ago. Teachers then, particularly those at boarding schools, used to tell their pupils it would send them blind and cause all sorts of terrible afflictions to try and frighten them so much that they'd stop playing with their sex organs in bed." She gave a throaty laugh. "It didn't work though. I mean, we've all got one, haven't we? And the next best thing to having someone else making it happy is to play with it ourselves."

They stopped in the middle of the field and rested under the shade of a large oak tree. Greg was so aroused that he completely forgot about the part he was supposed to be playing; in fact he really did feel like a young virgin about to be seduced by a passionate older woman.

"Why did they try so hard to stop it, then?" he asked.

She giggled. 'Because it turned them on, I suppose. We've all got dirty minds, you know, even teachers. To be honest, it really turned me on watching you.'

A broad grin stole across Greg's face as the meaning of her words, and the invitation behind them, became clear.

"Mind you," she went on, "some terribly horny things happened if the women teachers really fancied a boy. They would set out to catch him pleasuring himself every night, until there was nowhere that boy could go to relieve his frustration. That would go on for weeks, and the boy would be almost out of his mind with longing for an orgasm. He would be beside himself until one night, when he couldn't control himself any longer, he'd lie in bed and start stroking his cock. Then the teachers – there'd be at least three of them – would creep into the dormitory and catch

him. They would scold him and throw back the sheets, all the time telling him what a dirty boy he was while at every opportunity they'd be touching him up and feeling what he'd got. And, Greg," she added, her eyes shining with devilment, "you wouldn't believe what they'd do next."

"Tell me," he urged, his whole body trembling with excitement.

"Well . . ."

Lust was bringing a strange light into her eyes as Miss Phipps turned her back and slowly unfastened the buttons at the front of her dress. Greg let out an involuntary gasp when she slipped out of it, for her naked buttocks were perfectly rounded and her dense bush hung down from her crotch.

Her bra was made of white cotton and was embroidered with tiny red roses. Reaching behind, she undid the clasp and allowed it to fall to the ground. Greg could hardly wait for her to turn back, and he was panting with anticipation of her next move. But instead of revealing herself fully, she retrieved her dress and stepped into it.

A whimper of disappointment rose from his chest, but the sound became a deep sigh of surprise when she turned to face him. She had only fastened two of the buttons, and although they prevented the dress from opening up completely, he was still treated to a clear view of her large, firm breasts.

There was a look of sheer debauchery on her face as Miss Phipps picked up the bra and urged Greg to stand with his back against the tree and curl his arms behind him, around its trunk. He complied immediately for her eyes promised so much, and when he was in position she secured his hands with the bra. He could feel the heat of her breasts on the thin cotton as she tied knot after knot

around his wrists, and his cock stiffened inside his trousers as a delicious tingle ran along his spine.

"There," she said at last, coming to stand in front of him. "That's what they used to do to naughty boys who played with themselves. They used to tie them up – always claiming they did it to stop them masturbating, of course."

She was standing very close now, her husky voice drifting into his ear while her nimble fingers unbuttoned his shirt and acquainted themselves with the powerful muscles of his chest and stomach.

"You've got such a gorgeous body," she purred. "So muscular, so firm."

Greg was fast becoming intoxicated by her smell, and he moaned aloud when she unfastened the button of his jeans. Neither spoke again until she had stripped him down to his boxer shorts. When the jeans were thrown aside Miss Phipps stood back a step and gazed hungrily at his huge cock which was pushing impatiently against the blue shorts, eager to get to her promised treasure trove.

She giggled lightly. "Your shorts look like a sail with that massive shaft struggling to get out. Never mind, let's see if I can calm it down."

She nestled up to him, her lips playfully brushing his, her groin rubbing lazily against his erection. There was no need for haste now that she had him in her clutches; she could take her time and enjoy each erotic moment of their loveplay.

As their passions grew with the intensity of the kiss, the teacher's dress came apart at the front and Greg struggled against his bonds at the delicious feel of coarse pubic hair brushing against his thigh. Their tongues met and made love for many moments until Miss Phipps pulled away, moaning breathlessly.

"Oh, Greg," she sighed. "You've got such a big erection and it's all my fault. I disturbed you before the lovely thing could come, didn't I?"

A mischievous glint in her eyes defied the concern in her voice as her fingers toyed teasingly with the bulge of his cock which was still so annoyingly encased in the boxer shorts.

"Does it hurt, Greg? Oh, I bet it hurts."

"Yes," he panted.

And then his whole body went rigid with anticipation when he saw Miss Phipps reaching down for the plaything she desired. But her fingers fumbled awkwardly in the heat of passion, and he swore mildly as she struggled to find the gap in his shorts. His cock was so swollen, so desperate for her touch; and he was powerless to help, tied to the tree as he was.

Finally her cool fingers were grasping their prize, and the fluttering at her excited crotch reached such a level of bliss that she thought she might die with the joy of it.

'It's so big,' she murmured, almost swooning at the disgraceful sight of her hand poking inside the young boy's underwear.

She was desperate to see the gorgeous cock for a second time, and although her self-control hung in tatters, Miss Phipps managed to prolong the moment with one last lingering feel of the quivering rod. But then her impassioned vagina took firm control and forced her to push down the shorts and release the demon within their midst. She crouched down to pull them from his feet, and Greg squirmed against the tree as her warm breath enveloped his frustrated organ.

Her gaze positively devoured the lavish, pulsating cock. Its heavily veined surface promised satisfaction galore for

the waiting walls of her tunnel. And the glorious purple tip, tumescent for so long now, was still waiting for release and was certain to give freely of itself should a warm, dark cavern open up in its path.

But Miss Phipps knew she must advance carefully on that much needed shaft. After her long abstention from sex, the last thing she wanted was a frustrated Greg discharging his seed too quickly. Far better to release a little of the pressure first. She got to her feet and made a conscious effort to slow her erratic breathing.

"Yes, this is what those dirty teachers used to do," she cooed. "They would tie up the young boy, and he would be completely at their mercy."

While Greg gazed at her with pleading eyes, she started to pull his quivering cock with long, strong strokes until he was floating on a sea of ecstasy.

"And then those teachers – so virtuous on the outside but so filthy beneath the skin – would take their knickers off, one by one, and ravage him until their hairy nests were happy."

"Take your dress off," Greg murmured. "I want to see your hairy nest."

"Now I wonder if I should,' she teased. 'I'll have to think about that."

"Oh God, show me your cunt . . . please."

A luscious tremor passed through her middle at the thought of such a divine boy wanting to see her pleasure spot. It was almost a pity that his hands were secured, for she quite liked the idea of having her dress ripped off, and those strong young hands pinning her to the ground. Still, perhaps that could come later.

Without neglecting his cock, Miss Phipps unbuttoned her dress and allowed the wind to catch the flimsy material

and billow it open. As it flapped about on the breeze like a pair of gossamer wings, she rubbed her scorching slit on the stretched skin of his tip, and all the while increased her efforts on his shaft.

"And, of course, if the boy had a nice big one – like yours, Greg – then they'd keep going back night after night to satisfy themselves. And who can blame them? Cocks like yours don't come a girl's way very often."

She stole a look at his face and was overjoyed at the carnal bliss she saw there. Her raunchy words, together with her loving hand, were having a telling effect on the young boy. And as his lovely lips opened to let out a sexy sigh a torrid stream of milky seed left his indebted cock.

"Oh, that's wonderful. Greg. Come all over me."

It seemed that the fountain of sperm would gush forever, but eventually the torrent became a trickle and then his balls were empty.

Both boy and teacher were breathing heavily and both were lost in their separate worlds of ecstasy. Greg was savouring the delicious sensations still dominating the end of his cock, and Miss Phipps revelling in the heavenly feel of hot sperm clinging to her pubic hair. It found its way into her moist trench, to be met by her excited clitoris and her own sex cream, which gathered liberally at her opening.'

CHAPTER 11

Kate's pulse was racing, and her breasts were heaving in time with her frantic breath as the pages slipped from her grasp.

'Phew, I'd better start typing this,' she said, flopping back in the chair.

Once started, she found that typing the torrid scenes was equally as enjoyable as reading them and, as she settled happily into her temporary job, Kate found that the hours were simply flying by. She broke, rather reluctantly, at lunchtime for a snack of sandwiches and coffee; and at six o'clock she was still engrossed at the computer screen and had to almost will her hand to switch the machine off.

She was reaching for her coat when a knock came on the study door. It flew open before she could speak, and a girl poked her head around the door.

'Hi,' she said. 'My name's Roz. I'm the cook, bottle-washer, and general dogsbody around here.'

Her smile was so open and friendly that Kate found herself immediately warming to the girl.

'Do you do anything else?' she joked.

'Just the usual,' Roz said, with a sly wink. 'But I love that so much, I don't consider it to be work.'

She wandered across to the desk, her movements panther-like and sensual, and hitched herself up on its edge.

'I've got the flat upstairs,' she told Kate. 'I just wondered if you'd like to use it to clean up before dinner.'

'Thanks a lot. I'd like that.'

Kate sat back and studied the girl. She was about twenty-five and her body was slim, almost boyish, and looked fresh beneath the yellow linen shift which showed off her tan to perfection. Her short dark hair positively glowed with health, and matched the deep brown of her large eyes. Her face was simply beautiful. Kate should have been hotly jealous, but the girl's easy temperament oozed from her every pore, and made it impossible to dislike her.

'I hear you've been enquiring about Wilson,' she said.

Kate felt a bright flush creep into her cheeks. 'Yes, yes, I have. He's a friend of mine.'

'Huh, I doubt if Wilson has a friend in the world,' she countered, lightening her argumentative tone with a smile.

Kate shrugged and left it at that.

Up in the flat, which she found tidy and functional, Kate took a shower and washed her hair. Her knickers were now dry, if somewhat stained, but Kate had no option but to put them back on. She was glad of her solemn black skirt and white blouse because dinner turned out to be a very formal occasion.

The dining room was large and its opulent furniture suggested that Earl Barton was a very wealthy man. Roz joined them for the scrumptious meal which consisted of prawn cocktail for starters, lobster with a creamy sauce and side salad, and a wonderfully light strawberry soufflé for desert.

Barton sat at the head of the table, ministering to his guests as if he were a Lord of the Manor, and Kate and Roz sat on opposite sides of the enormous dining table.

Kate had with her the pages she had already typed and Barton studied them closely as he ate, bringing a silly nervousness to her stomach as if she were a school leaver desperate to impress her first boss.

After a while, he looked up and dabbed at the corners of his mouth with a white serviette.

'You've changed some of this,' he said, pointing to the pages.

'I have tidied some of it up,' Kate admitted. 'But I don't think I've altered the essence.'

'I agree, you haven't. Actually, I'm very pleased with what you've done.' He fell silent and took to playing with the stem of his wine glass. 'I think, Kate, that I should explain what happens here. Roz, whatever she tells you to the contrary, is my research assistant – and very good she is too.' He smiled at the girl and took a long drink of wine.

Kate took the opportunity to speak. 'Mr Barton, I take it that Susie, in your current book, is based on your daughter. Am I right?'

He placed his glass on the table, his long fingers still toying with the stem.

'You've very observant,' he said. 'Yes, you are right. It would seem that Donna has inherited her father's strong libido and is very fond of a sexy adventure. Everything you read in the book is true, if somewhat coloured by a writer's imagination.'

'I see,' Kate mused.

'Which brings me to my next point, that will tie up a lot of loose ends. I believe you're looking for Laurence Wilson—'

'He's a friend,' Kate began, lamely.

Barton held up a firm hand for silence. 'Please, Kate, do not lie. I know many people who are looking for Wilson.

Well, he stayed here and, yes, I do know where he went after he left. Now, I'm willing to divulge that information to you in return for certain favours.'

Oh, here we go, Kate thought wryly; I wondered when we'd get to the you-scratch-my-back-and-I'll-scratch-yours bit.

'It's not what you're thinking,' Barton said, catching her caustic look. 'My own sexual gratification does not come into the deal.' He paused. 'Actually, I want you to seduce my son and daughter. In any order you choose.'

Kate could feel her mouth sagging open, but she had to admit to herself that the proposition was of interest. How she had changed in such a short time. And how exciting life had become.

Roz moved silently around the table, refilling the wine glasses, and Barton chuckled gleefully.

'Well, at least you haven't stormed out which, I take it, means you are willing to discuss the matter.'

Kate nodded. 'I'm intrigued.'

'Good.' He paused again to sip his wine. 'As you say, one of my characters is based on Donna. But, alas, my daughter has an aversion to sex with other women, and as all my work is based on real experiences, this makes the character very limited—'

'But the girl hates me,' Kate interjected. 'I don't think she'll let me anywhere near her.'

'That should make it all the more challenging for you. Maybe you'll have to force her to start with.'

His enchanting eyes sparkled with mischief, and Kate found herself falling under his spell.

'She did have sex with Wilson, Kate, and she too knows where he is. Maybe she'll part with the information.'

Kate thought it over. If sex with Donna could help her

find the man, then she'd damn well have a go.

'But what about your son? Why do you want me to seduce him?'

'That is more personal,' he said. 'Matthew is shy, reserved – not at all like his father – and I must confess I wasn't at all bothered, until recently. You see, he spent an awful lot of time with Wilson while the man was enjoying my hospitality, and I'm concerned that the boy might be a homosexual. I am merely seeking confirmation that he's not.' He sat back in his seat and eyed Kate openly. 'So, that is my offer. You get to read a very good book,' he added, immodestly, 'and if you help Roz with the research – who knows? – you could well find yourself in it.'

'You know I've got a lot of money riding on finding Wilson?'

Barton nodded. 'I have been told.'

Kate sipped the delicious wine while she pondered the pros and cons of the man's offer. Finally, she said, 'All right, I'll do it.'

Barton clapped his hands excitedly. 'Good, very good, I'm sure you won't regret it. Now, what do you think of the book so far?'

'I think it's very horny,' she said. 'To be honest, it really got me going.'

The answer seemed to please him, and his chest swelled with contentment.

'Super . . . jolly good. And now, in keeping with tradition, it is time for me to claim the new typist's knickers.'

'Hold on,' Kate protested. 'You promised me I wouldn't be forced into anything.'

Roz laughed. 'But it's not at all like you think. Just slip your knickers off under the table and pass them to me.'

Genuinely puzzled, but not feeling in any way threat-

ened, Kate pulled her panties down and slipped them over her shoes. She then passed them across the table to Roz, who inspected them closely and handed them to Barton. He studied them for many moments, eyeing the stains with a tiny smile playing at the corners of his mouth, and then putting them to his nostrils and inhaling the strong scent of her love juice.

'That's nice, Kate, very nice,' he whispered. 'I have to be sure, you see. When I ask you if the book is good, you're bound by courtesy to say yes. But, like all writers, I'm riddled with insecurities and I have to be certain. Now I have seen and smelt your underwear, I am absolutely sure that you enjoyed reading my work.'

A few short days ago, Kate was a poorly paid private detective, living a drab life at her drab flat. But look at her now. She could not altogether believe the bizarre scene unfolding before her eyes. It was like something out of a film – one of those weird black comedies that she could never quite understand. And what happened next surprised her even more.

'I hope that during your stay with us,' Barton began, as he placed her panties in the centre of the table, 'you will learn there is far more to sex than the act itself – pleasurable as that may be. Sometimes the route by which you arrive is of equal importance. Let me demonstrate what I mean.'

He motioned to Roz who straightaway got to her feet and removed her short skirt. They were both aware of Kate's sharp intake of breath when the girl's flimsy blue panties came into view. The erotic mound of her pubis was clearly visible beneath the stretched fabric, as was the mass of dark hair which spilled from its sides.

Barton signalled to the two girls, and said, 'I'd like you

to come to this end of the table, if you would.'

Kate followed Roz, as if in a trance, all the time wondering what she was about to witness. When the dark girl positioned herself to the left of his chair, Barton took to feeling between her legs, pushing the silk of her panties into the heavenly crack which they concealed.

'Beautiful,' he enthused. 'As ever, my dear Roz, you are quite ready for any eventuality.'

She let out a divine giggle, quite clearly enjoying the probing at her groin. And when Barton left his seat she stepped back a pace.

'Show Kate what to do,' he ordered, as he sank to his knees and suckled at her crotch.

She let out a sexy groan, and then picked up a glass of red wine. Passing it to Kate, she murmured breathlessly, 'Pour it down my panties and let it trickle all over my crack.'

The girl held the silk away from her firm, tanned skin, and bit hard on her lip to stifle the cry which threatened to escape from her lips as the exploration between her legs grew more impassioned.

Feeling rather foolish, Kate tipped the glass and allowed the wine to flow slowly down the lower part of Roz's stomach. She watched, fascinated by the way in which it wove a path through the girl's black pubic hair in search of the lips of her vagina which opened up to let it pass between them.

Roz's head fell back as an ecstatic yell rose up from her throat at the feel of the cool liquid on her sizzling sex. Spurred on by her own throbbing vagina, Kate poured faster until a steady stream was gushing from the gusset of Roz's knickers and into the waiting mouth of Barton who swallowed the unusual drink with the utmost enjoyment.

Kate poured the whole contents of the glass over the same route, and her mouth watered at the tangy smell of the girl's love juice as it mingled freely with the wine.

'The perfect compliment to a nineteen-sixty-eight Burgundy,' Barton murmured, running his tongue around his lips. 'Maybe Kate would like to drink deeply.'

Knowing that she was in some ways on trial here, Kate realized that her reaction to this could influence her future with these strange individuals. And the challenging light in their eyes only confirmed that she was right.

Taking in a deep breath, she said, 'Yes, all right. I did feel the wine lacked a certain bouquet and flavour, but I'd like to take mine in a slightly different way.'

Their looks of interest made Kate bold, and with her confidence rising, she went on, 'I'm sure Roz wouldn't object to removing her knickers and lying on the table. Any more than you would object to showing me your prick – eh, Mr Barton?'

Roz was eager to kick off her panties, and they were laid to rest by the other pair on the table. Kate felt a tremor of excitement mushroom in her groin as Roz moved the plates aside and lay on the edge of the table, hitching up her skirt to display her thick bush and the pouting lips it so effortlessly concealed.

When Barton unzipped his trousers, Kate couldn't decide where to look first. She so liked the sight of Roz, prostrate and waiting, but at the same time could not drag her gaze away from Barton's hand which was guiding his masterful cock through open flies. She found herself experiencing the delicate fluttering between the legs that she had been reading about all day. As she viewed his eight inches of throbbing flesh, she almost ached to know how it would feel inside her seething cavern.

With an effort Kate managed to regain her composure, and she crossed to Roz and instructed her to place both heels on the table's edge and spread her knees wide. When Roz was in position, she took the glass of wine and very gradually allowed it to trickle over the girl's pubic forest. While the red river picked a gentle path through the thicket, Kate eased herself forward and lapped and sucked as it cascaded over the hilly terrain of Roz's tempting vagina.

The girl murmured and gasped wildly at the feel of those luscious lips exciting the nub of her sex and she wriggled about on the table top, causing the wine to splash and tumble into her hidden crevice, which opened up under the onslaught and revealed her Aladdin's cave. As she lay there, with her graceful legs thrust into the air, the wine formed a calm, deep red reservoir in that tropical haven, and Kate supped with all the vigour of one who had stumbled upon a lush, green oasis in the middle of a sun-scorched desert. Never before had she tasted so potent an elixir; the honey-sweet love juice which oozed from Roz's agitated crack contrasted perfectly with the dryness of the wine.

All too soon every last drop was gone and Kate smacked her lips with genuine appreciation as she rose to her feet and turned to face the lascivious Mr Barton. The sexy spectacle had left him drooling and rubbing away at his animated cock like a man possessed. Kate advanced on him with slow, deliberate steps, and the seductive smile on her lips brought an increased urgency to his hand-fuck. But she stopped him with a scolding, 'Tut, tut,' and stretched up to plant a fleeting kiss on his oh so desirable lips; moulding herself to him just long enough for Roz's mellow taste to register through the dizzy heights of his desire.

Only then did Kate give her full attention to his impassioned cock. She poured a little of the wine into the palm of
her hand and spread it along his whole length. His burning
tip was purple with rage at having been ignored, and Kate
all the while humoured it, cooing and coddling, as she
bathed it with the fruity drink.

The fiery shaft grew even larger, dwarfing her delicate
hand, as her frolicking fingers fluttered lightly back
towards his balls so that they too could be coated with the
wine. Satisfied with her work, and grinning inwardly at
Barton's bemused expression, she bent down and took
the shaft deep into her mouth.

An earthy groan started in his throat came out of
Barton's mouth on a strangled breath when his cockhead
nudged the back of Kate's throat just as her agile tongue
set to work on the veiny underside of his shaft. And then
she was sucking with a vengeance, pursing her lips tightly
to enhance the friction and heighten his pleasure.

Very soon the tangy flavour of the wine gave way to his
wholly masculine taste, and Kate revelled in the unmasked
smell of his maleness which was more intoxicating than
any alcohol. She longed to bring him to climax, but that
was not the point of the exercise. It was enough that she
had opened their eyes to her potential. The rest could
follow – there would be plenty of time.

'Perhaps the next time I can taste your sex cream, Mr
Barton. And I'd suggest that the wine should be a sixty-
nine. It would be far more appropriate.'

CHAPTER 12

Roz was still laughing when they got back to the flat.

'Earl does love to shock people, but you really turned the tables on him.'

'What's he like?' Kate asked, as she sprawled on the settee. 'In bed, I mean?'

'Brilliant,' she sighed, a faraway look settling in her eyes. 'He always satisfies me and, as you saw, he has so much to offer a woman. You know when that cock's in you, believe me.'

'I can believe it.' Kate lit two cigarettes and passed one across. 'Does he like a lot of sex?'

Roz exhaled gratefully, directing the smoke towards the ceiling. 'He's a randy sod. He can't get enough. I can't remember a time when he hasn't had a hard-on.'

'This research you do for his books,' Kate said, changing the subject. 'What does that entail?'

'Going with men and women, and then describing what happened to Earl.'

Kate's cheeks dimpled. 'Now that does sound like fun.'

'I'm glad you said that,' Roz said, 'because it is fun, and I was thinking of asking you to join in.'

'Oh, I'd love to. I can't think of anything I'd like more,' Kate gushed. 'But about his proposition – now, I'm not too bothered about seducing Matthew, but Donna . . . I've an

idea it's going to be very difficult to get inside that girl's knickers.'

Roz nodded her agreement. 'I've already tried, and once she knows you're interested she really flaunts herself, shows you her pussy at every opportunity. But all the time she's making a point of letting you know you can't have it.'

'We'll see,' Kate murmured, stubbing out the cigarette. 'Well, I suppose I'd better be going.'

Roz shot her a reluctant glance. 'Look, as from tomorrow you can stay here if you want to. After all, I do have a double bed. Oh, and Earl said if you do decide to stay, you can take tomorrow off, settle in properly. He can always get another girl from the agency – I mean, let's face it, if you help me with his research, you'll have far better things to do than sit in front of that decrepit word processor all day.'

'But I want to read the book,' Kate protested. 'I need to know what happens next.'

'Fine, I can read it to you tomorrow night when we're all having fun together. We've done it before, and it really does add something.'

Roz's gaze was fixed to Kate's face as she ground out her cigarette and crossed to her side. Kate sensed what might happen next, and found herself incapable of stopping it. Indeed, when tentative fingers pushed the skirt between her legs, feeling and groping at what lay underneath, Kate spread them in encouragement.

'You feel so nice,' Roz said, in a hoarse whisper. 'All through dinner I was wondering what you kept hidden beneath that long, straitlaced skirt, and now I know.'

'Why don't you feel it properly,' Kate invited. 'It's more than ready for some fun, I can tell you.'

Before the words had even left her mouth, Roz's eager

hand was pawing at the hairy patch, delving for her crack, which was sticky with the dew of her yearning. With the same hungry determination, Kate's hand disappeared up Roz's skirt, drawn there by the tight hole from which she had supped the wine.

'We mustn't go too far,' Roz warned. 'Earl will want us to have our first sexual encounter in front of him.'

'Just finger me then,' Kate implored. 'Let's finger each other while we're sitting here.'

Before the girl could utter her consent, Kate was familiarizing herself with the silky smooth walls of Roz's tunnel of love, thrilling at the tightness which trapped her fingers in that dark and mysterious place. And as she slid a fond finger deeper into the warmth, Roz did the same for her.

Kate spent most of the next day at home, attempting to sort out her motives for agreeing to go along with Barton's plan. Surely she had only consented to have sex with the man – not to mention pledging to seduce his son and daughter – in order to secure the one million pounds promised to her on finding the elusive Laurence Wilson? Surely?

That rather convenient explanation could well go some way to quashing her guilty conscience, but Kate knew in her heart of hearts that the real reason had its roots deeply laid in far more raunchy soil. The truth was that she couldn't wait to feel the full thrust of Barton's shaft in the depths of her vagina. She was longing to experience the exquisite joys of lesbian love with the delicious Roz while they indulged in erotic research for the book. And just thinking about seducing the untried Matthew brought a torrent of love juice gushing from her expectant crack. As for Donna, well, her chances of getting into that young

lady's knickers were slim, but as someone once said – it's not the winning, it's the taking part that counts. And Kate was definitely looking forward to the game.

Sex without strings, she thought happily as she packed her case. Would her life ever be the same again? And more important, did she want it to remain as it had been?

As she looked around the flat, Kate's gaze fell on her mahogany bookcase which wilted under the weight of the countless novels she had read in order to escape, albeit temporarily, from the humdrum and deadly-dull existence that was her life. At one time she had seriously thought about taking up knitting to while away the long winter evenings. My God, she thought ruefully, what would Roz make of that little gem?

When Kate stepped over the threshold and slammed the door, it felt as if she was drawing a line under the last twenty-five years of her life. And with suitcase in hand she skipped along the corridor heading for the street, and for the new world that was hers for the taking.

Donna let her into the mews house. As usual she was naked apart from the skimpy underwear which did little to cover her charms.

'I'll lend you a dress, if you like,' Kate quipped, as she rested the heavy suitcase on the hall carpet gratefully.

'Ha, ha,' the girl sneered. 'You really are a laugh a lifetime.'

She was slouched at the breakfast bar when Kate entered the kitchen.

'I've been reading about your exploits as Susie,' she said.

'And did they shock you?' Donna asked, with a taunting smile.

'Shock me?' Kate huffed. 'I would imagine that, without the aid of your father's rich imagination, your sex life must be so boring. After all, you are very limited in what you do.'

'And what exactly do you mean by that?' she retorted, quite stung by the remark.

Kate let out a husky laugh. 'There's no variety in it. All you seem to think about is cocks going up cunts, and that must get really monotonous after a time. Haven't you ever thought about trying something else?'

Suddenly Donna leapt to her feet and positioned herself in front of Kate, her panties pushed down around her knees.

'Like letting you have this, for example?'

Kate had to use all of her self control to keep her gaze away from the girl's gorgeous young pussy. If she showed the slightest hint of interest then, as Roz had said, Donna would flirt till the cows came home, so an altogether different tack was called for. Kate would ignore her completely, show no inclination at all to gaze at her lovely body. And then Donna might, she just might, start showing an interest herself. It was worth a try, at least.

'My, my, you are a conceited little bitch,' Kate remarked. 'Whatever makes you think I'd want what you've got? I'm very fond of having sex with women, it's true, but immature little girls who have hang-ups about their bodies just don't turn me on in the slightest. So I'd suggest that you put it away until you can find an equally immature little boy to play with it.'

'I can have any man I want, you cow,' Donna shouted, as Kate wandered out into the hall.

Round one to you, Kate, she thought carrying her suitcase up the stairs.

CHAPTER 13

Dinner was even more eccentric than it had been the previous evening. Roz had told Kate that they were to wear dressing gowns and nothing else. And when they entered the dining room Kate saw that Barton, already in his seat at the head of the table, was similarly kitted out in a white bathrobe with the monogram E.B. embroidered in navy blue on the breast pocket.

There was no conversation during the meal. By its end, Kate's head was spinning pleasantly from the effects of Barton's superior wine.

'I think it's time we retired to the secret room,' he announced grandly. 'Where we can all enjoy the carnal pleasures of the flesh.'

The secret room, Kate found, was behind the study. Its entrance was concealed by the wooden panelling on the walls which, at the press of a button, slid to one side to reveal a large area with white-emulsioned walls. There was no furniture, just bean bags spread all over the floor space.

'And now the time has come for us all to reveal to each other the full delights of our bodies,' Barton said, removing his bathrobe.

His penis, the massive proportions of which had remained in Kate's memory, was already thrusting madly, like a prize racehorse ready to run. And now that Kate

could see the whole package, she noted with awe that it was the perfect tool to complement such a well-developed and hugely attractive body.

Roz was the next to show, and she seemed to wallow in the admiring glances that swept over her slender form. Her skin was dark and completely unblemished by bikini lines. Here was a girl who worshipped the sun as God had created her – totally naked and free from inhibitions.

Kate envied her, for when she stepped out of her dressing gown there were plenty of inhibitions to bring a flush of embarrassment to her face. Although wishing wholeheartedly that she could shake off the last of the shackles from her former repressed life, she nevertheless stood before them with legs tightly together while their hungry gazes gorged on her splendid breasts.

'Show,' Barton breathed.

A lustful glow lit up his come-to-bed eyes as she opened her legs and fully revealed her inviting crack. Kate at last felt the remnants of her past float away like useless flotsam on a rough sea.

'You're beautiful, Kate,' he said, in that same breathy tone. 'You are so beautiful. And now, if you are willing, Roz would like to do something nice to you while I read from the book.'

Kate allowed herself to be led to the nearest of the bean bags. She lay on the floor and arched her back so that it could be manoeuvred underneath her bottom, and thrust her pelvis into the air.

Roz quickly knelt between her open thighs and straight-away took to toying with the triangle of soft hair which guarded her secret place with such devoted loyalty. The fingers pushed through the bush like worldly explorers; and every caress took them nearer and nearer to Kate's

pouting lips and the waiting love bud which shivered with sweet anticipation.

It was then that the fingers found her most sensitive spot and Kate gasped as a gigantic bolt of pleasure ripped through her groin. Then she was lost, boiling in a cauldron of Roz's making; each gentle caress, every subtle probe caused a tingling of such extreme bliss. Kate felt as if her centre had no substance and she was melting away under the girl's expert touch.

In the distance, paper rustled and Barton began to speak.

'Right, we left Miss Phipps and Greg in the field and we rejoin our sexy little Susie in Mr Steel's study.'

' "So, tell me how I can get out of it," the teacher asked hopefully.

"Well . . ." Susie giggled. "What if I told you all this was a joke, but it could become a nightmare if you don't do as I say?"

"I don't know what you mean."

"Just what I'm saying," Susie answered. "I've been a very naughty girl, actually. I've been teasing you, so I think you should punish me now. And if you do, I promise I won't take what I know to the Headmaster. What do you say . . . sir?"

"I can't afford to get into any sort of trouble involving my students," Mr Steel insisted.

"You're already in trouble," she reminded him. "But if you do what I want, you'll get out of it."

"All right," he said, resignedly. "What exactly do you want me to do?"

Susie leant across the desk, and whispered, "Pretend I'm a very young girl, and I've been sent to you for some

sort of punishment. You spank me and you cane me, but all the time you're getting more and more carried away. Have you still got a cane?"

"Yes, there's one in the cupboard."

"Okay, get it and let's start."

Earl Barton's well modulated and expressive voice gave full meaning to each word. As the conscious part of Kate's mind focused on his story she became more and more excited, for it was obvious where the scene was leading.

At the same time Roz's eager tongue and nimble fingers worked their magic at her crotch and soon led Kate to her first orgasm. She couldn't help but tell them loudly and in explicit detail about the delicious feelings in her crack, her heady groans interrupting Barton's telling of the story.

Roz was kissing her throbbing quim, soothing the ecstatic crack until it was quiet once more. And then, allowing it only a moment's rest, she continued her exploration. Her tongue pushed through the yielding doors and on along the moist cave as far as it could reach.

Kate writhed and gave herself fully to the wicked desires of her vagina. And as she headed for her second climax, Barton continued with the story, his words battling with Kate's laboured breath.

'The teacher's eyes appraised Susie's ripe young body. He certainly wasn't made of iron, and the prospect of what the girl was offering had cleared his mind of all other thoughts.

"All right, Susie," he said, beginning the improvisation. "You've been sent to me because Miss Phipps found you playing with yourself in the toilets. That's correct, is it not?"

Susie was standing before his desk, her head hung low

in shame. "Yes, sir. But I couldn't help it, sir. Since my tits have started to grow and my hairs have started to come through, I keep getting a terrible urge to touch myself."

"Well, it's an urge you must resist, because it is very, very wrong."

Mr Steel sounded highly embarrassed as he spouted on about Victorian values, and how little girls should keep themselves pure and not allow themselves to be led along a wicked path by their swiftly developing bodies. But what the hell? His own body was developing quite nicely, thank you – especially his cock, which even now was struggling against his groin within the limited space of his underpants.

"In the fullness of time," he went on, "you will understand why you feel like this. Now, you can choose detention, or—"

He paused, for his rampant shaft had anticipated his next words and was throbbing with expectancy. He swallowed, and cleared his throat.

"Or, I can smack your bottom."

"I want you to smack my bottom, sir," Susie replied. "Put me across your lap and smack my bottom."

"All right, if that's what you prefer," he said, trying in vain to keep his joy at the prospect out of his voice. "Come round to my side of the desk, then pull up your gymslip and lie across my knees."

Susie did as he asked with an almost indecent haste, and Mr Steel's eyes shone when he saw for the first time her sumptuous, fresh buttocks beneath the open lace-work of her red panties. He thought of this luscious girl playing with herself – *Oh Christ, how I'd love to watch that.*

Without a moment's hesitation, he brought his open palm lightly down onto her bottom; and he relished the

tingling in his hand as it made contact with the warm flesh. Susie wriggled on his lap, deliberately rubbing against his erection. The sensation brought a hushed murmur from his mouth, and a deep throb to his groin.

He gave her two more slaps, and after each she writhed against him, eroding his control.

"Okay," he said, in a choked voice. "I think I'd better pull your knickers down now, so the spanking will be more painful. Maybe then, young lady, you'll remember the pain of it next time you feel the urge to play with your cun . . . I mean, your sex organ."

"Yes, sir."

Susie left his lap and held up her dress for him to remove her panties. This was the moment she'd been waiting for, and he didn't disappoint. As soon as his gaze fell on her thatch of hair poking through the lace, his face turned pink and his breathing quickened. Susie hoped he might take her there and then – he seemed desperate enough.

The teacher's movements were faltering as he reached for the flimsy garment. He had never seen such a sexy sight. It was crazy to hope that she might be a virgin – Susie had probably been through most of the boys by now. But to have that young and perfect body thrusting beneath him; to push his cock between those gorgeous legs . . . He pulled down the panties with all the care of an archaeologist handling an item of world interest, and then she was displayed before him.

"Do you want me to lie on your lap again, sir?" she asked, her dress still held aloft. "So I can rub myself against you?"

Mr Steel spluttered. "Susie, you must not say things like that."

She gave a girlish giggle and scrambled across him.

"Spank me, sir," she pleaded, wriggling about.

"Open your legs then, so it'll hurt more."

Had he really said that? Oh, God help him.

Susie spread her legs and his hand almost strayed to her inviting slit, but he stopped himself in the nick of time and smacked her hard instead. Three more whacks followed, and his eyes never strayed from the fresh little nest which was only inches from his grasp. Already the pouting lips were wet with her love oil, and Mr Steel felt a trickle of sweat travel down his spine.

"There, that's all done," he said, in a strangled voice. "Now you'd better put your knickers back on and get off to your class."

"All the girls like you to spank them," Susie said, still holding up her dress. "They've all said they can feel you getting bigger while you're doing it."

"Now, stop it, Susie," he warned. "If you don't I'll be forced to cane you."

"But it's true, sir. I know all about sex. I've let three boys do it to me already. And I like watching their cocks get big as well."

"Right, I've just about heard enough of this."

The teacher jumped to his feet and turned the key in the lock. Next he hurtled across to the windows and closed the blinds.

"Okay, you've got me mad now," he said, breathing heavily. "You'd better take all your clothes off. And when you've done that and you're feeling really humiliated, you can bend over so that I can cane you."

"Oh, yes, sir," Susie giggled.

The outer clothes were off in a matter of seconds, and Mr Steel almost had a fit when he saw her breasts peeping

out above the tiny bra. Susie tingled with excitement. So she *had* chosen the right one. She just knew he'd love it.

When that was pulled off and thrown on the desk with her dress, she bent before him and cried in pain at the first blow from the thin cane.

"I don't really want to hurt you any more, Susie, but you must stop talking so dirty in my presence. Do you understand me?"

"But I can't, sir," she insisted. "I only got caught so you'd cane me. All the girls say you feel them up when you've finished. Feel me, sir. Please?"

When the cane swished again young Susie howled, and Mr Steel had the distinct feeling that the girl was enjoying the punishment, actually revelling in the discomfort.

"You can hit me as many times as you like, sir. I don't care. Jennifer Trasler said that after you'd felt her, you got your cock out and made her play with it until your stuff shot out all over her."

"You're asking for it, Susie, and believe me, you're going to get it."

And she was, too. Just as soon as their little game of charades was over she'd get it, good and hard. It was obvious now that she wasn't just teasing. The sexy bitch wanted it as much as he did.

"There, Susie," he said, dropping the cane and stroking her smarting bottom. "The pain should soon go away, and you can forget it ever happened."

"Keep on stroking me, sir. It feels so nice. I'm all hot and wet between my legs, sir, and my little slit's started to itch. Could you scratch it for me, sir? Could you?"

Mr Steel slipped his hand on to her waiting vagina, and as she whimpered with joy Susie felt his hot erection.

"It's so big, sir," she thrilled. "I'd love to see it."

Without further ado he unzipped his trousers and coaxed the hard shaft through his flies. Susie gave a wail of delight when she saw it.

"Bloody hell, it's massive," she gasped, slipping completely out of character.

"You like my cock, then?"

"It's fantastic."

"And do you want me to put it where it should go?"

"And where's that then, sir?" she asked, her eyes shining with devilment.

"Into your tight little cunt, of course," he said, grinning.

"Oh yes please, sir."

"Bend over for me, Susie – hurry. I've got something far nicer than the cane this time."

Giggling with delight, she bent over and parted her legs. Mr Steel positioned himself behind her and pushed his swollen cockhead into her tiny entrance.

"I hope it goes in, sir," Susie said, an edge of panic to her voice. "The others weren't anywhere near as big as yours."

"It'll go in, don't worry. Just relax."

He thrust forward an inch and then waited for her to open a little more before pushing all the way, and grunting with satisfaction as her passage expanded with ease to grant him entry. And then he was sliding back and forth along her clinging, well-oiled channel. Susie began to pant, and the sound made him push harder.

"Oh, sir," she cooed, "it feels so good. My cunt's so hot. It feels as though it's on fire."

He pushed harder still, and faster. He wanted the fuck to last forever, but all too soon her exquisite tightness defeated him and his milk was jetting into all corners of her velvety sheath.

"Wow, sir," Susie cried. "It feels lovely – all that hot sperm shooting inside me." '

CHAPTER 14

'That's it. That's it!'

Kate grabbed Roz's head and rubbed her erupting sex against the girl's responding lips until the orgasm had subsided.

'Oh, that was so good,' she whimpered.

Even when she released Roz and the girl had pulled away, Kate could not keep still. She turned over onto the bean bag and buried her face while the warm contentment continued to surge through her middle.

Barton said, 'I take it my sexy story was partly responsible for that?'

She nodded into the bean bag.

'If only more people would read dirty stories to their lovers,' he commented. 'Anyway, the next bit is boring, just what Susie says when she and Mr Steel return to their fantasy world. It was, I must add, written with a certain panache, but I shall bypass it.'

'I'll read next,' Roz offered. 'And Kate can pleasure you.'

Kate had hardly recovered from the violence of her climax, but was so worked up that she was now ready for anything. When she looked up Barton was lying on another, his big shaft pointing towards the ceiling. Kate feared that her shaking legs would be unable to support her weight, so she crawled between his open legs and took

the quivering member deep into her mouth.

Her mind went back to Maria and the lessons she had learnt at the woman's hand. A cock needs to be lubricated well, she told Kate repeatedly; and with that in mind Kate allowed saliva to trickle from her mouth until his shaft was soaked in it.

Just then something nice began to rub against her still ravenous clitoris, and she guessed it must be Roz's thumb. Oh, it was such joy. To have a delicious shaft to suck on while her love bud was rubbed into a frenzy was so wonderful. Surely paradise itself could not offer such pleasures?

But she was there to fulfil a mission, Kate reminded herself. While her own pleasure was important, Earl Barton's climax must be uppermost in her mind.

As Kate concentrated more fully on the job in hand – or to be more precise, the job in mouth – Roz began to read.

'Miss Phipps fondled Greg for a long time before releasing him; she needed to be sure that his shaft was stiff enough to give her what she needed. There was no need to worry, however, for the youthful cock stood resplendently at his groin. It was a positive work of art, with its graceful contours and subtle skin tones that grew deeper and more fiery the nearer they were to his noble tip.

When the cock was at last stretching its taut skin to its limit, and struggling and jumping within her caressing palm, Miss Phipps very slowly untied the knots in her rose-covered brassiere. Greg hindered her somewhat, struggling as he was. For so long her exciting treasure had been there before his eyes, so near and yet untouchable because of his bonds, and he could wait no longer to explore that inviting dip which was almost totally concealed by her pubic hair.

The second he was free, Greg pounced on that forbidden fruit but gently parted the bush, taking his time now that the moment had arrived, unwrapping her vagina as joyously as one would a welcome gift.

And then it was before him in all its fine glory. Reaching out a trembling hand he felt the glossy lips, and shivered with carnal lust as they parted straight away beneath his touch. His sperm was still on her sex, and his fingers were covered with it by the time they found her lustrous love bud.

Miss Phipps let out a bawdy curse and opened her legs wider when that sensitive nub was disturbed. And Greg, taking his cue from her violent reaction, rubbed at it with an almost childlike wonder, going faster and faster, harder and harder, until she was shrieking that it was good and bawling out expletives, not caring if anyone could hear.

Greg turned her around roughly so that her back was against the tree; the hard, uneven surface of the bark pressing into her delicate skin. The time for teasing foreplay was over and both of them were now frantic for satisfaction.

Miss Phipps spread her legs wide and, with words that would best befit a writhing whore, she howled for him to lick her carnal cavern as she pulled apart the doors to that tempting spot.'

As each word was uttered, Kate's aching vagina pulsated to an ever-increasing tempo, and she intensified the speed with which her steamy lips sucked at Barton's thankful cock. Her quicker movements had him squirming on the bean bag; and the more he squirmed the faster she worked, the friction of those shapely lips bringing even more blood rushing to that engorged rod.

Kate could well understand how the randy Miss Phipps must be feeling, for Roz, still pandering to her clitoris, was producing an erotic heat of such intensity that her crotch seemed to be floating away from her body – attached, yet adrift. It was as if her brain, fearful that the sensations would become too much for her to bear, had banished them to a safer distance.

Barton started to let out animal grunts as his breathing quickened and, with those lascivious sounds loud in her ears, Kate fought to concentrate on Roz's husky voice as she went on with the story.

' "That's lovely, Greg, so lovely," Miss Phipps moaned. "Get me ready for a good screwing."

The boy was using little technique, but none was needed here. The very feel of his tongue flicking along her wilful trench was enough to send her spirits soaring. Back and forth he travelled, from hungry opening to burning clitoris – back and forth, back and forth. He was like a dog, lapping at something which pleased it; and Miss Phipps would have welcomed a dog, if its tongue could produce such sweet sensations as those erupting in the wake of Greg's mischievous mouth.

She pushed herself into his face, demanding that he go faster. For she was nearly there, mere seconds away from orgasmic bliss. Greg's tongue fought back with violent devotion, and then she was sobbing with the joy of a climax which boiled over and sent hot contractions surging through her groin. On and on it went, never ending, as if her existence was one of perpetual orgasm.

But, finally, the heat subsided and the contractions slowed, leaving sweet contentment to settle upon her. It was a while, however, before Miss Phipps could confi-

dently stand on her trembling legs, and longer still before her breathing was sufficient to give voice to her bliss.

"I've never known anything so good, Greg, but it's only got me ready for what I really want. Hurry, Greg, hurry."

There was a frantic edge to her voice as Miss Phipps threw herself to the ground and lay with legs open and raised at the knee.

"I haven't had it for months," she breathed. "I can't wait any longer, Greg, I really can't."

His movements were as frenzied as hers as he manoeuvred himself on top and stabbed his weapon at her entrance.

"It's ready for you, Greg," she murmured, grabbing his hot, throbbing shaft and guiding it towards her sex-starved slit.

He rammed it in immediately, pausing only to relish the silky feel of her channel, and then he was fucking with a fury which brought ragged gasps from her moist lips. His initial frantic thrust was enough to release the first of her orgasms, so long repressed, and she urged him on, using every dirty expletive she could think of to heighten his arousal.

The shocking words were whispered in his ear, floating there on erratic breath while she fondled his anus, pushing the tip of a tentative finger into that dark place as the sheer ecstasy of orgasm after orgasm flooded over her body.

"I've never had such a good screwing," she whispered. "It's wonderful, Greg. Go faster, faster. I'll do anything you want, no matter how filthy it is, just as long as you keep giving me this."

She was babbling, and even as she begged him to go faster Greg slowed a little; his body, although young and super fit, was beginning to tire with the exertion needed

to satisfy the wanton woman bucking beneath him. His stomach muscles were screaming out and he was having to fight for his breath. Only the delicious tingling at the end of his shaft and Miss Phipps' dirty words were keeping him going.

"Go on," she encouraged. "Really go. My pussy loves it."

He began to groan, sweat oozing from his every pore. But the sensations in his cockhead were intensifying, building into a sweetness which promised complete fulfilment. And then he could stand it no longer – he needed to come. As his balls hardened and rose up in their sac, Greg let out a rapturous sigh and shuddered as load upon load of love seed exploded from his joyous tip and flooded the torrid tunnel of the prim Miss Phipps.'

Kate was sucking harder, faster, and Barton began to push back. She could feel his tip growing larger in her mouth and, letting go of his shaft, she opened her throat to its fullest extent and allowed him to slide in as far as he could go.

That new sensation alone was enough to bring a fountain of bitter seed gushing from his cockhead. Kate swallowed it all, grateful for the techniques learnt at Maria's side, and did not let him go until he was quite still.

The secret room reeked of raw sex, and Kate's burning crack longed for the one act which would finally make it happy. She fell back onto the bean bags, unable to keep her crotch still.

'I want it,' she murmured, shooting a lustful gaze at her genial host. 'Do it to me please, Mr Barton. I need it badly.'

While he approached, his formidable weapon still hard and more than ready to satisfy, Kate opened her legs in welcome and closed her eyes. She was longing to be

pinned down by the weight of his heavenly body, aching to be filled with his gigantic shaft.

'Let me put it in for you,' Roz breathed.

After reading the erotic story for so long, she was desperate to get her fingers around Barton's divine rod, and now it was in her palm she was in no hurry to give it up. She placed his tip at the glistening entrance to Kate's yearning crack and rubbed it along her wet crevice until she was almost sobbing with fury.

'Roz, don't tease me,' she yelled. 'Please don't tease. I can't wait any longer, just push it in.'

Her cry was one of absolute lust when the cock was allowed to thrust into her depths. Barton was altogether more accomplished than the young Greg of his story. He moved within her using effortless strokes, his body arching with every lift until the tip was almost free of its sheath. And as it returned, every one of her pleasure zones was pampered, not one was ignored along the length and breadth of her velvet box.

Barton knew exactly when to quicken his pace and bring orgasmic rapture hurtling towards her. He knew, too, when to slow into a steady rhythm and stop the climax in its tracks, leaving her with a sublime warmth which was bliss in itself. He used his technique for what seemed to Kate like an eternity, and she lay there quite content to let him set the pace, for the slow-quick-slow rhythm was designed to enhance her orgasms, rather than to tease. And it worked well. Kate reached her fourth thundering come before she stopped counting and simply surrendered to the fact that she was no longer in charge of the horny situation. She had been reduced to the animal which all humans become when they sense that carnal gratification is within their grasp.

She was aware that her body was moving in time with his, pushing back at the fierce thrusting, and knew that the only thing that could bring her total satisfaction was his hot cream jetting deep within her.

Barton gasped and groaned, stopped dead for many seconds. Then he was ramming into her at a ferocious speed. When sperm finally erupted from his tip, it felt to Kate that a dam had burst its banks. So powerful was the surge that she feared he would fill her to overflowing.

A dreamy fulfilment came over her, and Kate felt the weight leave her body as Barton fell back on the bean bags at her side. She was floating on a cloud, lost in her first real experience of complete satisfaction. She realised then that her life could never be the same again. Sex had become a driving force, and she would need it every day. The gates of a new life had opened up and she had walked through them into a land where physical pleasure was the main pursuit.

'Oh, yes, my dear Kate,' Barton said, his rich, deep voice cutting into her thoughts. 'You are indeed a very sexy lady.'

She opened her eyes to find him and Roz staring down at her, and she smiled.

'I want to seduce Matthew and Donna now,' she whispered.

CHAPTER 15

Kate had a long lie-in the following morning. She needed it – they all did. She awoke to find her arms entwined with Roz's, and a warm feeling mushroomed in her breast at the cosy intimacy they now shared.

When they had gone to bed, after leaving the secret room, Kate had had no need for lovemaking – all such desires had been richly accommodated during the amorous romp with Earl Barton. But Roz, who had received no stimulation from cock, fingers or mouth, had been content to pleasure herself with a huge pink vibrator while Kate had looked on.

Although extremely tired, Kate had found herself fascinated by the imitation prick. Its delicate humming had had an almost hypnotic effect on her; and watching Roz slide it in and out, in and out of her hungry slit had aroused Kate's sleepy crack.

As she gazed at her friend's gorgeous face, a mere pillow's width away, Kate felt so happy that she let out a soft, lilting laugh. The tiny sound was enough to lift Roz from her sleep, and she responded to it with a grin and a sleepy yawn.

'Good morning, lover. I'll get us some breakfast, shall I?'

She was soon back with a tray carrying a dish of bran

flakes with fresh fruit, and a glass of ice cold orange juice. She placed it on Kate's lap.

'I'll just fetch mine,' she said, smiling.

When she was sitting cross-legged and naked on the bed, munching her own breakfast, Roz said, 'You really are beautiful, Kate.'

'Roz, when are we going to get down to some horny sex?' she enquired. 'I will admit, I haven't done it properly with another woman yet, and I can't wait.'

'Let's make it tonight, then,' she responded, her eyes sparkling with happiness. 'I shall look forward to breaking you in.'

'Great. Tonight, then. And, Roz ...' She stopped, suddenly filled with a strong emotion. 'I'm so glad you're going to be my first.'

'So am I, Love. So am I.'

Kate took a sip of orange juice, and brought her mind back on to the job.

'Right, then, what can you tell me about Matthew and Donna?'

Roz swallowed, and sat for a moment, lost in her thoughts.

'Well, for a start, I think Earl's wrong about Matthew. I don't think he's shy, at all. I just think he needs a woman who'll show him how to put his dick in – it's as simple as that. I suppose that having Earl Barton for a father must be a terrible disadvantage. Everyone must expect him to know as much about sex as his Dad, and be as good at it.'

She thought some more, and then shrugged.

'As for Donna, well, I just don't know about her. She's such a surly young madam. I sometimes wonder if the exploits in the books are really based on her experiences – I mean, what boy in his right mind would want to have

fun with such a sullen little bitch? Anyway, Earl says the stories are true, so I reckon they must be.'

'I've been thinking about Donna a lot,' Kate mused. 'And I've got a pretty good idea what her problem might be. Anyway, I'd better shower and start the day.' She grinned. 'Are you coming to join me?'

'Try and stop me,' Roz laughed.

After the shower Kate put on a plain white bra with matching briefs and, after considerable debate, decided to wear a short pink cotton dress.

Out on the landing she had to hide a smile for Donna was leaving the bathroom, totally naked, at the very moment Kate walked past. Her teenaged breasts were indeed firm but not too large, and her hairy crack looked so ripe and inviting.

Much to the girl's annoyance, Kate hardly gave her a second glance as she strode off towards the stairs, and she let out a loud laugh at the sound of her bedroom door slamming angrily shut.

She was still giggling when she entered the kitchen. Matthew was already there, sitting in his usual spot at the breakfast bar and drinking coffee. Kate wondered momentarily if he ever did anything else.

'Hi,' she said, with a friendly smile.

This is going to be so easy, she thought, *all I've got to do is flash my honey pot and he'll come running after it – and then up it*. The giggle that she tried hard to subdue nevertheless found its way out, and Matthew shot her an enquiring glance.

'It's all right,' she said, 'just thoughts.'

She stood by the expensive kitchen units and studied him for a while.

'Do you ever read any of your father's books, Matthew?'

'Sometimes,' he admitted, reluctantly. 'But I always find them disappointing. After all, things like that don't happen in the real world, do they?'

The last few days had changed her mind about that, but she wasn't going to let on – not yet.

'I suppose there's something in what you say.'

'Do his works turn you on?' he asked.

'Oh, yes,' she said, her eyes flirting with his. 'But then again, that's not hard to do because I love sex.'

He smiled. 'You sound like one of the characters in Dad's books.'

'I suppose I do,' she said, slowly. 'But, Matthew, women nowadays aren't all pure and chaste – if indeed they ever were. Modern women will often take the lead in sexual matters. I know I do, and that adds to my enjoyment.'

The boy suddenly become reflective, and stared down into his coffee cup. Eventually, he said, 'You're leading me on, aren't you?'

'Are you a virgin?' she asked, bluntly.

He nodded. 'I suppose that means you're going to laugh.'

'Of course not. Why should I? I was a virgin once – there's nothing funny about it. The important thing is whether or not you want to stay a virgin. And if you don't, what are you prepared to do about it?'

He gazed at the wall behind her shoulder. 'If I told you I think sex should somehow be tied in with love, would you laugh then?'

It was perhaps the sweetest sentence she had ever heard, and she had not the slightest desire to laugh at it.

'I'd say that you're a truly romantic person, but it may

be as well to get some practice in, so you can fully satisfy that person you fall in love with.'

'But by doing that I'd just be using somebody else,' he countered.

'Not if that person's willing,' she argued. 'If she was getting as much out of it as you were, well, who's being used?'

'Where would I find somebody like that?'

'Some young men use a prostitute for that very purpose,' she said, hitching herself up on the work surface. 'But others find a slightly older woman who's simply looking for some sex fun.'

She opened her legs, giving him a good view of her tiny white panties, and she thrilled inside as his surprised eyes became transfixed on her crotch.

'There, now you've seen my knickers,' she said, her voice husky. 'And if you come to the flat this afternoon, I'll show you what's underneath them.'

Without another word, Kate eased herself off the work-top and sauntered out of the room. The seeds had been sown, and what came next depended on just how much her honey pot had attracted him.

She got back to the flat to find Roz in a state of high excitement.

'How would you like to be a call girl?' she asked, even before Kate had time to get inside the front door.

'It appeals,' she had to admit. 'This is research, I take it?'

'You don't think I'd sell my body for any other reason, do you?' she countered, with a look of mock horror.

'Okay, then, tell me what we're going to do.'

Kate wandered into the lounge and searched around

for her cigarettes and lighter. Roz followed her in.

'Well, it's rather a strange assignment,' she began. 'Apparently we're to be at the disposal of two very import-ant businessmen. And it's extremely vital to Earl that they're kept very happy. We'll have to do everything they want, no matter how kinky. And from what I can gather, they're seriously into the weird stuff. Still, we'll be quite safe so, what the hell, let's just enjoy it and have a good time.'

Kate at last located her cigarettes on the mantelpiece, lit two and passed one to Roz.

'It sounds like fun to me. I just hope I don't let Mr Barton down.'

'I'm sure you won't. Just do as I do, and you'll be fine. I've had jobs like this one before, and they always turn out to be the most exciting ones. It'll be great – don't worry.'

'Actually, I'll be getting a bit of practice in, soon. I've invited Matthew up here.'

Roz chuckled. 'Ah, so you're going to let him get his end away at last.'

'Not straight away,' Kate said, grinning. 'The longer he waits, the more he'll enjoy it. But I think I can safely say that he'll have some fun this afternoon. It should spur him on until all he can think about is my tight little crack.'

'And what about Donna?' Roz asked, reclining on the settee.

'I'm going to start work on that little madam right now,' Kate said with feeling.

'I hope you won't be in too much of a hurry to get these things done,' Roz said, suddenly serious. 'Once you find out where Wilson is, you'll be gone, I know you will. And I'll be so sad, Kate, I really shall.'

CHAPTER 16

It seemed that Donna had stormed out of the house after Kate had so purposefully ignored her young ripe body, so any plans in that direction had to be put on the back burner. Instead, she took a quick shower and prepared herself for Matthew's visit.

At a little after two p.m. there was a hesitant knock on the door. She opened up to find the boy standing on the landing, shuffling his feet and looking decidedly ill at ease.

'Hi, come on in,' she said with a warm smile.

As they walked into the lounge, Matthew was continually fiddling with his hands as if they had just sprouted and he was at a loss to know where to put them. Kate knew then that she would have to do something to relax the boy, and pretty quickly, or the whole afternoon would be a total disaster.

'Can I get you a drink?' she asked.

He nodded rather reluctantly, and she poured two large vodka and tonics, then sat on the settee and patted the cushion for him to join her. His movements were awkward as he sat by her side and took the drink.

'Well, it's good to see you,' she said. 'I didn't think you'd turn up.'

'I nearly didn't.'

That short sentence must have badly sapped his nerve,

for the moment it was uttered he gulped down half the drink and sat staring at the floor, gasping as if he'd run the two hundred yard sprint.

Kate stayed silent and waited for the alcohol to weave its magic, all the while watching for signs that his body was relaxing. Suddenly he was on his feet.

'I'd better be off,' he stammered. 'I really shouldn't have come.'

'Hold on,' she said kindly, grabbing his arm. 'You're supposed to be here for some sex fun. Why don't we have another drink and see how you feel then? If you still want to go – fine. If not, well, we could have a good time.'

'But I don't know where to start,' he said, falling back on to the settee. 'I'm all fingers and thumbs.'

His face was a picture of misery, and Kate's heart went out to him. How easy it was to forget one's feelings and apprehensions leading up to that first time. It had been years since she lost her virginity and, looking back, it had all seemed so simple, so natural. But was it? A distant memory stirred at the back of her mind, and with it came recollections of a pounding heart, acute embarrassment, and a morbid fear of failure.

What she had in mind for the boy would send his senses soaring, would bring him a joy never before experienced. He would love it, no doubt about that. But while she led him along the path to that wondrous place, Kate must remember to be gentle and let him choose the pace. She must view him as a fledgling bird which might scuttle away if frightened or humiliated. She reached for his hand and gave it an encouraging squeeze, a kindly smile brightening her eyes.

'I don't know about all fingers and thumbs,' she giggled. 'You'll be all dick by the time I'm finished with you, young man.'

She took his glass and went for a refill, shooting a surreptitious glance his way while she poured the vodka. The remark had relaxed him a little, and by the time she came back with the drinks, Matthew was at least looking at her.

'Now, we could play something like strip poker, but that takes too long. I know, how about tossing a coin? Whoever loses has to take something off. How does that sound?'

He took a long swallow of his vodka and nodded easily while Kate dug into her shoulder bag and rooted out a ten pence-piece.

'Heads, you win, and tails, I win. Okay? And whoever wins takes a garment off the loser.'

She tossed the coin and waited for it to land on the carpet. It was heads.

'You win,' she said. 'What do you want me to take off?'

Matthew licked his lips.

'Your dress.'

'Great,' Kate said, getting to her feet. 'Take if off for me, then.'

He went to her and pulled up the skirt, catching his breath when her long legs were revealed in all their shapely glory. Then he worked the dress up and over her head. Kate held her arms aloft and while he struggled to get it free, she rubbed her body against his, delighting in the fact that his penis was already nice and hard.

The dress finally came off and, laughing, she tossed the coin a second time, all the while aware that his eyes were eagerly acquainting themselves with the soft texture of her skin, which looked so richly tanned against the white cotton of her underwear.

'Tails,' she shrieked. 'My turn, now. I think I'll take your shirt off.'

Stepping forward slowly, so as not to panic the boy, she took her time unbuttoning the sports shirt before removing it with hands that brushed against him at every opportunity.

'You have got a beautiful body,' she purred, feeling his deep, hairless chest and his flat, hard stomach until his breathing quickened.

Matthew won the following toss of the coin and stood agonizing for many moments over what to remove next. She noticed that his gaze strayed repeatedly to her tiny panties, where the outline of her pouting vaginal lips showed through. And then his eyes would return to her bra which tried valiantly to restrain her large, jutting breasts as they rose and fell at a pace that matched her mounting arousal.

'Your bra,' he said, at last.

Once again her arms were held out as she turned her back and urged him to undo the clasp. Freed from their restraint, her huge mounds wobbled enticingly, and Matthew let out a gasp when she turned to show him her treasures. The breasts were superb; two lush mountains that a man could play with for hours on end. And the nipples were of the subtlest pink; a hue which even the great Van Gogh could not have hoped to capture.

Matthew reached out, longing for his first touch. When his fingers eventually met with the silky feel of those magnificent gifts, he was shaken by a tremor of passion so strong it brought a weakness to his knees and a throbbing ache to his cock. The fingers roamed over her skin in unceasing circles, round and round, getting ever closer to each pink gem.

'Why don't you suck them,' Kate breathed. 'Suck my tits, Matthew.'

An incredulous smile pulled at the corners of his mouth as the boy responded with a keen enthusiasm. His eagerness was touching and Kate silently pledged, there and then, to give him the very best of herself. Just as a mother holds and encourages a child throughout its first steps, then she would inspire Matthew to go forward with bold strides into a future made infinitely more desirable by the sexual confidence which he would gain from their lovemaking.

Matthew's mouth closed around her nipple and his eyes held a dreamy light as he suckled with an awkward urgency. Kate ran her fingers through his hair and guided him down to her stomach where he planted a multitude of tiny kisses on the lustrous skin, his soft lips leaving tingling goose bumps in their wake.

Down and down he went, en route to her panties, and Kate's breath grew more impassioned as he travelled ever closer to her waiting crack. Soon he was kneeling and nibbling at the cotton of her knickers, heightening the excitement within that carnal cavern with each teasing brush of his lips.

He was obviously acting on instinct, and his limited knowledge of the female body was clearly evident in the way he continually missed her sensitive spot. And yet it was his very inexperience which Kate found so arousing. A thousand pulses of pleasure rippled through her groin as he gnawed and kissed her most cherished prize.

'You've made it go all wet,' she murmured huskily as she held his head to her crotch, fearful that he would stop. 'It's covered with my love juice now. Can you taste it, Matthew? Is it sweet?'

The boy made no reply as he continued with his scrutiny of her private parts. Kate guessed that he could taste her

by now, however, and she rubbed herself against his lips again and again, encouraging him to sup well on her heady liquor.

'If I lose the next toss I'll have to drop my knickers,' she gasped. 'Shall we get on with it?'

Anticipation was bright in his eyes as Matthew rushed to his feet. And he didn't mind at all when the coin predicted a win for Kate – at least it meant she would remove his jeans.

There was an urgency in her movements now, an urgency which was at odds with the slow seduction she had planned. So, making a vain attempt to slow the trembling at her crotch, she silently upbraided herself and endeavoured to check her pace.

Kneeling at his feet, she removed his trainers and socks and helped him out of the jeans. Then, at last, Kate found herself staring at the huge weapon pushing out the front of his jockey shorts. It looked so inviting as it stretched the soft cotton. Its outline was clear to see, and only a woman of holy orders would possess sufficient control to resist putting out a hand and grasping the heavenly shaft.

Kate was not, and never would be, a nun. So her fingers were soon weaving around the solid weapon until she had a firm grip and had found the tip, still covered by the shorts and pointing towards her mouth. So much for making him wait, she thought drily, as her mouth closed around it.

She sucked him slowly, her lips barely brushing the material covering his cockhead. As she worked, the gentle throbbing of his shaft intensified until it felt like a pounding heartbeat which caused the mighty rod to thicken and rise up against her palm.

The soft cotton was soon covered with saliva and

moving freely back and forth, adding to the friction of her industrious mouth. The boy was whimpering and groaning, tossing his head from side to side as he wallowed in the sensations Kate was so successfully dragging from his sensitive tip.

Before long a jet of hot seed came gushing through the shorts and into her mouth. Kate eagerly lapped up each spurt, enjoying the bitter taste and yearning for more. Matthew's eyes were tightly closed and he was trembling when she stood up.

'Come on, Matthew,' she urged. 'This spin is for who takes their knickers off and shows first.'

She was pleased to see that his erection was only slightly sagging when the ten pence-piece spun in the air. The silver coin climbed and climbed, seemed to hang in space for seconds before beginning its descent. It landed on its edge, spinning rapidly, and then settled on the thick carpet pile. It was 'heads'.

'I've lost,' she exclaimed, jumping around with glee. 'Now you can take my knickers down. Or perhaps I should – that way you'll get a better look at what I've got. After that, I promise you can play with it.'

That was probably the easiest promise she would ever have to make. She couldn't wait to have those inexperienced fingertips delving into her writhing tunnel, couldn't wait to see the look on his face when he sees his first cunt, close up and in full technicolour.

'You take them down, then,' he said. 'I've never seen one before.'

Keeping her knees together, Kate slipped off her panties and then teased him for a few seconds before opening her legs and showing him her hairy bush.

'That's what my pussy looks like,' she whispered. 'I'll

show you how to play with it, if you like. I'll tell you how to make it happy.'

The shy, awkward Matthew had resurfaced by the time his hand went between her legs, and he roughly probed in the general area of her entrance.

'Ooh, gently,' she advised. 'Just stroke the hair around my little cunny until it feels really nice. That gets it excited, you see. It soothes it, gets it ready for a gorgeous cock like yours. Now play with my clit.'

She took his finger and placed it on the swollen button. 'That's nice . . . great. Just rub your fingertip over it. Lovely – that's it, keep doing it. Oh, good . . . good.'

Her love bud was beginning to itch and tingle, becoming larger and more demanding as Matthew toyed with it.

'Do it faster now,' she pleaded, placing her hands on his shoulders and spreading her legs wide. 'God, that's fantastic. Rub it very hard now, and make me come.'

His finger was a blur and his expression was one of pure delight when her love cream oozed out on to him as she reached her climax. Very quickly she closed her legs, trapping his hand until the warmth which was spreading throughout her groin finally cooled. Only when the waves of bliss began to subside did Kate open her legs and release him.

'Now finger me,' she said, in a breathless voice.

His hand was trembling as it brushed past the coarse forest which shaded her moist valley, but Matthew soon became bold when he stumbled upon the dip it concealed so well. He slipped a finger inside and shot an apprehensive glance at Kate, who responded with an encouraging smile.

She had never felt so sexy. Here she was with a handsome young virgin sliding a finger in and out of her hungry crack, and she was loving it. She contracted her vaginal

muscles and felt her yearning tunnel grip the finger with a frenzied passion. It was superb, absolutely superb.

But then Kate suddenly realised that she was getting all the pleasure at Matthew's expense. Yes, this was meant to be something of a training session, a lesson in techniques that he could take away and use on his future loves, but she was hardly being fair to the boy.

With that thought in mind, Kate reached for his jockey shorts and pulled them down around his thighs. His gorgeous rod, swinging before her, looked so ready to be taught, so eager to be shown the dark, sacred tunnel that it must conquer.

She fondled the thick shaft gently at first, rubbing with a tentative rhythm. Matthew's breathing was ragged and his chest was heaving, but Kate was thankful to find the tempo of his finger staying constant at her crotch.

'Use two fingers,' she said urgently, her hand now still while she waited for him to respond. 'That's good, now open them out.'

It took a few seconds for her meaning to reach him, and his gazed at her inquiringly as his fingers parted to a V sign.

'Perfect,' she purred, resuming her attack on his cock. 'Finger me again. Go—'

But her words were lost in the loud groans which rose up from the depths of her throat as Matthew's fingers continued with their heady labour. They moved confidently, touching every nerve ending, reaching every pleasure zone in the lusty walls of her vagina. The rapturous sensations made her pant like an exhausted animal. When total fulfilment thrust violently through her middle, it turned her legs to jelly and caused her groin to melt under its burning heat.

Matthew seemed a little bewildered by her animated ravings and rather in awe of the violent response that his wandering fingers alone had provoked, and his rhythm slowed. Kate grabbed his wrist with unseemly haste and forced him to keep up his delicious movements deep within her passage until the orgasm had burnt itself out. And her panting was still rapid even minutes after they had finished.

'Was that all right?' he asked, falteringly.

'Oh, Matthew, you gorgeous boy, that was more than all right,' she laughed, clamping a hand on her jerking crotch. 'I can honestly say that was more than all right.'

When the last of the spasms had stilled, she straightened up and there was a mischievous sparkle in her eyes as she gazed at him.

'Now, I may have remained quite ladylike and subdued while you were doing that,' she giggled, 'but, believe me, it was most satisfactory.'

He was still standing with his shorts around his thighs, and now that the moment of passion was over, Matthew felt rather foolish and unsure of his next move.

'Can I,' he stammered. 'I mean, can I ... well, you know—'

Kate's expression was blank, and she made much of attempting to guess his meaning. She knew what he wanted all right – her hot little box. But she couldn't resist a tease.

'What do you mean? Surely you don't want to screw me?'

He nodded eagerly.

'Oh, no, Matthew,' she said, shaking her head grimly. 'I never promised you full sex, did I? After all, you're much too young. I did only promise to take my knickers off for you—'

His look of abject disappointment made her want to chuckle but she suppressed the urge and gazed at him with what she hoped was motherly concern.

'I really am sorry, but I never meant to give you that impression.' She glanced at his cock. 'But you've still got a big hard-on, so what can we do about that? I know, would you like me to do the next best thing?'

His eyes lit up. He hadn't the slightest idea what the next best thing could be. Several possibilities sprang to mind, though, and all were very exciting. But whatever it was, he would throw himself wholeheartedly into it and to hell with the consequences. This is for you, dear wife, he thought with a satirical grin as he kicked off the shorts.

Kate was glad that she'd climaxed twice already, for the sight of his eager young tool made her insides flutter with longing. She went into the bathroom and searched the cabinet for a bottle of baby lotion. Shaking a little into her palm, she spread it liberally between her shapely things. Then, with its sweet scent mingling with the musty aroma of her love juices, she took the bottle into the lounge where Matthew was waiting earnestly. More of the lotion was worked into her palms, and his eyes widened with erotic pleasure when she started to stroke his quivering shaft.

'Your prick is simply divine,' she said, watching avidly as it bucked and writhed within her grasp. 'And you can bet that what I've got in mind will make it feel better than it's ever felt before.'

With a seductive smile on her lips, Kate bent over in front of him, her knees tightly together. She knew full well that this pose would give him a tantalizing glimpse of her bushy hair and trim buttocks, and she wished she could see his expression.

'Come to me,' she invited. 'Put your prick between my legs.'

His movements were clumsy but eventually he did as she asked, and Kate giggled inwardly when she felt the tip of his urgent penis press against the tightly closed entrance to her wet tunnel.

'Not in there, you naughty boy,' she scolded lightly.

Reaching behind, she guided his cock between her legs, where it stopped and slithered for a few seconds against her well-oiled thighs which pressed against him as firmly as the most grasping of vaginas.

Then he began to fuck, and tiny sounds of rapture left his lips as the feelings in his cock head grew more fiery with each forward thrust into that creamy channel.

The exercise was meant for Matthew alone, but soon Kate was responding to the luscious sensations created by his throbbing member rubbing to and fro against her wet pussy. She groaned loudly and encouraged him to push harder, touching his bulging tip each time it showed itself between her legs until it was forcing its way into her lightly clasped lotion-covered hand.

Matthew gripped her thighs and began to murmur, pushing harder all the time, eager now to fulfil the promise that bubbled in his aching testicles.

'Go on, shoot,' she yelled. 'It'll be lovely. Just let it go.'

And then he was coming. Kate positively marvelled at the amount of love seed which gushed through her fingers and ran in torrents down her perspiring thighs. Matthew kept on thrusting long after the last drop had left his ecstatic tip, and then he was still, grunting and sobbing with delirious contentment.

'Was that nice?' she asked, turning towards him. 'Was it, Matthew?'

The boy tried to speak but no words came, so he simply nodded as Kate crossed to the sideboard for a handful of tissues. And there was a faraway expression on his handsome face when she bent to clean herself up. She rather liked the feel of sticky sperm running down her legs, and loved the smell of it mingling with her own body scents.

'I think our next bit of fun should be had away from the house,' she said, wiping his cock clean. 'Is there anywhere quiet around here?'

'There's a lake over in the park,' he said, waving a hand vaguely in that direction. 'I go swimming there every day with my friend, Simon. Perhaps I could put him off and we could go there.'

Kate grinned as a plan formed in her mind. 'No, don't do that. Bring him along – we could all have a laugh – but just remember that I don't go all the way.'

He moved as if in a trance while Kate helped him to dress, making sure that she touched his naked flesh whenever possible.

'In the morning?' he asked, eagerly. 'We go swimming really early, before there's anyone else about.'

'Not tomorrow,' she replied, remembering the two businessmen she and Roz would be entertaining. 'The day after tomorrow, as early as you like.' She giggled. 'After all, we don't want anyone watching what we're doing.'

She walked him through to the hall, anxious to be alone so that she could plan his and Simon's seduction, and when she opened the door she was surprised to see Donna standing on the landing. Straightaway, the girl's sullen eyes swept over Kate's naked body.

'Been having fun?' she asked, a bitter note creeping into her voice.

Matthew ignored her, and after shooting a grin at Kate he wandered off towards the stairs.

'Of course we've been having fun,' Kate said, flaunting herself. 'That's what our bodies are for. It's a pity you're so uptight, Donna. You miss out on such a lot.'

The girl kept her gaze directed at Kate's pubic bush, making no attempt to look away or disappear down the stairs.

'It's only the same as yours,' Kate teased. 'The only difference is, I don't have your problems.'

'And how can you be so sure you know what my problems are?' she spat, finally managing to avert her eyes.

'I *do* understand, Donna,' she said, suddenly serious. 'And if you ever want to have a chat about it, then I'll always be here.'

Without waiting for the girl's reply, she closed the door of the flat.

CHAPTER 17

Roz was being rather secretive about the two business-men, and no matter how hard Kate pressed, she was only prepared to divulge that they were foreign and that all would be revealed in the morning. Kate left it there.

During dinner Roz chuckled constantly throughout Kate's detailed account of her time with Matthew, and the girl's eyebrows rose with admiration when she heard her further plans for the boy and his friend.

'You are a filthy cow,' she commented, when the tale was told and they were sipping their wine.

Kate was about to deliver a playful rebuke when there was a tentative knock on the door. Roz opened up and found a decidedly sheepish Donna waiting there on the landing.

'Is Kate in?' she asked, haltingly.

'Yes,' Roz replied, with a friendly smile. 'Come in.'

The girl was shown through to the lounge where she glanced around, ill at ease.

'Can I talk to you, Kate?'

'Of course you can.' She indicated the settee and waited for Donna to get comfortable. 'Is this about your problem?'

The girl bit on her lower lip and nodded.

'You know, don't you?' she said, her face a mask of misery.

'I've guessed that all those stories you pass on to your father are simply figments of your imagination. I'm right, aren't I?' She nodded. 'Now, correct me if I'm wrong, but I don't think you're a virgin.'

'No, I'm not,' Donna mumbled.

'But you don't enjoy it as much as you'd like,' Kate persisted.

'I don't enjoy it at all,' the girl admitted. 'But I love thinking about it, I love fantasizing about things I wouldn't dream of doing in real life. I suppose that's why Dad likes my stories so much, they're so dirty and such a turn on.'

'I see.' Kate motioned wildly for Roz to pour the girl some wine. 'Why don't you tell us one of your fantasies, so we can get a picture of the things you don't want to do in real life?'

Donna accepted the wine and took a long drink.

'Okay,' she said, clearly embarrassed but desperate for help. 'I'll tell you my favourite. Dad won't use it because the girl has to be forced, and he says that would be alien to Susie's character because she's always willing to do anything.'

Kate took the wine bottle and topped up Donna's glass.

'Go on, then,' she said. 'Just tell us the story as if it really happened to you.'

The girl took another long swig, and Kate was on hand to keep the wine flowing. Donna was clearly inhibited and had one or two false starts but, after her glass had been refilled a couple of times, she started to relax and made herself more comfortable on the settee, her short skirt halfway up her heavenly thighs and her baby-pink panties on open display.

'This story's about my teachers, Miss Phipps and Mr

Steel.' She gave a girlish giggle. 'You'll be thinking I've got a thing about those two.'

'They really are your teachers, then?' Kate quizzed.

'Oh, yes. I've spent years fantasizing about them. I'm always thinking up things I'd like them to do to me, really dirty things—' She paused, as if deciding where to start. 'Anyway, on this particular day I'm really confused because I've got a real crush on Mr Steel and I also feel very funny whenever Miss Phipps is near me. She keeps looking at me all the time, and once or twice her hands have brushed my tits while she's been leaning over my desk, you know, helping me with my work. One day she even cupped her hand around my left tit, but took it away immediately and said she was sorry, it was an accident.

'Anyway, like I said, I feel really confused because I know something's going on between her and Mr Steel, even though he's married. They always seem to be laughing at some private joke, and I keep seeing them having hushed conversations in various corners of the school. Once I even saw them kissing in the corridor when everybody else had gone. So one afternoon, at home-time, I decided to follow them and see where they go. I had to be very careful – I mean, if they'd seen me I'd have been in real trouble, wouldn't I? They probably wouldn't have noticed me anyway, though; they were too interested in each other.'

She paused for a sip of wine, and her audience waited with bated breath.

'Well?' Kate said. 'Where did they go?'

'They went across the playing fields, and once out of sight of the school, they put their arms around each other. I had to hide in some bushes when they stopped for a kiss and a cuddle. I was so frustrated and jealous, all at the

same time. Miss Phipps was rubbing herself against Mr Steel, and I could hear her telling him that her pussy had been itching all day because she wanted him so much. I knew they were going somewhere to have sex, and even though I was jealous I felt excited too, and I wished I could watch them doing it. I've never watched anybody before, and I thought I could pretend it was me they were having.

'I knew I was right when I heard Mr Steel say that they'd have to be careful and go somewhere where nobody could see them. Then they hurried across the playing field. I waited a few seconds before I dared leave the bushes, and I thought I'd lost them. I looked everywhere and I was beginning to panic when I heard Miss Phipps laugh. I looked around and realised they were in the hut where the groundsman stores his tools.'

'Ooh, that's novel. I wouldn't mind it there myself,' Roz said, grinning. 'Oh, sorry, Donna, carry on.'

'Like I said, Miss Phipps was laughing, and she said the tool shed was the right place for what he'd just shown her. There was a window on the side so I crawled round to it – I was holding my breath the whole time in case I made a noise. But when I got there, I found that the glass was so dirty and the inside of the shed so dark that I couldn't see a thing. Anyway, I pressed my ear to the glass and listened, and what I heard made the little crack inside my knickers go all wet and hot—'

'Well?' Kate said, her anticipation mounting. 'What did you hear?'

'Miss Phipps was saying how dusty it was in there and that perhaps they shouldn't be taking their clothes off. But from what I could hear Mr Steel just carried on stripping her, and she kept on giggling so she couldn't have been too bothered. She was saying, you still like it, don't you? –

and Mr Steel was saying, you know I do. He was going on and on about how bushy and tight she was. He must have had his finger in her by then because she was saying how nice it felt and how it was getting her ready—'

'What a shame you couldn't see anything,' Roz cut in. 'I'd have been really frustrated by now.'

'I was, believe me. Especially when she started playing with Mr Steel's big cock. And he has got a big one, you know – it fills out his tight trousers really nicely. All the girls are mad to see it. But getting back to Miss Phipps – she was oohing and aahing all over the place, telling him how much she loved to play with it and how she wished she could have it up her every night.

'Mr Steel, by this time, was making funny, strangled noises and his breathing was really quick, so she must have been rubbing him really hard. Then I could hear Miss Phipps urging him to finger her faster, and saying she was nearly there. I couldn't understand why I felt so worked up – after all, I couldn't see a thing. But there was something so exciting about Miss Phipp's voice; it was all breathy and urgent. And then she was crying out that she was there and it was beautiful – just beautiful, she said.'

'Here, have some more wine, Donna,' Kate urged. 'You're doing really well.'

'Thanks. It sounded like Miss Phipps was crying and I thought they must have done it. So I tried to peer through the window again but, like I said, it was too grubby. I could just make out their outlines though, and it looked like Miss Phipps was down on the floor, lying on her back. Then they must have moved around a bit and I could see Mr Steel lowering himself on top of her.

'I felt like screaming with frustration because I couldn't see what they were doing, and their voices kept over-

lapping so it was hard to make out what they were saying. I did hear Mr Steel telling her to spread her legs though, and I heard Miss Phipps say she'd guide him in. They both did a lot of grunting, and he was going on about how tight she was and how good she was to fuck.

'After that they didn't say much for a long time – it must have been ten minutes – but all the while they were groaning and sighing. And then Miss Phipps shouted out. Her voice was so loud it made me jump, and I pressed my ear to the glass. She was really panting, telling him she was coming again and imploring him to fuck her harder. Mr Steel sounded like he was working really hard, and Miss Phipps told him to pull it out and come all over her tight little crack. I was going mad outside that window because I'd have loved to have seen that.'

'What happened next?' Kate asked, while Donna took a sip of wine.

'It was a long time before they came out of the tool shed, and when they did they kept looking around to see if there was anybody about. I hid behind the shed, hardly daring to breathe, until they'd gone away.'

'Is that all?' Kate asked, softly.

The girl gave a vigorous shake of the head. 'Oh, no, there's far more, and I love thinking about what comes next.'

'Tell us, then,' Kate said, topping up Donna's glass. 'We're enjoying listening to this.'

Her glance flitted from Kate to Roz, as if checking that they were enjoying the story, and then she took a long drink before settling back with her eyes closed.

'I just couldn't sleep that night. I was tossing and turning in bed and my slit was itching to be touched. I tried to scratch it, but the feeling was somehow deep inside and I

couldn't reach it. The next morning I felt exactly the same – it was as if I was yearning for something. I didn't know what, but I did know it had something to do with the tool shed.

'Miss Phipps took our first class and I couldn't stop looking at her and remembering all those dirty words I'd heard coming from her mouth. My imagination was really running wild, and I couldn't stop thinking about what they must have been doing. Anyway, about halfway through the lesson she noticed me staring at her and she started paying me a lot of attention, as if I was her favourite. She came up behind my desk and pointed at something in my exercise book, and that's when her hand brushed over my breast again, and I went all weak. She smelt so nice, and her hair kept tickling my cheek. As she pulled her hand away, she touched my tit again, but this time she really felt it. She asked me if I liked it, and I said, yes, it made me go all funny between the legs. That made her smile. It was – oh, I can't think what you'd call it – a knowing smile, I suppose. And she asked me if I'd like to go to her flat during the lunch hour. I agreed straightaway because by now I desperately wanted to be dirty with her, and with Mr Steel.

'I whispered that I'd seen them in the tool shed and that I knew what they'd been up to. I don't know what made me do it, and as soon as the words were out I was terrified she'd be angry. She went really pale. I could see the colour draining from her face, underneath her tan. Anyway, she asked me if I was going to tell anybody, and I said no, but I also said that the next time they had sex I wanted to watch.

'That seemed to please her, and later that morning I saw her with Mr Steel – they were watching me and whispering. I heard Mr Steel tell her that I might be very

saying how nice I was. Her voice was all funny, really husky when she asked if I minded her doing that to me. All of us girls have got one, after all, she said. She dropped the toilet paper down the bowl but carried on playing with me. It was great having her fingers touching me – really dirty. I asked her if her slit was the same as mine and she laughed, saying she'd got more hair around hers.

'That made me curious, so I asked her if I could see it. She said she'd do better than that and strip off for me if I wanted. I nodded immediately, because I couldn't wait to see her without any clothes on. She stripped really quickly, and I couldn't believe my eyes – her tits were huge, and they wobbled about whenever she moved. She took off her knickers last, and I was amazed at how hairy she was. I wanted to touch her – I just couldn't help myself. It felt so hot, and the hair was so thick and coarse. Her eyes were shining and she made me take all my clothes off. I felt embarrassed, I must admit, and I kept apologizing because my crack wasn't as hairy as hers and my tits were so small. But she kept telling me to shush because I was gorgeous.'

Both Kate and Roz had noticed that the wine was beginning to slur Donna's speech, and also that the girl had taken to touching herself between the legs. The more exciting the story became, the longer she would leave her hand there. It was obvious that she was longing to play with herself.

They giggled softly, and Kate whispered, 'Why don't you finger yourself, Donna? Go on, we don't mind.'

By now the girl was drunk and no longer knew what she was doing. Her hand set to work inside her panties, and she sighed with pleasure, while Kate and Roz were treated to the spectacle of her sliding fingers, their youth and slenderness making the sight that much more erotic.

'I couldn't believe what happened next,' she went on. 'Miss Phipps asked me to smell her crack. I knelt down and she opened her legs. I was really nervous when I pushed my face into her hairy patch. It smelt divine and she kept telling me how good it felt. Then I heard someone come into the flat and I got frightened, but Miss Phipps told me not to worry. So I relaxed and carried on kissing her, getting closer and closer to the place with that gorgeous smell.

'She kept egging me on, pulling her hairs to one side so that I could find the crack. And it just opened up before my eyes, the lips were all wet and shining. Then I could see the hole – it was covered in white, juicy froth. Oh, that's gorgeous, she called out when I slipped my tongue into it, and the faster I licked, the more frenzied she became. Then she started calling out, like she'd done in the tool shed, saying things like "that's it, I'm nearly there, do it faster."

'When I pushed my finger into her slit, well, I thought she'd go berserk, and when I started rubbing her little bud she did go berserk, calling out and rubbing herself against my face. I could hardly breathe when she told me I was making her come because she held my face there until it was over and she started to calm down.

'When she finally released me, I looked around and saw that Mr Steel was standing in the doorway. He'd taken all his clothes off, and he looked fantastic. He's got a fabulous broad chest and loads of muscles in his stomach that none of the boys at school have got. I took a deep breath then, and looked at what I had been longing to see—'

'His cock, I bet,' Roz said to Kate, totally absorbed. 'What was his cock like, Donna?'

'It was so big. I just couldn't believe it, and I could see

that it was twitching even from a distance. Miss Phipps was just as pleased as I was to see him, and then she turned to me and said not to be worried because Mr Steel would never tell anyone that he'd seen us being dirty with each other.

'That was when she took my hand and led me to him. "He's got a big erection," she said, "because he can see what we've got between our legs and he's so looking forward to having our eager cracks." We all went through to the lounge and stood in front of the settee, and they both kept on touching my tits and my slit, saying how luscious they were and how nice it was that I'd agreed to come to the flat. Miss Phipps kept feeling my bum, too, really stroking it hard. I liked that, especially when she said I'd got a lovely arse and she couldn't keep her hands off it.

'Mr Steel was making me touch his cock, and although he was holding my hand and forcing me, there was no need because I'd wanted to play with it for so long. I liked the way it kept jumping in my hand, and I felt excited – aroused, I suppose – when it trembled every time I touched it.

'I couldn't believe these people were my teachers. They were so vulgar and did such dirty things, and all the while their breath was getting faster and faster until they were panting. Miss Phipps kept asking if I wanted something nice. I really had no need to act innocent because I really was, and by "nice", I thought she meant Mr Steel having sex with me. So I just said yes. Anyway, she made me crouch down in front of Mr Steel and he rubbed the tip of his cock around my lips. I'd heard about women sucking men off, of course, but I couldn't believe that's what they wanted me to do. Miss Phipps was cooing in my ear and

telling me to grab the nice, big shaft so that it couldn't go down my throat, and then I was to suck on the big tip. Just slide your mouth along it, she said, backwards and forwards, and run your hand along the shaft.

'She watched me long enough to see that I was doing it right – and the way Mr Steel was moaning and groaning made me think I'd got the hang of it – and then I felt her between my legs. She was lying on the floor and working her head between my thighs. I could feel her hot breath on my skin and I knew she was getting closer to my crack. Then her mouth was on it, and I'd never experienced anything like it. I went all tense to start with, but when she started licking me, all these lovely feelings went shooting along my legs and up into my stomach. Then, as if that wasn't enough, she poked a finger into me and I just flipped. I didn't think I'd be able to keep Mr Steel's cock in my mouth, but I did. In fact, what Miss Phipps was doing just made me rub and suck on it even harder.

'There was this warm feeling in my tummy, and it kept getting hotter and hotter. It was almost too good and, although I was loving it, I kept feeling the need to lift myself up and away from her. I was bouncing up and down on her face and she was telling me to keep still. Then it just exploded and spread all over my insides until I couldn't think. And at the same moment Mr Steel spurted into my mouth. There was so much of it, and I had a job to swallow it all, but I did. It was like nothing I'd ever tasted before, bitter and sweet at the same time.'

The girl was fingering herself fast now. The lewd expression on her pretty face distorted her mouth and made her speech difficult to understand. And from deep inside her panties came a loud slurping sound, caused by the three fingers she had worked within her passionate tunnel. Kate

knew that her climax was imminent and was desperate to watch.

'It's all right, Donna, don't stop,' she said, creeping forward. 'I'm only going to take your knickers off, so we can see what you've got.'

Her eyes were still tightly closed and, quite passively, she arched her back so that Kate could remove the panties more easily. Her vagina was soaking wet when she sighed and spread her legs.

'You want what Miss Phipps gave you, don't you, Donna?' Kate asked, in a low, sexy voice.

'Yes ... yes,' she said, a definite pleading tone in the words. 'That's what I want. That's what I've always wanted.'

'Just keep telling us the story,' Kate coaxed.

Roz moved forward to unbutton Donna's blouse and, as soon as her pert little breasts were uncovered, she teased the nipples with a relentless dedication. Kate, meanwhile, went between the girl's legs and forced her lips through the soft thicket until they were resting on her sticky honey pot. There, her tongue lovingly caressed the glossy hillocks, the brazen channel and the love bud, which looked for all the world like a colossal pearl nestling enticingly among the juicy flesh of a deep sea oyster.

Donna's voice was jerky and dripping with passion as she resumed the story.

'Mr Steel was still shaking when I stood up, and by the look on his face I was sure I'd pleased him. His gaze kept straying to the dip between my legs, so I opened my legs wider and let him see all that I'd got. His cock was still hard, and it started to throb again as soon as I flaunted myself at him.

'Miss Phipps was shouting encouragement. "Go on, have her," she was saying, "she's really hungry for it."

And I was. Oh, God, I couldn't wait. She made me lie on the floor with a cushion under my head, and by now I wanted to tease them, so I pretended I didn't want to have sex and I tried to look frightened while I kept my legs closed. And the more she begged me to open them, the more I shook my head and kept them shut.

"I don't want it," I whimpered, "my crack's too small for a big thing like that." Then she was whispering in my ear, telling me I'll love it once it's inside and making me happy. She promised me it wouldn't hurt. And after all, she said, she should know because she has it every day.

"Just open your legs, Donna," she kept on, "just open your legs." So I did, very slowly, pretending that I didn't really know what to do. Then Mr Steel grabbed my thighs and positioned his tip at the entrance to my wet crack. With one sure movement he pushed it all the way up, grunting when it was fully home. It felt so good ... *so* good. I couldn't wait, so I asked him to give me a good fucking. Well, that really started him off. He was pushing wildly, while Miss Phipps urged him on.

'I'd never experienced anything like the sensations that were building inside my crack, the feelings that his big sliding shaft were creating. When he gave me my first orgasm, my control began to slip, and I started to writhe about beneath him, and Miss Phipps' voice was really urgent when she shouted for me to push back. It took me some time to get the hang of it, but then I was moving in time with him, really screwing as if I'd been doing it for years.

'Mr Steel started groaning deep in his throat – those sounds and his breath on my face made me come over and over again. And when he gushed inside me, there was so much of it. I thought he was never going to stop shooting ... oh, oh Kate—'

Donna grabbed Kate's head and started rubbing her impassioned vagina against the full lips, harder and harder, until they began to do their job.

'I'm coming,' the girl screamed. 'I'm really coming. Oh, it's so gorgeous.'

Her body was a blur of movement and, when she finally stopped bucking, her sex juices were running freely down Kate's smiling face.

'Well, Donna,' she said. 'I think there's hope for you yet, girl.'

CHAPTER 18

The next morning Kate and Roz spent a whole two hours searching through wardrobes and drawers in the hope of finding outfits so spectacular that their foreign clients would be left speechless. The selection of underwear was easy: Kate chose frilly black panties and a low-cup brassiere with matching suspender belt and sheer silk stockings, while Roz opted for eggshell-blue g-string with a see-through stretch bra and flesh-coloured stockings held up by a delicate antique lace belt.

The perfect dress was far more elusive, however. As they continued their hunt, the conversation centred on the episode with Donna the previous evening.

After her first ever climax, the girl had positively raved, but as the elation wore off she started to worry that it might never happen again. Kate, in her unaccustomed role as mother figure, explained that sex was something a girl had to want for its own sake. It wasn't a bargaining tool that could be used in an effort to bring pressure to bear on another. If sex was entered into solely to exert power then it became less enjoyable, for it was being used for the wrong reasons.

Kate's comforting words seemed to satisfy the girl, but even so they had quite a job getting her to leave the flat, and it was well over midnight before they were alone.

'Well, that's Donna's seduction out of the way,' Kate said, agonizing between the powder-blue shift and the black business suit with the mile-long split up the back of its skirt.

'And what a seduction.' Roz enthused. 'I could have done with somebody like you when I was getting started.' She grinned. 'Come to think of it, I could still do with somebody like you.'

'Steady, girl,' Kate said, laughing. 'We've got the two businessmen to pleasure first. Then there's just Matthew and his friend to worry about. After that I'll have to know where Laurence Wilson is because, enjoyable as this job is, it's taking far too long.'

'Huh, you can't wait to get away from us, can you?' Roz huffed, her mouth a sulky line.

'It's not that, Roz, don't be silly. I just have to find him, that's all.'

'Shall we have some really steamy sex then, so that we don't forget each other?'

Maybe it would be appropriate to sixty-nine, Kate mused, with a cheeky grin. 'Oh, come on Roz, let's go to work, and sod the bloody dresses.'

E. Ross Publishers occupied a large and impressive building on the outskirts of town. Inside, the girls' high heels clicked a tattoo on the marble floor as the pretty receptionist led the way to the Managing Director's suite.

They were shown into a huge, plush office, and as Kate settled into a sumptuous leather chair she studied the man. He was around forty years old, with blond hair cropped short and a nice, if somewhat unusual, face, which seemed to bear a permanent friendly smile. He reached into the pocket of his smart, expensive business

suit and took out a large white handkerchief.

'Whew – you two look just right for the job,' he quipped, mopping his brow with exaggerated fervour.

'I take it, Mr Ryan, that E. Ross is not the name of your founder,' Kate said, with a grin.

He shot her a sexy wink. 'You take it right, young lady. When you're in the flesh business, you have to try every gimmick in the book.'

Kate noticed that he had a job to keep his eyes off her, so she deliberately made her manner flirtatious.

'And are we today's gimmick?' she asked.

'Yes, I have to admit that you are. Now, we've two Japanese guys over here from one of Japan's biggest publishing houses, and they're interested in taking Earl Barton's work back with them. No problem there – Earl's our biggest seller – but we want them to agree to take the rest of our list before we let them have him. Once again, no real problem – with Earl's sales potential, they'll agree eventually. But, at the moment, they're dragging their heels, and in this business, time's money. So, you two girls are sweeteners. If you give them everything they want, they'll sign today – no problem.'

Kate could hardly believe her ears. 'Are you saying that we'll actually be selling our bodies just so a handful of authors can get their books sold in Japan?'

'Yes,' he said, easily. 'But that's no problem, is it?'

'Not so long as we're getting paid enough,' she replied, jumping to her feet. 'Could I use your 'phone, please?'

'Sure.'

Ryan pushed the telephone across the desk, and Kate could hardly contain her annoyance as she punched out Earl Barton's number. It rang for almost a minute before the connection was made.

'Earl Barton,' he snapped. 'I'm trying to work here, for God's sake. I don't—'

'Yes, Earl, sweetie, and Roz and I are about to get our pussies shagged off by two Japanese men, just so that you and the rest of your fellow scribblers can rake in the money from Japan.'

'Ah, Kate,' he said, smoothly.

'Ah, balls,' she spat back. 'Now, you listen to me, I've taken care of your daughter. And your son will lose his virginity very early tomorrow morning. But if I'm to go through with this charade today, then I damn well better know where Wilson is – first thing tomorrow. Do I make myself clear?'

'It's a deal,' he assured her. 'Just do this for me, Kate – it's worth millions, and tomorrow I promise I'll tell you everything I know.'

She slammed down the receiver and turned to the Managing Director.

'Right, Mr Ryan, that's settled that. Now, what exactly do you want us to do?'

'Well,' he said, leaning back in his chair, his hands clasped behind his head. 'These two guys are off the leash. From what I can gather, this is the first time they've been anywhere without their wives in tow for twenty years, and consequently they've gone dick-mad. We've done the usual – strip shows, blue flicks, they've gone through dozens of call girls, but they still haven't enjoyed themselves enough to sign on the dotted line. It's your job to offer them something novel.'

Despite her initial misgivings, Kate was beginning to feel quite excited about the whole venture. Indeed, her vaginal muscles contracted sharply at the idea of overpowering a pair of wayward cocks when all else had failed.

'When do we get to meet these gentlemen?' she asked, wriggling in her seat as love cream seeped onto her briefs.

'Straight after the meeting.'

'No, Mr Ryan,' she said, holding up a hand. 'Let us serve tea at the meeting and – who knows? – maybe even you might learn something.'

The man looked intrigued. 'Whatever you say. Oh, by the way, neither of them speak any English.'

'What we've got up our skirts won't be bothered about that,' she said, with a scheming glance towards Roz.

The meeting was to take place in the board room which housed a long, dark oak conference table, around which stood a dozen chairs. At one end sat the Managing Director along with a member of his staff. The businessmen were positioned opposite, their clothes immaculate, their expressions fierce. A young female interpreter occupied a seat half way between the two groups. The Japanese were chatting in a highly excitable manner and the girl was translating it all into English.

She turned to Ryan and shook her head. 'They say it's too much money, and if you don't offer them a better deal, they'll leave immediately.'

The Director cradled his head in his hands.

'Tell them to go and fu—' He paused, and held up a placating hand. 'No, sorry, don't tell them that.'

He was about to go on when a door at the far end was flung open, and Kate strode into the room, closely followed by Roz. They were balancing trays containing cups of tea, and plates of biscuits and small cakes. Five pairs of eyes were glued to their images, for the girls had removed their dresses and wore nothing but their tantalising underwear. It was the suspender belts and stockings that seemed to

arouse the greatest interest from the foreign visitors.

They were served first, the cups of tea and plates of biscuits and cakes placed ceremoniously before them. Their eyes gleamed as they followed the girls' progress around the table. The translator was served next, and then the English Management team.

While arranging her bizarre plan with the Director, Kate was quick to realize that very careful planning was necessary for it to work, and she hoped that she had thought of everything, for it would be a pity to spoil an idea which had so much sexy potential.

She and Roz took their seats between Ryan and his cohort, then Kate leant forward straight away and took a chocolate finger from the plate. She held it aloft for a moment, seemingly intent on studying its sleek design, and then positioned it between her lovely lips and sucked until half had disappeared. It was an innocent gesture but so sexily done, and the men were silenced, mid-sentence, as they watched with mouths agog.

The biscuit was released from its silky sheath, and Kate winked at the foreigners as she brought it down below table height. There, away from the eyes of those so readily falling under her spell, she pulled the gusset of her panties to one side and inserted the biscuit into her vagina, sliding it to and fro and enjoying the sweet sensation as the creamy chocolate began to melt inside her slit. By the time she took it out, the finger was liberally coated with her white love cream which gleamed against the dark brown of the plain chocolate.

A surreptitious glance told her that Roz was doing the same. So far, so good. Next, she brought the biscuit to her nostrils and drank in her own luscious scent before rubbing it across the Director's lips. He closed his eyes and

bit into it, chewing greedily and expressing his pleasure with a long sigh.

The Japanese men were really jabbering now, their highly excitable voices reverberating around the large room. Kate took another biscuit from the plate and this time they ducked down to watch what she was doing beneath the table. And they were not disappointed, for she decided to give them a good show. Using deliberate movements, she pulled aside her knickers and rubbed the chocolate biscuit along her wet trench, caressing her rapidly swelling clitoris with it and moaning with lust. Even at that distance she could hear the ragged breathing of the businessmen. She was really beginning to enjoy the feel of the biscuit finger inside her crack, and she masturbated with it far longer than was necessary.

Ryan was eagerly awaiting his next snack – the thought of its perfumed love juice sent his taste buds into a frenzy of anticipation – and his mouth was open even before it was half way to his lips.

Above the excited chatter from the Japanese rose the cool voice of the translator.

'They want to know what you're doing.'

'We're serving morning tea,' Kate said, as she licked chocolate and sex-cream from her fingers.

A heated conversation followed between the men and their interpreter, and Kate watched with much amusement until they had finished.

'They want you to serve them morning tea,' the girl said, at last.

Kate motioned to Roz who followed her along the length of the table. When they reached the guests, the girls took up position on the table's edge, one either side of the men. They smiled down at them most politely, and then Kate

took hold of her gusset and exposed herself.

'My hairy treasure,' she said, enunciating the words carefully.

'Hairy treasure,' the nearest man repeated, with a vigorous nod of his head and a Cheshire cat grin. 'Hairy treasure.'

Kate's smile was fixed as she unwrapped a long, slim chocolate bar. Then, with her gaze resting on the man's animated features, she pushed herself to the very edge of the table and inserted two inches of it into her vagina. Her long, elegant fingers tenderly stroked the three inches that were protruding like a slim brown cock as she lay back on the table and beckoned for him to come forward.

The man's head went straight to her crotch, and he bit wildly into the chocolate bar, chewing quickly and swallowing the pieces almost whole in his eagerness to get to her pubic hair. Soon his greedy lips were touching her hot sex, his teeth drawing the rest of the exotic treat from her willing hole, his snake-like tongue chasing the chocolate residue deeper into her inviting cleft.

Kate was aware that everyone, even the chaste interpreter, had crowded around to watch her lascivious performance, knew too that Roz was duplicating her every action. With the small man still foraging at her groin, she removed her bra and covered the jewels of her breasts liberally with thick cream from the cakes at her side.

'Lick it off. Come on, lick it off,' she coaxed, pulling at the man's jacket collar.

Her words were alien to his ears, but her meaning became crystal clear when he glanced up to see Kate pointing eagerly to the creamy hills and running a lustful tongue around her sensuous lips.

His pounce was as quick and as accurate as a leopard's

and, with a lecherous grin which revealed a row of tiny, sharp teeth, he scoffed and gobbled the lot, stopping only long enough to draw a highly excitable breath.

While his mouth was glued to her right nipple, Kate manoeuvred herself around until his crotch was within reach, and she slipped a hand down to the protrusion which was growing larger with each erotic moment that passed. The man let out a babble of incoherent nonsense, and his eyes bulged in their sockets as he stared down at her foraging fingers.

He was panting rapidly, his hot, sweet breath wafting around her face, and he carried on jabbering to no one in particular as Kate pulled down his fly with a teasing laziness. Then, with movements that were equally slow, and with a devilish smile which knew no language barrier playing on her luscious lips, she delved inside. Her fingers closed purposefully around the straining shaft and, although the man was thrusting his pelvis forward and urging her in a torrent of hurried speech to pull him out, she took her time. She caressed and teased the throbbing cock in the warm confines of his underpants before working it towards the opening at a gradual pace which brought a frustrated flush to the man's highly animated features.

All eyes were on her invading hand – all, that is, except those of the man's colleague. His gaze was fixed firmly on Roz's fingers which were following Kate's lead at his own burning crotch.

Finally two compact but enormously desirable cocks were out on display. The female interpreter gasped and slavered at the meaty shafts, her gaze flitting from left to right as she stood between them, her eyes spoilt for choice.

Momentarily dismissing the delicious tremors dancing along the full length of her chocolatey tunnel, Kate took

time to familiarize herself with the handsome cock now resting in her palm. It was short but extremely thick, and looked enormous on so diminutive a man.

'Big cock,' she purred, while it jumped and throbbed at her touch.

'Big cock,' the man repeated, his face overtaken by a beaming grin.

A strange silence descended on the room, and was broken only by the occasional sharp intake of breath as Kate repeatedly dipped a finger into the cakes and spread thick, yellow cream from chunky root to bulging head of the endearing shaft.

When every inch was covered, she knelt before the man and tantalized him with the tip of her tongue, licking gently, and leaving glistening paths on the creamy landscape. Her flirting foray took Kate along the cock's trembling under-side with its thick, veiny surface, then on to his twitching balls where she changed her course and went up, up and around to the florid tip, which fought valiantly to get between her tempting lips.

At last the cream was cleared and the man let out a low moan at the touch of her snake-like tongue on his taut skin, made sweet by the tasty feast. And he ranted like a bedeviled soul when her mouth opened up to welcome his indebted cock into the comforting warmth of her throat.

Kate wanted the oral act to be over quickly. So as well as sucking hard, she rubbed the sticky shaft with a frenzied skill that would have impressed even the expert Maria, and soon her loving orifice was hit by the force of his erupting seed.

It took Roz a further two minutes to bring her partner to his climax, which was equally as violent, and he had hardly stopped spurting before entering into an earnest

discussion with his happy colleague. They whispered their demands to the flustered interpreter who looked around at the sea of faces.

'Do you want this wrapped up,' she said, 'or just the way they're saying it?'

'Just the way it is,' Ryan said.

'Okay, they're saying that they'll sign the contract, but first—' She stopped, and brought a hand to her flushed face. 'But first they want to fuck the two girls.'

'What do you say?' he asked, turning pleading eyes in Kate's direction. 'Forget the plan, eh? Just drop your knickers so we can get the deal stitched up.'

Kate grinned mischievously. 'Tell them it'll cost them another million.'

The interpreter translated and Ryan buried his face in his hands while the Japanese howled in protest.

'Tell them not to be so hasty,' Kate said, confidently. 'They don't know what's on offer yet.'

CHAPTER 19

There was an Olympic-sized swimming pool in the bowels of the publishing house, its water kept at a constant temperature at all times. E. Ross employed only the best, and the pool was just one of many perks which ensured that no one was ever tempted to move elsewhere.

Earlier that morning the water was drained away and replaced by several tons of mud on the orders of Kate. She stood now with the small party and watched as workmen darted to and fro, putting the finishing touches to her little scheme.

For the sake of decency, and in order to keep the Japanese men on the boil, Kate and Roz had been supplied with bathrobes, and as the puzzled workmen departed, these were slipped off and discarded. The girls wandered around the pool, gazing down at the deep mud while Ryan, with fingers crossed behind his back, announced the deal that was on offer.

'Are you sure you want to do this, Kate?' Roz asked, with a hint of doubt. 'It's going a bit far for research.'

'Of course – don't you? It really appeals to me and don't forget, you get laid in the showers first.'

As if on cue Ryan called over, 'They're going for it. Roz, you're needed. Now.'

With a playful smile Kate pushed the girl towards the

group who were now hurrying into the shower room to watch the sexy show. And as she listened to the ecstatic howls of the two men being made happy at Roz's hands, her thoughts turned to the interpreter. She was a pretty girl, shy perhaps, but it was obvious that she had one almighty crush on the Managing Director, and Kate was momentarily wondering whether they would strike up a liaison when joyous shrieks came from the direction of the shower room. She giggled, for it would seem that 'I'm coming' sounded pretty much the same in any language.

The Japanese men came out first and she marvelled at the muscular development of their small trim bodies. Their love weapons were still hard, despite the expert attention paid to them by Roz, and a heady expectancy hung in the air as they advanced to the pool's edge.

'Right,' Kate said. 'Have the rules been explained to them?'

'Yes,' the interpreter called back. 'If you can get from that end to this and climb out without them touching you, they get nothing. But if they prevent you from leaving the pool, they can do anything they want.'

'Spot on. Okay, let's get started.'

Kate descended the steps and tested the mud, which reached to the middle of her shins. It felt strangely sensual, and its earthy smell was cloying but served to heighten her arousal. She waited until the two men were on the steps before making her break, zig-zagging from left to right, her breathing soon laboured as the mud sucked at and hampered her darting feet.

Their wild shouts were almost behind her as she made her way towards the end of the pool which was so near and yet so difficult to reach in the tacky sludge. They were proving to be extremely nimble of foot and were upon her

in no time, tripping her from behind and sending her sprawling into the clinging mess.

She lay there spread-eagled and briefly dazed, but her senses returned abruptly when one of the men hurled himself on to her back and pinned her down while the other stripped off her knickers and held them aloft with a shout of triumph. Her bra was next to be torn away, and then Kate was roughly manhandled on to her back, the oozing mud seeping into her every crevice.

The men forced her legs open and, while one knelt on her shoulders, his testicles swinging an inch or so above her face, the other prepared to enter her. But as she felt his tip part the lips of her excited pussy, she decided to make the game more difficult and, without a second thought, sank her teeth into the bulging sac before her eyes.

For a split second the man was motionless, unable to believe that she would violate his precious balls in such a ferocious way, but then a crazy howl left his lips and he toppled from her, splashing into the mud and grasping his injured spot.

As soon as his weight was off Kate could see the startled expression on the face of the second man; the sudden commotion had caused him to miss his target completely, and his tip was now sliding ineffectually up and down her wet, muddy trench. Then he too was growling with pain when her foot came up and kicked him square in the chest.

He fell backwards, floundering in the muddy river while Kate struggled to her feet and moved away as quickly as she could. The Japanese were almost baying now, whipping themselves into a frenzy of madness. They were no longer men, but primeval animals involved in the pursuit of a

female who, if caught, would be shown no mercy until their desires had been totally satisfied.

They were gaining on her, and for the first time Kate felt fear rise in her throat. This had begun as a game but now, if those men caught her, they could do anything they wanted. Just what had she agreed to?

They were closer still, gaining with each laboured step, their hurried splashes moving ever nearer. And then the side of the pool loomed towards her. Thankfully, Kate reached up and gripped the top, her feet leaving the mud with slight plops as she heaved herself clear.

The men were almost upon her, so close that she could hear their hasty breath, but she was almost out of the pool and risked a quick look behind. It was then that a hand grabbed her ankle and pulled her back. Despite the cushion of mud, the fall winded Kate badly. But she rolled on impact, turning half a dozen times before coming to her feet, punching and kicking as the two men blocked her blows and grabbed an arm each.

Kate fought back, would not give in, but this time the men proved too powerful. They handled her roughly, seemingly unmindful of her safety. She was simply a toy, a plaything on which to vent their frustrations. And, worse still, their expressions told her clearly that they were enjoying the violence.

She managed to land a few more punches, but these did little more than bring awful lecherous smiles to their faces, and then her hair was grabbed from behind and her head forced back. The grip tightened until she feared that her hair would be pulled out from the roots but, oddly, instead of increasing her already spiralling fear, the pain sent a surge of sexual want coursing through her body. Those feelings of intense desire were so powerful that Kate was

tempted to turn the tables and rape the two men. But all the while her head was being pulled back, further and further, until she finally collapsed in a heap.

This time the men were taking no chances and, while one held her arms above her head, the other gripped her ankles and forced her legs apart, his eyes gleaming in his mud-spattered face as they swept over the prize at her crotch for which he had fought so hard.

He lowered himself upon her and placed the tip of his throbbing member at the entrance to her sex. And then, with a grunt of satisfaction, rammed it home. Kate lay still, not moving a muscle, and her face was devoid of emotion despite the fact that she wanted to call out in sheer joy at the pleasant sensations building inside her tight crack.

The man rode her well, making her climax three times before the tempo of his breathing increased. He started to moan repeatedly, his words meaningless staccato sounds, then suddenly he pulled out of her and rose to his feet while hot seed spewed from the end of his weapon and landed on her breasts and in her face.

The second man quickly took his place between her passive thighs. He was far rougher, perhaps because he could still feel the pain from her teeth in the sensitive sac that covered his balls. He gripped her buttocks, his fingers digging into her flesh and marking her while he rode her crack at a furious pace. And, as if to equal the score, he sank his own teeth repeatedly into her neck and the lobe of her ear. This was no idle nibbling to enhance their loveplay; his bites were vicious and designed to hurt.

Kate lay cocooned in her warm bed of mud, and sumptuous shivers rippled along her spine as he continued to gouge at her neck, his sharp teeth only enriching the divine

thrills coursing deep within her passage as his frolicking cock fucked in a frenzied rage.

Pain and pleasure played a divine duet and, with a speed which left Kate swooning, they merged into a gigantic climax, its intense heat stampeding towards her vagina until she felt that her middle was dissolving and becoming one with the cloying mud.

'I'm coming,' she shrieked, gripping the man's buttocks and riding the erotic wave along with him.

Her cries spurred him on, and soon he was emptying his balls into the pit of her cavern, load upon load of milky sperm filling her to the brim. He rolled off her and lay at her side, fighting to draw air into his overtaxed lungs, his cock momentarily subdued.

Kate got to her feet and gingerly fingered the side of her neck where a huge bruise was developing rapidly. Then, assuming that the game was finished, she pushed a path through the mud towards the steps to her right. But the men quickly followed and pinned her against the side of the pool.

'What do you want now?' she asked, a high note of alarm in her voice.

That earlier mood of hostility which had frightened her so much was now back, bringing a madness to their eyes and harsh, sadistic grins to their lips. They spun her around until her back was towards them, and then brutal fingers were probing between her buttocks, rubbing and poking her anus until she yelped with discomfort.

'Oh, no,' Kate protested. 'I draw the line at *that*.'

Her firm tone could have left them in little doubt that anal sex was not an option in this game of erotica, but they chose to ignore her and entered instead into an earnest discussion which ended with one of the men producing a

jar of grease from the top of the steps.

'Oh, God, no . . . I said *"No"*,' she shrieked.

But the man simply smiled, displaying once more his tiny rat's teeth, as he took to spreading the grease along his hardening prick. He knew not whether Kate's fear was real or otherwise, and he cared even less – a little resistance would make the fuck all the more enjoyable.

She tried to climb out of the pool but was immediately pulled back by his colleague, who grabbed her neck and forced her head down to her knees. It was then that Kate felt them spread the cold grease between her buttocks, and a jabbing finger drove the stuff into the tight, puckered opening of her arse.

Kate winced at the intrusion into her dark place, but any discomfort provoked by the wily finger was nothing compared with what was to follow. Something far bigger than a finger touched the taboo entrance, and before she could yell her distress, the cock was thrust in. Her agony was so sudden and so acute that Kate almost lost consciousness. But nevertheless she thanked God for the grease which at least allowed the demanding shaft to move in and out with some semblance of ease.

Unable to grip the shiny, tiled surface before her, Kate fell forward and allowed her body to relax against it, grateful for the coolness which brought a degree of relief to the anxiety which burned her cheeks.

She was howling her outrage at the two men, but even as she prayed that the ordeal would be over speedily, she realised that the fuck was altogether more desirable now that her tensions had eased. Indeed, as she allowed the pool wall to support her limp body, the friction of his cock was creating quite unbelievably sweet sensations in her anal passage, sensations made all the more divine because

they were unfamiliar, and the type of fuck forbidden, in her mind at least.

It occurred to Kate that her cries were making the man push harder, his pleasure doubly enhanced by the very fact that she was an unwilling participant in what was fast becoming a carnal rape. And as the feelings of pleasure increased with each firm thrust, she intensified her struggles until the man holding her neck had to tighten his grip.

While Kate spat vulgar expletives into his grinning face, an orgasm was building at her crotch. It seemed incredible, and yet it was true – her arse and vagina had merged into one huge tunnel of love, so that both were massaged with every fierce jab of the marauding shaft.

The more she screamed, the faster he fucked; and the faster he fucked, the more she screamed. This was her most exciting experience so far, and Kate wanted it to last forever. But her tightness was at last proving too much for the man and a war cry emerged from his throat when his balls gave up their precious gift to her animated depths.

Kate heaved a satisfied sigh into the side of the pool and smiled dreamily when the cock was pulled out. But there was to be little respite, for the other man was already greased-up and was pushing into her well-oiled channel the moment it was free.

This time, knowing what to expect, she stayed calm and thrust her buttocks towards him, allowing him full access to her sexy hideaway. The comforting warmth of her last orgasm still lingered around the periphery of her crotch, and the man needed only to thrust a couple of times in order to bring it flooding back, its force increasing ten-fold and dragging screams of ecstasy from Kate's smiling lips.

Her anal muscles, contracting wildly in their orgy of

pleasure, were playing the cock as nimbly as fingers on a flute. The man, already highly aroused, stood little chance of lasting as long as his colleague, and there was sadness as well as delight in his cries when hot sperm rumbled along her passage like a huge tidal wave.

And then it was all over. Kate turned to see that their lascivious expressions had vanished, the lustful light gone from their eyes. They were businessmen once more, their nakedness now incongruous. They even helped Kate out of the pool with gestures that were both humble and attentive.

With a quick nod of farewell the men left her and hurried across to the Managing Director whose avid expression was glued to the interpreter's lips as the men spoke rapidly and with more than a little emotion.

Ryan's features became animated and his handshakes were warm as he thanked the men profusely before backing towards Kate, still nodding his gratitude.

'Well done, Kate,' he said, smiling at the cloak of mud already hardening around her shapely body. 'They're going to sign, and they've given you a bonus of one hundred thousand pounds. They said they'd never enjoyed themselves so much.'

Kate's eyebrows arched appreciatively as she mentally banked the money along with the five hundred thousand already on deposit.

CHAPTER 20

It took well over an hour for Kate to get the mud out of her hair, not to mention the bush surrounding her extremely satisfied crack.

Roz and the interpreter – whose name they now knew was Penny – were in the shower room with her, and they both had tremendous fun drying Kate's pubic thatch with a hair drier. She positioned herself with her back to the wall, her legs wide apart, while the girls took turns in directing the warm air on to her crotch. Kate giggled and delighted in watching the lank, dripping hairs become a crinkly thicket once more.

'Did you enjoy watching the show?' Kate asked Penny, as she finished drying herself off.

'Yes, very much.'

The girl was laughing, but then the corners of her mouth turned down in a pout, and she said, 'Trouble is, I feel really randy now.'

'Oh, well, I'm sure that Mr Ryan, our friendly Managing Director, will be able to give you something to cure that,' Kate ventured.

Penny sighed. 'I doubt it. He's been trying to get inside my knickers for over a month now, but I've been playing hard to get and I think I've put him off.'

'I see,' Kate mused. 'Shall we try to do something about that?'

Penny's eyes lit up, and an expectant smile brightened her pretty face. 'What have you got in mind?'

'A good screw, of course. I'd rather like to watch, too, just to round the day off. Wouldn't you, Roz?'

'You bet I would,' she said, grinning.

Penny looked undecided. 'But I can't just walk into his office and say I've decided to drop my knickers after all.'

'Leave it to us,' Kate said, gathering the girls together. 'Now, what do you think of this for a plan?'

Ryan was seated at his desk, thoroughly delighted with the way things had gone. The signed contract was in front of him, and a broad smile was on his face when Kate and Roz sauntered into his office.

'That was really great, girls,' he gushed. 'They've signed the contract and E. Ross Publishing will probably make millions from this deal.'

'I'm glad you're pleased, Mr Ryan, but—' Kate paused, a look of mock dejection marring her beautiful features. 'Oh, I don't know, I just feel so disappointed about today, somehow.'

'But, why, Kate?' he asked, suddenly earnest. 'Everything went fine – it couldn't have gone better.'

Kate shook her head. 'Oh, yes, it could. You and Penny watched the show, but neither of you got horny, so I feel we failed to a certain extent.'

'But I did get horny. I got a massive hard-on,' he said, trying hard to placate. 'I've still got one, for that matter.'

'Why don't you show it to Penny, then?' Roz suggested. 'We couldn't get her going, so let's see if you can.'

A flush of embarrassment rose up in Ryan's face, and

he faltered a little, before saying, 'Penny wouldn't want to see it. I've been trying to screw her for ages now, but she's not interested.'

The girls took up position on the edge of his desk, their expressions highly sympathetic.

'Maybe you haven't tried hard enough,' Kate said. 'We've just been talking to her, and she's really hungry for it. She's on her way up now, so why don't you give it a try?'

Ryan looked from one to the other, and swallowed loudly.

'I'd do anything to get inside that girl's knickers, but she's driving me crazy. Every time I take a step towards her, she takes two steps back. She'll never go for it.'

'Don't worry, we'll help you,' Roz whispered. 'Just go along with what we do. Okay?'

'Fine by me,' Ryan said, fingering the bulge at his crotch.

Penny came into the office then, carrying three cups of tea on a tray. As she approached, the girls slid from the desk and Kate gave her a surreptitious wink as she pulled up a couple of chairs.

'We've decided we really hate you,' she said to Penny. 'Do you know, Mr Ryan just said he'd rather eat a chocolate biscuit from your juicy slit than from either of ours, any day of the week.'

The girl tut-tutted and let out a sceptical laugh. It was her attempt to appear completely indifferent in front of the amorous Mr Ryan, but she could do little to hide her strong arousal which reddened her cheeks and enlarged the pupils in her delectable eyes.

'Don't go on,' she said shyly, placing the tray on a corner of the desk. 'I've seen so many raunchy things today. A poor girl can only take so much.'

'No, I mean it,' Kate said. 'We're really miffed. Mr Ryan's been talking about you, non-stop. He says he gets a huge erection even just thinking about taking your knickers down.'

'Stop it, Kate, you're embarrassing me,' she said, giggling awkwardly and fanning her flushed cheeks with a folder from the desk. 'I don't like talking about things like that. I'm a very shy person.'

'Oh, come on, Penny, loosen up,' Roz coaxed as she sidled up behind the girl. 'Just take a deep breath and let him have a look at your legs.'

Penny let out an unbelieving shriek when Roz hitched up her skirt, lifting it high enough for her long and very shapely legs to be seen, but stopping short of exposing her panties.

'Look at him now,' Roz whispered in her ear. 'See the big bulge in his trousers? You're the cause of that. Nice, isn't it?'

'Please, don't,' Penny pleaded. 'If I let anything happen, Mr Ryan is bound to tell everybody.'

Kate skirted around the desk and asked the man to stand up. When he did, she bent down and took off his shoes. Then she cast her attention to his trousers which were soon hanging over the back of his executive chair, along with his sporty red and green Y-fronts.

She then motioned to Roz who straightaway lifted Penny's skirt higher to reveal the sexy bulge of her pubis nestling beneath pale blue Lycra panties. Ryan's impressive shaft trembled and expanded before their eyes, its inflamed tip throbbing and twitching as he fixed his gaze on the girl's highly desirable pleasure spot.

'Penny, do you want to play with him?' Kate asked, taking the cock in her hand.

'Oh, no,' she blustered, turning her head away. 'It's far too big. It must be a good inch longer than my boyfriend's. And it's far thicker, too.'

'Just play with it – what harm would it do? Every woman likes a nice big cock, and they don't come much bigger than Mr Ryan's, do they?' Kate made a grab for Penny's hand and placed it round the fine jumping shaft. 'Rub it for him – go on.'

Although reluctant, the girl began to masturbate Mr Ryan with slow, hesitant strokes.

'I really shouldn't be doing this,' she protested. 'But it's been such a randy day, and my pussy feels so neglected.'

'Let's show Mr Ryan what you've got for him, then,' Roz said, pulling the girl's panties down so that he could be further tantalized by her blonde bush. 'There, I do believe he likes it.'

The man was becoming more aroused with each tender pull on his cock, and he let out a deep moan when her erotic forest came into view. He gazed intently at Penny's crotch, hoping to penetrate the impregnable pubic cover and at last locate the crack which he craved so desperately.

'Why don't you let me take your knickers off?' Roz said to Penny, in a loud stage whisper that was guaranteed to reached Ryan's ears.

'Oh, no, no,' she responded, shaking her head violently. 'Not my knickers, Roz . . . please. If you take them off, I'm bound to do something I'll only regret later.'

Her struggles were half-hearted, to say the least, as Roz tugged at the delicate garment and threw it at Ryan's feet.

'Why don't you lie on the floor,' Kate purred. 'And then Mr Ryan can have a really good look at what you've got for him.'

Penny was still objecting, but the sharp quickening of her breath and her ragged sighs had more to do with hot arousal than with pious indignation, however much she might argue the opposite. A moment later, though, she was flat on her back with knees raised and her skirt up around her groin.

'I don't want to do this,' she murmured, breathlessly, her eyes heavy with desire.

The sight of her hairy vagina and her exquisite writhing body finally galvanized Ryan into action. He went between her legs with the speed of lightning and, still objecting, Penny arched her back and made it easier for him to find her eager entrance. She lay perfectly still while he rode her, not moving and showing no signs of pleasure.

'Please get it over with quickly,' she moaned. 'I'm sure someone's going to catch us, and I'll never be able to show my face again.'

Ryan was growling with frustration at her lack of passion. He drew back, completely withdrawing his impatient cock, and then thrust himself in up to the root. He used this rough manoeuvre time and again, until soft groans escaped her full lips and his shaft was treated to a sensual massage, courtesy of her enlivened vaginal muscles.

'Oh, God,' she murmured. 'That's so good. Oh, so good.'

Her delight was obvious to all, and it spurred Ryan on. He was giving Penny the fuck of her life, ramming into her for all he was worth, while her delicate fingers gripped his muscular buttocks and sent blissful tremors along his spine and down to those meaty balls, which were flapping all the while against her soft yielding flesh.

Kate knew that the girl was about to climax, and she watched, quite fascinated, as Penny began to buck wildly beneath the humping Ryan.

'Oh, what a lovely big cock,' the girl was screaming. 'Your wonderful cock's making me feel so good now.'

And then she was hit by the full force of a truly spectacular orgasm. Wriggling and writhing, she shrieked like a woman possessed and sucked on her middle finger as if it were a cock.

'Christ, I'm coming,' Ryan whimpered, as the finger disappeared between her sexy lips.

'Fill me with it,' Penny yelled. 'Oh, please, Mr Ryan, fill me up.'

And he did just that, his stupendous balls almost disappearing as they fought to empty themselves into her heavenly tunnel until every last drop was gone.

Kate grinned. 'I'd say that was the perfect end to a perfect day. Wouldn't you all agree?'

CHAPTER 21

When she rose at the crack of dawn the next morning, Kate was eager to get on with her next amorous adventure. She had lain awake for hours, her vagina trembling with anticipation of the pleasures that were to come.

Had Matthew and Simon managed to sleep? she wondered. Or had they too stared into the darkness, their ripe cocks flourishing beneath their quilts?

Although she was bubbling with excitement, a tiny part of Kate's mind focused on the fact that this was to be the last pleasant obstacle in the way of finding out the whereabouts of Laurence Wilson. The thought saddened her terribly, for she had enjoyed her stay. Still, life had to go on, and life with one million pounds in the bank could only be an improvement on her previously impoverished state.

Kate deliberately neglected to shower. She knew only too well that the boys would appreciate the sultry scent of her crack far more than the manufactured fragrance of Wild Rose shower gel, which was all she could find in Roz's usually well-stocked bathroom cabinet.

After brushing her teeth – an unwashed vagina was one thing, but halitosis was a definite passion-killer! – she changed into a simple sleeveless top of white cotton and skimpy pink shorts. Underwear, she had already decided, would only be in the way, so why bother?

Matthew was already waiting at the bottom of the stairs, and Kate felt a familiar and highly enjoyable fluttering in her groin when she saw him there, so cleanly scrubbed and expectant. He'd clearly had the same doubts about over-dressing, for he was naked apart from a pair of tatty white shorts that highlighted his deeply tanned and muscular physique.

'Hi,' he said, with a cheeky grin. 'It's only just getting light outside.'

'Let's go and swim,' she said, ushering him through the front door.

Simon was hovering nervously by the porch steps, and Kate fell in love with him at first glance. He was tall – about six foot-two, she thought – and whiplash-slim, but with a wide, powerful chest and well-developed muscles bulging on his arms and thighs. His long hair was dark brown and tied back in a pony-tail. But it was his face which caught her full attention; he was so drop-dead handsome that she almost swooned like a lovesick schoolgirl.

'Hello,' she smiled, eyeing the outline of an apparently enormous cock in his grey shorts. 'I'm Kate – nice to meet you.'

'Hi,' he said, his voice deep and smooth. 'Shall we go?'

They all three chatted as they made their way to the end of the mews and along an alleyway that led to the park. Kate thought how quiet and peaceful the city was without the non-stop, thundery noise of traffic.

The park was overgrown, and Kate took hold of the boys' hands as they picked a path through the long grass.

'So, what's Matthew told you about me?' she wanted to know.

Simon shrugged. 'Nothing, really. Just that you're fun to be with.'

His glance towards Matthew was fleeting, but it told Kate loudly that their sexy little romp had been relayed to him in minute detail.

'Oh, that's good,' she said, grinning inwardly.

She had already decided how to orchestrate their seduction. Two young virgins would appreciate an older woman who was raunchy and uninhibited, a woman who would offer far more than just the dick-up-pussy scenario which they were sure to assume all furtive sex was about.

'Hold on, I need to have a wee,' she said brightly, as they passed a large clump of bushes. 'Now, promise not to look, you two,' she added, wagging a warning finger while she backed away.

Once inside the dense foliage, Kate stopped to listen for any tell-tale rustling which would betray their presence. She wasn't disappointed; the boys were soon tip-toeing through the undergrowth with all the grace of baby elephants. She giggled lightly and, making sure that her back was towards them, dropped her shorts and started to urinate, watching the steaming water splash onto the hard ground and form a rivulet as it flowed away.

Kate dried her vagina with a piece of tissue, taking her time and allowing the boys a long look at her shapely buttocks before pulling up the shorts with sensuous ease. She turned then, and found that they had left their hiding place and were in the clearing, staring at her with huge, incredulous eyes.

'I thought I told you two not to watch,' she chided, good naturedly.

'We didn't really see anything,' Simon said, with a grin. 'You'd got your back to us.'

'And we only came in because we wanted a pee, too,' Matthew added quickly.

'Can I lend you a hand?' she teased. 'Do you want me to hold it for you, and shake it when you've finished?'

'You wouldn't dare,' Simon said, his face a picture of doubt.

'Try me,' Kate smiled. 'Come on, take your shorts off and I'll hold your cocks while you take a wee.'

The boys exchanged a quizzical look, but immediately scrambled out of their shorts. Kate let out a long ecstatic breath when their luscious young shafts sprang into view. Neither was fully erect. But even so, they set Kate's vagina trembling with lust as she stood between them, taking one in each hand and giggling merrily while they promptly emptied their bladders.

Under her gentle caresses the cocks began to grow, their foreskins pulling back swiftly and allowing the bulbous tips to grab centre stage. By this time their urine was shooting up in the air, two wicked fountains activated by her wanton touch. Kate let out a mischievous laugh when their flows became trickles and then finally stopped.

'Oh, what a shame,' she pouted. 'They're too hard to shake now, and I was really looking forward to that.'

Realising that the inexperienced duo would simply stand there, displaying themselves, she released them and plucked two long ears of grass that were laden with seed. Then, with a playful grin, she stood before them, her eyes drinking in their nakedness.

Their cocks were now fully erect and wholly magnificent – so very young and untried – an absolute dream come true for one such as Kate. Taking a grass in each hand, she traced them around the boys' bulging tips, then along the sensitive undersides of their tingling shafts until they were squirming and begging her to stop. Her exploration continued, however, and she teased their balls, tickling

between the cheeks of their bottoms until neither could keep still.

'Play with us properly,' Matthew begged in a breathless whisper.

'I couldn't do that,' she said, with mock severity. 'Now, come on, let's go for that swim.'

She threw down the grass and had started to walk away, when Simon called out, 'How about if we tease *you* with the grass?'

'You wouldn't dare,' she threw back, hoping frantically that they would.

When she glanced back to see the boys racing towards her, grasses held aloft, Kate took to her heels and ran across the park. It was just as well that the place was empty. Say a policeman suddenly appeared – how could she explain why she was running through the park, yelling like a banshee, with two naked boys in tow? It wouldn't be easy.

Giggling hysterically, Kate allowed them to gain a little ground, but just before they caught up she stopped suddenly and changed direction. Simon was quicker than she thought, though, and he grabbed her wrist and hustled her towards a tree. They were all laughing and fighting for breath by the time she was pinned against it.

Kate made little protest when Matthew pulled aside the leg of her shorts so that Simon could slide the grass inside, and she almost groaned when it bent on contact with her pubic bush.

Simon swore softly under his breath, and said, 'Take her shorts down, Matthew.'

'No,' she said, shrieking with delight when the boy fiddled with her zip. And she screamed and giggled when he pulled the shorts down around her ankles. Kate was

still feigning total indignation when, having found it impossible to open her legs fully and display her aching crack, she freed a foot and spread her legs wide as she leant back against the tree.

Now there was nothing to impede his progress, and Simon took full advantage as he ran the grass along her sticky trench. Its touch was almost imperceptible, and yet the sensations it produced were amazing. Soon Kate was breathing heavily and opening the lips of her vagina so that the tip of the grass could play on her quaking love bud. The whole of her sex seemed to come alive as her oh so sensitive nub was teased mercilessly until she was finally overwhelmed by a shuddering climax.

Her blissful cries echoed around the still-deserted park as the naked boys stood watching, their hands going automatically to their shafts which were now as solid as the gnarled trunk against which Kate was writhing.

'I want to screw you,' Matthew said heavily, stepping towards her, his cock held ready for action.

'No,' she said, still gasping for air as her thighs came together. 'Let's go for that swim.'

'Please,' they begged in unison. 'Let us have it.'

'I said "no",' she repeated, sharply.

But even as her face took on a fierce expression, her legs were slipping apart to expose her treasure once more.

'Listen, boys, all the men I know want my lovely cunt all the time, but I only let them have it when I'm really desperate for sex. At the moment I can take it or leave it, so the answer's still no. Okay?'

They looked so disappointed that Kate had to stifle a laugh, and it was then that she decided it would be fun to taunt them a little – it would make the sex a lot better, too.

'Besides,' she went on, 'you two are much too young to know what it's all about. I like men to lick me silly first, until I'm really screaming for it, and only then I let them have their ends away.'

'Okay,' Matthew said, dejectedly. 'Let's go for the swim.'

Simon followed him back to where they'd left their shorts and towels while Kate strolled towards the lake. She had left off her own shorts and was enjoying the feel of the soft breeze on her hungry sex, well aware that she wouldn't be able to hold out for much longer.

Eventually they caught up and, still naked, they walked either side of her, their silence deafening. Kate, however, was too engrossed in their handsome cocks to notice the dark clouds of disappointment that hovered mere inches above their heads. Indeed, the way in which those yearning shafts pointed proudly towards the heavens, their glistening tips begging to be sucked, suggested that her refusal had in no way cooled their ardent arousal. Thank God for that, she thought, happily.

'I never promised you full sex, did I, Matthew?' she said. 'In fact, I remember quite clearly making it plain that I wouldn't go that far.'

'But my balls ache so much,' the boy said, with a rueful grin. 'They feel like they're about to fall off.'

Kate was laughing loudly when the lake came into sight. It was a pretty stretch, with steep banks surrounded by trees. The water was crystal clear and sparkled prettily in the weak rays of the rising sun.

'Anyway, you didn't even give us a chance to lick you,' Simon grumbled. 'So how do you know we can't do it?'

Kate made no reply. Instead she took off her top and threw it aside as she ran towards the inviting water, her breasts rising and falling with each step. When she

entered, the water was warm to her skin and so pleasant. She waded out to a deeper spot.

The boys followed her in and she waited, treading water, while they swam towards her.

'Okay, let's see,' she said, brushing wet hair from her eyes. 'If either of you can lick my pussy under water for a full minute, then I'll open my legs for the pair of you.'

They let out ecstatic cheers and when Kate dived beneath the surface they followed her down and kept to her heels as she led them about twenty yards out to where the water was ten feet deep. There, she broke surface, took a huge breath, and dived again, her lovely hair fanning out on the rippling waves.

Matthew was right behind her and she turned to focus on his gorgeous shaft. Its size was distorted by the water and looked rather smaller but still hugely fuckable. Kate swam between his legs, then closed her lips hungrily around his bobbing tip, sucking heartily and rubbing its length with a tenderness which belied her feverish desires.

Simon was hovering behind her, sliding his artless tongue in and out of her delicious crack. She had never been licked under water before, and the teasing play of his inexperienced mouth together with the water continually lapping against her love bud was causing the most gorgeous feelings to build inside her tunnel of love. Its doors responded immediately to Simon's loving attention, and opened up fully so that his tongue could probe her hidden depths. And all the time she sucked and rubbed at Matthew's burgeoning cock, which was growing to positively gigantic proportions and dwarfing her tiny hand.

But then, with lungs that were almost bursting, she was forced to fight her way to the surface and gulp in the cool,

fresh air. The boys surfaced a moment later, their faces bright with youthful zest.

'That wasn't long enough,' she laughed, splashing water against their broad chests. 'Do you want to try again?'

This time Matthew was the one to dive below her, and Kate felt tiny air bubbles tickling the insides of her thighs as he exhaled. She spread her legs and waited for the exquisite touch of his attractive lips. And then he was there, finding her love bud with his first arousing kiss.

Her sex was fully open, its delicate petals pulled right back, the cave beyond dark and inviting. Matthew's caresses were surprisingly soft, but deadly accurate as they centred on the very nub of her joyful slit. Kate gave herself up to the superb sensations which turned her legs to jelly and her crotch to molten heat. But, quick to ensure that Simon would not feel neglected, she took to masturbating his mighty shaft, and giggled at the sight of his terrific balls.

Matthew surfaced then, his chest heaving as he pulled air into his aching lungs.

'Come here,' she laughed, reaching out for his cock.

He gasped and surrendered willingly to her expertise. Now she was pulling both along the road to their release, rubbing so hard that the water was frothing around their bodies. The boy's faces were masks of sheer bliss, and their expressions pleased her greatly as she increased her rhythm at the feel of their cocks hardening against her palms.

Simon was the first to climax. He whimpered, and when his shaft reared up, she gazed down into the clear water and watched his sperm float gently away.

She left him to languish on his post-orgasmic cloud and turned to concentrate fully on Matthew. The boy was so

carried away, murmuring and moaning and keeping his head above water with increasing difficulty. With both hands free, Kate was able to caress his testicles while she pulled his cock to climax. She gently squeezed the straining bags until they rose up in his groin and released a flood of milky seed.

'Well, how was that for starters?' she said, grinning.

CHAPTER 22

Kate swam back to the shore with long graceful strokes, and waded out of the lake with water cascading from her delectable body.

The boys splashed after her, and Matthew grabbed her arm. He was grinning.

'Right,' he said, lying back in the shallow water. 'You told us that if we could lick you for a minute while you were in the lake, then you'd open your legs for us.'

'But that's not at all fair,' she protested with a smile. 'It's not what I meant—'

'But it's what you said,' he interjected.

She knelt above his pouting face, and thought for a moment.

'All right, then, but I want it for a lot longer than a minute.'

She eased herself forward and lowered her crotch onto his warm mouth. Straight away, his delving tongue worked a path inside the perfumed cavern. And if that wasn't bliss in itself, she felt Simon's hot breath on her buttocks as he kissed the cheeks and slid his tongue along the satin-smooth skin. Matthew had found her clitoris by this time and was licking all around it, his tongue getting ever closer but deliberately staying just beyond the ticklish bud.

Simon was lapping avidly along the channel between

her buttocks, forcing her to move position and allow him to reach her anal opening, which was throbbing with the rapid pulse of passion.

As she moved, Matthew grunted his frustration and followed, his tongue now aiming directly at her clitoris. For several minutes he toyed with the tiny jewel, quite fascinated by the way his lips could bring such a strong reaction from Kate every time he kissed it. The merest touch would have her sighing with delight, whereas a lingering caress could send her swooning.

Simon was still exploring her buttocks and planting tiny kisses all around the tightly puckered hole. He seemed infatuated by the alien orifice and Kate was quite happy to let him satisfy his curiosity. After all, his inquisitive delving was bringing such divine feelings to greet those that Matthew was creating at her crack.

'This is all so good,' she purred.

And then she was trembling with joy because Simon had unexpectedly slipped a finger into the entrance to her pussy. He let it linger there for a moment, for he was intrigued by the warmth and utter softness of her clinging cavern. It was his first journey into the world of sexy slits, and he wanted to savour each new experience, revel in every unfamiliar texture to which Kate granted him access.

The passage was wet with the juices of her arousal. When Simon withdrew the finger, he found it was saturated with her milky dew. He was entranced, totally bewitched by this wanton woman whose body was theirs for the taking. With racing heart and quickening breath, he smeared her love juice around Kate's comely arse.

She hardly dared to breath as the finger pushed tentatively against her devilish hole. Ever since her encounter with the Japanese men, Kate had longed to experience

again those special, unbelievable sensations that came with such wicked use of her anus.

'Push it in, Simon,' she whimpered. 'Go on, do it.'

He did as she asked, worried at first that he would hurt her. But when his fumbling finger brought only growls of delight from deep within her chest, his confidence grew speedily, and in no time at all he was fingering her arse at a rapid tempo.

Matthew was still tonguing her clitoris. In fact, so deft were his movements that Kate doubted that she was the first to acquaint him with such wondrous activities. And while he kept up his assault on her bud, his middle finger was pushed to the far reaches of her cavern.

To be penetrated simultaneously at front and rear was fabulous, quite beyond belief, and Kate heaped her thanks on to the boys in a gush of giggling gasps. She wanted the double fingering to go on forever, but all too soon an orgasm exploded in her middle, leaving her breathless and limp and unable to take a second more of their exquisite torture.

The boys prised themselves from her grasping holes and stood around, obviously wondering what their next move should be. They waited for Kate to find her feet, and it was a good few minutes before she did.

'I really want it now,' she said, her voice low and seductive.

Without another word she lay down on the sloping bed of the lake with her face just above the water. Then, she opened her legs and raised the knees.

'I'm all your, boys. Who wants me first?'

Before Matthew could make a move, Simon went down and was guided towards her opening. Either his cock was swelling with anticipation, or the water had tightened her

crack, for they wrestled for quite a while before the gates to her pleasure palace opened up to his knock. But soon his powerful shaft was filling the length and breadth of her vagina, stretching the walls and rubbing every inch of her, not one of her pleasure spots neglected.

She whispered passionate words of encouragement into his ear until the sensuous feelings became too much for both of them. The fuck was divine, and they thrashed about in the water, drawing sweet gratification from each other's bodies. Mud from the lake bed was disturbed by their frenzied actions and it swirled around them, sticking to their skin and their hair, and bringing girlish giggles from Kate as she was reminded of her time in the mud-filled pool.

She was lost in the most violent orgasm she had ever reached when his hot seed exploded in the centre of her sex and hit her vaginal walls with such force that her climax spiralled to even greater heights and made her dizzy with satisfaction.

Simon rolled off, his sex urge completely satiated, and Matthew scrambled between her open thighs. Frantic now for total fulfilment, Kate arched her back and helped him into her craving cavern. Incomprehensible words tumbled from her lips as his sliding shaft pumped like a piston at her aching crotch.

All control slipped away as he rode her faster and faster, until she climaxed with a shuddering intensity that made her scream. Matthew was elated. His cock had turned the lovely Kate into a writhing whore. His cock, alone between her gorgeous legs, had conquered the tempting tigress. As this heady thought raced to the forefront of his mind, his industrious balls opened their doors and allowed a torrent of sperm to fill her loving cup to its brim.

When Kate finally came to her senses, Matthew was a dead weight on top of her. She pushed him off with a grateful grin and, staggering slightly, she made her way to the bank. Once on dry land, she glanced around to see if anyone had been watching their raunchy display. Luckily the park still seemed totally deserted, and she stood with eyes closed while her breathing returned to normal and the warm sunshine dried her skin.

There was an impish smile on her lips when she stooped down and emptied her bladder. And when she turned to see that the boys' cocks had sagged and shrunk to no more than three inches of limp flesh, a thought entered her mind.

'Ah, now I might get what I really wanted,' she said, coming up behind and grasping their defeated weapons.

She stood there with one in each hand and ordered them to pee. They were no longer the bashful boys of the past. Now, as their water gushed to the ground like torrential rain, they watched with huge enjoyment.

As soon as they had finished, Kate whooped with triumph as she shook the flaccid penises dry.

'Very nice, thank you,' she said, grinning. 'I've been looking forward to doing that.'

CHAPTER 23

When she got back to the mews house, Kate was surprised to find a letter from Earl Barton. She opened it with fingers that shook slightly, not altogether certain that she wanted to read its contents. It would tell her where to find Wilson, she was sure of that. And then – goodbye to Roz and to horny sex, and to all that she had enjoyed during the past days. Earl Barton and his family were strange, to say the least, but they were certainly fun to be with.

She was right. The letter gave her the address to which Wilson had moved, and it went on to say that she was expected there at six p.m. that evening.

Loathe to waste a precious second of what time they had left, Kate and Roz enjoyed a steamy sex session which lasted most of the afternoon, delaying their tearful farewell as long as they could.

Although Kate was sad to leave the haven of the house where she'd had more than her fair share of erotic games, she was however keen to move on to new adventures.

Who knows what might happen next, she thought happily, as she closed the lid of her suitcase.

The taxi dropped her outside a large house that stood resplendent in its own grounds. While the driver took her

bags from the boot, she stared awhile at the impressive building. It was a mini-mansion really, with at least ten bedrooms. And as her gaze roamed over the rambling lawns, her thoughts were taken up with four-poster beds, antiquated suits of armour ... and Madam rollicking in the bath with Johnson.

This place has definite possibilities, she thought, as a sexy smile dimpled her cheeks.

Kate was paying the taxi driver when a butler, so handsome in full evening dress, came hurrying down the wide stone steps to collect her luggage.

'If Madam would like to follow me,' he said with a deferential bow. 'Mr Williams is waiting to receive you in the study.'

As he led her through a vast reception hall, she could hear the roar of a powerful voice, and was intrigued when they stopped at the source of the sounds. The butler knocked briskly and entered the room.

'Miss Highlands,' he announced, backing away and motioning for Kate to enter.

Three pairs of eyes appraised her when she walked in with hesitant steps, her shoes sinking into the deep pile carpet.

'Hello, Miss Highlands.' It was the man with the booming voice. 'I'm Thackeray Williams, the actor. No doubt you've heard of me.'

He was a large man with rugged features that were attractive and utterly masculine. He strode forward and shook Kate's hand with a grip of steel.

'And these charming people are Robin Saunders and his wife, Diana,' he went on, waving towards the couple sitting on an impressive settee. 'Diana has a trim little body which Robin and I often share.'

'Is that supposed to shock me?' Kate asked, while she studied the other two.

Robin Saunders had a slim build and a good face with twinkling blue eyes. His smile was warm and seemed permanently fixed, and yet he had a habit of nervously running his hands through the thick mane of blond hair that tumbled over his forehead. Thackeray's description of the man's wife was hardly accurate. She was about five foot eleven, with a body of the most heavenly shape, and her gorgeous red hair framed a truly beautiful face.

'I hope you're unshockable, Miss Highlands,' Thackeray said, as the three continued to scrutinize her body.

'What do you think?' he asked the others.

'She's the right shape,' Saunders said, the twinkle in his eyes suddenly brighter. 'Even so, it depends on how she feels about sex, and whether or not she can act.'

'Hey, hold on,' Kate cut in. 'I'm here looking for a man named Laurence Wilson. I'm not here to audition for a part.'

Thackeray roared with laughter. 'I'm well aware of that, my dear, but – now, how can I put this? – we're talking about favours for a favour, if you see what I mean.'

'Oh, I get it,' Kate said, with a resigned sigh. 'Before I get any information, you want me to drop my knickers. I'm right, aren't I?'

'Absolutely, but you're to drop your knickers, as you so eloquently put it, in rather unusual circumstances.'

The large man strode purposefully to the drinks cabinet and poured four large brandies.

'But perhaps Diana should be the one to explain to you fully,' he said, passing the drinks around. 'So, Robin, if we leave these desirable women alone, maybe they can come up with some sort of arrangement.'

They left the room, still ogling Kate's shape. And as soon as the door closed behind them, Diana invited her to sit on the settee.

'Men,' she said lightly, as Kate made herself comfortable. 'They never quite grow up, you know. Every time they set eyes on an attractive woman, they can hardly wait to screw her.'

'Do they both screw you, or was the remark designed to shock?' Kate asked, between sips of the exquisite brandy.

'Yes, they do, frequently,' she admitted with a tinkling laugh. 'I do so love the sexy games those two play. They really spice up what could be an awfully dull life. Now, let me tell you what this is all about.' She paused to take a drink. 'Thackeray's directing a play in the theatre he had built in the cellar of the house. It's an awfully dirty play which will go on before a select audience. Believe me, Kate, there are lots of terribly famous people who are more than willing to part with a lot of money to watch a horny show – and I must warn you that Thackeray's play is really horny.'

Kate's mouth sagged open. 'Are you saying I'll be in the show?'

'You could be the star of it,' Diana beamed.

'But I can't act. I can't even—'

'Nonsense, Kate, we can all act. But you'll still have to audition for the part.'

'Am I really hearing this?' Kate muttered, tossing back the brandy.

'How sexy are you willing to be?' Diana asked, taking Kate's glass and going for a refill. 'By that I mean, what's acceptable to you? Some women just lie on their backs and open their legs when a man wants to fuck them. They

simply have no idea that they can participate in the fun. Are you like those women?'

'Oh, no,' she said, taking a fresh drink and reddening when her hand brushed Diana's. 'I can be a very dirty girl.'

'Good.' The woman sat down and sipped her brandy. 'There's quite a lot of oral sex in the play. Is that acceptable to you?'

'I've always thought that was what my mouth's for,' Kate quipped.

'Good girl.' Diana leant across and patted Kate's knee, her hand staying there for a few seconds. 'Do you mind me feeling your leg, Kate?'

She shook her head.

'Splendid. I'll tell you about Robin and Thackeray now, shall I? Every time they have me, the weave a little plot around it. It's usually something along the lines of, I meet a man and want to have sex with him, so I invite him home and it turns out that my husband has always wanted to watch another man screw me; it really gets him going, gets him ready for when it's his turn. You know the sort of thing, I'm sure.'

The brandy and the sumptuous surroundings were having a relaxing effect on Kate. Therefore, when she felt the woman's hand move ever so slightly along her leg, she felt no need to protest. Indeed, when Diana placed her glass on the carpet, Kate did the same and the two moved closer together.

'Does that sound like fun to you?'

She was so close now that Kate could smell her sexy aroma.

'Yes,' she whispered. 'I like that sort of thing.'

Diana kissed her lightly on the lips, as if to test her

reaction. When Kate didn't pull back, the kiss became more passionate. Their mouths opened and their tongues met, and all the while Diana's hand continued its journey up Kate's skirt. The kiss ended, and Diana's throaty voice was in her ear.

'You'll like Thackeray,' she murmured. 'He's got such a huge cock, and he's so inventive.' Her flirting fingers were exploring the tops of Kate's thighs. 'And Robin does so like a nice tight pussy.' The hand crept into her panties. 'Have you got a tight pussy, Kate?'

'Yes,' she breathed, opening her legs wide so that Diana's hand could probe her hairy patch.

'Oh, my dear, it's so bushy,' she enthused. 'The boys are going to love it.'

She pushed a finger into Kate's moistness, bringing a gasp from her lips.

'And it is tight,' Diana gushed. 'Believe me, it's going to enjoy what the boys have got for it.'

'Play with it properly,' Kate implored, moving her body so that she was sliding to and fro on the woman's foraging finger.

Diana gave a low, sexy chuckle. 'We mustn't go too far. The real fun starts when we've had a couple more drinks.'

Much to Kate's dismay, she removed the finger and jumped to her feet, an excited flush enhancing her already envious beauty.

'Stand up,' she said. 'I want you to unbutton your dress and take your panties off.'

Kate jumped to her feet and pulled at the buttons with quite scandalous haste, and there were delicious goose bumps of anticipation rising on her skin when Diana began to do the same. She hurried out of her panties, and watched with fascination as Diana pulled hers down and

stepped out of them with a graceful, almost balletic, motion. Kate's eyes widened at the ginger triangle between the woman's slender legs.

'Have you ever seen one this colour before?' she asked, clearly pleased by the reaction her sex had provoked.

Kate shook her head. 'It's beautiful.'

Diana took her hand and placed it on the thick red thatch.

'That's nice,' she breathed, as the fingers delved for her crack. 'It's just like being back at school. You show me yours, and I'll show you mine.'

Diana moved closer, and her soft breath on Kate's neck whipped up an arousal so strong that the girl shuddered at its intensity. And that arousal blossomed into a burning need when Diana reached for Kate's vagina, her fingers running slowly through the coarse hair before teasing the wet opening with her talented fingertips.

Kate surrendered herself willingly to the woman's exquisite pampering and was happy to return the pleasure, her nostrils thrilling at the earthy aroma drifting up from the woman's crack, which trembled beneath her touch.

'Did you ever do this with your girlfriends at school?' Diana whispered in her ear.

'Yes.'

The word was little more than a sigh, for Diana was coaxing sensations from her crack that even the sexy Roz could not manage.

'I did, too – all the time,' Diana said, her free hand straying to Kate's buttocks and stroking, her long finger-nails raking the smooth skin with an almost excruciating gentleness.

'We used to stand in the toilets and play with one another.' She laughed; it was a delicate sound which Kate

found utterly enchanting. 'I actually got a boy to join us once, and I played with his cock at the same time. That's when I got my first sight of a male climax. His sperm landed all over my stomach, and it was gorgeous to feel the sticky mess running down into my groove.'

That laugh came again, and took Kate's arousal to new heights.

'And do you know what I wanted? I wanted him to see to me, there and then. I wanted to stand in that tiny cubicle, which stank of bleach and urine, and feel his cock penetrate my virgin hole. And he did. As soon as I told him what I wanted, he was big and hard again. Then, he pushed me back against the wall – oh, he was so rough; it was divine – and I spread my legs and stood on tip-toe so that he could ease himself inside my crack.

'And, my God, did he go! My girlfriend was playing with herself as she watched, and I was glued to her fingers rubbing away with a girlish frenzy. We hadn't long learned how to bring ourselves off, and our poor cunts were sore more often than not. So, there I was, watching my friend hurrying towards her climax while the boy was doing what my fingers never could, and that's when I came. The orgasm just swept all over me, and I didn't know what I was doing. In fact, I was so carried away, I let the boy come inside me.'

Kate was groaning with bliss. Those mental images of the dirty young Diana flashing through her mind, and the constant fondling of her vagina, were sweeping her relentlessly towards her own climax. And she was almost there when Diana suddenly pulled away and chuckled.

'Kate, you're very sexy, but I can't let this go too far—' Her gaze fell to the girl's pubic bush which was saturated with the juice of her arousal. 'But, God, I'm so tempted. You're beautiful.'

She picked up Kate's panties and ran them beneath her nostrils before handing them across, her eyes half-closed with desire. Utterly disappointed, Kate pulled them on, trying desperately to ignore her complaining crack, which fluttered angrily beneath the lacy material.

She was buttoning her dress when Diana retrieved her own panties and offered them to her to smell. The heady aroma was intoxicating, and she drank it in greedily.

'You've made my knickers all wet,' Diana purred, brushing them over Kate's waiting lips.

Her head was spinning, and she started to plead loudly when the ginger nest was finally covered by black silk.

'Not yet, Kate,' Diana giggled. 'You must have patience.'

'But that wasn't fair,' she pouted. 'I suppose it was part of my audition—'

'It wasn't actually. I must confess I simply got carried away. But I'm so glad you responded in the way that you did because that's very important for the part.'

Securing this job was suddenly very important to Kate, and she said hopefully, 'Will you be in the play?'

'Oh, no,' Diana said, slipping on her dress and taking their glasses for a refill. 'The only other female part is being played by a very serious young actress called Trish Butler. Trish thinks it's all frightfully arty, and won't drop her knickers until the actual performance. So, I'm afraid that's how all rehearsals will be conducted – absolutely no sex.'

'That should make it interesting on the night,' Kate commented.

'I'll say. We should get some really raw screwing on stage.'

She handed Kate the fresh drink and sat down beside her. They both drank deeply, the strong alcohol warming

their insides and relaxing their over-excited bodies.

'There will be men in this play, I hope?'

'Don't worry, Kate, you'll get more than your share of cock. Both Thackeray and Robin are quite miffed at the moment, because Trish won't let them have it. They're acting like a pair of dogs sniffing around a bitch on heat.'

'Doesn't it disturb you – your husband having other women, I mean?'

'Good God, no,' Diana exclaimed. 'I like to see him having some fun, and besides, it leaves me with a lot of freedom to do my own thing. To tell you the truth, I still like it the way it was in the toilets at school, when I was broken in, standing there on tip-toes with my legs open. And, believe me, there are plenty of stage hands willing to oblige.'

Kate drained her glass. 'Okay, tell me what I have to do to audition.'

'Well, how does a wife-swapping party grab you? Robin will be playing your husband, and Thackeray will be mine. Your character's all for it at first, but now the time's here you're having a change of heart.'

'Hmm, that sounds like fun,' Kate said, with a grin. 'Lead me to it.'

CHAPTER 24

The dining room was extremely elegant, and was the chosen setting for their improvisation. Kate was sitting rigid on a corner of a large couch, with Robin Saunders facing her at the other end. The large space separating the two served to epitomize the huge gulf in relations between this character and his wife.

'Oh, come on,' he was saying persuasively. 'You were all for us having some horny fun with Thackeray and Diana. Why have you suddenly gone all cold on us?'

'I've changed my mind, that's all, Robin. It's a lady's prerogative, after all.'

Kate was very self-conscious. She had never acted before, and felt silly and uptight as she spouted the words. Nevertheless, she wanted to be in the play, and determined to throw herself into the part.

'But you promised,' he whined.

'I've just gone off the idea of us having sex together, it's as simple as that. I don't mind you having Diana, so go off and do it if you want.'

'If you don't mind that, then what is it? What's put you off?'

'I've told you, I just don't want to do it,' she yelled. 'It would make me feel silly.'

'Jesus Christ,' he spat. 'It's all arranged for tonight. You

know jolly well that they're on their way here even as we speak.'

'Well, you'll simply have to un-arrange it,' she screamed, really getting into the part.

Thackeray impersonated a doorbell off stage left, and he and Diana were soon being led in by a terribly flustered Robin. A heavy silence filled the room as the four seated themselves around the dining table to start their meal. The food was imaginary, but the white wine was real enough and Robin made sure it flowed freely.

'So, Kate's changed her mind,' Diana huffed. 'I must say, I'm really put out, I can tell you. I thought we were going to have a good sexy frolic. I'm even wearing my most revealing underwear, and now no one's going to see it.'

'Really, Diana?' Robin said, leaning forward eagerly. 'I, for one, wouldn't mind seeing it. My cock's been like concrete all week waiting for tonight.'

'She'll show you, if you like,' Thackeray said. 'Come and sit next to her. I was looking forward to a change of partner myself, but, well—'

They all shot reproachful glances in Kate's direction while Robin moved his chair next to Diana's. The woman was giggling uncontrollably and slapping playfully at the men's hands as they hitched up her skirt.

'Wow, suspenders and stockings,' Robin enthused. 'I just love them.'

'Oh, and I thought you wanted the hairy thing between my legs,' Diana teased. 'I'd hoped you'd got something big and hard that could satisfy it.'

'I have,' he said, shooting an imploring look at Kate. 'Darling, you said you wouldn't mind if I had Diana, so would it be all right—?'

'Go ahead,' she replied, haughtily. 'It doesn't make the slightest difference to me who you screw.'

'Good, that's the all-clear out of the way,' Diana said. 'Let's have some fun, Robin.'

She left her seat and removed her dress, swinging her hips like a stripper of little talent in a seedy back-street bar. Soon all three gazes were focused on the sexy red bra which hardly covered her amazing breasts, and the thin strip of lace passing itself off as panties. The set was complemented by a black lace suspender belt trimmed with tiny red satin bows, and black sheer stockings.

Kate's crack was positively oozing love cream, but in keeping with her character she rushed from the room with a petulant huff while the men threw off their clothes and directed lecherous leers towards the vision in bawdy lace who pranced enticingly before them.

When she returned moments later, with a look of contrition clouding her features, the men were naked and she couldn't help but gasp at the size of their excited members. Thackeray's was well over eight inches, and was thick and heavily veined. He was masturbating as a young boy would, pulling with guilty strokes while a naughty grin settled incongruously on his highly macho face.

Robin's cock was shorter but equally as thick, and its tip was the biggest Kate had ever seen. Diana was playing with it and cooing breathily. The way in which she pretended to acquaint herself with it was brilliant, and Robin was clearly enjoying her fingers' feverish tour, for his eyes were closed and his lips pulled back, and that ferocious cock head just carried on swelling.

'Two big dicks to satisfy,' Diana gushed. 'My little crack will be sore by the time I've milked you two dry.'

They all looked pointedly in Kate's direction.

'Come and join us,' Diana said, softly. 'You can at least watch, even if you don't take part.'

Trying hard to keep in character Kate wandered, spell-bound, towards them, her enthusiasm soaring at the sight of their naked bodies. She stopped in front of the group, unsure of her next move, and was therefore relieved when they gathered around her.

'Play with Thackeray's fine cock,' Diana encouraged. 'Oh, go on, Kate, you know damn well you want to.'

She grabbed Kate's hand and curled the fingers around his throbbing shaft, shouting with triumph when the deed was done.

'Good girl,' she said. 'Now, toss him off.'

Kate first of all felt the whole of the trembling penis, then stroked the bulging testicles which hung heavy with unshed seed. But it wasn't until Diana worked her hand up her skirt and into her panties to fondle her bottom that Kate started to rub. She slid her hand to and fro, quite intrigued by the way the thick foreskin never quite hid his engorged tip. It was as if the cock had outgrown its skin and it seemed impossible to Kate that the sexy coat would ever fit again.

Robin was busy unfastening the buttons of her dress, and although she was complaining, her words lacked conviction and were spoken with breath that trembled with excitement. Thackeray let out a complimentary gasp when her raunchy underwear was at last revealed, and she showed her thanks by increasing the speed of her hand fuck.

Her movements were animated, and all thoughts of acting forgotten, as she grappled with the giant at his groin. And she swore softly at having to release him in order to lose her dress. The bra was next to go, and her breasts

bobbed furiously as her hand movements grew more animated.

Thackeray was growling that his climax was almost reached, his head tossing deliriously from side to side, his legs trembling and threatening to buckle. All three were aroused by his erotic performance, and events were carried swiftly forward when Kate's panties were pulled down roughly so that her hairy nest could be pushed onto his throbbing tip. She thrilled at the feeling of his over-powering member nudging at her love bud, and moved her hips repeatedly so that the smooth wet doors to her tunnel could rub against it and add to his pleasure.

Thackeray growled again, and then his sperm was flying. The milky seed splattered out at all angles, catching her stomach, her thatch, her thighs, and dripped like watery sleet on to the fine carpet. She released him and, with a look of thanks, he sank into a chair.

Then, with a tantalizing smile, she scooped up the sperm from her pubic triangle and brought it to her lips. And Thackeray's eyes widened with lust as she lapped up the white, bitter fluid and licked her lips with obvious relish.

'Well, you are a dark horse, Kate,' Diana said. 'Here we all were thinking you didn't want to do anything like that. I think we'd better get her knickers off, boys, before she changes her mind again.'

Kate had never been so sexually excited. While they forcibly removed the panties, their hands rough and demanding, every nerve ending in her body seemed to be screaming for satisfaction. The moment her sodden briefs were pulled off, Kate was told to lie on the table, and she deliberately held back so that they could manhandle her into position.

Was she becoming addicted to rough treatment? Oh, what if she was? – it beat lying back and thinking of England.

'I think we can safely say that you've got the job,' Diana said, when Kate was flat on her back. 'But now you've got to have sex with all three of us.'

Her entire body shook when the beautiful woman knelt down in front of her, and she eagerly pushed herself to its edge and opened her legs wide. She expected Diana's expert tongue and fingers to start pleasuring her honey pot immediately, but Kate was about to learn a little about female to female foreplay.

Diana ran her tongue along Kate's delicious thighs, teasing her until she was panting. She could clearly hear the heavy breath of the two men as they stared down from either side of the table, watching as Diana's mouth travelled closer and closer to her twitching slit.

Then her breath was upon it, sweeping over the aching lips until they parted with a flourish.

'This should get you ready for the boys,' she said, exhaling sharply on to the spot and causing an ecstatic scream to leave Kate's lips.

Suddenly, Diana's long fingernails dug into her thighs and as Kate was about to object, the woman's mouth landed squarely at the centre of her thick bush. Kate was immediately thrashing about on the table, her groin racked with spasms of pure bliss, and the men were ordered to hold her still.

Taking an arm and shoulder each, they subdued Kate's movements but could not still the delicious torment, which rippled with ever increasing intensity along the whole length of her aching tunnel of love.

'Lick me, Diana,' Kate begged. 'I'll do anything you ask, but please, please lick me.'

The woman's tongue was hot and rampant when it pushed inside her warm earthy pit, and it charged along the grasping passage with all the vigour of a thrusting cock. Kate was floating, drifting on a cloud of delectable madness, and her pleasure was increased ten-fold when Diana's fingers joined in to lavish tender attention on her impassioned clitoris.

She was burning, being eaten up by a bliss so profound that she feared her body might implode at any moment. And it was then that the orgasm hit her, with all the force of a bomb blast, deep within her middle. Its scorching heat devastated all within its path, leaving embers of orgasmic fire in its wake. A second quickly followed, and then a third, each one leaving her breathless but doing nothing to calm the itch deep within her vagina.

Robin was the first to have her. He drove his penis to the far reaches of her cavern, his magnificent tip stretching and manipulating her pleasure zones in a way that had never been done before. She was babbling and raving to all and sundry while he thrust superbly, his rhythm not too fast but quick enough to send her senses reeling.

For ten minutes he pounded away, his diligent balls slapping with a delicious regularity against the highly-charged nub of her arse. Every orgasm inspired by his cock was loudly proclaimed by Kate. Her voice urged him on, eroded his self control, and soon he was shuddering with orgasmic bliss as his colossal tip gave up its treasure to her velvet sheath. Sperm was still flying from his indebted shaft when he withdrew, and it landed on the creamy skin of her thighs as he reeled away, spent but elated.

Thackeray was on her in a second, sinking his mighty cock into her warmth, right up to its hairy root, in one deft

action. The feel of his thick shaft almost sent her insane, for Kate was still hungry for sex and she begged him to make her come. But he teased, rotating his hips and toying with her, gauging how much she wanted of what only he could give.

'Please,' she implored him. 'Please.'

'What?' he asked, running his hands over her buttocks, feeling between the groove at her secret place.

'Screw me,' she cried, now completely at the mercy of her vagina. 'I want you to give me a good screwing.'

Unable to control himself any longer, Thackeray began to fuck with long, slow strokes of his enormous weapon. But these became progressively faster and faster, until his well-muscled body was a blur of action.

Kate was hardly conscious of the fact that she was playing with her breasts, squeezing the nipples and pulling them like miniature cocks. All that mattered was the sweet sensation which was taking her crack over. Total fulfilment swept through her as she climaxed, and she arched her body to meet his powerful thrusts. She whimpered when he pulled out, because she knew only too well that he had not discharged his seed.

'I want your come,' she murmured.

'You're going to have it, Kate,' Diana murmured, her voice hoarse.

When she opened her eyes, Kate saw that Thackeray was standing beside the table and allowing Diana to rub his cock to climax.

'Open your mouth,' she coaxed. 'Drink deeply of his precious seed.'

No sooner had Kate complied than Thackeray was ejaculating onto her face. Most of the hot sperm went into her mouth and covered her lips, but he was too excited to

stand still, let alone take proper aim, and the rest spattered on to her cheek. His cock was sagging as she ran her tongue around her lips, chasing the exquisite fruits of his passion and savouring the intoxicating flavour.

CHAPTER 25

Kate was given a huge bedroom all to herself. It was decorated in soft, utterly feminine tones, and had its own en suite bathroom. Exhausted by the sex romp, she was asleep before her head touched the pillows of the impressive king-sized bed. She woke next morning, apprehensive about the rehearsal in the one thousand-seat theatre.

Breakfast was informal and delicious, and afterwards she was led to the bowels of the house and ushered on to the stage to be introduced to the rest of the cast.

They sat around in a rough semi-circle for the first read-through of the play and, between reading her lines, Kate studied the others.

It was the two young men who grabbed her attention. They were both tall and slim, and extraordinarily good-looking. Between them sat Trish Butler, the arty girl mentioned by Diana. She was very slender and small breasted, with long black hair and dark, doe-like eyes. By the time they were halfway through the second act, the question that Kate was repeatedly asking herself was answered by Thackeray.

'If any of you are wondering why we haven't come to anything dirty yet, it's because all the sex is in the third act. It builds up into a climax which I'm sure you'll all

enjoy.' He roared with laughter at his joke. 'Right, children, it's time for coffee.'

Kate joined the queue at the drinks machine and, after collecting her coffee, went and stood in a corner with what she hoped was a friendly smile fixed to her face. Trish soon joined her.

'Hi,' she said. 'I was wondering when the horny stuff was coming in. I know you're not in the business, but you're good.'

Kate found herself blushing outrageously at the unexpected compliment.

'I understand we're not going to be rehearsing the sex,' she said.

'And no doubt you've been told that's because I'm such a strait-laced little mare who doesn't drop my knickers.'

'Well . . . yes,' Kate had to admit. 'At least, Thackeray and Robin hinted that that was the reason.'

Trish sipped her coffee. 'When you're in this business and you fuck, it's best not to do it with the director, because it soon gets around and then they expect it just for giving you a part.'

'I see. Well, I hope I get some during the week, because without sex I go mental.'

'Me too,' Trish said, with a smile. 'Hey, perhaps we should get together – as long as that sort of thing interests you, I mean.'

Kate grinned. 'Oh, it does, but I like a nice big prick, as well.'

The girl sighed. 'Yes, I must admit I like a varied sex life myself. That's why I'm a bit fed up – you see, I really fancy Thackeray and Robin.'

'We'll have to work something out then, won't we? There must be some way we can get you screwed by them

without it getting around that you fuck just to get parts. Let me think about it, Trish, and see what I can come up with.'

The third act was pure pornography. It read like a dirty video, and the whole of the cast were excited by the time the read through was over. Diana had sat in to listen, and by the end her face was as red as her raunchy underwear had been the evening before. When she hurried off the stage and almost flew out of the auditorium, Kate signalled for Trish to join her.

'Listen,' she said, 'I think Diana's gone off to have some fun. Shall we follow her?'

'You mean fun, as in sex?' Trish said, her dark eyes sparkling.

'The very same.' Kate let out a laugh. 'And from what she tells me, she likes her sex to get really dirty.'

'Let's go, then.'

They followed Diana backstage, where they found her chatting to a couple of burly stage hands who were supposed to be discussing the stage lighting. One was dark and fierce, the other fair and gentle; and both were gorgeous to look at. The area around them was dark, and the girls managed to get near enough to hear their words without being seen.

'So, I'll give you the lighting plan as soon as it's fully worked out,' Diana was saying, her eyes flirting with them.

'We'll look forward to it,' the dark bull of a man said.

It was plain that they were receiving her subliminal messages, and both seemed reluctant to leave.

'It's Act three I'm really worried about,' she continued, squatting on her haunches and unfolding a large plan which she placed on the floor.

The men followed her down, and tiny smiles hovered on their lips when Diana's short skirt rode up and revealed her white panties.

'Most of the tricky lighting is in that Act. We want the nude bodies to look good, you see, and we want the sex shown off to its best effect.'

She glanced up then to see the men staring at her panties, and she giggled lightly and brought a hand to her crotch.

'When I saw your naughty expressions then, I thought for a minute I'd forgotten to put my knickers on and I was showing you everything I've got.'

The men gulped and exchanged hopeful glances.

'I wish you were,' the dark man said.

'I'm sure you've seen one before, and they're all the same,' she said, smiling. 'It's only a tight little hole, after all.'

'I don't think they're all the same,' the man countered. 'Some of them are nice and hairy—' He paused, and added pointedly, 'And they like what men have got for them. Really warm and welcoming, they are.'

'Well, unless I'm mistaken we seem to have a you-show-me-yours-and-I'll-show-you-mine scenario here.' She giggled, holding their eyes with her own. 'Okay, then, who's going to be the first to flash?'

'Oh, I like to show mine off to its best advantage,' the fair-haired man piped up. 'And it's only at its best when it's seen something that's excited it.'

Diana's back was towards Kate and Trish, but they could tell by her movements that she was pulling her panties to one side and showing them her eager crack.

'Okay, so now you know it's a hairy one,' she whispered.

Their eyes were transfixed on the luscious cleft between her legs.

'And I can tell you, boys, it's more than warm, it's positively red-hot and it's always ready to welcome a cock that's big enough to make it happy.'

The men were on their feet in an instant, unzipping their trousers and coaxing out hard imposing shafts, hardly caring that anyone could walk past. There was nothing to choose between the two; both cocks were about seven and a half inches, and more than ready to give Diana the sex that she craved.

'Oh, goody,' she said, getting to her feet and scrambling out of her skirt and panties. 'I want it standing up against the wall.'

She positioned herself quickly and spread her legs wide, her thick red thatch on full display. The dark man stepped forward first and blocked the girls' view, but it was obvious that Diana was rubbing his trembling tip against her clitoris while the other man stood watching.

'That's so good,' she cooed. 'Now I'm nice and ready. Let me stretch up on tip-toe and then you can ram it in, boy. And, don't forget, give me all of your cock – I like it hard and fast.'

Kate's quickening breath matched that of Trish as they watched the man pumping away, thrusting into Diana with carnal grunts while she grasped his hips and implored him to go faster. Before too long a look of sheer delight spread over her lust-distorted features and she told the man over and over again that she was coming.

There was little doubt, given the man's moaning and groaning, that he was there too. Then with one last rapturous cry his seed spurted into her. But he was given little time to savour the moment for his friend, eager to enjoy Diana's excited love tunnel, pulled him off and positioned himself between her widely spread legs.

His movements were highly animated as he pushed his throbbing shaft deep into the welcoming slit, but his rhythm was slower, and he kept pulling back until he was almost out and then sinking himself into her warm, velvety depths yet again.

Now that some degree of technique was being used, Diana seemed to melt. Her head lolled back against the wall and her breath came in short, sharp pants as she waited for fulfilment to wash over her. Feeling that the time was right, the man began to move faster, the intense tingling at the end of his cock spurring him on.

'Go on,' she whispered. 'I'm nearly there.'

Diana held her breath – and Kate did, too – and then her legs were trembling and shaking and threatening to collapse beneath her.

'Oh, oh, I'm really coming now,' she breathed. 'I can't stop coming now.'

The man growled and then whimpered as he ejaculated inside her, the force of his last few thrusts lifting her off the floor as his balls released their very last drop.

It took all three a good few minutes to get over the amorous encounter, and Diana was the first to speak.

'Thank you, boys,' she said, pulling on her knickers with obvious difficulty due to the amount of sperm cascading down her thighs. 'I'd better tell you that I need screwing all the time, so you're going to see an awful lot of my aching quim this week.'

'When?' the dark man asked huskily.

'Same time, same place, tomorrow,' she said, winking lewdly as she got into her skirt.

Kate and Trish sank back into the shadows when she hurried past them, and they shared an unbelieving glance before turning back to the two men who, rather disap-

pointingly, had returned their thoughts to lighting cues.

'Let's go to my room,' Kate said, hurriedly. 'I'm so turned on, I can hardly think.'

CHAPTER 26

The girls were still in a highly excitable state when they arrived back at Kate's bedroom, both of them giggling and laughing, fit to burst. After a cup of tea and some ham sandwiches, they began to talk.

'Do you mind if we take things really slowly to start with?' Trish asked, while she dried the plates. 'Don't get me wrong, I adore sex fun with another girl, but I like a slow build-up so that by the end we can't keep our hands off each other.'

Kate's eyebrows rose knowingly as she washed the last of the cups.

'Okay, but we'd better get to it before Saturday, or we'll be having it for the first time in front of a thousand strangers.'

'I didn't mean that slow,' she said, laughing. But then she sobered. 'I'd much rather we got to know each other first, because I like some really strange things and I'd need to know if you're agreeable.'

Intrigued by that remark, Kate pulled the plug from the sink.

'And are you willing to tell me now what any of these really strange things are?'

'No,' Trish said, shaking her head teasingly. 'Tonight I'd like to concentrate on learning our parts.'

Kate laughed. 'Okay, then, you show me your parts and I'll show you mine.'

'You know what I mean,' she said, giggling.

They spent three hours working on the script and testing each other with their lines. Then they smoked cigarettes while Kate relayed all that had happened with Diana, Robin and Thackeray.

'You filthy, immoral, lucky cow,' Trish exclaimed. 'And to think – I was bloody well washing my hair while all that was going on. Oh, by the way, have you thought up any ideas for getting me laid by those two gorgeous hunks?'

'You'll have to wait and see,' she teased. 'But on Wednesday, you'll be the lucky cow, believe me.'

'Roll on Wednesday, then.'

'Now,' Kate said, getting to her feet. 'We have Morgan, the butler, at our disposal, so how about a brandy?'

She rang the bell and a few moments later Morgan appeared at the door. Kate asked him politely to bring up a bottle of brandy, two glasses and some dry ginger ale, and when he returned he was balancing all on a silver tray.

'Would Madam like me to serve the drinks?' he asked, his manner utterly formal as he placed the tray on the low coffee table.

'Please, and make them large ones.'

She gave him a warm, open smile and remained silent while he prepared the drinks.

'You must have been surprised by what you saw last night,' she ventured as he approached with her brandy. 'After all, I was lying on the dining table with my pussy in full view.'

Morgan gave a diplomatic cough. 'One sees many things in my profession, Madam, but one is trained to neither look nor make comment.'

She took the proffered drink with a nod of thanks. 'You may not be commenting, but last night you certainly had a good long look.'

A ghost of a smile touched his lips, as he said, 'I'm sure Madam is mistaken.'

He gave Trish her drink and then turned to Kate, the smile still evident. 'Will that be all, Madam?'

She inclined her head. 'For the moment, but I'm going to get behind that terribly proper manner of yours, Morgan, if it's the last thing I do.'

'I shall always behave in a manner that befits my position,' he assured her with a slight bow.

After the butler dismissed himself, backing obsequiously out of the room, the girls dissolved into fits of giggles.

'He's quite a character,' Trish said.

'Yes,' Kate agreed, 'and he's got a decent cock on him, if that swelling in his trousers is anything to go by.'

They had three large brandies while discussing the finer points of penises in general, and were quite pleasantly drunk when Trish announced it was time for her to leave and get some sleep.

'Can I use the bathroom before I go?' she asked, staggering slightly as she found her feet.

'Of course. Come on, I'll show you where it is.'

Kate wove an erratic path to the bathroom and waited outside while Trish went in, chuckling away merrily at nothing in particular. The door was slightly ajar, and from sounds drifting towards her, Kate pictured the girl lifting her skirt and tugging at her panties. Then the lavatory lid was lifted and water could be heard splashing into the bowl. A sudden shudder of excitement passed through her body and Kate, unable to control herself any longer, pushed the door fully open, causing Trish to start.

'I'm sorry,' she stammered, 'it's just that I love watching people while they're having a wee. It's ... it's something I've just discovered about myself.'

'Be my guest, then,' Trish said, pushing herself up from the seat, and exposing the water still pouring from her crack. 'It's all right, you know. We all have strange desires, Kate, and I don't mind you watching one little bit. In fact, I find it a turn on.'

Kate stared at the girl, quite fascinated as the flow became a trickle and then stopped. And she licked her lips hungrily when Trish wiped herself dry and flushed the toilet before pulling up her panties.

'I can't satisfy your fantasy, Kate, but I think I know exactly what you want.'

'So do I,' Kate admitted. 'I'm only just beginning to come to terms with it.'

The alcohol was breaking down all inhibitions, and as they wandered to the front door the girls held hands and fell against each other like young lovers do when mutual attraction drives everything else from their minds.

As Kate was about to reach for the latch, their lips touched briefly, and then the kiss turned into a fiery embrace which left them both breathless.

'Before I go, will you play with me through my knickers?' Trish whispered, opening her legs to welcome Kate's hand. 'Do you like what I've got?'

Kate could feel her coarse hair through the lacy material, and the breath caught in her throat when her fingers found the proud, pouting lips and finally the opening which, even through the panties, felt hot and demanding.

'It's beautiful,' she sighed. 'I want to play with it properly. I want to get my fingers into it, and give you a good time.'

Trish worked her hand up Kate's skirt and took to

moving the flat of her hand to and fro between her legs. The sensation of the coarse gusset sliding backwards and forwards over her nest made Kate gasp.

'Oh, Trish, that feels so good,' she purred.

'I've never told anyone about my deepest desires,' Trish confessed, in a hoarse whisper. 'But, for some reason, I need to tell you now. I want to be forced, Kate. What I mean is I don't want Trish Butler to be forced, I want to be a servile someone who has to do just what they're told, however dirty it is. And what's more I want to be punished if I don't do it properly.'

'Oh, God, Trish, that sounds fantastic,' Kate said. 'I'd love to punish you.'

The girl pulled away. The move was reluctant, but firm nevertheless.

'I think we'd better leave it there for tonight,' she said. 'We've both got a busy day tomorrow and if I get any more worked up, we're going to be awake all night.'

'Okay, you're right, I suppose. But, Trish, we'll have to make a date for it, because my poor crack's aching.'

Trish grinned. 'How does Thursday grab you? On Thursday night we'll have some really horny sex fun – yes?'

'Thursday?' Kate groaned. 'But that's three whole days away.'

'I know, but I did say I wanted us to get to know each other first. And you are supposed to be arranging my amorous romp with Thackeray and Robin for Wednesday, don't forget.'

'All right, but I'll have to get some sex before then – I'll go barmy if I don't.'

When the girl finally left, Kate went to bed. The sheets felt cold and lonely, and she tossed and turned for ages as

her groin ached with unfulfilled desire. Finally, she could stand it no longer and gave in to her complaining vagina. Three fingers were inserted, and were immediately pounced upon by the grasping passage, its muscles grappling with the substitute cock as they headed towards climax.

All thoughts of finding Wilson were banished from her mind, cast out by the sexy scenarios that flitted one after the other through her wicked imagination as she became more and more absorbed in her solitary pleasuring.

CHAPTER 27

The next day's rehearsals went well, with all the actors slotting easily into their roles. Kate would have enjoyed herself immensely if not for the fact that Trish seemed to be avoiding her. The girl's seemingly cool indifference bothered Kate, and it wasn't until late afternoon that she had an opportunity to question why.

'Trish, have I done anything to offend you?' she asked, as they waited backstage.

'No, of course not. It's just that, well, we were very drunk last night, and I think things got a bit out of hand.'

'Oh,' Kate said, her heart sinking. 'I thought that might be it.'

'You sound a bit disappointed,' the girl said, refusing to meet her gaze.

'That's because I am disappointed. Look, Trish, the idea appealed to me and I was looking forward to it.'

Suddenly Trish's face broke into a broad grin.

'Well, thank God for that,' she said. 'I thought that in the cold light of day you might have changed your mind, so I thought I'd give you a chance to get out of it.'

'You really are going to get punished, my girl,' Kate said, aiming a playful slap at her shoulder.

'Ooh, yes, please,' she replied, eagerly.

During a break, they watched Diana having her fun with

the two stage hands. This time she bent over so that one could take her from behind while she administered oral delights to the other. Kate's state of arousal soared while they spied on the trio. She had things planned for Diana the following evening, along with Robin and Thackeray – and Trish's slender and highly desirable body would be playing a major part in the production.

Later Kate had a light tea, for her main craving had nothing to do with food. Then she took a shower, dressed quickly, and settled down with her script. Quite surprisingly, she found she had a natural aptitude for learning lines, and had only to read through once for the majority to stay in her head.

It was the third act which held her attention, though, and she lingered long over it. The action was the dirtiest she had ever read, and she couldn't wait for tomorrow when they would start rehearsing it. The no sex rule still applied, so it was odds-on that the whole cast would be as horny as hell afterwards, which was probably why a drinks party had been arranged for the evening.

'And there's one very horny girl here tonight,' Kate murmured, as she rang the bell for Morgan.

Two minutes later, he glided into the room with a tray of brandy, ginger ale and glasses.

'I presumed that this was what Madam wanted. But if I am wrong, then I shall cater for whatever needs Madam has.' He set the tray down on the coffee table, and waited for his next order.

'Is that your job?' she asked. 'To cater for my needs? To pander to them, even?'

'A good butler must keep a guest happy,' he said, pouring a large brandy and standing almost to attention as he served her.

She sipped the drink. 'Talk to me, then. I'm lonely, Morgan.'

'If that's what Madam wishes.'

'What do you do for sex?' she asked, hiding a cheeky grin. 'I'd imagine that the things you witness in this house must leave you with a permanent hard on.'

'My sex life is my own business, Madam.' The words were not offered as a rebuke, and throughout his expression remained passive.

'Oh, now, come on,' she said, wagging a finger. 'You must keep your guests happy – that's what you've just told me.' She drained the glass swiftly and handed it back for a refill. 'Okay, then, let me guess. I bet you're into girlie magazines. I bet you study all those sexy pictures – all those girls showing off their tits and their luscious pussies – as if the show is for you alone. Then you read the dirty words, all the time stroking your big cock until you can't stand it any more so you have to jerk yourself right off. Am I right?'

He brought the drink to her, and hesitated before saying, 'One's sex life can be severely curtailed in my profession, Madam.'

'Ah, so that must be an admission that my assessment of your sex life is fairly accurate.'

He said nothing, but continued to stand before her, his unwavering gaze directed straight ahead. Kate realised then that she had never actively studied him, and when she started into his face was surprised to find that he was rather attractive.

Fortyish, she thought, and quite good-looking – why had she not noticed before? He had a heavy build, but it was all muscle and no fat. She assumed that, having spent years fading into the background, it was not often that his fine attributes were noticed.

That cock would never go undetected, though, however often his face was ignored. Her gaze drifted down to it, and she giggled lightly, for the bulge was growing even as they spoke.

'Am I embarrassing you, Morgan?' she asked, taking her drink and reclining on the settee.

'Not at all, Madam. It's my job to answer questions, however personal they may be.'

'Good.'

She took another sip – fine brandy could become a habit now she could afford it – and placed the glass on the carpet.

'I think the former visitor who stayed in this room must have shared your perverted tastes. I found some girlie magazines in the bedroom. Would you like to look through them? They're a real turn on.'

Morgan, for the very first time, began to look uncomfortable.

'Beg pardon, Madam, but I don't feel that would be a good idea.'

'Why ever not?' she said, stretching her arms languidly above her head, and opening her long legs at the same time. 'I've got an itch, Morgan. Be a dear and scratch it for me, would you?'

As she pulled up her skirt with a tantalizing slowness, the butler's eyes were glued to her thighs. He gulped loudly at the sight of her scant black panties, and fidgeted on the spot while she brought her bottom off the settee to pull the skirt around her waist.

'The itch is inside my knickers,' she whispered. 'Be a good butler and scratch it for me – eh, Morgan?'

His lustful eyes and the nervous twitch above them told of the battle taking place within him. But then, with a deep

sigh, he regained his composure and reached between her legs, his manicured fingernails gliding lightly over her panties.

'That's lovely,' she breathed, thrilling at his touch. 'But you're not quite on it yet. It's just inside the little crack.'

Guiding his hand, Kate urged him to push a finger into the silky material and up her sticky trench.

'It's just there. Oh, spot on, Morgan,' she said, as he started to rub her clitoris.

She allowed him to continue for a couple of minutes and then closed her legs, momentarily trapping the hand which was pulled away sharply as if fearful of being burned.

'Thank you, Morgan, it's fine now. But maybe we should look at those magazines – should I fetch them, do you think?'

'If that is what Madam wishes,' he said, his hand now at his crotch where it attempted to hide the enormous bulge which pushed out the thick fabric of his formal trousers. 'I only hope that I have eased Madam's discomfort at little.'

Kate left the settee and grinned inwardly, for his words carried a hopeful undertone which spoke louder than any polite sentence he could utter.

'My goodness, I do believe you're human, after all,' she teased. 'You're actually saying you enjoyed playing with my hairy pussy, aren't you?'

He gave a very controlled gasp when Kate unfastened her skirt and let it slide down and land in a heap at her feet.

'I cannot deny that I enjoyed pandering to Madam's needs,' he said, his eyes drinking in her shapely legs.

Kate thought it best to speed things up a little. Her vagina was screaming out to be filled, and so she stood in

front of him and pulled her panties' elastic right away from her body.

'That's all it is, Morgan,' she said. 'It's only what the girls in the magazines have got, only this one's real, this one can be played with. Do you want me to fetch the magazines, now?'

'Yes, please, Madam, I'd like that very much,' he said, craning his neck to catch a glimpse of her pubic thatch.

'Okay, but before I go I want you to do something else for me.'

She released the elastic and enjoyed his look of disappointment when her triangle was plucked from his sight.

'And what might that be, Madam?'

'Would you take all your clothes off for me? I'd be very pleased if you would, and I really don't want to make that an order.'

'I'll do that for you, Madam – certainly,' he said in a strangled tone.

He started to remove his black jacket, and was stopped immediately by Kate's strident voice.

'Oh, no, no, no,' she said. 'Your trousers and underpants first, I think. I do so want to see your big weapon.'

Morgan tried to be quick, but his hasty movements were hampered by eager fingers which fumbled with the clasp of his trousers. He let out a soft whispered expletive and immediately shot a contrite glance at Kate. Eventually the trousers were around his ankles, and white boxer shorts were pulled down to his knees. Kate marvelled at the size of his quivering cock, which bobbed towards her as if eager for her touch.

'My, it's even bigger than I'd hoped,' she said, squatting down to untie his shoelaces. 'Have I made it all big and hard like that?'

'Yes, Madam.'

Morgan's shoes were kicked off the moment the laces were undone. He knew that his hurried movements were totally out of character for a butler, but Kate's warm breath on the underside of his cock was making him frantic, and therefore his servility was swiftly quashed by desire.

'I am sorry,' she said. 'It must hurt such a lot when it's all worked up like that. I bet if you were by yourself you'd be making him happy by now. But I've kept you here.'

She pulled off his socks and almost tore at the rest of his clothes until he was naked. Already he was playing with his trembling shaft, fierce arousal making him unmindful of his position. He stroked it lovingly, running his fingers around the familiar and hugely-loved tip which bulged with want. Kate knew then that she would have little difficulty in making him do exactly what she desired.

His eyes never left her for a moment as she crossed to the bedroom and when she reappeared, holding up a magazine, a broad grin was upon his face. She sidled up to him, flicking the pages so that his eyes could feast on the naked female forms.

'Who do you want to see?' she asked. 'How about Mandy?'

She stopped at a page, and Morgan's breath was coming in ragged gasps as he devoured the picture before him.

'See? Mandy's a nice black girl who'll strip right off for you, while I read her naughty thoughts out loud.'

She pressed herself against him, making sure that her warm crotch was rubbing against his leg.

'Oh, yes, I'd like Mandy . . . oh, yes.'

'Right. Now, while I'm reading, there's something I want you to do for me.' Her hand slipped inside her panties

almost of its own accord, and went straightaway to her soaking wet vagina.

'And what might that be, Madam,' Morgan asked, excitedly.

'I've never seen a man toss himself right off, so will you do that while I watch? Please say you will, Morgan, dearest.'

'Oh, yes, Madam,' he said, before groaning gruffly when Kate caressed his aching shaft.

'It's all right,' she told him. 'I'm just covering it with love cream from my pussy, so that your hand will slide more easily.'

He groaned again and started to masturbate, his eyes transfixed on the picture of Mandy which Kate was holding in front of him.

She began to read. "Hi, I'm Mandy. I'm twenty-six years old, and my measurements are 39–26–38, so, as you can see, I'm a big girl. I know I've got all my clothes on, but if you turn the page I'll show you my tits."

Kate flicked the page, and they found Mandy reclining on a bed. She was naked apart from white knickers, and she was indeed well-built. Her breasts were enormous mounds of erotic flesh, firm and jutting; her large sexy nipples were a shade or two lighter, and they stood erect as if begging to be fondled.

"I like men to play with my tits," Kate read, her voice husky. "And men love to play with them. They like them because they're so big, and I just love to show them off."

Morgan was masturbating furiously now. 'Oh, Madam, this feels so good.'

She turned a few more pages and found Mandy lying on the bed, naked, with her spectacular legs spread wide and a sexy look on her face.

"Do what you want to me," Kate read. "Just anything. I don't care how filthy it is."

She put the magazine on the settee so that Morgan could carry on staring at the picture.

'Why don't you bring yourself off all over Mandy?' she encouraged. 'Why don't you spurt in her beautiful face?'

Her hand went between his legs to where his balls were jumping and jerking in their sac, and very gently she squeezed. Straightway his legs began to tremble and shake, and the hand gripping his shaft was a blur of movement.

'It feels so good,' he panted. 'So good, Madam.'

Kate pulled her panties down around her thighs and rubbed her hairy bush against his buttocks, covering them with her free-flowing love juices. Morgan gave a cry of uninhibited joy and then the entire contents of his heavy balls were spraying over the black girl's picture; her face, those fantastic breasts, and her long flawless legs were all covered with his thick, white sperm by the time his climax subsided.

'Thank you, Morgan, I really enjoyed that,' Kate said, as she bent to take off her panties.

He stood breathless, his chest heaving, and as he stared at the tight, sticky slit between her legs his drooping member rose up and became hard again.

'You've still got a big erection,' she marvelled. 'It's such a lovely cock. I don't think I've seen one quite so big before.'

His eyes pleaded with hers but, remembering his place, he remained silent.

'I've got that terrible itch again,' she confided, an impish smile on her lips. 'Would you scratch it for me, Morgan?'

He needed little persuasion, and was caressing her aching sex even before the words were uttered. Kate

placed her hands on his broad shoulders and spread her legs.

'Play with it for me. Slide your finger into my warm hole. Oh, that's it, now push it in and out.' Her head went back as delicious sensations accompanied his energetic hand. 'Oh, that's wonderful, Morgan, you've got me so excited. I can't remember ever being so wet before.'

He manoeuvred a second finger inside and worked them to and fro while she teased his shaft with the very tips of her fingers.

'I want you to do something else for me, Morgan,' she panted.

'Anything, Madam, anything.'

'Would it be in order to ask you to screw the arse off me?'

'Very much so, Madam.'

She pulled away from him and turned her back. Then, bending forward, she gripped her vaginal lips and opened the entrance to her yearning passage fully. Morgan gazed at it for many moments, as if relishing the pleasure that was to come, and then positioned his tip at the doors of her sheath and pushed inside. Its velvet-covered walls gripped his shaft as it slid in and out, and he grasped her thighs with hands that were hot and trembling.

Kate reached a powerful climax almost as soon as his thrusting cock began to pleasure her. And that peak had hardly dwindled when another began to build. Her second orgasm was much more intense, and soon the middle of Kate's body felt as if it had been consumed by a raging heat, its flames fanned into all corners of her groin.

She was urging him on, begging him to increase his speed and satisfy her fully. Morgan, in response, was fucking with a frantic urgency which rocked her to the

very core and sent orgasmic spasms searing along his rejoicing cock. The earthy smell of his sweat mingled with his strong male fragrance, and the heady mix pushed her over the brink of orgasm until she was yelling and crying and laughing with delight.

Now that her own fulfilment had been reached, her thoughts turned to his. With movements that were almost imperceptible, she closed her legs so that her wet tunnel grew tighter and tighter until it was clamped around his thrusting shaft. Morgan growled his approval of this new sensation, then almost dared not breathe as his own climax reared up.

'I'm coming, Madam,' he bawled.

'Oh, Morgan, shoot it up me. Let me feel your come.'

His actions were frenzied, and his sperm felt so hot as it pumped into her for what seemed like a wonderful eternity.

They stayed in their doggy position for a long time, neither moving, both fighting for breath and emitting tiny, throaty sounds of satisfaction. When Morgan eventually withdrew, Kate whimpered with regret as that delicious feeling of fullness was taken away from her crack.

'Will that be all, Madam?' he asked.

'For the moment, Morgan, yes.'

But before he could turn away, Kate was bending down and sucking his sagging cock into her mouth.

'Mmm, I just love to drink a man's come.' She smiled up at him, and winked. 'I'll ring when I need you again.'

CHAPTER 28

That notorious Third Act was in everyone's thoughts when dawn broke the next day. And the actual rehearsals were murder, for every time they came to a sex scene the actors had to call out from the stage what they would be doing on the night. And they couldn't just give a skeleton brief either; the whole scenario had to be explained fully for the benefit of those in the lighting box. There were many bulges in trousers, and much staining of knickers when the day's work came to an end.

It was six p.m. and Thackeray looked very hot under the collar as he stood centre stage and flicked through his notes.

'Okay,' he said, 'I think the best thing to do with Act Three is to make sure you all know your lines and moves, and then just let it happen on the night. Otherwise we'll all be working ourselves off all over the place.'

A ripple of laughter ran through the cast.

'All right, my loves;' he continued, holding up a hand for silence. 'You all know that we're going to have a little drinks party tonight, and if any of you feel like getting a teensy bit naughty during it, just go right ahead. But please forget all about the play and the situations in it.'

The cast melted away.

That evening, Kate saw Trish naked for the first time. Without an ounce of self-consciousness, the girl stripped off her loose-fitting rehearsal clothes in Kate's bedroom as she prepared for a shower.

Her slim legs were long and shapely, and the thatch of hair surrounding her vagina was flattened to her skin, completely saturated by her sexual longing. Her body was so slender and tantalizing with its trim hips and waspish waist, and its perfectly formed breasts that were home to quite delectable nipples. With her flowing black hair and her dark, desirable features she had the appearance of a little girl.

'You look nice,' Kate said. 'And you smell even better.'

Trish's hand went to her crotch and a finger was dipped into her tight slit.

'I can't believe how wet I am,' she said, bringing the finger to her nostrils and inhaling deeply. 'I always think it smells better when I'm highly aroused.' She held the finger out to Kate. 'Don't you?'

Kate brushed her nostrils over the tip and then took the whole of the finger into her mouth, thrilling at that first taste of Trish's creamy love potion.

'And it tastes even better,' she smiled, licking her lips. 'Now go and shower, you've got a big night ahead of you.'

Trish giggled. 'And tomorrow, I hope, when we have some fun.'

Whenever Thackeray Williams threw a party his catch-phrase was 'no expense spared' and therefore the alcohol flowed freely. The party was being held in a room on the first floor of the exquisite mansion and was soon extremely noisy. As bodies gyrated to the loud rock beat, an endless procession of amorous couples beat a path to the bedrooms;

and the more the booze was consumed, the more the beds came into use.

Kate and Trish mingled, danced and chatted until eleven o'clock, and then they strayed out into the corridor in search of a free room. After peeping into four and witnessing some very interesting sights, they found an empty bedroom with a large four-poster in its far corner.

Trish had deliberately gone easy on the drink, but Kate had been less restrained and was developing a definite stagger. Both however were doubled over with uproarious laughter now that the time had come to put their plan into action. Trish climbed on to the bed, her legs showing through the long slit in her ankle-length black skirt.

'Now, remember, all you've got to do is act pissed,' Kate said.

'Like you?' Trish retorted, with a grin.

'Cheeky cow,' Kate threw back as she stumbled towards the door.

'Hurry up, I'm randy,' the girl called to the closing door.

Kate wove an unsteady path back to the party. Across the crowded room she spotted Diana who was laughing with Thackeray and Robin. As she watched, the two men took turns to kiss and fondle Diana and her drunken shrieks could be plainly heard above the thunderous beat of the stereo. Kate picked a path across the rowdy dance floor and approached them.

'Hi,' she said, grabbing a glass of champagne from the tray of a passing waiter.

'Kate, my darling,' Thackeray said, his booming voice rather slurred around the edges. 'This terrible woman—' He caught Diana in an arm lock. 'This terrible woman is making indecent suggestions to me. You wouldn't like to bring your delightful little snatch along to make up a

foursome, would you?' He blinked and tried to focus his eyes. 'Or should that be an eightsome?'

Above their laughter, Kate said, 'I've got something far more interesting than that. You know you told me you've all got the hots for Trish—?'

'She's not giving it away, is she?' Robin asked, suddenly all ears.

'Not exactly, no. But she's in one of the bedrooms, out of her head on booze. If anything happened tonight, then I doubt if she'd be able to remember in the morning. And, believe me, she's in the mood for anything.'

'Where is she?' Thackeray wanted to know.

Kate hid a secret smile. 'Follow me.'

When they entered the bedroom amid a lot of drunken shushing, Kate saw that Trish was still in position on the bed. She deliberately stayed by the door while the other three carried on for a closer look.

'Are you all right?' Thackeray asked, his voice heavy with concern.

'No, I'm not,' Trish pouted, hitching herself up on to her elbows. 'I've lost my knickers. I had them on when I went to the loo for a pee, but now they've gone.'

Kate grinned. Trish was acting the part of a drunken woman to perfection.

'Let me have a look,' Diana soothed. 'You may still have them on.'

The woman's excited fingers undid the fastening of Trish's skirt and, with some difficulty, pulled it down and over her feet.

'God,' she breathed, as Trish opened her legs.

'See? I knew I'd lost them because I kept feeling my pussy, and it was nice.'

'Let's take your blouse off next, shall we?' There was a sexy edge to Diana's voice now, and her movements were almost frantic. 'Perhaps we should all undress and do something nice. Would you like that, Trish?'

The girl nodded, and within seconds of her blouse and bra being removed, three outfits were slung in a heap by the side of the bed.

'Why are we all naked?' Trish slurred, as if only now aware.

'Don't you worry about it, my love,' Diana said, putting a finger to her lips. 'We're going to make you feel really good.'

'Not sex,' Trish grumbled. 'I don't know anything about that but, do you know, tonight I feel I'd like to learn.'

'Oh, you gorgeous girl,' Diana cooed. 'Now, just open your legs really wide for me, and I'll get you ready for the boys. And perhaps they can get on the bed while I'm doing it, so you can play with their cocks at the same time.'

Trish gave a intoxicated chuckle as Thackeray and Robin hurled themselves on to the bed and knelt either side of her.

'Aren't they big boys,' she marvelled, stroking their straining shafts while they stared intently at the treasure resting between her open legs. But then it was blocked from their view by Diana whose mouth was now resting against its pouting lips.

'Oh, yes,' Trish sighed, spreading her legs as wide as she could when the woman's tongue snaked inside.

The tongue twisted and slithered in the hot passage, seeking out all of the girl's pleasure spots while Diana set her fingers to industrious labour along the wet trench in search of her love bud.

Trish was thrashing about, delighting in the ecstasy

caused by the erotic havoc of Diana's fingers and delving tongue. And all thoughts of toying with the boisterous cocks were chased from her mind as the pleasant sensation of an approaching climax coursed through her middle.

Kate was still watching from the doorway, and she realised then that Trish's sex urge was stronger than she could ever have hoped. It would take an awful lot of sexy games to satisfy that little madam. Still, the more the merrier, she thought brightly.

Diana was now kneeling between the girl's legs with four fingers inside her and the thumb of her free hand rubbing vigorously at her clitoris. The quivering gem was swollen and visibly throbbing with unfulfilled want, and Trish was reacting so fiercely to its pampering that the men were having to hold her down. But even the huge hands of two muscular males could not hold still the trim slip of a girl when she bucked and struggled in response to the turbulent orgasm brought on by Diana's foraging fingers and rotating thumb.

The eyes of all in the room, Kate's included, were alive with excitement as they anticipated the next move. When Trish was released, she stumbled to her feet and, resuming her drunken act, staggered across the room.

'Phew, I went all hot then,' she said, a hand flying to her fevered forehead.

'Come back here, my love,' Diana coaxed, a look of pure lechery on her face. 'Thackeray's got something that will make you go really hot.'

The girl lurched back towards them. 'Poor Thackeray and Robin. I was playing with their tools, but I had to stop because I went all funny and I didn't know what I was doing.'

She began to cry dramatically, and Kate marvelled at

the girl's natural performance which brought real tears tumbling on to her cheeks.

'Please forgive me,' she sobbed. 'You must be so angry. I know how it feels when you want to come so badly that it hurts, but the person you're with won't let you.'

Her wailing increased, and fresh tears traced a watery course from her large, sorrowful eyes.

'I'll do anything, if only you'll forgive me . . . anything. I don't care how dirty you want me to be.'

'Get on with it,' Diana hissed to the men. 'The party will be breaking up soon.'

'Shut up,' Thackeray snapped. 'I want to take my time with this.'

He signalled kindly to Trish who joined him at the side of the bed. The moment she was near, he took her tiny hand and placed it around his huge penis, the delicate fingers barely covering half its circumference.

'Do you know how to wank a man off?' he asked, his voice dripping with lust. 'Do you do it for your boyfriend?'

'No,' she said, her ardent expression like that of a child eager to learn. 'My boyfriend likes my pussy, and when he wants it I open my legs and let him have his fill.' She giggled. 'Sometimes he wants it so much that I don't even have time to take my knickers off – he just pulls them to one side and pushes himself in. He really loves my little crack,' she added, dreamily, 'but I've never wanked him off. Would you show me how to do it? Would you . . . please?'

Thackeray was positively leering at the girl. This was better than he'd hoped. Not only was she sensational to look at, but quite innocent, too. What fun they would have tonight!

'Of course I'll show you, my little love. And, don't worry,

I'm sure you'll be fine. Now, all you have to do is hold my cock really tight and pull then push, pull then push.'

The feel of her clumsy hand was sending giant waves of pleasure crashing to Thackeray's agitated tip, and he smiled encouragement at Trish when she glanced appealingly into his rugged face.

'You're doing extremely well ... extremely well,' he murmured, settling into the pillows. 'Now, if you could just stand back a little so that I can see your beautiful body—'

A wanton growl rose up in his throat as his gaze fell on her sweet breasts that wobbled and shook in time with the rhythm of her hand, and then travelled down to the comely forest of dark hair covering the treasure he would soon be enjoying.

'Am I doing it right?' she asked, as Robin approached from behind, his gentle caresses covering her creamy-white buttocks.

'Yes, yes, you're very good,' Thackeray assured her through tightly clenched teeth.

'Oh,' she said, with a delightful chuckle, 'Robin's playing with my bottom, now, and I like it very much. No one's ever touched me there before. I'm really starting to enjoy all this – I really am.'

Robin sank to his knees and parted her buttocks, and Trish let out a sexy breath when his tongue was made to roam along the groove.

'Robin,' she shrieked with joy, 'fancy licking me there! It feels so nice, though. Honestly, I just don't know what's come over me tonight. I won't even let my boyfriend lick my pussy—'

Thackeray was emitting lascivious grunts as her hand began to move with startling speed.

'And, look, my hand's going really fast, now,' she said,

her voice bristling with wonder, 'You will tell me if I'm not wanking you off properly, won't you, Thackeray?'

His 'yes' seemed to stick in his throat, so he nodded wildly instead.

'Please put your tongue into my naughty hole, Robin,' she implored, that little girl voice causing Kate to swallow a raucous laugh. 'I want such dirty things, tonight, and I don't know why.' She gasped. 'Oh, Robin, that feels divine. Lick it faster.'

Thackeray was panting hard and then, with a deep-throated growl, he ejaculated. His sperm jetted towards her in a perfect arc and came to rest on her stomach. Trish giggled heartily as she watched it stream down to her pubic bush.

'Thackeray, that was wonderful,' she marvelled, wide-eyed. 'I've never seen a man shoot his come before. But do you know, it's got my naughty crack all excited again. It feels all funny – sort of hot and itchy.'

'Bend over,' Robin urged. 'I'll make it feel better for you.'

She did so immediately, but kept her thighs tightly closed.

'Is that all right?' she asked, sweetly.

'Fine, but you'll have to open your legs. That's it, just spread them.'

'What are you going to do?'

'This,' he said, grasping his quivering cock and positioned the tip at her yearning entrance.

'That big thing will never go into my pussy – I'm far too tight,' she said. 'It's so much bigger than my boyfriend's, and even he fills me up.'

Robin's shaft disappeared inside her an inch at a time. And it wasn't her tightness which restricted his thrust, but her playful vaginal muscles that welcomed the strapping beast with the most ferocious of hugs.

'Oh, it's gone in,' she shrieked. 'I can't believe it. Oh, goodness, and now you're screwing me with it. Robin, dear Robin, I don't think I'll ever want a small one again, because your divine prick is making me come already.'

He was fucking with a feverish passion now, gripping her tiny waist and giving her the full length of his shaft on every push until Trish was screaming for more. She climaxed twice, and each time described in graphic detail the sensations that were overwhelming her juicy little peach. Each of her blissful cries made him fuck harder until he was pumping at a terrifying rate.

'I'm coming,' he yelled. 'I can't hold out any longer.'

A sound resembling a girlish squeal escaped from his throat as Robin's balls gave up their treasure. But, even before he had time to discharge his full load, Thackeray was pulling him away, and thick blobs of sperm hit her trembling buttocks as he stepped back.

Thackeray was installed in her velvet tunnel before Trish even had time to beg for his giant of a cock, and she laughed merrily at the feel of it stretching her to impossible limits and activating pleasure spots that even she was unaware of.

'Oh, Thackeray, that's sensational,' she told him. 'My horny crack can't get enough cock tonight.'

Kate watched in awe while the man slammed into Trish like a soul possessed. He was totally out of control, truly enraptured by the girl's tight hairy nest, and by the thought that he was taking advantage of a tipsy innocent girl.

It took him ten minutes to reach his climax, and by that time they were all crowded around the copulating couple. When it was obvious that Thackeray's moment of joy was near Diana spoke in that low throaty tone which was hers alone.

'Take it out, Thackeray, darling. When it starts shooting, take it right out.'

He screamed that he was there, and withdrew from her fulfilled passage with an animal snarl. Love seed flew from his tip and was still oozing out when Diana grabbed the shaft and placed it at the entrance to Trish's arse so that he could push a little of it in and empty the rest of his sperm into there.

The girl was in raptures and wholly in favour of that unexpected turn of events, and she fucked the inch of animated cock with a vengeance, greedy as she was for every last drop from his lustful loins.

'Thank you ... all of you,' Trish said, as she straightened up. 'That was so good. I really don't know what's come over me tonight. I think I had too much to drink.'

With a dreamy smile she staggered to the bed and collapsed on to it. Her eyes closed straightaway, and she seemed to be falling into a drunken sleep.

'We'd better get dressed and get back to the party before everyone goes,' Diana said.

She was already struggling into her clothes, her gaze now and then turning eagerly towards the door, and Kate imagined that a fair number of the stage hands would be very happy by the time the party did break up. It was a theory confirmed by the fact that Diana didn't bother to put her panties back on when she dressed. Thackeray and Robin appeared dazed as they replaced their clothes at a far more leisurely pace, and soon all three were filing out on to the landing. No sooner had the door closed on them than Trish began to laugh into the bedclothes.

'You filthy little cow,' Kate lightly scolded. 'You were lapping that up.'

'I bloody well was,' she admitted, sitting up and beaming

at Kate. 'That was the best time I've ever had. I was surprised how much I liked it up my arse – I must get it for real some time.'

'You really can act, you know. You looked pissed out of your skull.'

That remark pleased Trish, and she smiled her thanks.

'That's what you're all about, isn't it?' Kate said. 'Being forced to do it, or too drunk to realize what you're doing. Is it because you don't want the responsibility of saying yes?'

'Oh, God, no analysis tonight, please,' she said, jumping off the bed. 'I feel too good to start delving into the whys and wherefores of everything.' She looked pensive all of a sudden. 'Kate, there's nothing wrong with wanting an arse fuck, is there?'

'No, of course not. I reckon anything's okay as long as it's what you want. And, don't worry, I'll make sure you're tied up or held down and then, when it's all over, I'll punish you for being a dirty little girl.'

'I can't wait, I really can't. I want it so much. And I don't mind how much you mark me. I can always cover it up with stage make-up.'

'What an incorrigible girl you are . . . Come on, get dressed and let's get out of here.'

Kate moved about the room, collecting the girl's scattered clothes, and there was a thoughtful look on her face when she returned the pile to Trish.

'By the way, would you mind if a man joined us tomorrow?' she asked, her hands running over the girl's buttocks. 'He could supply you with your newly-acquired fantasy.'

Trish trembled beneath her touch. 'Oh, Kate, that exactly what I want.'

CHAPTER 29

Hours later, alone in her room, Kate showered and styled her hair carefully, then slipped into a comfortable pink bathrobe. Once settled on the settee she rang the bell for Morgan, who arrived minutes later carrying a single brandy on a silver tray.

'I assumed that Madam would want a drink, so I took the liberty of pouring one.'

'Thank you, Morgan, that was nice of you.'

She took the glass and was about to sip the dark brown liquid when she noticed that there were streaks of white floating on its surface. A look of amazement widened her eyes as she gazed up at him.

There was just a hint of a smile on his face, when Morgan said, 'Madam did indicate that she loved to drink a man's seed so, being an attentive butler, I arranged it.'

'You sod,' she laughed.

Holding the glass in both palms, Kate put the rim to her mouth and closed her eyes as the erotic cocktail burned a sumptuous trail to her stomach.

'Delicious,' she said, smacking her lips appreciatively. 'I shall expect you to do this with every drink you serve me from now on, Morgan.'

'Most certainly, Madam. It will be my pleasure.' He gave

a slight bow and eyed her long legs which were on display beneath the short bathrobe.

'Will you do something else for me now?' she asked, draining the glass and licking all around the rim.

'I was hoping that Madam would ask,' he murmured.

She let the bathrobe fall open and showed him her body. And, pleased to see that his gaze went immediately to her triangle of glossy hair, she opened her legs to give him a better view.

'My pussy badly needs some sex fun, but I want you to do something else for me, Morgan. Now, you know Trish Butler, obviously . . .'

'Yes, I do, Madam.'

'Well . . .'

By the time she had finished outlining her plan, Morgan had a full, throbbing erection that he found impossible to keep inside his trousers.

Trish behaved as if she had an almighty hangover the following morning, and nothing in her behaviour suggested that she could recall any of the events of the previous night. There was plenty of nudging and lots of furtive whispered conversations taking place between Thackeray and Robin, who no doubt believed that they had escaped the ugly scenes which could so easily have resulted from their unsolicited attentions.

As a result, the rehearsals went very well and, as soon as they were able, Kate and Trish visited the wardrobe department. There they asked for some 1920s costumes, explaining that they were needed for a party they were to attend. The elderly wardrobe mistress was most accommodating. Yes, of course they could borrow the costumes, and how exciting the party sounded. They could keep the

clothes as long as they needed, she told them, as long as they signed for them first.

Ten minutes later, with the outfits safely installed in large plastic bags, the girls arranged to meet in Kate's room at seven that evening. Morgan was to take the evening off and join them there for a drink.

'Right,' Kate said, giggling frantically, 'it's time to get our costumes on and really party.'

They had tremendous fun with the old-fashioned underwear, which consisted of huge knickers and large-cupped brassieres. Kate had chosen a smart two piece suit, the skirt of which came down around her ankles, while Trish had opted for a maid's uniform which also had a full length skirt.

When at last they were pleased with their appearances, they went into the bedroom where Morgan was already resplendent in his period suit. He was sitting in a chair, skimming through a newspaper, and he looked up when the girls rushed in. His expression was one of appreciation as Kate took the chair beside his and picked up a sewing basket that she had placed there earlier.

Soon Trish was serving them tea, and whenever she moved around the room, their eyes followed her hungrily. Flustered, and quite obviously embarrassed, the girl curtsied and hurried away.

'Don't, John,' Kate scolded. 'I know exactly the kind of wicked thoughts that race through your mind whenever your eyes settle on that poor girl.'

'But don't we always have fun with a new servant?' he said, dropping easily into his new character. 'After all, they have to do something to show their heartfelt gratitude to us for giving them a job.'

'Emily's different,' Kate said, her tone hushed. 'She's so much younger than the others, for a start. She may well tell her parents, and think of the trouble that would cause.'

'She wouldn't dare breathe a word,' Morgan said, sitting back and folding his paper. 'Are you trying to tell me you don't want to get her naked so that you can have your fun?'

'Of course I do,' she threw back. 'Every morning she comes into the bedroom and helps me to dress. Oh, John, when she's so close I long to slip my hand up the leg of her knickers.' She paused in her sewing. 'And I know she plays with herself in bed at night.'

'What? You mean—?'

'I mean, she gives herself a good fingering, that's what I mean.'

Morgan smiled. 'Maybe we should watch tonight, and then in the morning a severe reprimand may be in order.'

'You may well be right, dear, as long as we go about it in the right way Emily won't be able to tell her parents because they'd probably give her a good thrashing if she did.'

It was supposed to be hours later when they pushed open the bedroom door just enough to peer through the gap. Trish – happily into the part of the gullible Emily – was in bed, the sheets pulled up to her throat. Her legs were open and raised at the knees and it was obvious to the spying pair, given the rhythmic movements of the blankets, that she was masturbating quite vigorously. She was moaning and sighing amid feverish gasps as her fingers moved with effortless ease along the juicy cleft between her legs.

They were both breathing heavily when she climaxed with a violence that raised her from the bed, a hand

clamped in her mouth to stifle an ecstatic scream. Morgan quietly pulled the door shut.

'I don't believe the little slut,' he marvelled. 'To look at that angelic face, you'd think butter wouldn't melt in her mouth.'

Kate took his arm. 'Come on, I think it'll have to be your special favourite tonight.'

'Oh, yes,' he said, his eyes bright. 'Do you think Emily would allow me to?'

'Perish the thought, dear,' Kate said, highly shocked. 'We're the only people in the world to do that – surely?'

'We'll have to see, won't we?' he mused. 'She's got such a trim little body. I'm going to find her very hard to resist, I can tell you.'

The scene changed to Kate and Morgan's bedroom the following morning. Kate was alone, and dressed only in her underwear. Trish entered, carrying the two piece suit on a hanger.

'Ah, Emily, what a good girl you are,' she said. 'Come here, I need to talk to you about something frightfully important. I've been noticing certain stains on your bed linen, so last night I opened the door to your room and I saw—' She paused, and wrinkled her noise as if against an unpleasant smell. 'I saw you doing something to yourself, something not very nice.'

Trish blushed quite brilliantly. 'I'm sorry, ma'am. I . . . I won't do it again.'

Kate put a finger to the girl's lips to silence her. 'I haven't finished, yet. Now, I want to tell you something – the master was with me, and we've decided that we can either punish you ourselves, or tell your parents and let them do it. Which would you rather it be?'

'I'd rather you punished me, ma'am,' she said, hanging

her head in shame. 'My father would kill me if he found out I'd done that to myself.'

'Yes, I can understand that,' Kate sympathized. 'Sex is such a terrible thing. It makes even the most moral of souls do things they wouldn't normally dream of doing. And afterwards, of course, they're deeply ashamed.'

'Yes, ma'am.'

'Now, it's very important that you tell me exactly what you're thinking about when you're playing with yourself. Are your thoughts always filled with men?'

'Yes, ma'am.'

'Never women? Be honest, now – you're never dreaming of doing it with another woman?'

The girl reddened and shuffled her feet, cringing with embarrassment.

'Sometimes I do, ma'am,' she blurted out. 'When I'm doing it, all sorts of strange thoughts come into my mind. I don't seem able to control them.'

'I see.' Kate paced the bedroom. 'Look, the master and I are very modern in our outlooks. After all, this is 1922, and I must confess I understand how you feel because we enjoy sex, therefore we'll make the punishment as light as possible.'

'Thank you, ma'am.'

'Good, that's that out of the way,' Kate said, with a huge smile. 'I'm going to take my knickers off now, Emily, and I want you to tell me if you like what I've got because should you agree to be nice to me I might persuade the master to make your punishment lighter still.'

Trish's eyes shone when Kate's hairy patch came into view, and they twinkled even more when she took off her bra.

'So, now you can see everything, and you can touch me

280

between the legs, if you like,' she said, her tone full of hope. 'Because I was thinking about you all last night, and I couldn't sleep for wishing you were there in the bed with me.'

Trish took a hesitant step forward and stroked Kate's enticing crack. Her caresses were tentative to start with, but as Kate's jerking breath became hot against her cheek she slipped a finger into the crack and pleasured it eagerly.

'How lovely,' Kate gasped, stepping back and cupping the girl's animated features in her hands. 'The master has a truly enormous rod, and he gives it to me every night. But I do love to have a young girl like you fingering me.'

'I thought I was the only one who liked this, ma'am. I used to look at you in your fine underwear, and get really worked up.'

'Go faster, Emily. Do it faster,' Kate urged. 'Make me come, you lovely girl.'

'I'll show you what I do to myself,' the girl whispered hoarsely, as her free hand searched out Kate's scorching clitoris and stroked it lovingly.

'Oh, that is so beautiful,' she sighed, throwing back her head. 'At last, a girl who knows how to satisfy her mistress.'

Her joyous cries brought footsteps pounding on an imaginary staircase, and then Morgan was bursting into the room.

'She's made me come,' Kate enthused. 'And she's willing to let us do what we want with her, so there'll be no need for punishment of any kind.'

'But, ma'am, I want to be punished,' Trish blurted. 'I used to love being caned at school. The teacher used to make me take my knickers off, and I'd get all worked up. I used to break the rules on purpose, just so that he could hit me.'

'Your teacher made you take your knickers off, eh?' Morgan said, as he hurried to the wardrobe and fished out a thin bamboo cane. 'And did he do anything else?'

Trish gulped; could her dream be about to come true?

'No, sir, he didn't,' she said. 'But I wanted him to. I used to wriggle my bottom against him between every stroke.'

Morgan swished the cane, bringing it crashing down into the palm of his hand, as he said, 'You'd better take your dress off, young lady, and then you can bend over.'

Trish almost tore at the buttons of her frock and allowed it to fall to the floor. Their gasps of delight at the sweet ripeness of her body were wholly real, and they both strained to glimpse the crack of her sex which was plain to see, even beneath the large knickers.

'Bend over,' Morgan said.

When she was comfortably in position, he brought the cane down on to her backside with much force. She howled, the pain and her distress all too real, but even so she wiggled her buttocks invitingly.

'Again,' she sighed. 'Hit me again – harder this time.'

The cane swished through the air and another stinging, smarting blow landed. Still bending, Trish unclipped her brassiere and struggled out of it, her small, perfectly formed breasts dancing in time with her impassioned breath.

'I'll leave your knickers on, so that I don't mark you too much,' Morgan said, his voice catching in his throat as he eyed the girl bending brazenly before him, desperate to see what lay hidden beneath the green drawers.

His hand roamed over the thick material and dipped between her buttocks, tracing along the channel until it found her pubic hair.

'My God,' he breathed, 'it feels so wet, Kate. Her knickers are sticking to it.'

'Hit me again,' the girl pleaded. 'But this time do it on my bare bottom.'

Kate eased forward, her movements made awkward by excitement. Indeed, she remarked, 'I'm all fingers and thumbs,' as she pulled down the girl's pants until they were around her neat little ankles. She stepped back then and joined Morgan as he stared agog at the smooth white buttocks that bore ugly red marks where the cane had struck, and her tasty vagina that nestled in its bed of dark silky hair.

She was begging the master to cane her again, but it was Kate who took the weapon of punishment and landed three heavy strokes, leaving angry red wheals on the flawless skin as a demented expression marred her ecstatic features.

'You naughty girl,' she shrieked between each blow. 'How dare you get your master and myself all worked up with your depraved and shocking behaviour in bed last night.'

The cane swished again, and Trish yelped but her smile grew broader.

'Yes, my girl, that was only what you deserved,' Kate said, taking the cane in both hands and bending it almost double. 'And now you must please us, because if you don't I really will thrash you.'

'I'll do anything,' Trish said, her face radiant with bliss as she felt her smarting buttocks.

Morgan undid his flies and coaxed his rock-hard cock through the opening. Straight away, Trish's hand flew to her mouth, her eyebrows rising with surprise.

'But it's so big,' she exclaimed.

'Take your knickers right off, girl,' Kate said, 'so that the master can get a proper look at your cunt.'

Trish gave a delightful laugh as she hurriedly stepped out of the pants and opened her legs. Her eyes were glued to the enormous shaft which poked disgustingly from the trousers, and she was thrilled to see it harden still more as Morgan gazed admiringly at her hairy nest, his features red with lust.

She reached down and opened up the doors at her entrance, teasing him with the sight of her tunnel. Morgan took off his thick leather belt, his gaze unwavering, and undid the buttons of his trousers. When they were in a heap around his feet, Kate implored the girl to take off his shoes quickly.

Trish was forced to kneel down and remove the shoes and socks, and when they were neatly positioned to her left, she looked up and found herself face to face with Morgan's quivering weapon. It was mere inches away from her perfectly formed lips, and she lavished compliments on its size and smell.

Kate gripped the girl's hair at the back of her head in an effort to keep her still, and then Morgan rammed his bulky cock towards her lips.

'Open your mouth and pleasure it,' Kate coaxed.

But Trish chose to disobey, and instead she kissed the shaft and ran her hot tongue along its sensitive underside, thrilling at the earthy, unwashed smell that drifting up from his balls. Kate released her hair and, with her movements now unimpeded, she worked her mouth between his legs and gently sucked on one of his aching testicles while he groaned his thanks and almost sank to his knees, so divine was the sensation.

Kate lay on her back and eased herself between Trish's

open legs, forcing the girl to change position until she was squatting over Kate's face, the entrance to her spectacular crack just above her mouth.

'Lick it,' Trish implored, during the few seconds her mouth was not in use.

While Kate's hot jerking breath teased her yearning crack, the girl returned her full attention to Morgan's cock and worked her tongue into the tiny slit at the centre of his tip. Sheer delight bubbled inside her at the sound of his delirious cries, and at the feel of Kate's tongue lapping at her love bud and teasing her entrance which by now was saturated with heady love juice and warm saliva.

Trish gripped the penis and moved it gently to and fro, all the while kissing its head as she worked him off. Morgan rotated his hips and constantly thrust forward, pushing more and more of his torrid tool into her soothing mouth. Eventually the whole of his seven inches was sliding between her lips, and Trish gripped its root while Morgan grabbed her head to hold it still and fucked her mouth with vigorous strokes.

By now Kate's delving tongue was sending strong surges of pleasure through Trish's body. Morgan worked his fingers through her glossy hair, twisting thick locks of it until the pressure began to hurt her scalp, while he continued to slide his pulsating member to and fro in her comely mouth.

The gorgeous ripples of pleasure in her crack grew ever bigger, until a tidal wave of orgasmic bliss swept through her groin. And her pleasure was further enhanced by Morgan's demented babbling, which told that his peak had almost been reached. She promptly let go of his throbbing cock so that it could slide to the far reaches of her grasping throat. While he thrust with new enthusiasm, she rubbed

herself wildly against Kate's lips, unable to keep still as she rode the waves of her powerful climax.

At the same time Morgan's seed hit the walls of her throat and she swallowed each dynamic spurt quickly, gulping it down in readiness for the next.

'That was so good,' he murmured. 'I've never known a young girl who could suck cock like that.'

She beamed with pleasure, savouring the taste of his organ and the bitter tang of his love cream while Kate pulled herself free and got to her feet, her face flushed with excitement.

'She's so ripe, John, and she tastes wonderful. And just look at you,' she said, with a sexy laugh. 'After all that, you've still got the horn. I just know you won't lose it until you've had everything you want.'

Kate led Trish to the bed and ordered her to lie on it.

'I'd much rather get on top,' she said. 'I know how to give a man a good time in that position.'

Hurriedly, Morgan clambered on to the bed, his lusty tool standing to attention, ready and willing for her to lower herself on to it. She merely straddled him at first, rubbing his hot tip against her trembling clitoris. A torrent of love juice was escaping from her tunnel and streaming down his shaft, and their murmurs of mutual bliss met and mingled in the quiet of the room.

Trish took hold of the cock and slipped it between the wet lips of her crack, allowing him to sink into her from below. She began to ride immediately, bringing loud grunts of satisfaction from his throat. Morgan gripped her buttocks and forced her to quicken her pace until sweat was trickling down her back.

Sensing her own moment of fulfilment was close, she moved faster of her own will, welcoming the warm feeling

in her groin with an elated shout. She worked her hands between her legs and toyed with his anus while he fondled hers, working the tip of his finger inside and making her whimper with ecstasy.

'He's got something far bigger than his finger to shove up it,' Kate whispered lewdly. 'I let him have my arse three times a week, and he simply adores it. He can shoot his spunk up there, you see, without getting me pregnant.'

'I'm coming,' Morgan panted. 'I'm coming.'

Trish pulled herself off at the very moment when a fountain of seed left his indebted tip, and she watched with lust-filled eyes as he grabbed his tool and rubbed with a fiery passion while he lay back, his mouth open and eyes closed, coaxing the last of the hot come from his straining sac.

But still his cock would not sag. It pointed towards the ceiling, proud and confident, its tip an angry red.

'Come on, Emily,' Kate said. 'It's time to bend over for your master, and let him have his fun.'

'Oh, no, no,' the girl cried, shrinking away. 'I've always vowed I would never do that for any man.'

Kate grinned and made a grab for Morgan's leather belt.

'You ungrateful little hussy,' she hissed. 'From now on it will be part of your job to let the master have whatever he wants. You will also get into bed with me every morning, and you will not leave it until I'm satisfied.'

She wrapped the belt around her hand twice, and then swished it through the air. It made a cruel cracking sound and although Trish cringed upon hearing it, the corners of her mouth turned up in an unconscious smile.

'Now, bend over,' Kate snapped. 'I'm beginning to think that we'll have to beat you at least once a week.'

Trish was trembling as she bent over and gripped her

shins – trembling with desire. She screamed loudly when the thick leather slapped at her buttocks, but then she began to squirm under each blow and tiny groans of contentment left her lips on ragged breath.

'Thrash me,' she whispered. 'I really enjoy it. I'm always ready for sex, but I do love to be punished, too.'

Kate kept up her assault on the girl's painfully tender buttocks, and added to her discomfort by aiming the odd blow at her willowy thighs. Trish reacted violently with horrendous shrieks, but still she asked for more. Morgan, in the meantime, had smothered his cock with grease and was aching for the delight that awaited him.

The torture ceased, and Trish was left to writhe in her delicious distress while Kate took the jar from Morgan and slapped a large helping of the cool lotion onto the smarting injuries which covered the girl's soft skin.

'There, Emily,' she soothed, 'that should make it all feel a lot better – take away the pain. My, my, though, we had no idea you were such a wicked girl.'

'I've always been a wicked girl,' she said, the comforting cream making her purr like a contented cat. 'Even when I was at school, I used to go into the woods to watch the boys playing with each other's cocks. It was really filthy, seeing them make each other come.'

She flinched slightly when Kate's cream-covered finger circled her anus and dipped inside.

'Don't mind what I'm doing, Emily,' she said. 'This will get you ready for the master's big tool.'

Her finger slid in and out of the tight orifice, and all the while she tut-tutted. 'Boys playing with each other until they shoot – whatever next? It was never like that in our day, was it, John?'

Morgan made no reply, for he was past listening. His

gaze was rivetted to the hole being made available for him. And not before time; his yearning balls, which had laboured so hard already, were once more eager to empty their contents, and his shaft was straining at its root.

'Oh, your finger feels so nice,' Trish breathed. 'I didn't think I'd like it, but I do.'

'I knew you would,' Kate said, with a smile. 'But these naughty boys in the woods – did they ever catch you spying on them?'

'Yes, they caught me once, and three of them pulled my knickers off and had me, one after the other.'

Suddenly Kate's finger was gone, and something far bigger was seeking entry. Morgan pushed inside with a loud grunt, amazed at the ease with which her dark hole accommodated him. Trish whimpered at the discomfort, but it was merely a token sound, for her loins were alive with excitement and eager to savour this utterly alien sensation.

She relaxed her muscles and, allowing the grease to do its work, gave in to her enjoyment, which increased with each push of his thrusting rod. Her arse tingled and brought shivers of delight to her spine as the heavenly friction built up and, paradoxically, led her ever closer to a stunning vaginal orgasm.

The shaft slid in and out of the tight hole with a relentless energy, and Morgan grunted and growled as each thrust took him nearer to his own spectacular release.

'She feels superb,' he panted. 'I can't wait much longer – I've got to come.'

His grip on her thighs was vice-like, his fingernails bruising the flesh and causing the girl to almost swoon with the joy of it all. Fierce expletives left his mouth as his balls rose up, ready to discharge, and then he stopped.

Trish was quite startled and was about to beg him to start again when she felt his first sperm jet exploding on to her inner walls. He was moving and baying like a dog, his full load gushing inside her.

They were all three still and silent for a long moment and then Trish, still in her bending position, said, 'You bitch, Kate, I thought you were going to take the skin off my arse with that belt.'

Morgan withdrew from the sweet pit of her buttocks, still groaning with satisfaction.

'That was truly out of this world,' he murmured. 'I'll definitely be doing that again.'

Kate grinned and stroked Trish's bottom with a soothing hand. 'I couldn't resist it, honestly,' she said, with little compassion. 'You were just begging for a good beating.'

As quickly as they had found their new characters, they slipped back into their own.

'I'd better go and take a bath,' Morgan said, on his way to the bathroom. 'That is, if Madam will allow me to.'

'Of course, Morgan, take as long as you like.' She turned to Trish, and laughed. 'You really got me going with that tale about the boys jerking one another off. You just wouldn't believe the pictures that brought to my mind.'

'But it was true,' she said, flinching as she sat on the bed and directing a belligerent 'cow' towards Kate. 'That's how I got myself broken in, by the three boys.'

'God, I'd give anything to see something like that,' Kate said, wistfully. 'The boys doing it together, I mean.'

'I'm sure it goes on around here. We could always look around.' Trish's eyes searched her thoughtful face. 'If you were staying, that is, but I heard you'd be leaving straight after the play.'

'How did you hear that?' Kate asked, somewhat surprised.

'But it's common knowledge,' Trish said, suddenly flustered. 'Everybody knows that you're only here to find a man named Wilson.'

Kate let out a long weary sigh. 'So much for my prowess as a private detective.'

CHAPTER 30

It was the final scene of the play, and Kate was waiting in the wings for the cue to her last entrance. The whole production had gone extremely well and her main worry, that the first two acts would not hold the attentions of the theatre-goers, had proved to be unfounded. Although there was no sex in those acts, the dialogue and suggestive moves led brilliantly towards the sultry third act, and all in the audience were in a high state of anticipation by the time the action arrived.

They were in no way rowdy, but the high charge of sexual excitement that coursed through the auditorium during the erotic bits could have been cut by a knife.

I bet there's plenty of hard dicks and wet knickers out there, Kate thought, as she waited.

She was fully dressed in panties and bra and long blue dress that came to the middle of her calves, and was feeling particularly randy, for none of the hot sex had yet come her way. Her dripping pleasure spot was aching for it, and the stabbing pains were beginning to affect her upper thighs. Never in her life had she wanted sex so much.

The play's story was a simple one, and was built around three sisters who had inherited a fortune. The sisters were played by Trish, Kate, and an actress called Jenny. Trish and Jenny's characters had sunk into a world of high-living,

booze and sex that was fast becoming more and more depraved. But Kate's character was resisting, hard though it was. She had watched her sisters having all sorts of fun with a worker on the estate, a lad called Jed, who was not overly intelligent but very well endowed. Unable to endure the raunchy practices taking place before her eyes, she had gone off to her bedroom intent on indulging in her secret, solitary pleasuring.

The lights went down, and when they came up again Kate was on stage, pacing about and touching herself between the legs every so often through the thin material of her skirt.

'No, I mustn't,' she scolded herself, in a loud stage whisper. 'But my little pussy's going insane for something nice.'

She undid the fastener of her skirt, and the audience gasped in unison at the sight of her sheer blue panties and the wisps of pubic hair escaping from their sides. Her constant fingering had pushed the gusset into her yearning cleft, and even those in the balcony could make out clearly the outline of her engorged vaginal lips. Kate continued to pleasure herself, her fingers caressing and fondling through the panties.

'This is gorgeous,' she murmured.

She was stroking with uninhibited passion now, her teeth biting into her bottom lip as her hand stole wantonly down inside her knickers and a finger quickly inserted into her burning slit. She could hear a tide of heavy breathing rolling in from the auditorium as her finger set to work, the busy hand pushing out the front of her panties while she brought herself to a swift climax in front of a thousand strangers.

It was the most violent she had ever experienced, and it

left her with legs that could barely support her weight and lungs that were heaving in their efforts to drag in air.

The lights went down, and Kate left the stage as Trish, Jenny and Jed made their entrances. When the lights came up, the three were naked, and Trish was on her knees in front of Jed, studiously sucking his huge organ while he moaned and sighed.

'Oh, please,' he begged, in a strong country accent. 'Make it shoot.'

Trish took her mouth away and said, as if speaking to a child, 'Not yet, Jed. This lovely big shaft of yours has got to wait tonight. There's somewhere really special we want it to shoot into.'

The boy tried to push it back into her mouth, but she moved and he uttered angry gibberish as he stabbed ineffectually against her neck.

'Don't,' she said, laughing. 'I think we'd better wait for you to calm down. Then, while Jenny rubs her hot cunny on the backs of your legs, I'll rub your tool until you're all worked up again. Would you like that, Jed?'

'Yes,' he pouted. 'Play with it now.'

'I'll stroke it for you, shall I?' she said, in the same pandering tone. 'And you'll have to tell us again how it feels when you come. Okay?'

Jenny stood behind him and grasped the root of his shaft, all the while massaging the backs of his thighs with her pubic bush while Trish administered light caresses to the jerking cock.

'Tell us, Jed,' she said. 'How does it feel when we let you put this heavenly thing inside us?'

'It feels great,' he stammered, 'because you're both so tight. I think I'm going mad when it slides inside, and I can't stop shoving it in, again and again and again. And

what with you and Miss Jenny saying all those dirty things about how big it is and how it satisfies you so, well, a man can only take so much.

'That's when the end starts to tickle, and that only makes me want to go faster. But the faster I go, the more it tickles, but by this time I can't stop, I've got to keep shoving it in or I'll lose the tickle – and although I can't stand it, I don't want to lose it. So, I have to go quicker and quicker, until I shoot.'

'Oh, doesn't that sound like fun, Jenny? We like it when you tell us how it feels, Jed. Okay, now I'm going to rub it for you and while I'm doing that I'm going to tell you what we want you to do.'

She took hold of his cock and pulled on it with a lewd passion, her rhythm increasing until the boy closed his eyes and let out blissful moans that had the audience wriggling in their seats.

'Are you listening, Jed? Can you hear me?'

He managed a nod.

'We want you to show this to Miss Kate,' she said, with a wicked giggle. 'Oh, I can tell you like the idea, because you've gone even harder. Then, when you've shown her what you've got, we want you to tell her how we've tormented you, tell her we teased and wouldn't let you come. Say that you feel really awful, and ask her if she'll make you happy.'

She was rubbing hard now, and Jed's head was lolling from side to side. His performance was utterly realistic, and Thackeray knew then that his 'no sex during rehearsals' rule had paid off. The audience were totally enthralled and were almost willing the boy to come, but just as his climax approached, Trish stopped and let him go.

'Why didn't you finish it?' he cried, tears of frustration

springing into his eyes. 'I can't stand it any more. Why didn't you finish it off?'

'Go to Miss Kate,' she said, firmly. 'Go and ask Miss Kate to bring you off.'

The two girls laughed mischievously as he left the stage, his huge shoulders hunched with despair.

'Our dear sister is in for the shock of her life, I fear,' Jenny remarked.

'Isn't she just?' Trish replied, with an impish grin.

The audience knew that the end of the play was near, and most were already on the edges of their seats. As soon as the lights came up to reveal Kate alone on the stage, a ripple of applause ran through the vast auditorium.

She was lounging in a towelling robe now, and her dress and underwear were thrown casually across the bed. The loud knock on the door made her jump.

'Come in,' she called.

When the naked Jed burst into her room, Kate let out a scream of surprise.

'Jed,' she mouthed, her eyes wide with horror. 'What on earth do you think you're doing?'

He blurted out his story, while she eyed the throbbing shaft between his legs.

'They tormented you like that? Oh, you poor thing,' she said, her tone highly sympathetic. 'But, Jed, you shouldn't listen to them, you could get yourself into real trouble.' Again her eyes feasted on his quivering shaft. 'I mean to say, whatever made you think I'd be willing to let anything sexual take place between us? You know I'm nothing at all like my sisters. I . . . I could report you to the police.'

Although her tone was adamant and her resolve strong, her yearning crack was weak and it rose up and demanded

to be satisfied as she sat mesmerized by the beautiful sight of his unclothed body.

'I don't know why I let them talk me into it, Miss Kate,' he stuttered. 'They just got me so worked up, that's all, and I didn't know what I was doing. And I've always fancied you, see? I stand sometimes and look at your knickers when they're on the washing line. And my cock always goes rock hard when I think about how nice they'd look on you.'

'Jed,' she cautioned, rapidly, 'you shouldn't be telling me this.'

'I can only apologize, Miss Kate,' he said, his cheeks reddening with shame. 'I suppose I'll get the sack now, will I?'

She gave him a reassuring smile. 'No, Jed, I shouldn't think so for a minute. I'm very fond of sex, despite what my sisters must think, and to have a naked man in my room, telling me how much he fancies me, well, it's very flattering. And in any case, it was my sisters' intention to get you into trouble, so let's show them it hasn't worked, shall we?'

He nodded, but there was a quizzical expression on his face as Kate crossed to the bed and retrieved her panties.

'I never knew you liked looking at my knickers on the line,' she said, smiling. 'Do you ever think about what lies hidden beneath them?'

'Yes,' he admitted straightaway. 'And I think about you taking them off, as well.'

She let out a teasing laugh. 'Oh, poor Jed, no wonder you get yourself all horny. And I must admit you're making me feel horny, too.'

She ran the panties under his nostrils, and thrilled at his blissful expression. 'That's how they smell when I've been wearing them all day.'

Jed inhaled again the heady perfume, and his handsome face fell when the panties were taken away.

'Now, I'll let you keep this pair, if you like.'

She opened the dressing gown just long enough for the audience to get a tantalizing glimpse of her pussy hair while she wiped the silky panties along her wet crack, and then she turned back to the boy.

'There, now they're covered with my love juice.' One again they were put to his nostrils. 'Do they smell even better, now?'

'Oh, yes,' he said, breathing in the yeasty aroma.

The panties were traced around his mouth, dragging erotic sounds from his throat, and then the wet gusset was pushed between his earnest lips so that he could suck on it.

'You've got such a big cock, Jed. I really can't keep my hands off it a moment longer.'

Kate began to fondle him, first of all toying with his bulging testicles and then sliding her fingers over his pulsating shaft. Jed was begging her to rub it for him, pleading with her to feel him properly. With a sexy light in her beautiful eyes, she took the saturated knickers and wrapped them around his hardness. Then, very slowly, she slid them to and fro, egged on by his shouts of ecstasy. And with her free hand she opened her dressing gown and displayed herself to him.

'There you are, Jed, that's what I let a man have whenever I feel like a good screw.'

The vision of her hairy patch pushed him over the brink, and his whole body shuddered and shook as he ejaculated into her palm.

'Oh, good boy, Jed,' she said, softly. 'Think about what you'd really like to do to me, and enjoy your come.'

Rather than bringing any relief to the boy, his orgasm seemed to heighten his arousal, and there was a demented look on his face as his rough hands pulled the dressing gown from her delicate body. He began to growl when he got his first glimpse of her nakedness, and he drooled at the sight of her swelling breasts and the pouting lips of her sex.

'Now, Jed, I want you to take my little cunt. Take it like a real man should.'

He pushed her back against the wall, all the time whimpering with unfulfilled lust. They were both so eager for full sex now, and Kate wasted no time in spreading her legs. But, even standing on tip-toe, she was not tall enough to allow his quivering member to find her welcoming hole.

'Oh, Jed, it won't go in,' she called out in exasperation. 'Let me bend over for you.'

He was trying to enter her even before she was fully bent over, his eager tip sliding between her glistening buttocks.

'Please . . . please,' he babbled, over and over again.

But then the head of his jerking cock touched her nest, and Kate reached behind to guide him to his final destination. He thrust hard, and was fully installed within a second.

'Your knob's so big, Jed, it's really stretching my poor little pussy,' she groaned. 'It's so big that it hurts, but I want it so much . . . so very much.'

They were positioned in profile to the audience, so that everyone had a perfect view of Jed's energetic penis jabbing into her, then pulling back and thrusting forward once more. Neither of them were in any hurry to bring this amorous scene to an end, and their cries of passion were in no way made for the benefit of the onlookers.

Kate climaxed three times in all, and an excited hum went through the audience when Jed's cock began to swell and his balls began to rise. He was no longer an actor playing a part, but a real man led by his amorous cock. His thrusts were harsh and powerful, and they almost brought Kate to her knees, but she withstood the onslaught and helped him towards his rapturous moment.

They were both lost in the wanton act, both letting out abandoned cries when Kate reached out for the wall and placed her palms against it, steeling herself for the end of his totally rampant fuck.

'Go on, really give it to me,' she urged, her senses reeling as his shaft expanded deep within her middle, stretching her grateful passage more than it had ever been stretched before.

'Oh, brilliant fuck,' she loudly enthused. 'It's a brilliant fuck.'

Jed's body went rigid, and then he was coming inside her. Almost at once he withdrew, so that everyone could see the hot sperm flying from his tip.

The audience rose to its feet as one, their tumultuous applause and their appreciative cheers ringing loud in the actors' ears. Kate straightened up and then, grabbing Jed's still shooting shaft, she rubbed it feverishly, milking every last ounce of come from his voluptuous balls.

The standing ovation, which lasted long after the house lights came up, was truly deafening, and the company was forced, quite happily, to take six curtain calls. Kate and Jed were still naked, and a number of excited women rushed on to the stage and stood before them, clapping and shouting their admiration.

Jed still had a hold of Kate's hand when they left the stage. In the wings, he gazed down and smiled at her.

'Thanks,' he said. 'I don't know how much of that was acting—'

'None,' she assured him, eagerly. 'I've honestly never enjoyed a fuck as much as that.'

'Pity it's not a week's run,' he said, grinning.

Kate let out a lilting laugh. 'If it was, I wouldn't be able to stand up by the end of it.'

Thackeray rushed backstage, kissing and congratulating everyone, but quickly working his way towards Kate.

'Darling,' he gushed. 'What a truly divine performance. I just knew you had it in you.'

'*I* knew I had it in me, I can tell you,' she quipped. 'And I wouldn't mind it there again.'

He roared with laughter, and then sobered. 'Actually, there might be a possibility of that. You see, there was a very rich Arab in the audience tonight, and he's asked me for a big favour. If you help me out, I'll give you the address that Wilson went to when he left here.'

'What does he want me to do?' she asked, wearily.

CHAPTER 31

Kate and Jed had been told to wait in one of the bedrooms. They were still unclothed, and had been given strict orders not to shower or wash. After about ten minutes they heard urgent footsteps approaching along the corridor, and then two Arab gentlemen came into the room, closely followed by a woman. The largest of the men – a bulky giant with huge muscles that spoilt the cut of his expensive business suit – stood at the side of the door, his massive arms folded.

'Our bodyguard,' the other man explained. 'Do not worry, he will not interfere in any way.'

The wealthy Arab was swarthy, with a large hooked nose. His clothes, and those of his wife, were of Western style and thoroughly modern.

Harrods' finest, Kate thought enviously, before remembering that she too could afford such sumptuous outfits as that which graced the woman's perfect figure.

The woman appeared timid and for the most part she stared at the carpet, only occasionally sneaking a glance at Jed's half-erect penis. She was perhaps ten years younger than the man, and was tall and slim with a dusky maiden's appeal.

'Now,' the Arab said, rubbing his large hands together. 'I don't know what you've been told, but my wife and I both

enjoyed the play, and it most definitely had the desired effect on our loins, believe me. My wife likes sex to be energetic, just as yours was on stage, while I enjoy the gentler arts of the mouth and hands to give me pleasure. In view of that, we find it convenient to get other people to supply us with our needs. In our own country we are regarded as royalty, and therefore cannot afford to be involved in any scandals, so I will offer you both one hundred thousand pounds to fulfil our desires and afterwards keep your mouths well and truly shut.'

Jed's jaw hung open in disbelief, and he glanced towards Kate who was swallowing hard, her large eyes blinking rapidly.

'Do you want us all to perform in the same room?' Jed asked, at last finding his voice.

The man smiled. 'Yes, you see, that is a large part of our satisfaction. My wife likes sex, but unfortunately it is a custom in our country that a woman should not be seen to enjoy it. So, she may appear to lack passion, but she will be wholly pleased with what you have for her.'

His eyes narrowed sharply as they focused on Jed. 'So, that is it. If you both agree, we will disrobe and proceed.'

'Yes ... yes, I agree,' Jed was quick to say, while Kate merely nodded her willingness.

They shuffled awkwardly on the spot while the man and his luscious wife undressed. The man did so with great nonchalance, taking off his suit and carefully folding the trousers before placing them tidily on the end of the bed. Then he removed his shirt and tie with equal care, and last of all discarded his boxer shorts.

His dark shaft was fully erect, its taut skin smooth and shiny. It was nowhere near as big as Jed's, but still a respectable seven inches. Kate would have no complaints

when this extraordinary scenario was over, she was certain of that.

By this time his wife was down to her bra and panties.
She licked her lips, her tongue running over them in a
slow, sensuous manner, and then reached behind to undo
her bra and slip it off. Her breasts were firm and jutting,
her dusky skin positively gleaming in the flattering light
from the overhead chandelier.

Jed inhaled sharply, his penis now fully erect and throbbing, the veins on its surface jumping as hot blood coursed
through them.

'How nice it must be to have a cannon that can fire its
shot so many times in one evening,' the man said, with a
tinge of regret in his voice. 'Alas, when a man passes
fifty . . .'

He shrugged, and the sight was so pitiful that Kate's
heart went out to him. She suddenly saw the problem.
The woman was so much younger than her husband and
obviously highly sexed, but at the same time was afraid to
show too much passion when with another man for fear of
offending him.

'Your wife has a beautiful body,' she remarked. 'I would
very much like to see her enjoying sex fun before you and
I indulge ourselves. That would enable me to heighten
your pleasure.'

'Alas,' the Arab said, 'sex is something that neither of
us fully enjoy any longer. It is merely a release that our
bodies tell us we need every so often.'

'Nonsense,' Kate exclaimed. 'Will you put yourselves
into our hands for just one hour? Will you let us teach you
how to enjoy the pleasures of the flesh once again?'

'Please let us try this, Omar.' The woman's voice, which
had been unheard until now, was as delectable as her

shape. 'I long to use all of those dirty words that we are forbidden to use in our own country.'

Her husband seemed to be thinking it over, his dark eyes flashing.

'All right,' he said, at last. 'I will allow it, but only this one time.'

Kate rang for Morgan who immediately delivered brandy, glasses, and a giant-sized carton of fresh cream, gliding between the group as silently and unobtrusively as a ghost.

Jed took the woman's arm and led her to the centre of the room. She was as nervous as a tiny kitten, and equally as sweet. Speaking almost in a whisper, so as not to frighten her, he asked for her name. Her response was meek, for she was unused to speaking to males.

'My name is Salome,' she said, her amazing eyes still cast to the floor.

'Salome . . . what a fantastic name! Well, Salome,' Jed said gently, collecting the tub of fresh cream, 'I would like to do something a little unusual.'

Kate had settled with Omar on large cushions that were strewn around the perimeter of the room. He was sitting cross-legged, and she took up his penis and stroked it tenderly, her fingertips lightly running along its whole length while they watched the other two.

Jed dipped his finger into the cream and applied a mountain of it to each of Salome's nipples. She shivered at his touch and at the coldness of the cream which clung precariously to the jewels of her breasts while she shot a hesitant glance towards her husband, eager for his approval. He nodded his consent and the woman visibly relaxed.

Still loath to alarm this most timid of females, Jed very

slowly bent forward and gently, with almost imperceptible gestures, licked the creamy hills at her bosom, his tongue dipping into the rich banquet and tormenting now and then the sensitive tips of her tempting buds. She threw back her head and emitted a surprised gasp, her hand automatically reaching for his thick shaft, but stopping just short of it.

'Why don't you play with it, if that's what you want?' he coaxed. 'Kate's playing with your husband's – see?'

With a deep sigh she gripped him, relishing the feel of his handsome cock, a feel that had always been denied her. Not only was she an Arab woman, but an Arab of royal distinction, and therefore the pleasures of the flesh were of small importance when compared with the many and varied duties that went with her public office.

'God, you're gorgeous,' Jed breathed, finishing his feast and reaching once again for the cream. 'Let's do something that's really dirty now, shall we?'

'Let's,' she smiled, seemingly unable to leave his weapon alone.

He scooped a large amount of the cream on to his finger and pulled at the elastic of her panties.

'We'll cover your hairy slit with it,' he told her, his hand delving down into her knickers and spreading the cool substance along her hot trench.

Salome giggled and squirmed at first, but gave a sharp intake of breath when he started to pay attention to her quaking clitoris.

'I can smell how aroused you were while watching the play,' he said, his voice husky. 'It's made you all wet and ready for sex.'

When he withdrew his hand and let go of her panties, her pouting expression told Jed loudly of her disapproval.

'Don't worry, there's plenty more to come,' he said. 'What I'm going to do is suck the cream through your wet knickers. That way I'll be able to taste your juices at the same time.'

He lay on the floor and instructed her to squat over his face. She seemed reluctant at first but her jumping crack was making its presence felt so, with movements that were utterly graceful, she lowered herself upon him.

Jed was as expert at this manoeuvre as he was with a straightforward fuck, and Salome moaned with delight as he sucked the cream through the material of her panties, his hot breath causing a profusion of blood to come rushing to her vaginal lips which were already desperate for stimulation. Soon she was panting with a mounting desire that she had never before experienced.

Omar's breath had also quickened, and Kate continued to roll the shaft of his throbbing penis between her palms, every so often delving into her wet crack to collect her love juices, which were speedily transferred to the bucking cock. She crouched beside him, keeping one eye on Jed and Salome. Tiny waves of excitement were coursing through her groin as she watched the woman pull her gusset aside.

'Lick it clean for me,' she begged. And from the sounds that left her lips, it was clear that Jed obeyed her breathless command immediately.

When he had finished, she rose to her feet and took her panties right off. Her pubic hair was still thick with cream and Jed automatically stooped to suck it off, but she clamped a hand over her hairy bush and thwarted his attempt.

'No, I want your prick in my pussy,' she breathed.

Such words, leaving so beautiful a mouth, sounded

unbelievably dirty, and the fact that this was probably the first time she had dared to utter them made them more so.

Omar was holding his breath, and Kate knew it was time for her mouth to get busy. Managing to tear her eyes away from his wife who was now lying on the floor with her legs spread wide and imploring Jed to ride her, she gave her full attention to his cock. She worked her way between his legs and started by kissing his bulging tip. He exhaled and, to the accompaniment of Salome's sexy sighs, she ran her tongue along the hilly underside of his penis until his thighs were trembling rapidly.

'Oh, that is good,' Salome cried out. 'Rub your tip against my clit. That is what I have always wanted, but have never dared to ask for.'

Her breathless panting seemed to fill the room, and Kate noticed that the bodyguard had needed to loosen his tie and unbutton his shirt at the collar.

Salome continued to cry out, the new sensations in her crack effectively chasing away decades of restraint.

'Now shove your big cock into me,' she commanded. 'My cunt cannot wait any longer.'

Kate sucked Omar deep into her mouth, closing her soft lips around him tightly, to resemble a grasping vagina, and all the while she fondled his quite heavenly balls. His head lolled back, but his eyes remained firmly fixed on his wife, who was thrilling to Jed's expert attention. Kate was sucking harder and faster, sliding her hand up to tease his arse. Omar moaned and shifted his position to give her better access to his sensitive opening.

'Faster, Jed, faster,' Salome was begging. 'My little crack is on fire. It has never felt like this before.'

Kate could hear them thrashing about, flesh hitting flesh, and guessed from the sounds that Salome was quite

actively pushing back as her orgasm moved ever nearer.

'I have come,' she shrieked, in an incredulous tone. 'I have come.'

Omar's shaft was being treated to a most spectacular mouthing now. Kate was sucking rapidly and rubbing his shaft, which glistened with her saliva. She gathered some of it up and slipped it between his writhing buttocks, hoping to break through the man's inhibitions and get him to react. His legs were shaking violently, but still he maintained an outward show of composure, while his wife had totally lost hers.

'Yes, yes, yes,' she was screaming out. 'Shoot your come into my tight little hole.'

At the sound of Salome's spirited outburst, Omar's control was finally beginning to erode. His breathing became rapid while he watched his wife still squirming and bucking beneath Jed, both of them in the throes of mutual orgasm. Kate's wet finger probed his arse while she sucked avidly and continued to work his tool with her hand.

He murmured something in Arabic which she didn't understand, and then his entire body went rigid and he started to pant like a winded animal.

'That is it,' he cried out. 'I am going to come.'

His passionate cry excited Kate beyond all expectations, and she sobbed with joy when his lovely sperm exploded in her throat. She swallowed eagerly, her contracting throat muscles teasing his animated tip beyond the Arab's wildest dreams and causing his climax to last for what felt like an eternity.

No one moved until the erotic sounds of heavy breathing – the bodyguard's included – began to subside. Then Kate struggled to her feet, still licking sweet sperm from her lips.

'I think it would be most proper for you to dress now,' Omar instructed his wife.

'Whatever you say, my love,' she said, back to her servile ways. 'I will do so immediately.'

'Thank you, thank you both,' he said to Jed and Kate, with as much passion as if he were thanking them for a cup of coffee.

He crossed to the bed, the hefty muscles on his back rippling with every move, and retrieved three envelopes from the inside pocket of his jacket.

'As promised,' he said, turning back, 'you both have a cheque for one hundred thousand pounds for your services. And in the third envelope, Miss Highlands, is an address which Thackeray asked me to pass on.'

CHAPTER 32

The Grange. The very name spoke of opulent wealth, and the house more than lived up to the promise. Set in rolling open countryside, about ten miles from the city, it was of Tudor origins, its white façade criss-crossed with black timbers. Kate had difficulty in thinking that anything seedy or untoward could happen there.

She rang the front door bell and stepped back outside the porch to admire the climbing roses which littered its walls. Presently, the door was opened by a good-looking man. He was around early forties, and was tall with brown hair that fell sexily over his forehead.

'I'm Kate Highlands,' she said, with a friendly smile. 'I believe I'm expected.'

'Kate,' the man said, smiling back and offering his hand. 'I'm Lance Devlin.'

His handshake was warm and lingering.

'Come in, why don't you?' He stood aside and allowed her to enter the hall. 'I don't suppose this is the time to beat about the bush, so I'll get straight to the point. You're here on a favour for favour basis. If I tell you where Laurence Wilson is—'

'I'll have to drop my knickers for you,' she interjected, sharply.

He let out a boyish chuckle, and allowed his gaze to roam over her body.

'Quite,' he said, 'and I do find the way in which you phrased the offer extremely tempting. Come through into the lounge.'

He led her into a cosy room that was decorated and furnished in an olde worlde fashion.

'Very nice,' she remarked, glancing around as she took a seat beside the inglenook fireplace. 'Now, let's get this straight – you say that you have need of my body, and I take it the deal involves my having to remove my underwear for others to dip their fingers – among other things – into my honey pot.'

He let out an infectious laugh, and settled himself in the seat opposite.

'Yes, spot on,' he said. 'My wife, for one.'

Kate's eyebrows rose questioningly.

'I deal in gold bullion,' he explained. 'The social side of my life is very important to my business, and the more adventurous of my clients like to be entertained in a world where anything goes. I have to be pretty inventive, and the more outrageous the amusement the happier my clients are. One of our regular playtimes involves our wives having a little girl-to-girl fun in front of their husbands.'

'And your wife isn't willing to go that far – is that it?'

He nodded. 'Actually, she refuses point blank. Oh, don't get me wrong, she loves sex and throws herself into it wholeheartedly, both with me and with my male clients. But as for girls – she strongly draws the line there.'

Kate took time to digest this.

'Earlier on you said your wife, for one, would be using my body. So that means there are others.'

'Yes, Kate. My wife harbours a fantasy about the stable lad—'

'Oh, Christ, not another virgin who needs to be broken in,' she interjected, wearily. 'I've done that so many times during my search for Wilson, that I'm surprised there are any virgins left in this country.'

'No, it's not that,' he assured her. 'The boy's not a virgin. I just want you to find a way for my wife to enjoy herself with him.'

'So, you want me to seduce your wife, then enter into a game in the stables – and for what? I think you'd better tell me what I'll be getting out of it. More, I hope, than where Wilson went when he left here.'

'Much more,' he said, leaning forward. 'I can send you directly to the man who knows where Wilson is now. He'll tell you on the same day you carry out your favour for me.'

'After I've removed my knickers for him, no doubt.'

'Probably,' he said, grinning. 'But I promise you'll know all on the same day, Kate.'

She thought about the one million pounds, plus the two hundred thousand she had so far made from selling her body.

'You're not willing to pay me a fee for this, I suppose?'

'No,' he said, slowly shaking his head. 'But I've noticed that the Mini you drive has seen better days. I could make you a present of a brand new Jaguar that's surplus to requirements – if you add just one more favour to your list, that is.'

'And that would be what?'

'That you help me to live out a fantasy of my own.'

She inclined her head. 'You've just made yourself a deal.'

* * *

Devlin's wife, Angela, was not what Kate had expected. She was in her late thirties, sophisticated and elegant, but great fun to be with. In fact, Kate hit it off with her straight away; and it was not hard to imagine that her husband's male clients would be well pleased to have her administering to them. She was tall, with huge breasts that in no way sagged, an impossibly slim waist, and wide hips that swayed invitingly when she walked.

After dinner, while her husband was dealing with some business, she invited Kate into the drawing room for a drink. Brandy was poured, and soon her cultured veneer began to wash away under its influence.

'I know why you're here,' Angela told her. 'You're supposed to seduce me.'

Kate laughed. 'That's one of the reasons. And if you let me, you won't be sorry, I'm the best screw there is.'

'And all this time I thought I was,' Angela giggled. 'Huh . . . men. All they think about is their dicks. They never dream of wondering what a woman might want from sex.'

Kate sipped her drink. 'That being?'

'Oh, I don't know.' She stretched out on the sofa, her thoughts wandering. 'Fun, I suppose, and adventure. It shouldn't always be a case of dick up pussy until you both come. I'd really like something different.'

'Like what?' Kate probed, hoping that the woman would say girl-fun.

'Look, if I tell you, promise you won't repeat it.'

'Of course I promise,' Kate smiled. 'Who would I tell anyway? It's none of my business what you daydream about.'

'Well, the thing is, we keep six horses here, and one of the stable lads . . .' She mimed a swoon. 'I'd simply love to offer him sex, really filthy illicit sex, just to see what he'd do.'

'Don't you know?' Kate said, her eyes widening. 'He'd unzip his trousers and take his prick out like a shot.'

'I suppose I already knew that,' Angela said, before draining her glass. 'But I'd really tease him first. Oh, I know what I mean, but I can't explain it.'

'Why don't we do it?' Kate suggested. 'And then you can show me.'

Angela's eyes sparkled. 'All right, but we'll have to think of something he can eavesdrop on, just to get him going.'

I know just the thing, Kate thought, the very thing.

CHAPTER 33

Kate wondered whether four-poster beds were set to become a fixture in her life. The guest room at The Grange had a huge one installed in it, and she spent an extremely comfortable first night cocooned within its cosy confines. After showering in the en suite bathroom, she prepared to go horse riding with Angela over the rolling hills of the surrounding countryside.

Kate had imagined Dave Perry, the chosen stable hand, to be gawky and countrified, inexperienced and boyish, so she was happily surprised at her first sight of him. He was well over six feet tall, with broad shoulders and pleasing, sensitive features. He was a little shy and withdrawn, admittedly, but was both articulate and hugely polite.

The women were wearing tight white blouses and their black jodhpurs fitted like a second skin, highlighting the delightful clefts between their legs. The young man immediately showed immense if somewhat surreptitious interest in their bodies, and Kate let out a relieved breath for it was obvious that he would be a positive walk-over. When the horses were saddled and mounted, Dave led them out into the yard.

'Well, what do you think of him?' Angela whispered, as they headed for the fields at a snail's pace.

'My little slit, it say "yes",' Kate laughed, giving her the thumbs-up sign.

They rode for an hour, and by that time both the women and their horses were bathed in sweat. At the edge of a small copse they dismounted and secured the animals to a tree.

'Riding always makes me horny,' Angela said as she stretched out on the grass and lit two cigarettes. 'It must be because of what rubs against the saddle.'

Kate giggled and accepted the proffered cigarette. 'You seem like a very sexy lady to me.'

'Oh, I am. Lance and I have a very open marriage, and it works brilliantly. One thing I always say is, there's nothing quite like a good bunk up. Do you know, three of my son's friends have had me – they have little technique but so much enthusiasm. Lance's always trying to get me into bed with his clients' wives—'

'But you don't fancy it?' Kate asked lightly, as she stubbed the cigarette out on the hard ground.

'Not really,' she said, looking directly at Kate's thighs. 'But then I think, am I really against it, or is being pressured into doing it putting me off?'

'Shall we start back?' Kate said, determined not to apply any pressure.

They arrived back at the stables and chatted with Dave for about ten minutes before going off to Kate's room. Once there, Angela proved straightaway that she was not in the least bit shy by stripping off completely after declaring her intention to shower. Kate watched avidly while the woman threw off her blouse and jodhpurs. Her shapely breasts were firm, and they glistened with sweat which trickled down over her flat stomach.

When she moved to take off her panties, Kate took a

deep breath and prepared herself for that first peek at the treasures of her crotch. Then that breath escaped on a highly appreciative sigh, for the woman's pubic hair was clipped quite short and did little to conceal her proud, pouting lips and the interesting dip between them. Kate could smell the vagina's alluring scent, and her own crack promptly responded by jumping and twitching within her tight jodhpurs.

'You look nice,' she remarked pointedly, while removing her own clothes.

When she too was naked tiny waves of pleasure shot through Kate's body for she noticed that Angela was glancing repeatedly at her luscious breasts and at the copious bush that protected her slit.

'So do you,' Angela said eventually, in a low throaty tone. 'Maybe we should dry each other off after we've taken our showers.'

'We could, or I could towel you down now,' Kate flirted. 'I could get all of that nasty perspiration off your body, and then the soap would lather more easily.'

'All right,' Angela said, her eyes coyly lowered. 'But I'm not going to do anything, you understand. I just want to have a giggle.'

'Understood,' she said, laughing inwardly as she hurried into the bathroom for a large, fluffy pink towel.

Angela stood stiffly to attention while Kate rubbed vigorously at her back, towelling the flawless skin with an easy, impartial zest. Her shoulders were dried next, and then the towel was taken down to the small of her back and on to her buttocks. It was then that the woman's breath began to quicken.

'Right, now for the front,' Kate said, reaching from behind to rub Angela's breasts, a playful smile coming to

her lips when she felt the nipples harden.

Every so often she made sure that her pubic bush lightly touched the backs of Angela's legs, the coarse hair tantalizing the skin. And then she was down on her knees, innocently running the towel up the woman's legs, but lingering at the top and brushing between her open thighs. Finally she stood up.

'That's you all done,' she said, laughing inwardly at the disappointment so evident on Angela's face. 'Unless you want me to wipe between your legs, that is.'

'Yes, I do,' she said, the words hardly audible. 'That's where I feel really filthy – all sweaty and hot.'

'Let me come round to the front, then,' Kate said brightly, 'so that I can see what I'm doing.'

Hoping to conceal her own spiralling arousal, Kate positioned herself in front of the woman, making sure that their breasts touched often as she stroked the towel between her legs, rubbing the fluffy material backwards and forwards over her pubic bush.

Angela let out a shuddering sigh, and when Kate turned to give her a smile their lips came together almost of their own volition. The kiss was light, a fleeting encounter, but when Angela responded it became long and lingering, their tongues happily meeting as they delved.

The towel slipped from Kate's grasp, and her fingers went immediately to Angela's yearning sex, where they explored the velvet skin with an eagerness that betrayed her own hot desires.

'You've got a beautiful cunt,' she whispered when the fiery kiss ended.

'Will you play with it properly?' the woman asked, her tone urgent.

'Don't be in such a hurry,' Kate cautioned. 'Let's take

our time. Why don't you feel mine to see if you like it?'

She spread her legs and her eyes implored Angela to feel her riches. Already her love oil was flowing and moistening the insides of her tremulous thighs.

'It's fantastic,' Angela enthused in a throaty voice. 'You're so bushy and so wet. I couldn't drag my eyes away from it.'

Kate's free hand stole behind the woman's back and took to stroking her buttocks with a gentle motion, making her whole body shiver and shake.

'This is all so exciting for me,' Kate murmured. 'I'll be the first woman ever to finger and lick your delicious little pussy.'

'Do it to me, now,' Angela implored. 'I can't wait much longer. I've never felt so horny.'

'Sit on the sofa, then, so I can get to you properly.'

The woman ran to the sofa and almost flung herself on to it, bringing her heels up onto the seat with a hasty keenness and opening her legs wide. Kate knelt before her and started to tease the opening of her crack with a fingertip while her hot breath played on the wet lips until they parted willingly to reveal the glistening love bud at their heart.

'You smell divine,' she said, exhaling sharply and making Angela squirm. 'I want to drink your sex juice.'

When the words were out, her tongue lapped at the clitoris and her finger eased itself into the tight love channel and masturbated with such expertise that Angela was soon grunting with delight.

Kate knew it would not be long before she climaxed, and decided there and then to bring it about rapidly. By the time I'm finished, she thought, Angela won't know what's hit her. She rubbed the love bud hard and fast

while her tongue probed into the sweet-smelling chamber beneath it.

'I'm coming,' Angela cried out. 'I can feel myself spurting.'

She grabbed the back of Kate's head, fearing that she would take away those teasing lips before her satisfaction was complete, and then lay there howling with pleasure when the full force of the stupendous orgasm raged throughout her groin. Afterwards she lay on the sofa, her eyes aglow.

'That was really wonderful, Kate. Do you want me to do the same for you?'

'Not yet. Let's save it, shall we? Perhaps we could use it to get you laid by Dave.' She grinned. 'We could take a shower together, though.'

The idea certainly appealed to the woman, and she immediately pulled Kate towards the bathroom and turned on the shower. They stepped inside, holding hands and giggling as the warm water tumbled and hissed its way over their shapely contours. Turning their faces towards the gushing jet they lathered the soap, and then Kate directed the water away from themselves while they spread the perfumed bubbles over each other's bodies, Angela all the while taking her lead from Kate.

First their breasts were covered with the white foam, their hands loitering longer than was necessary, massaging and sliding around in circles, straying down onto their stomachs and enjoying the feel of wet, soap-covered flesh. Then they washed each other's bottoms, lathering the soap until it became a frothing mass, exchanging grins at first but then whimpering at the feel of busy fingers between their buttocks. Simultaneously their hands were attracted to the flattened hair at their groins, and they shampooed the pubic forests until both were breathing heavily.

Kate took the shower head from its holder with fingers that were shaking slightly, and she directed the water over Angela's body, laughing raucously when the woman shrieked with joy at the water jet pointing towards her nipples.

On Kate's instructions she turned her back and leant forward. Then, once in position, Kate aimed the hot water between her legs and over her buttocks. Angela sighed with pleasure while it played on and stimulated her hairy nest and anus.

There was a high flush on her face when Angela started to wash Kate and she never missed a chance to touch her, chasing away the soap with eager hands and thrilling at the feel of her goose-pimpled flesh. The shower jet had felt so good between her legs and she now returned the pleasure, aiming the harsh flow directly onto Kate's soapy crack.

At first Kate laughed and screamed with amusement, but then the feeling began to arouse her and she pushed her vagina against the rough face of the shower head, rubbing against the raised holes from where the water flowed.

'God, this is really getting me going,' she breathed. 'It's gorgeous.'

'You are a filthy cow,' Angela said, with a note of admiration in her voice.

'I love my cunt,' Kate said. 'And I like to find new ways of making it happy.'

When she had finished her novel masturbation, Angela turned off the water, and said, 'Well, I think we've done all we can with a shower head.'

'I wouldn't agree with that,' Kate replied, taking it from her.

She promptly positioned it at the entrance to Angela's vagina, bringing an alarmed shriek from the woman's lips.

'Oh, no, Kate, not that.' But even as the words were spoken, she was spreading her legs. 'It's too big to go in, surely?'

Kate nudged at Angela's tight tunnel and gently worked the shower head inside.

'How does it feel?'

'Oh, Kate, it feels so good . . . so big and hard.'

With a lewd expression brightening her features, she worked her body to and fro.

'Just like Dave's tool will be when he shoves it up you,' Kate intoned. 'After he's watched me seduce you in the stable, he'll go mad for what you've got for him.'

'I'm coming again,' the woman yelled, moving faster now that the shower head could slide easily along her lubricated tunnel.

She stopped suddenly, let out an ecstatic cry, and then leant back against the wall tiles, totally breathless.

Kate grinned. 'Now we've definitely done everything there is to do with a shower head.'

CHAPTER 34

It was late evening when they wandered across to the stables. Dave looked gorgeous; he was stripped to the waist, and his powerful chest muscles moved sexily as he forked hay into one of the stalls. The girls passed him, their eyes flirting with his, and Kate felt the familiar stirring in her loins as they stopped in the shadows at the end of the block.

'Dave,' Angela called, signalling for him to join them.

The boy put down the pitch fork and sauntered over.

'Kate and I came in here to have some fun,' she said, completely matter of fact. 'Now, I'm sure you won't tell on us, but would you mind keeping guard?'

Confusion clouded his face. 'What? You mean you're going to—?'

His words tapered off when Kate started to undress, deliberately taking her time, her movements kittenish and highly enticing.

'We're going to have a little frolic,' she said as she pushed her tight skirt to the ground.

Dave was eyeing her underwear as a thirsty man would a long cool drink, and then his head swivelled round, his expression one of total disbelief when Angela pulled off her dress.

'Don't look so worried,' Kate soothed. 'Actually, we had

a little bet. Angela reckons that if you saw us having fun and knew we were both available for a good screw, you wouldn't take advantage because you're too nice. But I said, once you saw our hairy cracks you'd react just like any other man.'

Dave's eyes nearly popped out of their sockets when their bras were removed. Kate just smiled, and stood stroking her breasts in front of him.

'Why don't you take your jeans off?' she murmured.

With his gaze still pinned to their wondrous nipples, Dave unfastened his jeans and stood rigid while the girls helped him out of them. His big tool was making the front of his boxer shorts stand out, and his hand went involuntarily to the bulge.

'That's better,' Kate said. 'Now I think it's time to show our pussies, Angela. So, whose does Dave want to see first?'

'Both of them,' he stammered.

'I don't know – two women who can't wait to drop their knickers for you,' Angela teased. 'You are a lucky man.'

She pushed her panties down around her knees, and flashed him a provocative smile. 'That's mine, Dave, and it just loves cock. Kate's been playing with me all afternoon, but now I'm so ready for a man, I hurt.'

Kate wasted no time in taking off her knickers and displaying herself. Dave's eyes strayed from one hairy patch to the other, his breathing now ragged, the swelling in his shorts even larger.

Kate pouted. 'I'm beginning to think you were right, Angela. He's not going to take advantage of us,' she said, hitching herself up on the side of a stall and opening her legs wide. 'Never mind, though, you did promise you'd lick my pussy for me, so I'll just have to make do with that, I suppose.'

Angela hurriedly stepped out of her knickers then knelt in front of Kate and planted kisses on her pubic bush. Dave watched the brazen display for several minutes, tampering with his cock more eagerly when Kate's head lolled from side to side, and groaning with desire when she gasped repeatedly in response to Angela's rough tongue finding her clitoris. Then her probing fingers were exploring Kate's sex channel and her sumptuous breasts danced a delicious jig as she squirmed against the sweet agony.

'Oh, that's so good,' she cried out.

Dave was shuffling his feet and bending closer for a clearer view of Angela, hard at work between Kate's legs. He could see her three fingers sliding in and out of the wet crack, their slurping sounds filling the entire stable block.

Angela jumped to her feet, intent on finding a more comfortable position, and her bottom was thrust into the air. Managing to drag his gaze away from Kate's vagina, Dave studied the well-rounded buttocks, the sparse pubic undergrowth with the glistening dip in its middle.

'Take her, Dave. What's stopping you?'

Kate's husky voice made him jump, and he gulped when her meaning became clear.

'She thinks about you all the time, you know. She's told me she yearns for your cock – she can't think about anything else. Even when her husband's giving her a good stiff one, she closes her eyes and imagines he's you.'

Dave's hands were trembling as he pulled off his boxer shorts, and his huge, quivering shaft was obviously taken with the idea, but still he looked undecided.

'She's there for the taking,' Kate encouraged, her words almost choked by a fast-approaching orgasm. 'Angela will spread her legs really wide for you. She's really panting for some hot sex.'

There was a growl starting in Dave's throat as he lunged
forward and – just as Kate had predicted – Angela's legs
opened up for him. The raunchy way in which she
displayed her sex took him beyond the point of self-control,
and he aimed his tip at her entrance and thrust inside with
a loud grunt. His face was a picture of carnal bliss and the
sight of it, together with Angela's energetic tongue and
fingers, brought Kate to a shuddering climax.

She relaxed and, with her friend's head resting on her
still-jumping pussy, she settled back to watch Dave, who
was pounding away at her crack with apparently limitless
energy.

'I'm coming . . . I'm coming.'

Angela's hoarse voice was almost lost in Kate's hairy
bush, but the sound spurred Dave on. He pushed harder,
his shaft swelling and seeking out her pleasure zones, his
balls jumping and jerking as they prepared to spill their
hot seed into her velvet passage.

Kate tingled with delight when Angela's teeth sank
into the skin of her pubis for, although painful, the
sensation was highly erotic. And she giggled when the
woman gave a violent shudder as an electrifying orgasm
overtook her.

'That's it, Dave,' Angela yelled. 'I'm there. I'm there.'

In the second that those words were uttered Dave's
thrusting shaft exploded within her depths. He was almost
sobbing with exertion and ecstasy when he pulled out,
milky seed still jetting from his tip, and rubbed at the happy
cock until his balls could produce no more.

Angela straightened up and turned to watch him, holding herself between the legs, still savouring the beautiful
sensations. Kate stayed where she was on the side of the
stall, her legs still open, until Dave regained some degree

of control. His tool had begun to sag, to wilt, and Kate smiled inwardly.

'Come here, Dave,' she said.

Dazed, he approached and stood between her open legs. She touched his back, her fingers tracing along the line of his spine. Sensing what she wanted, he glanced down and frowned.

'But I've lost my hard-on,' he said, apologetically.

'That's all right,' she grinned. 'It'll go in.'

Taking a firm hold of his shrivelling shaft she placed it at the doors to her cavern. Her hips came forward and he sank into her. Immediately she started to work her powerful vaginal muscles, squeezing and massaging the flagging flesh while she whispered in his ear.

'Is this the first time you've had two cunts to play with at the same time?'

He nodded, and then let out a deep groan when her tongue flicked into his ear.

'You'll have to train up a bit, then, because from now on Angela's going to let you inside her knickers every day, and while I'm here I'll drop mine whenever you want.'

Kate thrilled at the feel of his cock coming to life in the far reaches of her tunnel, and she continued to egg him on in the same sexy whisper.

'We'll do anything you want. We'll suck you ... oh yes, I see you like that idea because you're really getting hard now. We'll suck your cock until it spurts in our mouths.'

Dave whimpered.

'Yes, until it spurts in our mouths,' she repeated, working her hips to and fro until she felt his foreskin pull back and his bulging tip emerge. 'Oh, super, now you're ready to screw me.'

He was slower this time, using long leisurely strokes

that made her moan and cry out. Angela stood beside them, her close presence adding to the lewdness of the scene.

'Go on, Dave, give it to her faster,' she breathed. 'Really screw her, Dave.'

He increased his rhythm, pushing into her hard, telling her how tight she was and how good it felt. Finally, Kate could take no more and she gave in to a stupendous climax, panting and screaming as she pushed back, her jerky movements bringing on a second powerful orgasm.

She gripped his young buttocks and urged him on. Indeed, her noisy encouragement was disturbing the horses, and they stamped their hooves and whinnied with alarm. Angela, however, was deaf to the scuffles as she lightly squeezed his aching testicles while she too coaxed him to climax.

Dave began to moan, the feelings at the end of his shaft driving all else from his mind. And then he was shooting, his whole body trembling and shaking while Angela's frisky hand helped to milk him.

'I think I can safely say I've won the bet,' Kate grinned.

CHAPTER 35

The next day Lance Devlin presented Kate with a dark grey Jaguar car.

'Nice,' she exclaimed, circling the vehicle and shivering with excitement. 'It's really nice.'

'Fancy a test spin in it?'

His tone of voice told her loudly that some time during the drive she would be expected to remove her panties and earn the car.

She laughed. 'Why not?'

After driving a battered Mini for so many years, the Jaguar was a dream come true. Its leather upholstery hugged her body, and its engine's purr was hardly audible. After a pleasant hour, driving along the leafy lanes, she had mastered the controls and was already feeling at home behind the wheel. Her skirt had ridden up around her thighs, and Devlin kept glancing at her stocking tops with their sexy pink suspenders.

'I had sex for the first time in the back of a car,' he said, reflectively. 'So many years ago—'

'And you'd like to recapture the magic,' she grinned. 'So I'd better look for somewhere to pull over.'

'It's more than that,' he admitted after a time. 'She was a married woman with a lot of experience and I was just a kid.' He laughed. 'I knew why I was there and I was more

than willing, but it was so exciting not knowing quite what to do.'

'Okay, so you want me to play the older woman,' Kate ventured.

'She was our next door neighbour, actually,' he said, a wistful light in his eyes. 'And I suppose you think I'm every sort of a prat.'

She shot him a sideways glance. 'Not really. I mean, sex is all about fantasies really, isn't it? Just tell me how you want me to play it and we'll take it from there.'

She listened and, while he explained, that wonderful tingling began inside her panties.

They found a field which was shielded from the road by a high hedge, and Devlin raced out of the car and opened the gate for her to drive in. She pulled up and waited for him to join her. As he climbed into the passenger seat, she forced herself to drift into the fantasy.

'Do you want a cigarette?' Suddenly, she tut-tutted. 'What am I saying? You shouldn't smoke at your age.'

'I do, though,' he countered, shyly. 'I am sixteen.'

'Yes, of course.' She sighed and lit two cigarettes. 'There,' she said, passing one across, 'and don't tell your Mum I gave it to you.'

He took a drag and exhaled. 'Why have we stopped here, Aunty Joy?'

'I love it when you call me Aunty Joy,' she said, hoping the remark would explain her laugh which was provoked by the absurdity of it all.

'I know you're not really my Aunty, but that's what I've always called you.'

'Ever since we've lived next door to your Mum. Now, that's been what? Five years? And in that time I've watched you grow into a fine strapping lad.' She drew on the

cigarette. 'We've stopped here because I'm a married woman and if people saw us together, they'd talk.'

'Why?' he asked, innocently.

'Because—' She giggled. 'Because of the things men and women do to each other. Now, come on, I'm sure you're not as naive as you're making out.'

'What? Sex, you mean?'

'Yes, sex.'

She stubbed out the cigarette and then brushed her hand across his lap, letting it linger there for a few seconds before removing it.

'I'm sorry, I shouldn't have done that. But I've been thinking about you so much just lately – ever since that night when I came into your bedroom and saw you in bed. You were naked – remember? – and the duvet had slipped off so I could see your cock.'

He put out his cigarette with fingers that shook.

'I wanted to play with it,' she went on, 'but I didn't dare because your Mum was downstairs, and if she'd caught me, well—'

'I wish you had,' was his enthusiastic reply.

'If I did, you'd never tell anyone, would you? I could make it feel really nice if you'd promise never to tell.'

'I wouldn't tell, ever,' he said.

Her hand found his lap again, but this time she was fingering him, gauging his length.

She smiled. 'Mmm, nice. It's gone hard now. Why don't we get on to the back seat where there's more room, and then you can show it to me.'

They scrambled out of the car and were soon installed in the back. With frantic movements, she helped him out of his trousers, her eyes never leaving his tantalizing weapon.

'It's so big,' she enthused. 'It's far bigger than your uncle's.'

She stroked the shaft until it was throbbing, and when her hand snaked around it and started to rub, he whimpered with delight.

'I knew you'd like this,' she whispered. 'There are so many things an experienced woman can do to make a big dick like this feel happy. She can work it off with her hand, or she can suck it—'

He groaned.

'Or better still ... I've got somewhere warm and soft that you can put it in. Show me where this big cock should go – come on, show me.'

His movements were clumsy and so like those of a young boy as he worked a hand up her skirt, and Kate found herself warming to the theme. A soft sigh left his lips when his fingers touched the silk of her panties and fondled the warmth beneath them.

'That's it – the nice little thing in my knickers that can't get enough sex.'

He worked his fingers under the gusset while she continued to rub his shaft. Soon he was moaning uncontrollably.

'I'll let you do it to me,' she murmured, 'just so long as you don't tell anybody. If you like, I'll teach you all about sex.'

'I promise, I promise,' he sobbed. 'I'm going to come, Aunty, and it's so much nicer than when I do it myself.'

'Good boy,' she giggled. 'Come all over my skirt.'

Sperm flew from his tip, and Kate momentarily slipped out of character when it hit the back of her lovely car seat. But then, what the hell? It should easily sponge off.

'Was that nice?' she asked.

'It was fantastic,' he said, his breath coming in quick gasps.

'I had to make you shoot,' she said, 'or you wouldn't have lasted long enough to satisfy me. My, you are a dirty boy – you've still got a big hard-on.'

Kate arched her back and took off her panties, making sure that he had a good view of her hairy nest as she did so.

'Do you like it?' she asked, sitting back and pulling up her skirt. 'See? There's my crack.'

'It's beautiful,' he marvelled. 'I've never heard it called a crack before.'

'Stroke it for me,' she said, reaching for his hand and placing it on her hairy patch.

His trembling hand explored it, rubbing the pouting lips and finding the wet entrance, and sank a finger deep inside. Kate opened her legs wider and leant back in the seat.

'Oh, that's nice,' she said, grabbing his wrist and making him go faster. 'Get me ready for your cock.'

'I'm so excited, Aunty. I really want to do it.'

'All right, just this once I'll let you do it straight away.'

He withdrew his finger and manoeuvred himself between her thighs, his weapon larger than ever now. Grasping it by the root, he stabbed it at her vagina in an amateurish attempt to find her entrance. Kate was happy to guide him in, and placed the tip between the wet craving lips.

'Do it now,' she whispered. 'Push it into my cunt.'

He almost cried out with bliss when he sank into her silky channel and began working his cock to and fro.

'Ooh, Aunty,' he kept calling out.

'Slow down,' she urged. 'I don't want you spurting again until my cunt's really satisfied.'

Her voice and the words she was using made him move even faster and fulfillment soon beckoned, so Kate pushed forward to meet his thrusts in an attempt to grasp it. Warm sensations surfaced in her middle and fanned out over her body until she was panting.

'Good fuck ... gorgeous fuck,' she murmured at the feel of hot seed streaming into her.

Kate was surprised to find herself reluctant to let the fantasy go when they finally disentangled themselves, and it was with real regret that she allowed him to ease himself off.

'You were so good,' she said, 'that I'm going to let you keep my knickers as a souvenir.'

'Was it really alright?' he asked, still in character. 'Did I do it alright? Was it as good as when Uncle does it to you?'

'Your cock's bigger than Uncle's, and he does it to me every night.'

His chest swelled with pride at the compliment to his size, but then he noticed her slightly distant expression.

'But it wasn't better than when Uncle does it?'

'The thing is, we do a lot of things to each other that you're far too young to know about. Things that help to satisfy us.'

'Like what,' he was eager to know.

'Things we couldn't do in a car,' she replied in a hushed whisper. 'Really dirty things.'

'Like what?' he repeated.

'I couldn't possibly tell you,' she said, lowering her eyes. 'You're much too young.'

'Please, Aunty. Please?'

'Okay. For a start, Uncle licks my crack.'

'Let's do that then,' he said, his features highly animated.

'I don't think there's room in the back of a car.'

'Please, Aunty—' A calculating expression came to his face. 'If you don't let me do it, I'll tell everybody what we've done.'

'You wouldn't do that, would you? But you promised.' Her eyes widened with mock horror. 'Oh, yes, you would – I can tell by your face. So, I've really no choice.' She giggled and spread her legs. 'I can see that from now on I'll have to do anything you want.'

He knelt eagerly at her crotch, enthralled by the closeness of her pubic forest as he buried his face into it.

'Gently,' she advised, stroking his hair. 'Just run your tongue along the slit until you get used to the smell and the taste. Oh, you've found my clit already, you wonderful boy.'

She twisted her fingers in his hair and writhed in her seat as what felt like mild electric shocks raced through her groin.

'Now lick the tight hole,' she pleaded, her voice jerking. 'Push your tongue right in and really lick it.'

His hand strayed between her buttocks and made her gasp with joy.

'Oh, you are learning fast,' she told him in a sexy whisper. 'And from now on I shall have to do anything you want, however dirty it is, because if I don't, you'll tell.'

His lips and his athletic tongue soon had her bucking wildly beneath him, and he kept up his attack until her orgasm dwindled and died.

'Good boy,' she murmured. 'Now, come on, it's your turn. Sit down and see if you like what Aunty's going to do.'

He sank into the sumptuous seat, his shaft big and hard again. It trembled and quivered as she knelt between his legs, letting her warm breath play on his heavy balls. She

ran her lips over them, just brushing the wrinkled skin until he was twisting about on the seat. Then she ran her tongue up the sensitive underside of his shaft and finally pushed her pursed lips down over his tip.

She sucked hard until it was almost time for his release. His heavily-veined penis was throbbing, and she could feel it vibrating in her mouth. His head was tossing from side to side and he groaned as she slid a finger between his buttocks. Immediately his heels came up onto the seat to give her better access.

Kate found toying with his anus highly arousing and she released his shaft and rubbed it while her mouth glided towards the puckered hole, her tongue darting out to tease its opening.

'Lick me there, Aunty,' he begged.

'I couldn't,' she breathed. 'It's too much for you to ask.'

'I'll tell,' he panted. 'I'll tell if you don't.'

There was a smile on her lips when Kate forced her tongue into his tightness, and she twirled it around and rubbed his cock faster and faster until he was screaming with ecstasy and ejaculating his load into her hair. She quickly lifted her face and grinned as it splattered on to her cheeks.

'Thank you, Kate,' Devlin said, the game of fantasy now over. 'You cost me a lot of money, but you've been worth every penny.'

She took it that he was referring to the car, and was surprised that someone of his obvious wealth should regard the price of a Jaguar as a lot of money.

'I aim to please,' she said, smiling. 'I aim to please.'

CHAPTER 36

Back at the house it was once again time for goodbyes. However, Kate was not too sad for she now had the address of a nightclub where Laurence Wilson could be found.

As she drove the Jaguar back towards the city her thoughts turned to James Dixon and the lovely Maria – the two who had sent her on this quest. She would be seeing them soon to collect the five hundred thousand pounds still owing.

She pulled into the large car park at the rear of the club and her high heels sounded on the tarmac as she hurriedly made for the main doors. Once inside she went straight to the reception desk which was staffed by a distinguished man in full evening dress. He looked up as Kate approached.

'I'm looking for a man named Laurence Wilson,' she told him.

'Really?' he said, his tone noncommittal.

'Yes, I've been told he's here, or that you know where he is.'

'That's as may be,' he said, tapping the side of his nose. 'And what would this information be worth to you?'

Kate was reaching into her shoulder bag for money when she noticed the man appraising her body.

'I don't believe this,' she shrieked, her mouth sagging open. 'Are you asking for sex?'

He shrugged. 'A favour for a favour.'

'No,' she said, shaking her head. 'I'm not doing it. It's definitely out.'

'Then you don't want Wilson that badly,' the man said, his bored expression fuelling her anger.

In her mind's eyes, Kate saw half a million pounds slipping away. 'Do you know where Wilson is?' she asked.

He nodded.

'All right,' she said, sighing. 'Where do you want it?'

He jerked his thumb over his shoulder. 'In the back room.'

'Let's go,' she said, skirting round the desk.

'Sandra,' the man shouted, 'take over here.'

A young girl came hurrying towards the desk as Kate followed the man into a tiny room behind the partition.

'Drop your knickers and bend over,' he said with little ceremony.

Kate stepped out of one leg of her panties and leant forward, hitching her skirt up as she moved. The man was straightaway groping between her legs, his hands rough and demanding on her hairy vagina.

'Nice,' he said, his voice husky. 'Very nice, and more than ready for my dick.'

Despite herself, Kate felt love juice spilling out on to the tops of her thighs while the rasping sound of his zip filled the tiny space. Suddenly the whole incident became wildly exciting. Here she was with a perfect stranger, bending over with her knickers around her ankles, within a few yards of where others were walking in and out of the club.

Something warm and extremely hard nudged the entrance to the vagina. Then the man was gripping her thighs and ramming into her with a mighty thrust.

'You're so tight,' he grunted, working himself to and fro.

She could feel the thick veins of his shaft rubbing her aroused tunnel, causing it to become more wet and clinging. He was fucking far too fast for her to reach fulfilment, really pumping into her with rapid grunts and moans, so she used her vaginal muscles to grapple with his thrusting weapon. He was almost fighting for breath now, his fingers digging into her soft thighs.

'You filthy cow,' he muttered. 'You dirty little whore.' And then he exploded inside her.

She let him finish spurting before pulling away, and then she reached down for her knickers and wiped them across her still-yearning crack until they were covered with the heady mixture of sperm and her own sex juice.

'For you,' she said, handing them to the man. 'A present from a filthy cow.'

He took them and rubbed them around his swollen shaft.

'Thank you,' he said. 'That's something I've always wanted to do.'

She gave a slight curtsy. 'My pleasure. Now, Wilson, where is he?'

'Go back to reception and take the first flight of stairs on your right. He's in the room at the top.'

'Thanks.'

'Can I just do something else before you go?' He extracted a wallet from his inside pocket and withdrew two twenty pound notes. 'Can I pay you?'

With a puzzled frown Kate took the money and was stuffing it into her shoulder bag as she entered reception. She positively bounded up the stairs and flung open the door at the top. A man was sitting in an armchair, its back towards the door.

'Laurence Wilson?' she called out.

'No, I'm not.'

The man turned around, and there was a smile on his handsome face. It was James Dixon. Just then Maria, naked and beguiling, appeared at the bedroom door.

'What's happening here?' Kate asked, totally startled. 'What the shit's happening here?'

Dixon rose from the chair. He too was naked, and Kate thrilled at the sight of his magnificently muscled torso.

'Kate,' he said, kindly. 'I'm afraid you've been a victim of deception.'

'Have I now,' she spat, slamming the door shut.

'Yes.' He gave her a disarming smile. 'You see, Wilson doesn't exist. When you started using the 69 Club, which I'm sure you know has an upstairs brothel, certain members of the male clientele expressed an interest in your body for sexual purposes. But, unfortunately, your body was not for sale. These men are very rich and because they couldn't have you, they began offering vast sums for me to procure you.'

Kate looked from one to the other, a frown marring her beautiful face. 'You mean you invented this story about Wilson so you could sell my body?'

'Yes,' Maria said. 'We thought if we offered you a million pounds to act as a detective, then you'd accept.'

'So all those people I had sex with paid you money?'

'That's right. Mind you, there were a couple – a butler and a stable lad, I believe – that were entirely your own idea. But as for the rest – Barton, the publishers, the play,' he spread his hands, 'they all paid handsomely. In fact, your share of the money is perhaps only twenty per cent. As I said, they are very rich people.'

Kate laughed. 'You bastard.'

'Did you enjoy it?' Maria asked.

'Enormously,' she admitted. 'I think I must have fitted into the part well because your doorman's just paid me forty pounds for sex.'

'He's not the doorman,' Maria said, a smile hovering on her lips. 'He's a very wealthy barrister who wanted a naughty girl.'

Kate viewed their naked bodies. 'He left me really horny and dying for a good come.'

'That will be taken care of,' Dixon told her. 'But first some champagne to celebrate our successful business arrangement.'

'I feel a little overdressed,' Kate said, above the popping of the cork.

Maria grinned. 'That's easily remedied.'

Kate took off her clothes; not in a slow, sensuous strip tease, but hurriedly, eager to be naked as the others were.

'It's nice to see your hairy crack again,' Maria said, helping her off with her bra.

Dixon carried the champagne across, all the while eying Kate's body, which she was quite happy to display. His shaft was now huge and ready for the delights that only her tight little slit could bring. Kate fondled him lovingly, stroking and rubbing gently while they sipped the sparkling wine.

'We know what you want, Kate,' Maria whispered as she stroked her hairy patch from behind.

'I want sex all the time,' Kate replied, gasping as the woman's finger found her opening.

'All nicely soiled already,' Maria cooed, inserting a second finger and briskly setting to work. 'No, I mean we know what you really want.'

No one could ever guess that. Could they? Suddenly

the fluttering in her groin increased and the trembling in her carnal cavern became more insistent.

Kate's glass landed with a dull thud on the carpet as she spread her legs and rested her head on Dixon's shoulder while she played with his aggressive shaft. But then, as she was hurtling towards her much-needed climax, Dixon grasped her hand and brought it to a halt while Maria's welcome fingers withdrew.

'Come into the bathroom, Kate,' he coaxed. 'Let us give you what you really want.'

They put down their glasses and led her into the bathroom. She followed like an innocent child, hoping that the present waiting behind the door was that which she truly craved.

They made her get into the bath and sit on its edge. Maria sat across her legs, facing towards her.

'And now,' she said, kissing Kate lightly on the lips. 'I'm going to give you what you want.'

Kate murmured a frantic 'yes' as Maria's urine gushed on to her thighs. The woman lifted herself up slightly so that Kate could see the stream of water pouring from her. It played on her legs and lap, but all too soon became a slow trickle and then stopped altogether. The women groaned in unison when it was over.

Her eyes were closed, and when she felt Maria's weight leave her, Kate glanced up to see Dixon standing before her, his weapon visibly throbbing within his grasp.

'Yes,' she pleaded. 'Go on, do it.'

Water shot from the split in his purple tip and it splashed on to her stomach, leaving a warm trail as it ran over her pubic hair.

'Direct it onto my cunt,' she begged.

He adjusted his aim until the water was hissing onto

her vagina. Kate squirmed, her legs trembling. She hoped it would never end, but all too soon it did and she whimpered in complaint. But then Dixon lay down in the bath and he beckoned for her to join him. With a tiny cry of joy, Kate squatted over him, her hairy spot almost touching his bulging tip.

'Do it on his cock,' Maria breathed. 'Do it all over his cock.'

A second later Kate's hot urine was cascading over his jumping penis. She placed her fingers in the flow, playing with it, making it trickle onto his huge testicles. With the water still flowing, she pushed her hot crack onto his rigid shaft and then started to fuck.

'I'm coming already,' she told them, blissfully.